Praise for

Caine's Reckoning

Named the Readers' Choice Best American Historical by All About Romance and Best Historical Romance by Romance Reviews Today.

"Sarah McCarty's new series is an exciting blend of raw masculinity, spunky, feisty heroines and the wild living in the old west…with spicy, hot love scenes. Ms. McCarty gave us small peeks into each member of the Hell's Eight and I'm looking forward to reading the other men's stories."
—*Erotica Romance Writers*

"Intense, edgy and passionate, this is old-school historical romance at its finest."
—*RT Book Reviews*

"*Caine's Reckoning* is a can't-put-it-down adventure story…. Superb writing and characterization, along with a well-described setting, bring the story alive and pull readers into the action. This exceptional first-in-series book has this reader eagerly anticipating future stories and earns it the RRT Perfect 10 rating…a hands-down winning tale that is not to be missed."
—*Romance Reviews Today*

"Though Caine and Desi alone would have made this a wonderful romance, the many other men of Hell's Eight are an integral part of the series and we are certainly left anxious for the next installment."
—*A Romance Review*

"This was a very good book…very worth the time. Ms. McCarty weaves a tale of depravity and redemption…. This is the book for you, folks, if you're a fan of westerns, historicals, redemptives…I scarfed it down in a day and really enjoyed the hell out of myself while doing it."
—*The Good, the Bad, the Unread*

Also by

SARAH
McCARTY

TRACKER'S SIN
TUCKER'S CLAIM
SAM'S CREED

SARAH McCARTY

Caine's Reckoning

ISBN-13: 978-0-373-77625-2

CAINE'S RECKONING

This edition published by arrangement with Harlequin Books S.A.

For questions and comments about the quality of this book please contact us at Customer_eCare@Harlequin.ca.

www.HQNBooks.com

Printed in U.S.A.

ACKNOWLEDGMENTS

For Sunny for yanking me out of my comfort zone and into the mainstream. For Roberta for catching me and guiding me through skepticism. For Susan for taking my dream and shaping it into what should be, rather than just what could be. Thank you.

To Lori H., Caine's Woman of Reckoning,
for the support you've given, the laughter you've shared
and for that sharp wit that no doubt keeps the men
in your life on their toes. May life bless you with the same
generosity and joy you give to so many.

Caine's Reckoning

1858: Texas Territory

1

He hated the sound of a woman's scream.

Caine pulled Chaser up short. The black Appaloosa's hoofbeats ended in cadence with Tracker's and Sam's horses. After fifteen years together, there was no guesswork to the men's moves. They were a team.

The high-pitched scream came again, cutting through the cold morning air, hovering a desperate moment on the heavy mist before dropping off with eerie abruptness.

Tracker took the blade of grass he'd been chewing from between his teeth. "Looks like we've found them."

"Yup." Caine pulled his rifle from the scabbard, scouting the surrounding area. There weren't that many areas a man could hide here in the flatlands.

Sam tipped back his hat, his blue eyes glittering like cold ice. "About the only place that offers protection is that cluster of trees yonder."

Caine didn't need to hear the grim edge to the statement to know what that meant. If those were true Comancheros who'd stolen the women, they'd already been spotted. The women were as good as dead, and that scream had merely been a baited invitation to a trap. However, nothing in this whole kidnapping spoke of the snake-in-the-grass intelligence Comancheros were known for. Greed, yes. The women stolen had been the youngest and prettiest, but there was a certain lack of intelligence displayed in taking the sheriff's wife. Even if he had been out of town at the time. There were some things a smart man didn't do, and one of them was stealing a lawman's woman.

Tracker slid off his horse, stepped forward and squatted next to hoofprints in the mud. He flicked aside some debris and touched the base of an indentation.

"Same notched shoe?" Caine asked.

"Yup." Beneath his hat, Tracker's long black hair blew back from his face as he followed the trajectory of the tracks to the cluster of trees, revealing the hard ridge of scar tissue puckering the dark skin of his cheek. A scar he'd earned at the age of fifteen when he'd extracted justice for his mother from the man who'd raped her. He pointed to the copse of trees halfway up the rise.

"They're in there."

Another scream tore through the morning calm, this time rising and falling on a ruptured, barely recognizable *"No!"*

"Shit." Sam flipped the strap on his holster. "Stopping to fuck with a posse on their tail? I've a mind to complain to the padre. It's a waste of time sending us out to round up this bunch when any kid in knee pants could do the job."

Remnants of the scream echoed off the surrounding hills, raising the hairs on the back of Caine's neck. Right along with memories he'd rather have stayed buried.

"Gotta admit that much stupidity fairly begs a man to put it out of its misery."

"That it does." Sam checked the cylinder of his pistol,

the easy nonchalance of his attitude belied by the grim smile lifting the corner of his lips. Nothing irritated Sam more than a stupid outlaw. "But seeing as they chose to bring their law-breaking to our land, I suppose it won't overwork us none to teach them a lesson."

The same tug of cold intent in Sam's smile flowed through Caine's blood, sharpening his senses, giving a home to the anger that had festered without satisfaction for the last fifteen years. They'd fought long and hard for a place to call their own, carved two thousand acres out of these canyons with their sweat and blood. This was their home, and the only law that existed in it was the one they enforced. And on Hell's Eight land, a body could do a lot of things, but hurt a woman and live wasn't one of them. "I don't suppose it will."

Sam dropped his revolver back into his holster. "I'll head 'round."

"You want the sentries, Tracker?" Caine asked, as Sam loped off, circling to keep the slight rise between him and their quarry.

Tracker stood and put his hand on the worn leather-wrapped hilt of his knife. "My pleasure."

Silhouetted against the morning mist, he looked every bit of his reputation—a big, mean nightmare come to life. His dark gaze fixed on the copse of trees, his focus already on the battle to come. If Tracker ever allowed one of the sentries to see his expression, the implacable intent there, the man would piss his pants. Too bad Tracker never let them see his face. Caine levered a bullet into the chamber of his rifle with the snap of his wrist. He'd pay money to see that. "Then I guess that leaves the how-de-do's up to me."

The barest hint of a smile touched Tracker's lips. "Enjoy yourself."

CAINE CREPT ON HIS belly to the edge of the low ridge overhanging the small clearing. Tipping back his hat, he looked directly below to the small group in the hollowed-out bank in the curve of the stream. Stupid did not begin to describe this bunch.

One of the five men they were tracking held a gun loosely on three women who cowered in terror against the earthen bank. Three more outlaws were engrossed in trying to catch a blond-haired hellion knee-deep in the rushing stream, pitching curses and stones at their heads with assorted degrees of accuracy. If she'd once worn a dress, it was long gone. Her bloomers and camisole were plastered to her compact body, her small breasts and mound clearly delineated by the transparent material. The provocative display no doubt contributed to the idiocy of the men, one of whom chose that moment to rush the woman. She jerked to the side, her long hair obscuring her expression as he grabbed her arm and pulled. Instead of fighting, she went with him, planting her feet when he stumbled on the uneven stream bed, bringing her knee up hard enough to feed the guy his balls for breakfast. She should have run, but she was a fighter and clearly had a fighter's instinct to finish the job. As the guy sank to the ground, hands clamped over his balls, she kicked out again, catching him on the chin. He went over like a felled ox, water splashing high. Out cold.

Caine raised an eyebrow as she turned on the other two, feet braced, daring them to come after her. A smile tugged past his fury. Hell, if they delayed a bit, the little spitfire might just take care of this mess for them. A barely perceptible thud to his left deepened his smile. But it wouldn't be necessary. Tracker was nothing if not efficient and that thud was the first sentry. One down.

Two more to go. Caine inched closer as the outlaws on the edge of the stream shifted position. The bigger of the two said something to the other, his heavy beard obscuring the shape of the words. In response, the smaller man pulled off his hat, revealing a thin face scraggled with beard. He slapped the hat against his thigh. Whatever the suggestion had been, the smaller man wasn't cozying up to it.

"Just rush her for Christ sake," the redhead guarding the other women shouted impatiently, punctuating his point with a wave of his rifle that had the women he was guarding screaming and covering their heads with their hands.

"If you want her rushed, Red, do it yourself," Scraggle Beard hollered back. "I like my balls right where they are."

"Do I have to do everything myself?" Red aimed his revolver at the two men. They went absolutely still. With a flick of the muzzle, he ordered, "Get out of the way."

The two men stepped aside, relief seeping into the set of their shoulders as Red centered the muzzle on the blond woman. "Get out of the stream."

The blonde's response to that flat order was a flip of her head that had her hair whipping back over her shoulder, revealing a delicately shaped face devoid of color but full of determination.

She didn't move a foot, nor say a word, but if there was ever a combination of gestures that said *go to hell*, it was the lift of that small, pointed chin and the narrowing of those big eyes.

Over the rushing of the stream, Caine heard the faint click of the gun hammer locking into place. *Shit.*

"Now."

Caine had never seen a more stupidly brave woman.

Instead of obeying, she squared her shoulders. Courage was one thing but she was just about begging the man to pull the trigger, and for that she needed her cute little ass paddled. Caine notched the barrel of his rifle between two stones and took aim as Red straightened his arm.

The blonde narrowed her eyes and stretched her defiance out to the last possible second before, with another toss of that wet mane, she sloshed out of the stream. Water dripped in a small river as she stomped up the bank. She came to a stop three steps from Red, chin still high, shaking like she had the ague. Goddamn, if she didn't drop with pneumonia before the day was out, they would all be lucky.

"See, boys, nothing to be afraid of," Red sneered, releasing the hammer and lowering the revolver to his side. "Just a pretty little whore displaying her goodies for our pleasure."

The "boys" converged on the woman, grabbing her arms. If looks could kill, Red would be dead and the "boys" not far behind. The bearded man grabbed the woman's hair, yanking her around as he ripped the chemise from her body. Her screech echoed around the clearing. With the speed of a rattler, she sank her teeth into his hand, hard enough that his holler followed hers. Scraggle Beard jerked her back. She didn't let go, just stretched out between the two men, hanging like a crazed coon, anchored by her teeth and the grip on her arm.

"Fucking shit! Stop yanking on her before she bites my thumb clear off!"

Scraggle Beard froze. The bearded man brought his hamlike fist down on the woman's back. Her knees buckled, but she held on. No matter how the man shook his hand, yanked and threatened, she didn't turn him loose. Son of a bitch, she was something.

Caine adjusted his aim. "That's right, hellcat. Keep them busy just a little bit more, just until Tracker gets those sentries." He tightened his finger on the trigger. "Just a little bit more, and I'll settle this for you once and for all."

As if she heard, the woman clung to the outlaw, flopping where he shook her, getting a bit of her own back the only way she could, clearly stuck on her course of action with no real way out. If she let go she'd be helpless, if she held on, she was an easy target for his fist. The man brought his fist up a second time. Caine sighted the gun. That was one blow that wasn't going to land.

Tracker's signal trilled through the clearing, sharp and sweet. Followed immediately by another. Caine fired in rapid succession. Simultaneously, three shots shattered the rain of curses streaming into the clearing, followed quickly by a fourth. The men dropped, the blond woman with them. Caine leapt over the ledge and slid down the muddy slope, sending loose rocks tumbling before him. He reached her side in a few rapid strides. No way had he hit her. He'd placed his bullets precisely where he'd wanted them. So had Sam and Tracker. He'd lay money on it. All of the Hell's Eight were known for their accuracy. That fifth shot had him worried, though. That shot hadn't come from any of their guns.

The closer he got, the smaller the woman got. Fine bones, fine build. He stepped over the outlaw at her side, the screams and cries of the other three women no more than the buzz of insects. Blood splattered on what he could see of the little blonde's arms, but he didn't think it was hers. The impression of fragility increased as he cupped her shoulders through the wet mass of hair. Shit, there wasn't anything to her beyond grit and determination. And temper, he decided as he tugged up and she snarled. She was still biting the man. "You can turn him loose now, ma'am."

There was a pause and the tension under his hand eased. He pulled. She sat back, wiped at her mouth with both hands before huddling into a ball, looking for all the world like she'd start plastering herself with mud to cover up if he didn't present an alternative fast. Then she looked up at him and sucker-punched him with the eloquence of those big eyes. Everything she felt inside, everything left out of her remarkably composed expression, whirled in the deep blue depths—shame, anger, hope and fear.

"Who are you?" she asked, through the chattering of her teeth.

"Caine Allen, Texas Ranger." He'd tip his hat if he had a free hand. Though she was all but naked and covered in blood, she had an air about her that reminded a man of his manners. The introduction didn't ease any of the turbulence he read in her eyes.

"Father Gerard asked me to come fetch you home," he added, shrugging out of his wool-lined leather duster and wrapping it around her, drawing her into his body heat. She fit against him nicely.

"Is he dead?"

It was hard to acquaint the quavery whisper with the woman who'd faced down three grown men with nothing more than her temper and teeth. He took in the fallen man's blank stare, the hole dead-center between his eyes and the blood pooling beneath his head. "If not, he's doing a fair imitation."

"Oh."

If he hadn't been studying the blue tinge under her skin, he would have missed the subtle tremble that ran through her and just mistaken it for another of the cold chills shaking her from head to toe. Winter was wrapping up, but spring had yet to put in an appearance and the late March wind was cold. He helped her up and forward, moving her away from the blood toward the other women. She'd fought like hell, but as soon as reaction set in, she'd be wanting the company of her own sex.

To their right, there was a series of splashes. He looked up. Tracker stood over the man in the stream.

"That the last of them?"

"Yup." Tracker bent and grabbed the man's arms, hauling the body out of the water.

The cold damp of the woman's hair soaked through his shirt as she turned her head to stare at the gruesome sight. Another almost imperceptible shiver racked her frame. Caine turned his body, shielding her from the horror.

Her "Good riddance" caught him by surprise. He tipped her chin up, checking her expression. Her face was tight with strain, her pale lips drawn to a narrow, bloodless line, but she was still with him. "It is that, ma'am."

She cautiously moved her chin off the shelf of his finger, her wary gaze locked on his as if afraid to move too fast. He guessed he couldn't blame her for that—being kidnapped out of her bed and subjected to attempted rape probably made a woman six ways of cautious. He dropped his hand to her back, keeping her against him as the chill from her body seeped into his.

"'I need to sit down."

He just bet she did, but a good twenty feet still separated them from the women. He would take on many things without batting an eye, but a hysterical female wasn't one of them. She stopped at a fallen tree.

"This is good."

For such a delicate little thing, her voice had a pleasing depth and a seductive, husky rasp that made him think of dark rooms, soft whispers and hot sex. His cock, semi-hard from the battle, surged to fully erect as the soft scent of lavender teased his senses. He shifted his position so she wouldn't notice the purely male reaction. A woman who'd just escaped rape would not welcome any sign of a man's interest, no matter what side of the law he sat on. "No offense, Miss...?"

Instead of immediately supplying her name, she hesitated and frowned. For the space of two heartbeats she left the blank empty, then with a nearly imperceptible shrug she answered, "Desi."

Unusual, but it suited her in a strange, boldly feminine way. "Would that be Miss or Mrs.?"

Another pause. "Miss."

Unmarried. His luck was picking up. He motioned with his hand to the women on the opposite edge of the clearing. "I'm sure you'll be more comfortable with the others."

She shook her head, turned out of his arms and sank down, clutching his coat around her and repeated, "This is good."

"Yes."

He let his hands slide up her back as she lowered herself, feeling her wince as she reached the log, the action no doubt compressing her ribs. "You sure you're okay, ma'am?"

"Yes."

Remembering the blow she'd taken, he didn't find that short, breathless assurance comforting. He ran his right hand down her spine over the jacket, spreading his fingers wide, counting her ribs as he went, immediately locating the damaged area by her soft gasp.

"She all right?" Sam asked, strolling up to their side.

His "No" overrode her "Yes."

Sam, damn his hide, had the gall to look amused at the contradiction. Caine pressed along her sixth rib. She twisted away. He paused. "Maybe you'd feel better with one of the women caring for you?"

She hunched her shoulders into the heavy duster and shook her head. Her chin was set in that way he already recognized meant stubborn. "I'm fine."

He checked the other side as best he could through the coat.

"Denying what needs to be done doesn't end the need for the doing."

Her fingers made deep dents in the coat's leather sleeves. "Why not?"

He shook his head at the illogic. "Because I said so."

"I don't hold you the final opinion on what's so."

He just bet she didn't. "Now that's a shame, because right now I'm the one calling the shots."

Her chin came up in that way that just begged a man to make a stronger point. "For now."

"I'm thinking if anyone's going to do anything, it's going to have to be you," Sam added.

Caine threw him a questioning glance, slipping his hand under the coat and testing the extent of Desi's tenderness with one hand while keeping her put with the other on her shoulder.

"Seems the other women don't want to associate with—" a jerk of his thumb indicated the woman beside him "—her."

If he hadn't been touching Desi, he wouldn't have felt her start.

"They got a reason for that line of thinking?" Caine asked. From what he could tell, Desi was the only one worth associating with. Any woman who could spit in the devil's eye had his admiration.

"Apparently, she has a history of tempting men," Sam said.

"You're shitting me, right?" Caine glanced down. Desi didn't look up, just shook her head, which could have been an answer either way, shivered and then tugged the coat collar higher.

"They seem mighty convinced of their notions," Sam offered without inflection.

One glance at the sullen faces of the three women standing shoulder-to-shoulder arguing with a nonresponsive Tracker put credence to Sam's claim. "Is that what they're clucking about over there?"

"Yeah. About nonstop. Seem to think the more words they throw at a man the more sway they have."

"Tracker must be in his glory."

Sam smiled that cold smile that didn't reach his eyes. "He says to tell you he's about ready to cut out some tongues to get some peace."

Desi jumped and cast Tracker a wary look. He couldn't blame her. Tracker had a lethal just-give-me-a-reason attitude about him that could clear the roughest saloon with just a glance. The scar on his cheek did nothing to diminish it.

Caine smoothed the heavy mass of hair off Desi's cheek, absorbing into his palm the trembles the shook her. The "Easy, I've got you" welled out of nowhere, a murmured reassurance connected to a foreign sense of possessiveness. Sam cocked a sandy eyebrow at him, a bit of amusement lightening his gaze as he pulled out his makings. He gestured to Desi with the packet.

"I get the impression this one could spout gospel and those three would label it devil worship."

Beneath Caine's fingers, the woman's muscles tightened to rock hard ridges. "Jesus H. Christ."

Sam rolled a smoke, the sharpness in the move the only indication of his disgust. "It gets better."

It would. "What?"

He reached into his pocket for a lucifer. "They're requesting you return them to their homes immediately."

"That's the plan."

He struck the lucifer on the side of his boot. "But they don't want her brought along."

"What do they think I'm going to do, leave her as a treat for whoever comes calling?" Desi flinched. He caught a flash of blue as she cut him a glance from under her lashes. He took his hand out from under her coat. As she pulled the lapels closed, he stroked her back, gentling her worries. He wouldn't leave her.

Sam lit the cigarette. "Don't think they'd be averse to the idea."

"Goddamn!"

"I don't mind." The soft statement rode his exasperation, feeding it.

"Well, I sure as he—" he caught himself in time "—heck do."

Sam flicked the match to the ground and took a draw on his smoke. "The women claim they won't go if she goes with them."

"So?"

"Just checking how you feel on that."

Beneath his hands, Desi's bones felt as delicate as bird wings. It was hard to believe she'd fought as hard as she had or been so successful with so little, but sometimes it wasn't the size of the dog in the fight as much as the size of the fight in the dog, and this woman had plenty of fight. He admired that. "Tell them when I say mount up, they'll mount, or they'll walk tied behind, but one way or another, they'll go."

A strident screech from one of the other women snapped his head around. From the pitch he would have assumed the camp was under immediate attack, but in reality, the only one who looked threatened was Tracker. Even from where he stood, Caine could see the anger roll off the women flanking him. The vehemence. Hands waved, fingers pointed, and then, as if it would add emphasis to their point, the women moved in.

Tracker drove the three women back with a slice of his hand and a sharp utterance Caine couldn't make out. Turning on his heel, he stalked toward them, his long black hair fanning behind him, emphasizing his irritation. He touched the brim of his black hat in deference to Desi as he got close, his expression displaying none of the anger Caine could see simmering under his skin.

"This the one the padre was concerned about?"

"Yup. Desi, this is Tracker Ochoa."

Caine couldn't blame Tracker for the shake of the head. It was hard to reconcile Father Gerard's description of "a fragile flower of womanhood" with the hellion who had held off three men with nothing more than sheer grit.

"Hell of a fight you put up, ma'am."

Desi ducked her head. Her "Thank you" was a wisp of sound as she all but disappeared into the coat. If she was hoping to dispel interest, Caine could have told her she was angling down the wrong path. The contradiction of all that fire banked behind a wall of demure shyness was the perfect recipe to raise a man's interest. Tracker's more so than most. For all that he was one scary son of a bitch, he was the softest man Caine had ever seen when it came to women.

Tracker jerked his thumb over his shoulder. "The ladies demand to talk to—" he lifted his nose and pitched his deep baritone to a high falsetto "—whomever is in command." The irritation in the imitation reflected Tracker's sentiments on the matter. Whereas Desi had earned the big man's respect, the other women had apparently stirred up nothing but disgust.

"Appears to me they're not in a position to demand anything."

"Give them a chance, they'll argue that into the ground."

Caine didn't intend to give them any chance at all. Giving Desi's shoulder one last reassuring squeeze, he stepped back, settled his Stetson on his head and bit back the anger that rose too swiftly these days. "Then I guess this is their lucky day. I'm available."

DESI BREATHED A SIGH of relief as Caine took his hands off her shoulders. He was simply too much, from the way he watched her with those intense green eyes that seemed to uncover everything she wanted hidden, to the way his chin squared beneath his generous mouth. Everything about him was raw and untamed and uncompromisingly masculine. The lines that bracketed that mouth could indicate either a tendency to frown or smile. Truth be told, she couldn't imagine so intense a man smiling, but at the same time he didn't have that negative feel to him that she associated with bitterness. The hat he kept pulled low over his coffee-brown hair only heightened the impression of power. Angled low over his brow, it shaded his eyes and emphasized the command set into the rugged structure of his face. He wasn't strictly handsome, but she bet there wasn't a woman in the territory who didn't stop and speculate when he passed. He had a presence that just screamed danger, while at the same time that innate strength beckoned with the seductive lure of safety. Both messages were delivered with equal strength, leaving it to the imagination which trait would be the one a woman would find in her bed should she be reckless enough to extend an invitation.

Not that she would ever extend an invitation. Desi shivered. The last year had cured her of all girlish illusions to the true nature of men, and as soon as she located her sister, she was going to find at least one place in this world where she could live her life in peace.

Desi watched as Caine crossed the clearing to talk to her fellow captives, his long legs eating up the distance with amazing ease, his muscled buttocks, perfectly outlined by the straps of his chaps, flexing with every step. Nothing in the easy roll of his gait or the set of his wide shoulders indicated impatience, but he *was* impatient. She'd felt it in his touch a second before he'd stepped away. Part of her hoped he'd unleash that frustration on Mavis, who seemed to feel it was her God-given right to be judge, jury and executioner over all that came into her domain.

Desi grabbed another fold of the coat into her fingers, the lingering warmth from Caine's body welcome, the surge of his scent not as unpleasant as it should be, and watched as Mavis drew herself to her full height. Tall for a woman, with big bones and an hourglass figure that men admired, Mavis had presence and she was used to getting her way, in one manner or another.

Her two friends, Abigail and Sadie, stood in her shadow, as always, adding their will to hers, blindly following her lead. As one they stood, watching the big

Ranger's approach. From the expression on Mavis's face, he was about to get an earful. The woman wanted Desi gone—had been campaigning for it for a year—and clearly saw this as a chance to obtain their goal.

Desi would have gladly granted Mavis's wish, but there'd never been an opportunity. Until now. This was her chance. She couldn't mess it up. A shudder came out of nowhere, a debilitating mixture of cold and panic starting in her core and radiating outward.

"Don't you worry, ma'am," the blond man said, the kindness in his drawl at odds with the hard implacability of his expression. "There isn't a soul born who can tell Caine Allen what to do. Those women can fuss all they want, but when the dust settles, you'll be riding with us."

That was not what she needed to hear right now. "I don't want to go back there."

All that statement got her was a raised eyebrow from the sandy-blond man as he blew out a stream of smoke, along with a "Can't say that I blame you" from the savagely handsome, completely terrifying Tracker.

She stood, checking the sway in her movement through sheer force of will. Between James's efforts to starve her into compliance and the fight with the outlaws, her strength was going fast. "I need some privacy."

Her blush wasn't entirely faked. No matter what she'd learned to think of as normal in the last year, discussing her bodily functions was not one of them.

Tracker's hand immediately enveloped her elbow. "This way."

She couldn't help her instinctive flinch. His expression went from impassive to stony with a twitch of an eyelid, but he didn't say a word, just drew her along with him.

She went, her lip between her teeth. She had an unreasonable sense that she'd hurt his feelings. She wanted to tell him it wasn't him—the fact that he was obviously Indian, or his scars. She resented any man's touch, but she didn't say anything. Couldn't. These remnants of softness left over from before had to be squashed before it killed off her last opportunity, because if she didn't escape now, the only way out from the hell of her existence would be death. Either by her own hand or another's. It didn't matter. She couldn't continue this way anymore.

Guiding her across the uneven ground as if she were the finest of ladies at a social rather than a scandalous woman naked beneath a coat, Tracker helped her over a log, steadying her on the other side, keeping her close as he took her to the copse of trees where the outlaws had tied their horses. The snorts and whickers were welcome indicators that the horses were still there. Maybe her luck was changing.

She stopped before he could guide her through the thicket at the edge. "Thank you."

He released her elbow. "Give a holler when you're done, and I'll come help you back. No need for you to pick up any more bruises than you've already got."

He'd been holding her elbow because he was worried she'd fall, not because he was keeping her hostage…? The realization broadsided her. Desi ducked her head, hoping Tracker would take the gesture as one of embarrassment at the subject matter rather than guilt at her assumptions. "Thank you."

Casting one quick glance over her shoulder, she stepped through the bushes, making sure he wasn't following. Tracker stood where she'd left him, leaning against a thin tree, tossing that ugly knife in his hands, flipping it end to end before catching it. Desi shuddered, imagining him in a rage, and ducked through the brush. She had no intention of calling for him. This was her chance, and she was taking it.

2

You cannot expect decent women to be seen in the company of someone like her."

The way the older woman, Mrs. Hatchet, referred to Desi set Caine's back teeth to grinding. And it wasn't because of the nasal twang to her voice or the highfalutin way she pronounced her words. It was her absolute belief that because she had a husband to shield her that she was better than other women who'd run up against the hard truth of this land. Specifically, Desi.

"Lady, what I expect is silence and obedience." He jerked his thumb over his shoulder, indicating the open range beyond their sheltered spot. "In case it's escaped your notice, we're in the middle of Indian country. Those gunshots are going to attract every Comanche out there, so what I expect is for you to use the next few minutes getting ready to ride, because as soon as we gather what we can off those bodies, we're lighting out."

"You're robbing the dead?"

If a man had made such an accusation, he'd have punched him in the mouth for both the insult and the stupidity behind it. But the insult came from a woman, which tied his hands. "I'm taking what we need to survive."

Caine spun on his heel. Son of a bitch, he was never taking a wife if he had to put up with crap like that on a daily basis. He expected to see Desi waiting for him with Tracker and Sam. She wasn't. Sam was at the edge of the trees, checking out the action on a revolver while Tracker was efficiently going over the rest of the possessions looking for anything useful.

"Where's the woman?"

Sam flicked his used-up smoke into the stream, a genuine grin on his lips. "With the horses."

"What's she doing there?"

"Escaping." Tracker dumped out a saddlebag. "I figure we've got about twenty minutes before she sweet-talks that big mustang into opening its mouth for the bit."

This he had to see. Caine cut through the scrub brush to the horses. Evidence of Desi's attempts was everywhere. A bridle dangled from a horse already tacked out in a nose band. A saddle lurched off the side of a hardy paint mustang with the conformation of a runner. He stepped up to the brown-and-white paint, patting the deeply muscled chest that said he could go for miles without foundering. He ran his hand down its spine, murmuring soothingly as it fussed and gathered his scent, studying the tracks in the muddy ground as he righted the saddle.

Bare footprints littered the mud in mute testament to Desi's frustration. Sure as shit, she didn't know anything about tack, but that hadn't lessened her determination. The tracks spun in a circle, deepened as she'd put her weight squarely on both heels, and then took off in a straight line. The depth and distance between the prints indicated she'd been in a hurry.

Caine looked up the rise. He flipped the paint's stirrup onto the saddle, kneed him gently to warn him to cut the crap when he sucked in wind and tightened the cinch when he blew out. With an easy leap he was in the saddle, a smile on his lips as he studied those tracks. Damn, if she hadn't had the guts to light out on foot.

He spun the paint around and urged him up the rise. The outlaws might have been stupid, but they'd known good horseflesh. The paint responded as if he hadn't just finished a hard ride, driving fast up the hill, eager to run, dancing in a circle when Caine pulled him up at the top.

It wasn't hard to find Desi in the scraggly sea of winter dead brush. The bright sun shone off her blond hair like a brilliant white-gold beacon. He shook his head. She was heading due west, straight into Indian country. Caine gave the paint its head, smiling as the horse plunged down the rise. A man just had to admire the amount of gumption that drove a woman to take control of her future despite the odds or a poor sense of direction.

He was about forty feet behind Desi before she looked back. He had an impression of big blue eyes in a white face and a startled expression before she took off, bare feet flying across the ground, hair streaming behind her. Caine leaned over the cow pony's neck. The animal surged forward. Human or cattle, it didn't matter to the horse. He knew his job. Chase, catch and maintain. He did it well, dispelling the myth that paints made poor cow ponies.

The paint caught up with Desi in less than a minute. Caine reached down, snagging the back of the too-big coat, lifting her up. If her first screech didn't draw every Indian and bandit for twenty miles, the second surely would. It was all he could do to lift her onto the saddle as she struggled. Damn, who knew one small woman could hold so much wiggle?

"Hold still, damn it!"

If anything, she struggled harder. "Let me go!"

"No." He gave her a shake. "Settle down."

She braced her foot on his, lightening his load. Her arm wrapped around his, her fingers tangling in the excess folds of his coat, slipping off his shirtsleeve before grabbing desperately at his wrist.

"I'm not going back!"

"Well, you're sure as shit not heading out on your own."

"Watch me!"

She wrenched to the left and to the right. The pony danced beneath them as the coat flapped against his sides. A hard shove and she almost succeeded in unseating him. One minute he had more woman than he could contain and the next he held an empty coat. Caine swore, dropped the coat and leaned back. The pony sat on its haunches, slid ten feet and spun, lunging anew after Desi, who ran ahead, her fair skin glowing in the sunlight, looking like one of those golden nymphs he'd seen paintings of in that fancy whorehouse up Chicago way.

The woman's determination was no match for the paint's speed. In about three heartbeats, he was running beside her, adjusting his stride to match her panicked darts, crowding her to where Caine wanted her to go. Over the thunder of the pony's hooves, Caine could hear her labored breathing, her desperate sobs. Damn it! Why was she making this so hard?

He leapt off the pony's back and hit the ground running, catching her around the waist as he spun, cushioning her against his chest as he took the brunt of the fall on his back. He crossed his arms over her torso, keeping free of her teeth, trapping her feet with his legs, letting her exhaust herself with her struggles until she was tired enough to find reason.

It took about four minutes for her to figure out she wasn't going anywhere. When she did, her body just collapsed against his, her skull thunking on his collarbone one last time, her hips settling into the cradle of his groin, her buttocks cushioning the hard length of his cock. Not by a twitch of an eyelash did she let on that she knew what was poking at her down there. She simply turned her face west and stared as her labored breathing pushed her ribs against his.

"You 'bout ready to see reason?"

"I'm not going back."

Her body was about played out, but her stubbornness sure wasn't. "Why not?"

She crossed one arm over her breasts. "I'll die there."

Her body shook with shivers. He slid her off to the side, keeping her anchored with one arm as he sat up.

"That's a mighty serious accusation."

"It's the truth."

"Tell me why."

He stood, grabbing his hat before pulling her up with him, admiring the way her breasts swelled over the ridge of her arm. Her hand slipped, treating him to a glimpse of one hard-tipped peak. She was a pretty little thing, all pink and white with a nipped-in waist and rosebud nipples. His cock, hard and aching from the chase, pulsed in response to the inadvertent display.

The order flowed over Desi's calm, digging down into her determination, undermining the confidence she'd cultivated. What would be the point? The truth would only ensure he sent her back. She glanced around his arm to the long stretch of prairie, followed the flight of a bird as it swooped down over the grass, gliding on the wind.

Free. For one heartbeat she'd been like that, the future she'd wanted for herself there, just over the horizon. The bird disappeared into the haze, the spread of its wings blending into the rise of the hills. No matter how hard she strained, she couldn't follow it.

She took a step toward the horizon, wanting more than anything to vanish with it, far away from here. From the hell her life had become. Pressure in her arm drew her gaze down. Caine still held her. His fingers were suntanned and rough, looking very dark against the white skin of her upper arm. Smudges of dirt marred the sides, but, overall, they were surprisingly clean. The nails were pared short.

They were the hands of a hardworking man, bearing the scars and nicks of his life. Her gaze dipped down to the knife in his gun belt and then back up to those scars. A hardworking man and maybe a killer. Everyone knew Rangers were one short step up from the men they hunted—which could be her second piece of luck. If she couldn't count on his honor to gain her freedom, maybe he had a disreputable side she could exploit.

She tugged at her arm. Wind whipped her hair over her face, blocking her vision, but she didn't need to see the shake of his head to know his answer to her silent request. The tightening of his fingers said it all. The shifting of his stance reminded her he was still waiting on an answer. She'd definitely give him one, but not the one he wanted. Not the truth. That would cost her too much.

Pushing her hair out of her face, Desi raised her arms so her breasts were showcased, grabbing the heavy mass into a ponytail, relaxing her stance and expression to one she hoped looked welcoming. Flirtatious was going to take some working up to. "I'm looking to move on."

She bet he was a hell of a Ranger. He wasn't doing anything more than staring at her, and she could feel the need to confess welling.

"There isn't much west except Indian country."

She shrugged, letting her body relax against his. The hilt of his knife dug into her side. The pain blended with the agony in her soul. The muscled planes of his body were an unyielding wall of power, the ridge of his cock comfortingly familiar in the face of so much intimidating strength, and for once she was glad of the experience she'd acquired in the last year. There was nothing more pliable than a man with rutting on his mind. She tilted her head back, letting her hair slide over her shoulders, knowing how the thick, silky length intrigued men, ignoring the cold and the agony of her torn feet as she stepped into his embrace. What was one more scream among the soundless ones she'd already uttered? She kept everything but soft invitation out of her tone as she pointed out, "And California."

His eyes narrowed, but his arm came around her, his hand spreading on her spine, taking her weight. "You've got gold fever?"

He made it sound like a bad case of ague. "I don't know anyone who doesn't want to be rich."

"You'd do better to find a husband."

She was never going to be dependent on a man's whims again. She shoved the anger down, hoping that flicker of his eyelids didn't mean he'd spotted it. Right now she wanted him concentrating on sex and what he'd have to agree to do to get it. She shrugged, rubbing her breasts up and down his chest with the gesture, smiling internally as his cock leapt against her in response and added a bit more husk to her voice. "It's as easy to love a rich man as a poor one."

His other hand joined the first on her back. The warmth of his body encouraged her closer more persuasively than the press of his fingertips. "Money won't keep a woman safe."

"Now there, I disagree." She opened her hand, holding his gaze as she placed her palm to the right of his shirt placket, running her tongue over her lips as her fingers teased between the buttons, catching on the tight curls covering the swell of hard muscle. "With enough money, a woman can buy all the protection she requires."

That twitch of his eyebrows could have been amusement or disbelief. "You're planning on buying a man?"

"I prefer to think of it as—" she flipped the button open and slid her hand all the way inside, her palm shaping naturally to the curve of his pectoral as she tilted her head to the side, raising her eyebrows suggestively "—renting his skills."

"Skills?"

The quickened beat of his heart belied the flat neutrality of his question. He wanted her. The truth was in the hard gleam of his eyes and the sharp jerk of his cock. She lowered her lashes the way she'd been taught, letting her lips relax into a seductive pout, working a few more buttons open. "A woman often has needs only a man can fulfill."

His hand dipped to the hollow of her spine while the other curled under her chin, bringing her gaze dead center to his. "And you intend to buy them as you need them?"

She nodded as she tugged his shirt free of his denims, reaching around him to work it loose at the back, using her eyes and expression to enhance the suggestion in her words. "I find it a more productive method."

"And we're in negotiations now?" His grip shifted off

her chin, sliding across her neck, the rough calluses of his fingertips sending shivers of sensation blending into the shivers of cold as the wind blew. He didn't stop until his hand cupped her skull. She gave him responsibility for supporting her as she cuddled into his heat. He took it easily, confirming her belief that he was a man used to being in control. She'd have to play this very carefully.

"Oh, definitely."

The lines fanning out from the corners of his eyes deepened with amusement. "Sweetheart, I can see from here you don't have any money."

That hint of a smile took his face from harsh to sexy, sliding beneath her armor to find the woman she'd once been. The woman who'd believed in happily ever after. The woman who would have been instantly drawn to that mix of power and humor. The woman who would have given him the flick of her fan that would have encouraged him to come call. The woman she'd thought long dead and buried. The woman who thought all there was to seducing a man was a bat of an eyelash and a coquettish smile. That woman had learned a lot.

"But I do believe I have something you need." Desi dropped one hand from Caine's chest to his groin, following the bulge down his thigh, blinking when her hand traveled a lot farther than she'd anticipated before finding the fat head through the tight cotton. She gave it a squeeze, fascinated as the muscles in his throat worked as he swallowed. She'd never deliberately set out to seduce a man before. The thrill of power took her by surprise. "And I'll trade it for what I want."

"Which is?"

Confidence bubbled at the tension in his drawl. "Out of Los Santos."

"Take off my shirt."

The order landed wrong. She was the one in charge. "In a minute."

His hand came back around her head, more imperative than seductive. "That wasn't a request."

As if she didn't recognize an order when she heard one. Desi rubbed her palm lightly over the spongy head of Caine's shaft, looking for and finding that response again in the shift of his hips and the rapid beat of his pulse. She was used to men who grabbed, crushed and thrust at the first hint of desire. Caine's restraint was... fascinating. "I'm aware of that, but I want to play a bit first."

"You can play as soon as you get warm."

That pulled her up short. He wanted her comfortable? He hadn't finished the sentence before he was shrugging out of his shirt, taking his support away as he removed his arms from the sleeves. She just stared at him as she pointed out the truth. "But you'll be cold."

He lifted his eyebrow at her as if she'd said something totally ludicrous. His "I've been cold before" wrapped around her along with the shirt, enfolding her in the soft, warm wool and the knowledge that he was worried about her comfort. He was a very strange man.

She caught the edges before it could slip from her shoulders. She took a cautious breath. Threading through the faint smell of sweat and horse came that uniquely intriguing scent she associated only with him. Beneath her determination, the girl she'd used to be struggled for attention.

She squashed her flat. She couldn't afford to kill off this opportunity with idealistic moments. Caine was a man, and she was a woman. What was going on here was a bargain as old as time. Just because she wasn't hating it didn't change anything.

Her knees bent with the security she found in this up-front, honest negotiation. "Then I guess it will be up to me to warm *you* up."

On the way down, she couldn't help but admire his form. She'd never seen a naked man on this side of forty, and Caine was a very well-made man. The bulge of his pectorals curved to the broad ridges of his abdominal muscles. His shirt hem brushed her calves, sending a shiver of unfamiliar sensation up her spine as she followed that thin valley between his stomach muscles with her lips counting the hills on either side as she went. One, two, three. The well of his navel tempted her tongue to linger and flick. The inhalation of his breath proved an incentive to tease.

The gap that spread between the waistband of his pants and his flesh became an invite to explore. She caught the faint line of hair that started below, trapping a strand in her teeth, tugging it instinctively, smiling when he sucked in a harsh breath. He wasn't so different after all.

Caine's hand cupped her skull, once again applying that subtle direction she was coming to expect. She opened her mouth, pressing a hot kiss to the hard flesh of his abdomen, tracing a scar with her tongue until the smooth center ended just to the left of his navel in a rough pucker of healed flesh.

Thumbs under her chin pressed back, putting an inch between her mouth and his stomach, but never surrendering control, holding her in place for his pleasure. "Unbutton my pants."

She reached for the gun belt, flicking her tongue over her lips as she did, feeling his gaze as intently as a touch, the ache in her nipples a foreign, distracting sensation she pushed aside. "Leave the guns," he said, surprising her. She glanced up. He was staring at her with her eyes gone dark with passion and something else she couldn't define. "They might come in handy."

She didn't know whether to be comforted or dismayed he was still so aware of their location and the risk.

It was harder to get his pants undone with the heavy weight of the guns dragging on the belt, but he didn't fuss or swear, just waited patiently, his thumbs stroking her cheeks as she wrestled with the task. Around them the grass rustled with the passing breeze and birds chirped in a soothing melody she clung to, not understanding nor trusting the undercurrents that made this time feel so different.

She finally got the top two buttons undone. The next three relinquished the battle with an eagerness that reflected the increase in Caine's respiration, the only indication beyond his engorged cock she had that he was aroused. His stoicism annoyed her on some deeply feminine level she didn't begin to understand.

His hands left her cheeks just long enough to lower his pants the inches she needed to free his cock. And they definitely needed to lower. The thick shaft was too hard and too long just to pull out. A minute of expectant silence surrounded them as inch after inch appeared until finally, the broad head fell into her hand, swollen with passion, rigid with need, too heavy to stand upright. Dear God, she wasn't sure she'd be able to make him fit. She gave him a tentative squeeze, running her tongue over her lip.

His hand dropped to her shoulder while the other curved under her jaw, steadying her through the awkward moment.

"Hungry, baby?"

She shook her head on an instinctive "no."

His weight shifted and the whole atmosphere of the moment shifted right along with it. Desi's sense of power blinked out as if it'd never existed, and she was, once again, just a pathetically weak woman on her knees before a man who held all the cards.

"That's what I thought." The hand under her chin turned her face up to his, and she knew what that something else was she'd seen in his gaze. Pity. Her nails dug into Caine's thighs as he said, "Seems to me a woman must be pretty damned desperate to be willing to freeze her ass off bargaining with a stranger this way."

She closed her eyes as emotion washed over her in a sick wave. She didn't know what was stronger, despair or horror, just that both were potent contributors to the humiliation that had a stranglehold on her voice. "Maybe I'm just a natural born whore."

The statement she wanted to sound cold and matter-of-fact came out high and strained. Caine cocked his head to the side. His thumb stroked the corner of her mouth. "It's been my experience there's no such thing. Just women who've run out of options."

The downward tug on her arm was order enough. He didn't need to add the "Stay put."

He made himself decent with that efficiency of motion she was beginning to associate with him. His hand came back under her chin. She followed the silent direction. She had the sense he saw in her eyes everything she tried to hide—the pain, the despair, the stupid endless hope. "Tell me why."

She couldn't. He wouldn't believe her and even if he did, he wouldn't be able to help. He would be honor bound to uphold the law once he knew the truth. "You don't need to know why."

If his frown was any indication, he wasn't used to being denied.

"I'm a Texas Ranger. If you need help, I'm here to provide it."

She looked past him to the horizon. "We've already settled what I need."

"Indian country is no place for a woman."

But it was the only chance she had. She licked her lips. "You promised you'd let me go."

"No. I promised I'd get you out of Los Santos."

"But it was a trick." Acceptance flowed from her in a shuddering sigh. Just another trick.

Caine didn't hide from the truth. "Yes."

He'd needed to know what he was walking into. Desi's desperation combined with the padre's told him all he needed to know. The woman needed help. Badly. "But it's leading to a promise."

"What kind of promise?"

There was no challenge in the question, no hellfire and brimstone defiance, just more of that damn hopeless acceptance. The merciless sunlight reflected off the moisture gathering in her eyes, tears he knew she'd rather die than have him see.… Ah, hell. There was no going back for either of them.

He rubbed his thumb across her lips. "A Hell's Eight promise. One you can believe in. From here on out, Desi, you've no need to run. I won't let anyone hurt you."

She shook her head, her big blue eyes begging his. "Just let me go."

"No." Sending her off into Indian country with no protection would be tantamount to murder. Caine helped Desi to her feet, steadying her as she swayed. He jerked his chin to the west. "Whatever you're running from, it's not worse than what you'll find out there."

"You don't know anything."

"I know you belong with people who care for you."

"My people are dead."

"Your guardian, then."

Her upper lip curled in a sneer. "No, thank you." He made a note of her disgust as he dragged her along behind him toward the paint. The uneven tugging of his hand had him looking back. She was limping. He stopped. "Let me see your feet."

She didn't hesitate, merely lifted her left foot with an obedience that was oddly disturbing. He took it in his hand, the high arch and fine bones making him want to hold her safe. The state of the sole made him wince.

"Show me the other."

With that same obedience she lifted the other. *Shit.* They were both bruised and scraped but the right one was torn to shreds. Guilt roughed his temper. She'd been hurting and he'd let her play sex games. Not that he'd meant for things to go that far. He'd just been measuring the extent of her desperation when something else had risen between them. Something hot, dark and possessive. As a result, he'd acted as he never had. That fact wasn't sitting any better with him than the fact that she'd been hurt in the first place. He pressed lightly to the side of the deeper cut. Fresh blood welled. He met her gaze. "You should have said something."

She shrugged. "It doesn't matter."

He didn't like the resigned tone of her voice any more than he liked that disturbing obedience. Desi was a woman of fire, not calm. "It matters to me."

He dropped the reins and put his hands on her waist. His thumb and fingers met above her hips. The edges of her ribs cut into the sides of his palms as he lifted her onto the horse. Whoever had care of her wasn't doing their job. She was too thin.

As soon as her cute butt hit the saddle, she was kicking away at the horse's sides, trying to set the pony into a run. The paint snorted and tossed his head but didn't bolt. Caine picked his reins off the ground, patting the horse's neck as he danced under the conflicting messages.

"He's trained to stay put when the reins hit the dirt."

That just might have been a curse Desi uttered under her breath. It annoyed him that she just didn't let go with that temper. A woman like her shouldn't be hiding her light or trying to be less than she was. She should be shining brightly, letting that fire lead the way, burning any man lucky enough to be in her path with all that tempting passion.

He clucked his tongue, leading the pony to where they'd dropped the coat. Desi hunched in the saddle, her arms crossed over her chest, her expression sullen. The wind bit into his skin but not as much as the nagging suspicion tore at his peace that he was missing something important. He grabbed up the heavy coat and held it up to Desi.

"I'll trade you the coat for my shirt."

"You're getting the worse of the deal."

"Maybe, but it's the one I'm proposing."

She took the coat and held it against her chest, glaring at him as if he hadn't already seen all there was to be seen. "Turn around."

Caine sighed and gave her his back. First cloth rustled and then leather rasped against the saddle as she donned the coat.

The wind blew across the grass in a play of light, as he ran the facts as he knew them through his mind. She was a young woman without family. Attractive, headstrong and a touch wild. The other women hated her, claiming she wasn't fit company. There was only one thing that got good women's tails in a twist like that. The saddle creaked. The pony snorted and then, silence. He turned. Desi was bundled to her neck in the coat, which looked like it could about wrap around her twice. His shirt lay across the saddle. He grabbed it and shrugged it on. As he buttoned the front he said, "The women back there don't like you much."

Her gaze focused on a point past his shoulder. "No."

"You give them cause?"

"No."

"Are you the whore they say you are?"

The coat rustled as she jerked and cut him a glare. "I just attempted to...pleasure you with my mouth in a field. What do you think?"

"I think you're not the first woman left with only her body to barter. This country's hard on women."

"Not all women."

"No, but it chews up and spits out those without a man."

Her jaw muscles flexed. Her mouth worked. He patted her thigh. "Something you don't have to worry about anymore."

He stepped to the side, facing the paint. "Scoot up."

"What?"

He moved her hands to the pommel on either side of the horn. "Lever yourself up there."

Eyeing him with a clear suspicion that said he was up to no good, she supported her weight on her arms. In a smooth swing he was behind her, taking advantage of the distraction of the horse's dance to hook his arm around her waist, lifting her up as he swung into the saddle before settling her down onto his lap. She grabbed his hand as he gathered the reins, her short nails pressing against his skin as if she couldn't decide whether to claw or cling. Caine kneed the paint into motion, taking the decision off her hands.

A trot was never the most comfortable of gaits and the hardest for an inexperienced rider to adjust to. After about the third bone-jarring clop, Desi was bouncing like a sack of grain. He tucked her back against his chest. "Relax into me."

The glance she shot him over her shoulder clearly showed she wondered what good that would do, but she did, and followed the coaxing of his hand to curve her spine into his chest. He nudged the paint into a canter. He didn't think she breathed the whole way across the meadow. Resting his chin on her shoulder, he murmured in her ear, "I don't bite."

Desi jumped as if he just had. Then her spine pulled taut and that chin tilted up. "Would it make a difference if you did?"

The full-out attack knocked a smile loose. He did like a woman who didn't duck, hide or play shy. "I'm willing to try it if you are."

"Why?"

He took a deep breath. She smelled of sweat, fear and that tantalizing touch of lavender. "Because you've got grit and fire and are about the prettiest thing I've ever seen."

"You don't know me."

"And you don't know me, but I promise you, I'll keep you safe, and you don't have to bargain with anything to make it happen."

"You promised me out of Los Santos."

"Don't worry, I keep my promises."

Her grunt let him know how little stock she put in that.

The pony stumbled. She lurched to the side and he yanked her back. The coat splayed open, giving him a clear view down between the plump inner curves of her breasts to the small indentation of her navel and the temptation below. He brought his hand up. She stiffened and grabbed his wrist. He let her cling while he closed the gap. They came into sight of the others while he was tucking in the lapels.

The dramatic gasps of the women drew a disgusted glance from Tracker who was repacking the saddlebags. Clearly, the three thought he'd been in the bushes making time with Desi rather than chasing her over every bump in the ground. The fact that they wouldn't be far wrong stung his pride. Sam looked up from where he was covering the bodies with blankets and debris. The makeshift covering would hide them long enough for them to get clear of the area. More than that they didn't need. Everyone knew where Hell's Eight land began and ended. And if they didn't, he and the men wouldn't waste time making the knowledge public.

A mutter of *whore* drifted in on the breeze. Said in a feminine voice and laced with disgust, it hit Desi with the force of a blow. If Caine hadn't been holding her, she would have doubled over. Hot color rose to flood her neck and cheeks until it finally engulfed her entire face.

If they were in a bedroom and she was dropping her clothing piece by piece, he'd probably find that blush damn charming, but here in the open, with the inspiration being the censure of three women he didn't give two shits about, well, it didn't sit well. "Sam, you got any of that salve left?"

"In the saddlebag."

He slid off the horse, keeping his hand on Desi's thigh. Even through the coat the firm curve tempted him to slide his hand down the six inches necessary to touch bare skin. She had very soft skin. "Bring it over along with some water, would you?"

"Coming right up."

Murmurs from the women sidled across the distance. "Disgusting." Followed by, "Even in front of decent women, he can't keep his hands off her." With every word, the muscles beneath Caine's hand tightened. The paint grunted a protest as Desi squeezed those thighs in reaction to the insults. He looked up, expecting to find that chin set proudly. Instead, it was lodged somewhere down between her collarbone.

Shit. "Want me to cut their tongues out and leave 'em as buzzard bait along with the rest of the refuse?"

He had to wait a second but then her eyes met his. They were packed with a whole lot of anger and maybe just a touch of humor.

"I think that would just make the buzzards sick."

Yup. Definitely a sense of humor. Fire, grit and humor, all wrapped up in a pretty-as-a-picture package. And he'd woken up this morning thinking it was a day like any other. Just goes to show how far off a man could be in his estimations.

"Now, I definitely think you have the right of that, ma'am," Sam strolled up with that easy way he had, that smile that women fawned over on his too-handsome face and real warmth in his normally cold eyes. In his hands he had a poncho and the salve. Desi's response was a minimal twitch of her lips, but that she responded at all nicked Caine on his tender side.

Caine angled in, cutting off Sam's approach. Unlike

Tracker, who'd accepted his claim with little more than a flick of an eyebrow, Sam stiffened. That was the thing about Sam and what had earned him the nickname "Wild Card." There was no telling which way the man would jump, just a damn certainty that when the bullets cleared, he'd be standing on whatever side he'd decided was right. Sam tossed him a poncho.

Caine held out his hand for the salve and canteen. Sam hesitated another second, his gaze meeting Caine's in a clear challenge. They'd known each other since they were ten, survived hell together, saved each other's asses more than once, been the only thing either could depend on for the last fifteen years, but in that moment Caine knew the truth. He'd fight Sam for Desi. And he'd take the battle however far he had to in order to guard his claim. Hell of a thing for a man to realize in the middle of nowhere.

Sam held his gaze for a couple more seconds. Though he wasn't pushing it now, the message was clear. He had every intention of being competition. Damn!

Sam tossed Caine the salve before turning to Desi with a smile and a nod of his head.

"Sam MacGregor." He jerked his thumb over his shoulder. "Don't let those biddies get under your skin, ma'am. There's no one here who gives their opinions any weight."

Desi took a slow breath as the handsome man made his interest known, concentrating on making that one breath perfectly even in a desperate attempt to avoid bolting. She didn't want him to want her. Frigid water pouring over her foot ruined her concentration. She took another breath and tried again as Caine cleaned the area with the faded red handkerchief he'd removed from his neck. Through it all, the blond man watched her, study-ing her reaction.

Big as the other two, he was the handsomest of the lot, but that cold air of lethal efficiency he wore like most people wore a smile was scary. A woman would have no say in his bed. Metal popped against metal as Caine opened the tin of salve. Much as she was trying to avoid looking at either man, she couldn't stop herself from looking at Caine when he pulled her foot away from the horse's side.

If the other two men scared her, Caine terrified her to her bones. Danger lurked around him in an invisible shimmer, so much a part of his presence, she didn't even think he realized it. She knew he could kill as easily as he changed his socks, and she knew he wouldn't worry overly much about it when he was done. Survival was a matter of course to him. He was a lot like the land that way—rugged, deadly and uncompromising. Those who understood that and respected it would survive. Those who didn't, would die.

She watched as he threw another silent challenge at Sam and held her breath through the outcome. Oh, God, there wasn't a thing to stop them from taking what they wanted except maybe the presence and disapproval of Mavis and her friends. As a shield it was an extremely flimsy one and once they got to town even that would disappear.

She realized Sam was still looking at her, waiting on an answer, a slight frown putting a crease between his startling, slate-blue eyes. She blinked slowly, strug-gling for some sort of neutral response that wouldn't increase his interest. The only thing that came to mind was "Thank you."

She dug her nails into the leather pommel as he continued to study her. If these three succeeded in getting her back to town, the situation would only get worse. She knew what James would do. He was too smart to cross men like these. He'd give them whatever they wanted with a smile and an eye to survival.

She locked her gaze over Caine's left shoulder, focusing on the winter-killed grass at the edge of the frigid stream. No matter what, she couldn't let them get her back to town.

Sam was still looking at her. She could feel his gaze like a touch. She didn't know what he was looking for or what he expected, but she sincerely hoped he gave up looking for it soon, otherwise she was going to break and the whirlwind of emotion twisting inside would rip free. If that happened, she didn't know how she'd ever get it back under control.

The salve stung as Caine worked it into her cuts, giving her something else to focus on. She winced, and Caine paused.

"I'm being as gentle as I can." The apology in the flatly worded statement brought her gaze down. Caine's attention was on her foot. Despite the fact that her bare leg was inches from his face and she could see the bulge of his manhood where his chaps hugged his hips, there was nothing lecherous in his touch. Only caretaking with a hint of...tenderness? The sheer absurdity of the notion brought her up short. That soft part of her was once again chasing rainbows. Men like this weren't tender, and even if they were, it wasn't the kind of emotion they wasted on women like her.

Sam turned to Caine. "Beyond the horses and a couple decent guns, there wasn't much worth saving off that bunch."

Caine didn't look up from his treatment of her foot. "Not a shock there."

"One of the horses is wind broke."

Even Desi knew what that meant. Her brother had once, in ignorance, bought a horse with that condition, ridden so hard and cared for so poorly that he couldn't exert himself without fighting for breath. Her father had had one of the guides put it out of its misery. There was no mercy for the weak in this territory.

"Damn. Which one?"

"The sorrel. It's a shame, too. He's got a nice gait on him and a real pleasant how-de-do."

Caine patted her thigh almost absentmindedly and ducked under the paint's neck before taking her other foot into that inexorable grip and dousing it with more of the icy water. "You like him."

It wasn't a question so much as a statement of fact. Sam shrugged. "Just hate to see good horseflesh abused."

Caine ran his finger down the center of her right foot in an ethereal caress, sending strange tingles upward and outward. She couldn't help her shiver. She didn't know if the quirk of his lips was for her reaction or Sam's.

"I don't suppose it would hurt to bring him along. As long as we don't run into trouble, he should be fine."

Sam nodded. "That was my thought." He jerked his head in the direction of the other women. "Suppose I'd better go help Tracker get that lot saddled up."

He sounded like he'd rather be nibbled to death by ducks. Not the reaction Mavis and her friends were used to getting from men.

"Better you than me."

Desi looked down as Caine probed the edges of the deep cut near her arch. "You're not going to put the horse down?"

She couldn't see his face for the brim of his hat, but his attention was clearly more on her foot than her words.

"Not without need."

She would have thought the fact the horse couldn't pull his weight constituted need. Fleeting pressure on her ankle was her only warning before he worked the ointment into the wound. It hurt nearly as much as getting the injury in the first place. Her exclamation was involuntary. His response disconcerting.

"Easy, baby." The stroke of his hand on her calf was both soothing and absurdly comforting. She yanked back, but she couldn't break his hold. Caine's palm curved around her calf. He massaged her leg while standing so close the heat from his body warmed her cold skin. The pain eased.

At her terse "Thank you," he touched her tightly curled toes in a way she could only describe as tender. Except this was not a tender man. She relaxed her foot, watching him carefully. Her reward was another squeeze of her calf and the resetting of her leg against the horse's side. He was definitely a confusing one, though.

Caine tugged the reins over the horse's head and dropped them to the ground, his mouth creasing at the corners with the hint of amusement as he ordered, "Stay put."

And also an irritating one, she decided. Even if she leaned forward the reins were out of her reach, which meant she had no choice but to stay where he'd put her. Caine headed toward the area where the rest of the group waited, mounted. Each step was infused with that combination of strength, grace and confidence that once would have filled her with interest. He stopped at the side of an all-black horse, with white hindquarters covered with black spots, and opened the saddlebags. The horse snaked its head around, teeth showing. With an ease that spoke of long practice, he smacked it across the nose while pulling something free of the bag. Not brutally, but more in the way of a warning. As he tied the bag shut, the horse gathered its haunches as if to kick. Another light slap, this time on its hindquarters, and the horse settled down. With a comment to the women who were waiting in various degrees of comfort on their horses and a pat to the black horse's shoulder as if what had passed between them were some sort of game, Caine headed back, tucking something into his back pocket before taking whatever he'd grabbed from under his arm.

When he got close enough, he held up a brown wad of material lying on top of a pile of leather. "Thought you might like these."

The first "these" were woolen socks, the second, high-topped moccasins.

"They'll be too big."

He shrugged and tucked the moccasins under his arm. "They'll do the job until you get your own clothes."

"I don't have any." The confession slipped out before she could catch it, snapping his gaze to hers. She quickly waved to the items in his hands. "Moccasins, I mean."

"Uh-huh." He cupped her foot in his hands, warming it between his palms a second before bending to blow. His breath was hot and moist, scalding in comparison to the chill she felt to her bone. Before she could come up with a suitable protest, he worked the sock over her foot. As soon as he came around to the other side, she tucked her foot back against the horse's withers.

"I can do it myself."

"Not without risking falling off that horse, and I'd say at this point you have enough bruises."

As if that settled that, he hooked his fingers around her

ankle and drew her foot forward. She suffered through another warming before he slid the sock on. He tipped his hat back when he was done. "Admit it, that feels better."

Even though she didn't like the proprietary way he handled her body, she couldn't deny how good it felt to have her flesh covered. She hated to be cold. "Yes, it does."

He slid the moccasin on, tying the fringed top above her knee, his touch impersonal again. "Good."

He went back around the other side, moccasin at the ready. She experimented with bending her right leg. She couldn't straighten it all the way. She tried to flex it again as he slipped the other moccasin on. "I can't walk in these."

He tied the second moccasin with the same impersonal efficiency as he had the first. "But you can ride, which is more important."

"What if we need to run?"

"If it comes to a footrace, we're both dead."

He pulled worn leather gloves from his back pocket. With a curl of his fingers, he ordered her to hold out her hands. She did, cautiously, not liking the emotion flirting with the perimeter of his stern features. He slipped the gloves on her hands and then, before she could pull back, looped a long piece of rawhide around both her wrists, flipping the string between her before she could protest. When he put her bound hands on the saddle horn, there was no mistaking the emotion tugging at his mouth. Amusement.

He tipped his battered brown hat and grabbed up the reins, leading the paint toward the black-spotted horse. "Just in case you were thinking of running from me."

3

Well, at least she was consistent. Caine shifted Desi as she sat sideways on his lap, pulling the thick collar of his coat up over her cheeks, protecting her from chill as they rode into the wind. Adjusting his own poncho, he glanced over at Sam, and damn, he wanted to laugh all over again. Sam was as wet as Desi and mad enough to chew lead and spit bullets. Served Sam right, though, for thinking Desi had even a passing acquaintance with the word quit.

Untying her hands at the river crossing had been Sam's first mistake. Thinking a fear of drowning would be a deterrent to trying to escape had been his second. Hell, for that much foolishness he deserved a cold ride back. Water seeped from Desi's clothes through Caine's denims as he scanned the countryside. They'd saved half a day by cutting through Hell's Eight land and slipping through the cave at the back of that box canyon, but he didn't like how quiet things were. The hair on the back of his neck was standing up straight, which always meant trouble brewing.

He didn't have to look far for the cause. The women's kidnapping had been too haphazard to have been carried out by experienced men, which meant they must have been hired by experienced men, meaning there were likely real Comancheros sitting out there without their income. Not good. Chaser, sensing his tension, snorted and did a quick sidestep. Desi's fingers dug into his shirt.

"Easy."

Both woman and horse ignored the order. A tightening of the reins brought Chaser in line, but Desi was going to take a bit more effort. She shifted on his lap, looking over his shoulder.

"When we get back to Los Santos, you're going to be owing me a new pair of moccasins."

Her wiggling stopped and that peculiar stillness that came over her when she was riled and hiding it froze her up. "I'm sure you can soften them up with a bit of saddle soap."

"Now why would I be doing that since it was your harebrained idea that got them wet?"

"It wasn't harebrained, it was…" The sentence trailed off. She tucked her head and that wealth of hair fell over her face, obscuring her expression. He tipped her chin up. She didn't duck his gaze, just glared at him, blue eyes dark with fury and frustration. And under it all, something he was sure she didn't want him to see.

"Desperate might be the word you were looking for." Only desperation could drive a woman to turn her horse into deep water, clinging to the animal's back with the same reckless courage that had the horse following the command.

Her lips set in a flat line. She jerked her chin, but he didn't let her hide, just held her there, studying the subtle nuance of her expression as she wrestled with her demons. "The closer we get to Los Santos, the more desperate you get. Care to tell me why?"

Cold resentment pushed out every other emotion in that face that made him think of warm smiles and sultry invitations.

"I already told you."

Yes, she had, but he'd like a bit more detail. He reached back into the saddlebag and pulled out a stale biscuit and some jerky. "Seeing as that's the case, I expect you'd like a last meal?"

Her stomach rumbled. She held out her bound wrists, arching her hands back to facilitate being untied.

"Uh-uh." He dropped the food onto the plateau formed by the oversized gloves. "I learned my lesson watching you teach Sam to swim. Those hands stay tied."

She rested her hands on her lap, making no attempt to eat the food, presenting him with a clear view of her profile; small nose, pointed chin, smooth forehead and full lips that practically begged for a man to plant a kiss on them. He tapped the biscuit, knowing damn well she understood the order. Not by a twitch of those thick lashes did she acknowledge his presence. Another smile tugged at his lips.

"You keep this up and in about four miles, I'm going to start noticing you're snubbing me and my feelings are bound to get hurt."

Nothing. He hitched her back a bit and, keeping one hand on the reins, picked up the biscuit with the other. He held it to her mouth. Her stomach rumbled louder, but those kissable lips stayed tightly closed. She swallowed once. Twice. A person had to be damn hungry to salivate at the thought of a day-old biscuit. "When's the last time you ate?"

Her lips barely moved as she imparted the information, no doubt worried he was going to shove the biscuit in. "A few days ago."

Damn. "We were told you women were taken some-time last night."

Outlaws often did their dirty work by the big Comanche moon that lit the plains like daylight.

She shrugged and turned her face into his chest, stomach rumbling, throat rippling, defying common sense. He lowered the biscuit and shook his head. "You are one stubborn woman."

"If you put me on my own horse, you won't have to endure my company anymore."

He had to smile at her persistence. "Now why would I do that? It's not so often I get to hold a pretty woman in my arms that I'm eager to give up the pleasure."

She rolled those big eyes and snorted indelicately. "I'm dripping wet, smell of horse, blood and other unpleasant things."

"No arguing, you *are* a bit ripe." Her outraged gasp caught on his sense of humor and gave it a tug. "But compared to that dead deer I hauled last week, you're a clear step up."

That fast, the steel left her spine. She shrugged down into the coat like a cake gone flat. He wondered if she'd actually been fishing for a compliment.

He returned the biscuit to her mouth. "I'm adding prickly to your list of attributes."

She shot him a glare.

He shook his head. "Not eating won't prove anything, and will just leave you too weak to fight."

She snapped a bite, narrowly missing his fingertips. He waited until she got four good chews in, just enough to have the hard tack spread through her mouth before adding, "Truth be told, though, I don't think I've ever had a prettier woman keep me company in the saddle." If looks could kill, he'd be dead. She struggled to get a retort with the hard tack gluing her tongue to the roof of her mouth.

He dropped the biscuit into her hands and untied the canteen. Pulling the cork free with his teeth, he held it to her lips. She swished the first mouthful around before swallowing. After that, she just drank like there was no tomorrow. He pulled the canteen away, anger churning in his gut. If he'd known what bad shape she was in, he would have insisted she eat and drink back at the river and to hell with her stubbornness or the risk. "I take it that it's been a while since you've had a good drink?"

"Our kidnappers weren't overly concerned with the niceties."

"None of us had a drink because of her," Mavis called over the snort of the sorrel she was riding. Her dark hair was pulled back in a makeshift bun, her clothes as properly straightened as they could be after the day they'd had.

Since Tracker had seen to the other women's needs earlier while Sam had been fishing Desi out of the San Antonio, Caine didn't see a need for her outrage. Apparently, Mavis didn't agree. She pointed at Desi and kept going. "She's always causing trouble, bringing shame down on us all. No matter how often my brother disciplines her, she continues with her promiscuous ways."

Desi's face closed up tighter than a drum. She stared out across the rolling plains, shutting the other woman out. Shutting him out. Caine pulled the coat collar up to shield her as Sam rode her. Sam took one look at Desi's posture, grabbed the sorrel's bridle and shook his head.

"For an attractive woman, you sure are ugly," he informed Mavis as he led her horse away. Mavis didn't take kindly to that verdict and her argument was both loud and heated until Tracker shut her up by pointing out that she was drawing Indians.

Caine waited until she was out of earshot. "That woman has a belly full of hate for you."

He didn't think Desi was going to answer, but finally, she did. "Yes."

"Her brother is your guardian?"

"Yes."

"How'd that come to be? You kin?"

"No. But the circuit judge felt it was in my best interest to have one."

"And he picked her brother?"

"Yes."

"How old are you?"

"Twenty."

"And they thought 'best' was a guardian for a grown woman?"

She shrugged. "The town fathers felt I had wayward tendencies."

"By wayward, I take it they felt you were forward with men?"

"Yes."

"And what did you do to make them think that?"

Her expression grew tighter, more defensive. "Nothing."

He believed her. Desi was more likely to remove a man's balls than to delight in the fact that he had them.

"For a circuit judge to make a decision like that about a grown woman there had to be proof of a need."

Nothing moved on her except her mouth. "*They* had a lot of proof."

He didn't miss the emphasis on they. "Who are 'they'?"

"The town fathers," she said with no emphasis on

anything, as if reciting the facts. As if she expected him to believe the nonsense she was spouting.

"Why is it so important to you that I believe the worst of you?"

"It saves time."

He took the canteen back and handed her a piece of jerky, settling her more comfortably against his chest. She could try until hell froze over, but he was never going to believe she was the forward type who needed a guardian to keep her behavior in check.

"Well, time I've got plenty of, so I guess it doesn't matter if you waste a bit of it."

LOS SANTOS WASN'T AS big as San Antonio, but it shared the same Franciscan heritage reflected in the fact that the church overshadowed every other building in the complex. The steeple could be seen for miles, and when the setting sun glinted off the inlaid tiles around the towers as it was doing now, it served as a beacon, drawing folk in from near and far.

Partial walls protected the town's most vulnerable sides, but not much else stood in the way of defense. The size of the town itself was its best defense. Ten miles west of San Antonio, situated on a broad bend of the same river and boasting close to one hundred residents—all heavily armed—not many saw it as a prime target. Not when there were so many other smaller settlements and ranches cropping up on the outskirts. As they approached, the church bell rang and residents poured into the street.

"There's Bert!" Mavis cried as a broad, hatless man came out to the middle of the street. She stood in the stirrups and waved her arms. After a second, the man shielded his eyes against the glare and then turned and shouted before running toward them, sunlight flashing off the star pinned to his chest.

Abigail and Sadie just as eagerly searched the crowd, standing in their stirrups until they, too, spotted their loved ones. Waving and crying, they yanked at their reins until Sam and Tracker turned their horses loose and let them gallop ahead to meet their kin.

In contrast, Desi didn't even look up, just turned her face into his chest and took slow, even, very careful breaths. Caine brushed her hair off her cheek, dipping his fingers to the base of her neck, sliding his thumb around to the hollow of her throat, feeling the rapid beat of her pulse. For all that she sat calm and composed, she was terrified.

Tracker rode up beside him. He jerked his chin at Desi.

"She doesn't look none too happy to be home."

Caine nodded, curving his hand over her shoulder, the rounded point fitting precisely into his palm. "I noticed."

"I don't see anyone stepping forward to greet her."

"It's only been a minute." Though he knew what Tracker was getting at. It seemed hard to believe that anyone missing Desi wouldn't be at the forefront of the watch for her return.

"I don't like the feel of this."

He didn't, either. "She's got a guardian appointed by the circuit judge."

Sam rode up on the other side, the same concern in his gaze as in Tracker's.

"The padre that sent us after her?"

"No. Mavis's brother."

Tracker snorted. "Now, why doesn't that make me all warm and toasty in my gut?"

Probably for the same reason it didn't make him. The women had reached the men. There was a lot of cheering and hugging as everyone crowded around, wanting to hear the details of their rescue. A man separated from the crowd, the brightness of his white shirt against his paisley vest almost blinding as it reflected the rays of the setting sun. He stood apart from the crowd, legs spread, arms folded across his chest. Waiting.

Sam pushed his hat back off his brow and rested his forearm across the horn of his saddle. A body would have thought him completely relaxed, unless they noticed the repetitive opening and closing of his fingers. Anyone familiar with a gunslinger's habits would recognize what he was doing. Sam wasn't getting a toasty gut, either. "Looks like someone's waiting on her return."

Tracker spat his disgust. "A gambler."

"Could just be a fancy dresser," Sam offered, testing the fit of his revolver in the holster strapped to his leg.

"Yup." Caine pulled his rifle from the scabbard and rested it across the saddle between the pommel and Desi's hip. She cut him a startled glance. He squeezed her shoulder. "Is that your guardian, Desi?"

She didn't turn her head, didn't answer, but her respirations came two beats faster than normal. Finally, she nodded.

Tracker frowned. "What kind of judge gives guardianship of a young lady to a goddamn gambler?"

None that Caine knew. "Any chance you remember the name of the judge who heard your case, Desi?"

She would never forget. Not the way he had sat up on the church altar as though he were God on high. Not the way he'd acted the all-knowing, benevolent wise man, nor what had come after. "Judge Harvey Clayton."

All three men swore at once.

"Well, that puts a clearer shine on things," Sam muttered.

Caine rested his chin on her head and continued to stroke her arm with his fingers while, with every clop of the horses' hooves on the wet ground, they got closer and closer to James. Desi closed her eyes and worked harder at getting her hands out of the gloves. By keeping her wrists apart after Sam had retied her, and letting her hair drip on the leather, she'd managed to stretch the ties some as they absorbed the water.

She risked a glance out of the corner of her eye. James was waiting and he wasn't happy. He only stood that way when he wasn't happy. Oh, God, she needed to get free. She worked her hands more frantically inside the gloves, pulling so hard the ties cut into her skin through the leather. She bit her cheek against the pain.

Caine's strong hand settled over hers, engulfing her hands and wrists in the warmth of his touch. Again she got that conflicting message of threat and comfort. He squeezed, defeating her efforts with disheartening ease. She looked up. She couldn't read a thing in his expression, partly because of the glare of the sun, and partly because he was just too good at hiding what he was thinking.

She tugged at her hands. Another squeeze and a shake of his head told her he knew what she was doing. The horse stopped. She heard James approaching. She'd sat and waited too many times like this not to recognize the sound of his tread. He always scuffed his foot on the third step.

Caine straightened. The rifle barrel pressed into her hip as he changed the angle.

"Ranger."

James's voice was smooth and well modulated. Pitched

to inspire confidence. He stepped into Desi's view. His facial muscles were set in the same open, confidence-inspiring expression. His ability to charm people while hiding what he really thought was what made him such a successful gambler. He touched the brim of his hat with his finger. One finger. Her flinch escaped her control. "Desi."

Caine's grip on her shoulder tightened. He didn't have to worry. She would never throw herself into this man's arms.

James nodded to the other two men, who fanned out on either side of Caine. "I want to thank you all for bringing our Desdemona back to us."

Tracker was the one who answered, a chill underlying his deep drawl. "It's our job."

James's smile was easy and appreciative, as if he'd been longing to have her back. He probably had been, which accounted for the sincerity she sensed. "I hope she wasn't too much trouble."

"Why would you think she'd be any trouble?" Caine asked.

"Pretty as she is, surely you've noticed she's not quite right in her head."

As naturally as most people breathed, James slipped the lie into the conversation. Against her shoulder, she felt Caine stiffen. She straightened her spine, shifting away from the illusion that his strength was hers. It was starting again, just like it had before. The innuendo, the twisting of the truth until everything she'd done in self-defense was nothing more than another example of her instability.

She curled her fingers into fists as the rage beat against the futility of effort. Lawman or not, with her back-ground, Caine wouldn't listen to her, let alone believe her.

What was the word of one deranged woman compared to the word of so many upstanding citizens? When push came to shove, he'd given her to them.

Caine's "Can't say that I have" caught her totally by surprise, the same way Tracker's "Bullshit" and Sam's "For Christ's sake" did. Usually, when men came up against James's confidence and smooth manner they went along with him. Caine and his men were the first who hadn't, and she didn't care if it was their naturally perverse nature or genuine belief that drove them to do it. She was just glad they had. It gave her a minute more of hope.

James looked her up and down, the concern never leaving his expression, but that twitch at the corner of his eye let her know that he was annoyed. He stepped in, holding his hand up to Caine. If Caine hadn't chosen that moment to hook his foot over her ankle, she would have kicked James in his teeth.

"James Haddock. Desdemona's guardian. And I'm glad she's been having a good day."

Caine made no effort to shake James's hand. "I wouldn't exactly call it 'good.'"

"That probably wasn't the best choice of words."

If anything, the solid wall of muscle against her side got harder. Desi tilted her head back. Caine was staring at James with that impassive face that gave away nothing. To him or to her.

"What would be a better choice?" Caine asked, his finger touching her cheek, the calluses on his fingertip feeling strange against her skin before recurving his hand round her shoulder. Though it was illogical, she felt safer with it there.

"Stable maybe?" James's sigh was sympathy personified as he stepped back. Behind him, spectators gathered. Most of them just bored townsfolk, but a few like Bert, Bryan and Carl had an interest even if they weren't going to reveal it. She shuddered. They would never touch her again.

"Ever since her *ordeal*," James continued, taking a step closer. "There's been no knowing how she's going to be one day to the next."

Desi sucked in a breath and held it, pointless outrage surging. Again. Caine unhooked his leg from over her feet.

"Ordeal?"

"I'm afraid so."

She curled her hands into fists, knowing what was coming. How it was going to end. Caine's chin bumped her head lightly and then his lips brushed her ear. "Breathe, Desi."

She didn't think she was ever going to breathe again.

"Ever since she came to us her mental condition has been...delicate."

"I am not insane." For once she wanted to say that and have someone really believe her.

"Of course you're not," James agreed immediately, that smile she hated stretching his lips and that warning tic pulling infinitesimally at the corner of his eye. "You've just had a tough time recovering from your experience with the Comancheros last year."

Shame and anger warred for dominance. Everyone knew what Comancheros did to captives. Everyone knew how filthy they left a woman. Forever tainted. Scorned.

"That true, Desi?" Caine asked, no discernible inflection in his voice.

"I'm not crazy."

"I already know that. I was questioning the part about the Comancheros."

There would be no point in denying it. The sheriff or the priest would back up James's claim. She dug her nails so hard into her palms they ached. "Yes."

"Damn, I'm sorry, honey."

Honey? When had she become *honey?* She took one deep slow breath, then two.

"Is that how you lost your parents?"

She didn't bother with three. Simply gave up the struggle for calm. It just wasn't possible with the threat of her return hanging over her head and Caine bringing the pain of the past to the fore. "Yes." And her twin sister. She closed her eyes on that memory.

James took a step forward, and the snap of a twig under his foot jerked her eyes open. This time Caine didn't put his foot over hers as he came almost into reach. "We've done our best by her."

"That's true," Sheriff Hatchet said, coming up. "The girl was wild when she first got here. No one could get near her. There was talk of sending her back east to one of those asylums until James here agreed to take her on." He slapped James on the back. "Don't know how he did it, but he worked wonders with the girl." He shook his head in amazement. "Pure wonders."

"Did he work wonders on you, Desi?" Caine asked, still with no inflection in his voice to give her an idea of what he wanted her to say.

"Her name is Desdemona," James corrected before she could answer.

"The girl spoke clear enough when she introduced herself."

That came from Sam.

James took a step nearer. The side of Caine's hand dug into her hip as he adjusted his aim. James stopped midstride. He blinked, then slowly raised his hands and reversed his steps. The fear on his face gave Desi no end of satisfaction.

"Ranger," the sheriff interjected. "James is the girl's legal guardian. If you have a problem with that, you'll need to take it up with the circuit judge next time he comes through."

The saddle creaked as Caine shifted his weight. "I'm thinking maybe I will."

"I assure you, Ranger, we've only had her best interests in mind."

"Can't help it if it strikes my suspicious bone funny when the territories' crookedest judge gives a pretty young girl to a gambler for caretaking."

"Can't argue with the results," the sheriff pointed out.

"I guess that would depend on which angle you were viewing the results from," Caine countered.

To her surprise, Caine slid the rifle under her hands, pushing it forward until the smooth stock pressed against the heels of her hands and the hammer caught on her gloves. "You want to weigh in on James's caretaking, Desi?"

She looked up at him only to find him staring down at her, green eyes serious. He couldn't mean what she thought he meant. "I can shoot him?"

He nodded. "Anywhere you want."

He had to be joking. She fumbled through the gloves to get her finger around the trigger. However, if there was a chance he was serious, she wasn't missing out. Hate welled up, spreading outward in a cold, dark wave.

Could she do it? Did she have it in her to kill him and to hell with the consequences?

She tilted the gun. It wobbled. Caine steadied it for her as she lifted it and sighted down the barrel at James's face, savoring the terror in his expression, remembering how it felt that night he'd begun "working wonders" with her. Remembering how helpless she'd felt. So damn sick and afraid. So betrayed.

The sight at the end of the muzzle dropped over his torso. She followed the line of buttons on his vest until she came to the waistband of his fancy black broadcloth pants. From there it was only a matter of two more inches before she reached her destination. There. Right there was where she wanted the first shot to go.

James swore and backed up, stumbling over his own feet. With Caine's help, she kept the rifle trained as he landed on his butt in the mud. The sheriff grabbed for his revolver, but before he got it clear of his holster, she squeezed the trigger, keeping her eyes on the target, wanting to see the bullet hit. Wanting the satisfaction.

At the last second, the gun tilted down and there was an explosion of mud that sprayed between James's feet. While she stared, not understanding, Caine removed the gun from her hands.

"Guess that answers my question."

But it didn't answer hers. She wanted the gun back in her hands. She wanted one second more. She wanted James dead. She stared at the gloves overwhelming her hands and felt Caine all around her. Another man using her to get what he wanted. "Why did you stop me?"

The quaver in her voice was barely perceptible but Caine heard it. Desi had a belly full of anger and no outlet. He tipped her face up. The pain and rage in her eyes ate at his gut. "I figure you've got enough scars, you don't need the kind killing a man can bring."

"I wouldn't mind."

He released her chin and moved the rifle out of her reach, aiming it at the men rushing up from the edge of town. "I would."

He squeezed with his right knee and Chaser turned into the oncoming crowd. "You best be telling those men to holster their guns, Sheriff, or this town's going to be short some of its important citizens."

"You can't just come in here and start shooting people, Allen."

"Unless you're going to stop me," he told the older man, "I can pretty much do whatever the hell I want."

And what he wanted right now was justice.

"He's got a point," Tracker drawled, a revolver in each hand, his horse tossing its head as the tension built. "We just start shooting up towns whenever we get the urge, eventually someone's going to slap up a wanted poster with our pictures on it."

"Not that I particularly mind," Sam added, his new revolver in one hand and a shotgun in the other. "Hell, we've skirted the wrong side of legal all our lives, but you know damn well they aren't going to do our handsome faces justice on those damn posters and that would pain me."

"What would you suggest?"

"We should just take the girl and leave."

Caine pretended to consider the suggestion as the sheriff—as crooked a son of a bitch as Caine had ever seen—settled his weight into his boots with misplaced confidence. "There are ten of us here and only three of you, son. I think you'd better settle down."

Caine had no intention of settling down. A short,

stocky figure in brown robes pushed through the crowd. Caine bumped Desi's butt with his thigh to get her attention. "Desi, I want you to slide on down now and go stand with Father Gerard."

He didn't want her anywhere near him if shooting commenced. He held her wrists as her feet touched the ground, stretching her back, forcing her to look at him. At the base of her throat, where the coat parted, he could see her pulse pounding. She was afraid but game. A woman a man could depend on.

"No running. Not this time." He held her gaze, trusting Tracker and Sam to guard his back. She finally nodded.

"Give me your word." A flare of surprise crossed her face, and then that chin set and she gave a short nod.

"Good." He let her go. She limped over to Father Gerard, her steps awkward due to the way he'd tied the moccasins and the cuts on her feet. As soon as she reached the priest, he put his arms around her. She held up her hands. The older man went to work on the knots. Across the small distance her triumph was palpable. Caine nodded, ceding her the small victory. Then he turned back to the gambler. "I'm revoking your guardianship."

"You can't do that." A portly man who shouldn't have anything to do with the discussion broke in. Immediately, another man shushed him. Both were better dressed than farmers. All confident. None of them should have cared one way or another what happened to one small woman with no family or influence.

I'll die there.

Desi's words took on deeper meaning. An ugly suspicion took root as he pulled the puzzle pieces together. Mavis's unreasonable dislike. The sheriff's interest. The judge giving her over to the gambler. Father Gerard's veiled innuendos about circumstances and his request for Caine to watch out for her personally. Son of a bitch. He didn't like the conclusion he was reaching. He waved the rifle barrel at the fat man. "Who are you?"

The man paled but didn't back up, obviously under some illusion that Caine would suffer a pang of conscience at plugging him. "Bryan Sanders. Representative of Steel, Jones and Steel."

"And who are they?" From the cut of the man's clothes, "they," were well-heeled.

"A group of gentlemen with financial interests in the region."

"Bankers." Sam spat. Sam liked bankers about as much as he liked gamblers.

Caine considered himself to be more open-minded, but in this case, he had to agree. He was developing his own dislike for the fat banker. "It must have been real tempting for y'all, having a pretty young woman come through, no family to speak for her, no one to turn to, traumatized by her experiences."

The women pushed in from the edge of the crowd. One gasped. Another murmured. The banker drew himself to his full height, his jowls jiggling with his outrage. "I don't think I like your innuendo."

"Hate to break it to you, but your likes and dislikes aren't high on my consideration list."

"What the hell are you getting at, Allen?" James asked, getting to his feet, wiping mud from his pants.

"We took her in, saved her from those devils. Gave her a home. Community."

Chaser stepped sideways as a horse bumped him.

"Priorities, Caine."

He spared Tracker a glance, who in turn jerked his chin in Desi's direction. Her face was bleached white as she stood there, dwarfed by his coat and the truth she didn't want known. Her chin lifted high as her gaze met his, but he got the impression all that was holding her up was that damn pride as the women murmured among themselves, enjoying the scandal he'd begun.

Caine bit back the rage burning in his gut. Tracker was right. First things first. "We're taking Desi with us and if anyone has anything to say against it—" he levered a bullet into the chamber, letting the fury roll through him in an open challenge ". —step up now so we can get the discussing behind us."

To his surprise it was Father Gerard who stepped forward. "I can't let you do that, Caine."

"I don't rightly see where you can stop me, Padre." More titters spread through the crowd.

"I cannot let an unmarried woman go off with three men, lawmen or not."

"Whatever we have planned, it's better than what's here."

The stocky priest shook his nearly bald head. "It can't be allowed."

The longer they stood there, the more dutch courage the men were getting and the more trigger-happy fingers were twitching.

"If you take her like this, she'll still be James's ward, and still his by law."

Caine kneed Chaser in a half circle, drawing his revolver. "Any who want to dispute my claim know where to find me."

"I'm not going with you."

He wasn't surprised when Desi's protest was the only one spoken. There were times when a deadly reputation came in right handy.

"Ten months ago when I saved your life, Caine Allen," Father Gerard continued in his calm way, "you told me I could ask a favor anytime, and it would be granted."

"I did." Caine had an idea where this was heading.

The priest's next words confirmed his suspicions.

"A husband's rights supersede all others."

Caine took aim at a young wrangler on the left edge of the crowd. "Don't do it, son."

He cut Father Gerard a quick glance. "You don't call in markers on something like this."

The priest shrugged, coming closer, letting go of Desi's hand when she planted her feet. "You'll have to forgive me. This is my first time."

If it was the priest's first time, he'd eat his boot. The cowboy holstered his revolver and held up his hands. Caine backed Chaser up two steps. "I thought it was a sin for priests to lie."

"And I thought Rangers always kept their promises."

They did—he did—but as much as he admired Desi's courage, he wasn't about to marry her. Although the thought wasn't as distasteful as it should have been. "Marriage is a forever thing, Padre."

"Yes."

"I'm not a forever kind of man."

"Then perhaps it's time you changed."

"Might be too late in the day for that miracle."

"Are you going back on your promise?"

This time Caine cut a glance at Desi. She was staring at the smiling gambler with resigned horror, sure Caine would go back on his word to the priest and to her. Jesus, he wanted to walk Chaser over there and kick those damn shiny teeth down the gambling bastard's throat just for looking at her. "No."

"Without my approval this marriage can't take place," the gambler piped up, clearly looking to shorten his life.

A shotgun cocked on Caine's right. "Then give it." Sam's was short and to the point.

He didn't give his approval, but he shut up, which was all the same to Caine.

Caine clucked his tongue, guiding Chaser to where Desi stood. He holstered the rifle and motioned for her to hold up her hands. He pulled his knife from his boot top and cut through her bonds. "A woman shouldn't get married with her hands tied."

"I don't want to marry."

Neither did he, but neither of them had much of a choice. Forced by circumstance and honor, there was only one path for both of them. "Would you rather stay here?"

"No."

"Then we get hitched."

He waited for the priest to reach them. His robes flapped around his legs in the breeze. He should have looked ridiculous, womanly in the garb, but he didn't. He looked what he was. A man at peace with his life and the choices he'd made. Caine envied him. He couldn't remember a time when he'd felt calm.

Since the day the Mexican army had slaughtered their entire town, shouting "Death!" as they'd murdered men, women and children alike, he'd been consumed with a rage for justice that wouldn't let him rest. The same rage flowed over him now as the men he'd mentally marked gathered together, voices rising and falling in an angry cadence, occasionally punctuating their frustration with sharp gestures. His finger ached on the trigger of his revolver. It'd be so easy to take them out. To save everyone the expense of a trial for what they'd done to Desi. So very easy to make them suffer.

"Vengeance is mine, sayeth the Lord."

Caine didn't take his eyes off the men, controlling Chaser's impatient prance with a light touch on the reins. "This time, Padre, the good Lord is going to have to get in line."

4

Desi huddled deeper into the warmth of her borrowed coat. She pulled the collar up against her cheeks and watched as Caine hunkered down beside the saddlebags and fished something out of the depths. Firelight flicked shadows over his big form, elongating his silhouette into the deeper gloom between the rocks. Making him more than he was, but more distant, too....

"You hungry?"

The question was tossed over his shoulder.

"I'm fine."

He paused. The glance he cast her was knowing. "I seriously doubt that."

The shame of that burned to her soul. There weren't words strong enough to cut him down. She lifted her chin and pulled the cold around her, letting it seep into the well that wedged permanently in her soul. "Nevertheless, it's true."

He took his big knife out of its sheath. The rasp of metal on leather was loud. He opened the packet on the ground. Firelight caught in the blade and reflected back as he brought it down. He took the food and held it out to her. "It's not too tasty, but it will fill the hole in your gut."

She looked at the handful of dried meat, then back up at him. It was going to take a lot more than jerky to fill the hole in her. She let go of the edge of the coat, watching his hands as she reached for the meal. Watching for any sign of meanness. She was hungry, but not hungry enough to be stupid. She stopped halfway there. Caught between hunger and wariness.

Around them there was only darkness. Just she and Caine trapped in this intimate insubstantial circle of light. Tracker and Sam had gone back to town to get her things. She'd told them it wasn't necessary, but they'd insisted on some notion that a woman needed her things about her. Maybe a woman did, but her things had been stripped from her long ago, and all she had now was her pride, determination and...her husband. Caine's fingers twitched and she jerked her hand back.

She took a breath, eyes locked on his hand. Beyond that twitch of his fingers, he didn't move.

"You'd do better to watch my eyes."

The low, drawled comment was as startling as the twitch of those fingers.

She clutched at the neck of the coat again, watching his hand, her heart beating too fast to breathe right.

"What?"

"If you want a heads-up when I'm about to turn ornery, you'd do better to watch my eyes."

She had to look then. Caine was watching, no expression on his face, no discernible indication of what he was thinking. Just watching her as if she were some sort of puzzle he intended to figure out. She hated the way that made her feel. Helpless, stupid, easy prey. She snatched the food from his hand, almost whimpering with the stress as her fingers touched his, expecting him to grab her wrist as she grabbed the food. He didn't move, and his hand stayed where it was even after she had tucked her hand back into the shelter of her body. She forced a normal tone. "What good would it do me to watch your eyes when it's your hand I'm worried about?"

"It'd give you that split-second warning that could make the difference between life and death." He waved to the food in her hand with the knife before going back to the chunk and cutting off another piece. "Eat."

Her throat was so dry she didn't think she could work up the spit to swallow, so she just sat there, huddled by the fire and waited for Caine to turn his attention to something else. She waited in vain. He brought the meat to his mouth and took a bite, revealing strong white teeth and the hint of a smile. He motioned to the food pressed into her middle. "It's not going to soften up no matter how hard you squeeze it."

She wasn't just squeezing the meat, she had a death grip on it. And he was right. It wasn't softening up. Feeling like a fool, she brought it to her mouth. She took a bite, chewing it. It was tough and grainy and sat like sand in her dry mouth. There was no way she could swallow it. She chewed until her jaws tired, and it still didn't soften.

Caine turned away. Shadows from the fire stretched like dark flames up over his shoulders, blending into the deeper shadow cast by the brim of his hat. He was a very powerful man. She remembered how he'd held off the town, how comfortable he'd been in enforcing his will. Fighting him over food she needed wasn't a battle in which she wanted to engage him. She glanced down and chewed more.

A canteen appeared in her line of vision. "This might help."

She took it carefully, but without the hesitation of

before, which made her feel better. She hadn't become a total coward.

The water was cool and fresh. He must have refilled it before the others left, because not at any point since had she been left alone. The meat softened, and she swallowed. Her stomach rumbled with eagerness as the small bit of food landed. Caine's laugh hit her pride like a blow.

"Been a long time since I heard anyone's stomach get excited about jerky." The humor in his words didn't linger in his expression. His mouth was set in a straight line and his eyes narrowed. Worse, they were back to studying her in that way that made her throat close. She brought the jerky back to her lap. "I can't eat with you watching me."

She expected him to argue or to spit out a "Tough." She did not expect him, after a brief pause, to hand her his piece of jerky and to turn his attention to the tiny fire. "I don't want your food."

"There's more coming."

But not for a while. "I can wait."

"Gypsy, there's not enough meat on your bones to wait five minutes, let alone an hour."

Despite the fact she didn't care what he thought, it stung that he saw her as scrawny. "I've always been lean."

He turned back. "Maybe so, but now you're in need of fattening up."

For the slaughter. The phrase cut through her mind. "It's not your problem."

"You're my wife. Everything about you is my problem."

"We're not really married."

She suddenly had his full attention. "Sweetheart, I

made a promise to the padre and to God. It doesn't get more married than that."

"I meant you don't have to stay married. You can get rid of me anytime."

"Really? And here I thought we were hitched for life."

She gripped the meat so hard, her short nails cut through the tough strings.

"Uh-huh." He indicated the barely touched meal. "Your stomach will be happier if you eat that rather than play with it."

"They'll come after me."

He took the canteen from her hand and took a swig. She watched his throat work over the edge of the poncho. Watched his Adam's apple bob up and down. Where was his worry? He had to be worried. "James and his friends are not nice people."

He handed the canteen back to her. When she took it, his hand came up under her chin, tapping the bottom, bringing her gaze up.

"One of these days I want you to tell me how 'not nice' they were."

She shook her head. She would never tell anyone how it was.

He continued as if she hadn't denied him. "But for now, you just need to know that they are no longer a threat to you."

She bit her lip. She couldn't believe that, either. James, Bryan and Carl had enjoyed having her at their disposal too much to just let her be spirited away. And they thought too much of themselves not to take it personally that she had been. Still, Caine had risked his life for her. She owed him at least a warning. "They'll kill you."

Unbelievably, he smiled. A genuine smile full of amusement. "They're welcome to try."

He didn't understand. "They won't be up front about it."

He dropped his hand from her chin. "Never thought they would be."

God, he was arrogant. "If you let me go, they'll leave you alone."

He picked up a stick and snapped it in two. "If I let you go, you'd have no protection."

"I could hide."

"Sweetheart, no matter where you ran, men would find you and you'd be back in bed."

"I don't want a man."

He added small sticks to the tiny fire. "I don't remember mentioning that you'd be there willingly."

He fed the fire another stick.

"I won't be taken again."

"On that we agree. My wife stays with me."

He was really stuck on the wife thing. It obviously meant more to him than it did to her.

"I wish you could forget that we married."

His gaze traveled slowly down her body before taking an equally slow trip back up. She knew she looked like hell, and knew he couldn't see a thing through the bulky coat, but she still felt like she was standing before him naked, with no secrets and no protection.

"That's not something I have any interest in forgetting."

He wanted her sexually. No doubt he relished the fact that she was at his disposal, probably even expected her to just lie back and spread her legs so he could take his pleasure. She glared at him, anger serving as her friend, giving her the strength to say, "I'll fight you."

His eyebrow kicked up. "Did you fight them?" With everything she'd had, which hadn't amounted to anything in the long run. "Yes."

His head canted to the side. "Did it do any good?"

Up until they'd tied her, it had. "No."

He handed her back the canteen and placed his fingers under the back of her other hand, pushing the food to her mouth. His voice was incredibly gentle when he asked, "Then what makes you think I'm going to be worried about you fighting me?"

Nothing. Nothing at all. She sank her teeth into the meat, gnawing on the realization that what she thought or wanted didn't matter here any more than it had mattered anywhere else. And with each chew, she was aware of how he watched her. The food coalesced in a hard lump in her mouth. Caine passed her the canteen. She didn't lift it to her mouth. There was just no way she could swallow anything with his words sashaying through her head. She turned and spat the food into the dirt. His sigh brought her right back around again.

"I can see I'm going to have to change my ways around you if I don't want you wasting away."

"You don't like skinny women?"

"What I like or don't like is immaterial. I'm married." He motioned to the food in her hand. "You going to eat that?"

Was he planning on making her? "I couldn't."

"Because I made you mad?"

What did he want? A yes? A no? She settled on a shrug.

He took the food from her hand and wrapped it up. It seemed to take him forever to put it away in the saddle-bags, though his movements were smooth and efficient.

It was just her own sense of time that was off-kilter. A twig snapped in the darkness beyond the small circle of light. Her heart leapt in her throat.

Caine settled back against the boulder, resting his arm across his bent knee, looking so powerful that the rifle propped by his side appeared superfluous.

"Relax."

"I can't."

He sighed and angled his hat down. "What worries you more, them or me?"

Him, definitely him. "You."

"Why?"

A stark, bold question by a stark, bold man. She licked her lips, debated answering, but there was something about the set of his mouth that made her think he'd force the response. "I know what to expect from them."

He pulled the saddlebag over to him and fished around in one of the outer pockets. "What makes you think I'm any different?"

She licked her dry lips again, took a sip of water and forced herself to answer. "I don't know."

"That would be my point. You don't know." He pulled out a package wrapped in brown paper and untied it carefully. "I could be a real sweetheart between the sheets."

Sweetheart or devil, she didn't see how it made a difference. She took another sip from the canteen, at a loss as how to answer.

"Give me your hand."

She instinctively tucked it into her stomach. He shook his head, reaching for it, pulling it forward until it stretched between them, palm up like a sacrifice. She tugged. He didn't let go. The corner of his mouth twitched as he looked up at her from beneath the brim of his hat. "Trust me, you don't want to do that."

She watched as he put the brown paper in her hand. It was light and solid. He closed her fingers around it and let her go.

"I figure that will go down easier than jerky."

Desi propped the canteen on the rock beside her. She parted the brown paper. Inside lay three heart-shaped confections. A fourth, more oddly shaped piece was smaller than the other three. Dark, rich and shiny, they lay like the perfect temptation in her palm.

Chocolate. Dear God, chocolate. She brought the package up close enough to take a deep breath of the heady aroma. It flowed through her system along with the memories of happier times, when she and her sister romped through the family mansion, running from room to room with reckless abandon. Never appreciating how good they had it, longing for the adventure they didn't know could turn into a disaster. Chocolate had been an expected daily treat. They'd pitched tantrums when they hadn't gotten it. In their innocence and bliss they'd never appreciated what a luxury it was to have it at all. She touched the irregular fourth piece with her finger. It had several vertical slices. Like someone had chiseled bits and pieces off it over time.

"My mother always swore by chocolate in times of stress."

She looked up. It was Caine's chocolate. He had to have been the one to chip off those tiny pieces. It was obviously something he valued and savored. She wrapped the package up, biting her lips against the pain it caused, and handed it back to him. "I can't take your chocolate."

Just as calmly he pushed her hand back toward her.

"Why not? Don't you like it?"

"I love it."

"As I want you to have it, where's the problem?"

She didn't look down as he unwrapped the paper again. "Why?"

"Because you're my wife," he said, nudging it toward her, "this is our wedding day and thirty years from now when you reminisce to our kids about it, I'd like for you to have a pleasant memory to pass on."

She didn't know what to be shocked by more. The fact that he thought so far down the road or the fact that he thought about her at all. She took two of the whole pieces of chocolate and held them out.

He shook his head. "I gave them to you."

He said that as if he couldn't care less about the sweet, except she held the evidence to the contrary in her hand. She tucked her pinky against the chopped piece, running her fingertip across the irregular ridges. The chocolate was dear to him, a prize he savored. "You like it, too."

"That I do."

"I can't take something you value."

"Why don't you take a nibble before making a statement like that."

He was tempting her. With chocolate. A devil in dirty clothes and a battered hat and more muscle than she could shake a stick at. The chocolate began to warm to her hand. Soon it would make a mess. "I don't want it."

"Now, that's a lie."

She cut him a glare.

"Now what?"

The truth just burst out. "I don't want to be beholden to you!"

His laugh was unexpected. "Are you telling me all it

takes is giving you a sweet, and you'll be in my debt? Gypsy, it's going to be darn easy being married to you."

He was right. If she couldn't even manage this small courtesy, she was going to be very easy to manipulate. However, now that she'd dug this hole for herself, she wasn't quite sure how to get out of it. She settled for a blunt, "No."

He took the two pieces of chocolate. "So maybe if we share, it won't offend your sense of proper?"

This time the look she cast him was puzzled.

He shook his head. "As much as this might ruffle your sense of how it's going to be, I don't want to be at war with my wife."

So he'd made her a peace offering with what he had, giving her something he valued. Sharing. It wasn't such a bad way to start things. She took back the smaller piece and replaced it with the larger one.

His left eyebrow went up. He flicked a finger in the direction of the smaller piece. "You're getting the short end of the stick."

She didn't think so. "Maybe I want you to have a happy memory, too."

Even as she said it, she knew it was true. She might not have had the wedding of her dreams, she might be married to a total stranger, but he'd risked his life to save her twice, and he was her husband. Just in case she lived long enough to think back on this day as a memory, she wanted to see herself as more than helpless debris tossed along the current of her life.

Caine took the candy. One glance at his expression made her glad she'd made the gesture. The harsh planes had mellowed into an expression of satisfaction. He held up the candy like a man making a toast. "To a happy future."

She noticed he didn't say together. She touched the broken piece to his whole one. "To a happy future."

He caught her hand before she could put the candy in her mouth. His fingers wrapped around hers, holding her steady as he leaned in. She watched as his mouth opened. The gleam of his teeth was faint in the firelight. His lips brushed her fingers, firm but surprisingly soft as he took a bite.

"To seal the deal."

"That was mine." She licked her lips as a fine tingle shivered up her arm. "You gave it to me."

"Nah, that was clearly mine." He touched one of the nicked edges. "I put my mark all over it."

"It's still mine now."

He shook his head again, a smile flirting with the corner of his mouth. "Wrong again." His finger touched the corner of her mouth, drawing those strange tingles there. "Once mine, always mine."

He held one of his chocolates against her lower lip, pressing in gently as she absorbed his statement. A comfort or a threat? When she didn't open her mouth immediately, he worked the chocolate in deeper using gentle side-to-side motions that spread the melting confection along the lining of her lip. The taste of his skin blended with the taste of the sweet. His gaze held hers, the green of his eyes almost black in the faint light. "To seal the deal."

She took a bite, letting the flavor flow through her mouth. It was rich and sweet and so good. She swallowed. The taste of man and chocolate blended in a pleasant combination. She blinked. It was such a foreign concept to think of anything to do with a man being pleasant.

His smile was strangely gentle as he sat back against his rock and fed another stick into the fire. "I'm not an ornery man, Desi."

What was she supposed to say to that? She settled on "Thank you," which sounded ridiculous even to her own ears.

"I don't have any intention of being an ornery husband."

Again, she didn't have anything to say. The smile that twitched his lips should have warned her but it didn't. She was too distracted by the taste of chocolate, the taste of man and the confusing image he presented that was so different from what she thought he'd be. "But I do plan to be real sweet between the sheets."

SAM AND TRACKER SLIPPED back into camp with the same stealth with which they'd left. Two dark shadows, as comfortable in the dark as they were in the light.

Caine nodded as they dropped their saddlebags on the other side of the fire. The set of Tracker's shoulders spoke volumes. Something had happened in town. "Did you have any trouble?"

"Nothing we couldn't handle."

Sam took out his makings. "Sure enough that town needs some cleaning up."

Across the fire, Desi stiffened. She was watching Tracker and Sam with a dread that didn't make sense.

"And Desi's things?" A woman needed her things about her, familiar geegaws and such that made wherever she landed home. He'd never met a woman who didn't put a lot of stock in her personal treasures, and he had no reason to feel Desi was any different.

Tracker sighed and pulled out a brown, wrapped

package and crossed the small distance, standing over Desi where she sat on the low rock, looking big in comparison, which might explain the anxious expression on her face, but he didn't think so. There was more going on here than what anyone was letting on.

"I'm real sorry, ma'am. The bastards got to your things before I could retrieve them, but the mercantile had some ready-mades that might do."

Desi took the package with hands that trembled. Caine could put that tremble down to fear, but he hadn't lived this long by guessing wrong. "Thank you."

There wasn't a more shaky bit of gratitude ever expressed. Tracker held the package a little longer than necessary, drawing her gaze. "You're welcome."

Sam rolled his smoke, his eyes on Desi, too. "You might not be able to believe this right now, seeing as where you came from, but you can relax now."

Something was definitely up. "Is there something that happened in town that I should know about?"

Tracker shook his head, his long hair sliding over his shoulder. He stepped back. "We handled it."

Caine glanced over at Sam. "What did you handle?"

"What needed it." He pitched the unlit smoke into the fire.

It wasn't like Sam to waste a smoke. A glance at Desi didn't reveal any more than Tracker and Sam had. She just sat there clutching the package to her chest, all hunched down as if she wanted to disappear. Shit!

"I'm thinking maybe I should have been the one to fetch my wife's things."

Tracker's gaze flicked to Desi as he said, "I'm thinking things worked out the way they should have."

Maybe. Caine asked Desi, "What do Sam and Tracker know that I don't?"

She licked her lower lip the way she did when she was nervous. "I have no idea."

That was a bald-faced lie. He cupped her chin in his hand and brought her face up. She'd tell him and then he'd handle it. Her lids flinched but the rest of her expression stayed stubbornly set. "Now, try telling me the truth."

"Leave her alone, Caine."

He didn't let go of Desi's chin or take his gaze from hers. "This is between me and my wife, Tracker."

"Some things don't need telling."

He didn't agree. The haunted look in Desi's eyes drove him to know. "I'll be deciding that."

Denim rustled as Sam stood. "No. You won't."

Caine straightened, letting his hand slip from his wife's chin. "Who's going to stop me?"

Desi gasped as Sam took a step forward. "If you can't resist being an ass long enough to find the respect you owe your wife, I guess I will."

"I don't think so."

A soft sound had him looking down. Desi was backed against the boulder doing her level best to fade into the rough rock, her blue eyes wide and locked on him and Sam, but he wasn't exactly sure she saw him. There was a wildness to her gaze, an inward focus that reminded him of battle-crazed men lost to reality. She clutched the package to her. He stepped back from Sam. Sam's gray eyes cut to Desi and then back to him. "Leave it alone, Caine. At least for now."

"She's had about all she can take," Tracker added.

Caine could see that. He hunkered down in front of Desi as he asked them. "Tell me one thing, when the time comes, did you leave one for me?"

"We did better than that." Sam added, "We left you three."

"Good." He needed to know there would be a place to release the rage that consumed him. "Desi?"

She didn't answer the call, didn't look at him. He rubbed the backs of his fingers across the backs of hers, his nails hitting the paper on the package, the rustle of the paper sounding loud in the sudden silence. "Sweetheart, you haven't finished your chocolate."

A long pause and then she blinked. She looked down at her hand. "Oh, no."

Smears were on her fingers and the brown paper. "You'd best eat it fast before it makes a mess of your new clothes." Her lashes lifted and he was staring into her big blue eyes and all the devastating sadness she normally hid.

"I was going to save it."

"I'll get you some more." He wasn't sure where he would find it or how he would pay for it—they were building the ranch and not established—but anything that took the sadness from those blue eyes was worth it.

She opened her hand and stared at the mess. He caught her wrist and brought her hand to his mouth. He pressed a chaste kiss on the edge of her palm. Chocolate spread to his lips. He backed off, licking his lips. "It's still good."

He brought her hand to her mouth. "Eat it while I get supper."

She glanced toward the jerky. It didn't take a genius to interpret what she was thinking. *No, not jerky.*

"Oh, we can do a lot better than jerky," Sam disappeared into the darkness and came back carrying two large oval tins with handles. "The padre's housekeeper sent a bunch of tamales and pork stew along with tortillas and—" he lifted a square basket "—wedding cakes." Desi stopped licking at her hand. "Oh."

Oh, indeed.

"Maria said it wasn't proper you didn't have a wedding supper."

Caine took the basket with the cakes in it from Tracker and put it beside Desi. "Maria cooks like a dream."

"Learned everything she knows from Tia."

"Tia?" Desi asked.

"Tia's been taking care of us since the massacre."

"Massacre?"

She was beginning to sound a bit like a parrot but Caine couldn't begrudge her. After the day she'd had she had to feel a bit like she'd been tossed from a coach going at full speed and was now just bouncing around in the aftermath. "We all used to live in the same town. After the massacre took our families, we banded together."

"We didn't know shit about surviving," Sam interjected, opening a tin.

"Damn near starved to death," Tracker agreed, getting out a metal coffeepot. "Best thing we ever did was to try and steal tortillas from Tia's windowsill."

Caine rubbed at the back of his neck with the memory. "That woman wields a mean broom, though."

"That she did," Sam agreed, pulling out husk-wrapped bundles. "Lined us up against the wall of her home and lectured us a good hour while dinner simmered in the pot. Quoted the bible one minute and threatened our manly charms the next."

"Damn longest hour of my life," Caine said, remembering the hunger that had driven him to steal, the shame at being caught by a good woman who quoted the bible, but most of all he remembered how good that damn meal had tasted after he and the others had worked another hour to earn their place at the table.

"Does she still live with you?" Desi asked.

"Hell, yeah."

"Runs Hell's Eight with an iron fist." Sam popped the top off the second tin. The rich scent of spicy meat stew filled the air.

"She's family."

"Yes." Maybe not by blood but by everything that mattered, Tia was family.

Desi's face took up that guarded look he didn't like. He took the package from her hands and set it aside. It wasn't hard to see where her thoughts had wandered. "She'll like you just fine, Desi?"

Caine reached back for his saddlebag and fished out his tin plate and spoon. Tracker poured some stew onto the plate and tossed on a tortilla. Sam added a tamale. Caine glanced over at where Desi sat dwarfed by the coat. "Add another tamale on there."

Sam followed his glance. "Yeah. She could use some fattening up."

Shit, Caine hoped Desi hadn't heard that. It only took a turn to see that she had. That full, totally tempting mouth was set in a flat line and those eyes were shooting daggers at him again. He sighed and handed her the plate. "He wasn't slinging mud. Just concern."

She took it. "It doesn't matter."

He noticed the fine tremor in her hands as he let go.

Hunger, fear, anger...? Hell, there were too many reasons that could cause that shaking to pinpoint just one. She didn't immediately grab up the spoon.

"Maria said to tell you she didn't make it too spicy, ma'am," Sam offered.

Desi appreciated that. She'd only met the woman once, early on before James had understood how determined she'd been to escape. Plump and colorful, happily married to the town's blacksmith, she'd been a too-cheerful reminder of all Desi had lost. Desi's renewed defiance after the one time she'd delivered food had ensured James had never let Maria back again. "Thank her for me, please."

"You can tell her yourself," Caine inserted in his low drawl. "She comes out to Hell's Eight once a month in good weather to visit Tia."

Which meant there was no chance she'd find any peace at Caine's home. Desi clenched the spoon in her hand. The food that had her stomach rumbling a moment before was suddenly as appetizing as glue. No woman wanted her male relations taking up with a whore. If Tia was as formidable as the men implied, she'd spend her days paying for her crimes against decency and her nights paying for Caine having to marry her. The future did not look good. She kept her voice even as she said, "Thank you, I will."

She stared beyond the firelight, to the wildness beyond. It matched the wildness she felt inside. She just wanted to be free. Free of men's demands, society's scorn and the personal pain that ate like acid at her soul.

"Desi?"

She resented Caine's interruption as much as she resented her circumstances. "What?"

He placed his fingers under the plate and pressed, until she either had to lift the plate or wear the contents. She lifted. His cool green eyes met hers with a confidence she wished she could borrow.

"I promise you, nothing's going to be as bad as you're imagining."

5

It wasn't as bad, it was worse. Desi stared at the bedroll set on the opposite side of the fire from everyone else, the distance emphasizing this was her wedding night. She'd come back from changing into her new clothes and found this. The euphoria and contentment from her full stomach faded. She glanced across the fire to where Caine stood talking to Tracker and Sam. While she didn't consider twenty feet a token to privacy, Caine probably did. Men, she knew, didn't mind other men watching them stake their claim. She'd hoped it would be different if she were a wife, but she glanced at the double bedroll again and knew that had been a vain hope.

The Hell's Eight men did everything together. Legend said they were ghosts of warriors past come back to right wrongs. Others said they'd made a deal with the Devil to survive when the Mexicans had wiped out their town. No one ever said they worried over much about what was proper or respectable. And she was a whore in the eyes of everyone around her. Maybe even in her own heart if she dared to check, but she wasn't checking and she wasn't believing it. That being the case, she wasn't behaving like one.

Deliberately, she picked up the closest half of the bedroll and moved it four feet to the left. She would have moved it farther if a shadow hadn't come between her and the firelight. A booted foot settled on the far corner of the bedroll. She didn't need to look up to know who that boot belonged to. She'd spent all day today while riding, watching that boot rock in the stirrup. The three horizontal scrapes across the instep marked it as Caine's.

"You worried about catching on fire?"

"No."

She gave the bedroll a yank. It came out from under his foot easier than she'd expected. She hit the ground hard enough to leave bruises on her fanny. She also managed to move her bedroll and extra two feet.

His shadow stretched over her, then his hand, and then the amusement in his drawl. "The heat of the fire isn't going to reach this far."

She accepted his hand. "I don't mind."

He didn't let go as he bent down and grabbed the bedroll. "I do."

She snatched it out of his hand, draping it over her arm as she smoothed the wrinkles out. "Then you can stay over there." She didn't dare look at his face as she added, "I don't mind."

He took her hand again. His thumb stroked over the back of it. "I must be in a real contrary mood tonight because I mind."

Anger surged from deep within. "Why, because you'll miss out on an opportunity to show your friends how well you fuck?"

That thumb didn't even break rhythm. "And here I was thinking I won't get a wink of sleep watching my wife shiver in her blankets."

She wrenched her arm from his grip and stomped

back to his bedroll. She threw the blankets down atop the saddle. "Do me a favor."

He came quietly up behind her, but it didn't matter. The man had too much presence to sneak. The hairs on the back of her neck always warned her when he was around. "What?"

"Don't try to dress it up prettily."

"Dress what up?"

She glanced across the fire. Tracker and Sam were staring hard at the flames, pretending not to be aware of what was going on. She lowered her voice, "What's going to happen here tonight."

She couldn't see his eyes under the brim of his hat, but she could see the quirk of his lips. "You got something against sleep?"

She turned and slammed her hands on her hips, anger writhing through her like a living thing. "Stop it. Just stop pretending. If all you were planning to do was sleep, we wouldn't be over here and—" she kicked the pile of blankets "—we wouldn't be sharing a bedroll."

A log popped on the fire. She jumped and spun around. By the time she turned back, Caine was right there, close enough that the edge of his poncho touched her coat. His coat. She swallowed and risked a look at his face. He didn't look angry, but with him, who could tell? His hand lifted. She flinched. His eyes narrowed. She braced her spine for the blow that was coming. His fingers grazed her jaw, slid along the bone, feather-light, but the drag of the rough callus left no doubt he was strong. His thumb came to rest against her mouth as his fingers cradled her cheek.

"The bedrolls are over here because we thought you might be a bit uncomfortable without privacy. The bedrolls are together because it's damn cold and you've taken enough chill for one day, and also because you're my wife, and my wife sleeps by me."

"Why?" It felt strange to speak against his thumb, but she didn't let that stop her.

"Because it's my right to protect you."

She pulled back against his hold. "I don't need your protection."

"Too bad. You've got it anyway." He motioned to the right. "You got any business to take care of before we call it a night?"

The blush rose despite her desire to contain it. "No."

"Good." He bent, and with a few flicks of his wrists, resettled the blankets. "'Cause I'm beat."

"Don't you have to stand guard?"

"It's my wedding night. Tracker and Sam are giving me the night off as a wedding present."

Just what she needed. She glared at the two men. "What was my present?"

His lips quirked and he pushed a strand of hair behind her ear. "Me."

It just burst out. "I got shortchanged."

Unbelievably, he laughed. "I imagine you see it that way now."

He sat down on the blankets, sliding his hand down her neck, her shoulder, her arm, hooking her wrist in his grip when he reached the ground and tugging her down. "But you won't always."

He had no idea what she thought and what she planned. She fell, more than sat, beside him. He caught her the way he always did, as if nothing ever threw him off guard. He lay back against the saddle, his hand anchoring her wrist. "Lie down. Morning will be here before you know it."

An owl hooted in the distance. The first she'd heard

this spring. Was it a good omen or a bad one? She didn't know, but looking at the sheer size of the man waiting for her to bed down beside him, she had to pray it was good.

"I don't have a pillow."

He patted the broad expanse of his shoulder. "I've got your pillow right here."

He expected her to sleep against him. She bit her lip. The wind blew, rattling the bushes. A cold chill went down her spine. Caine's smile faded to a frown. He pulled her toward him, lifting her arm over his head, directing her fall toward his chest, not giving her an opportunity to twist away.

"If you don't get tucked in here fast, you're going to freeze over faster than a stream in winter."

He let her go when she was lying along his side, her cheek on her hand on his shoulder. "Sleeping like this is going to break my neck."

One big hand came across her chest, pulling her into his torso as he hitched up. Her shoulder tucked under his arm. She had no choice but to drop her hand. Her fingers caught in the folds of his poncho. As much as she tugged, she was stuck under her own weight, elbow wedged to the ground, head at an even more awkward angle. His coat, made for a much bigger person than she, bunched up over her face. There was a deep masculine chuckle and then several tugs. The coat opened inch by inch, revealing the same amusement in his eyes that had been in his voice.

She frowned back at him. "This is not an improvement."

Another button popped and the gap widened, enabling her to see his expression. Caine was smiling. A full-fledged smile without the usual reserve.

"I can see that."

Another tug on the coat had her yelping. The buttons were now caught in her hair.

"Now for sure I know this coat is male."

She twisted about trying to get a hand free to get to her hair only to find his hands in the way when she eventually got herself clear.

"This would go a lot easier," he told her, "if you'd stop trying to help."

"I'm trying to keep from being snatched bald." Another tug had her wincing.

"No danger of that."

She was so sick of him pretending to be nice to her. "Because you intend to be careful?"

He was shaking his head before she finished, that full smile diminishing to the level of a grin. "Nah." The tension released on her hair, leaving only a sting behind. "There's no danger for the simple reason you've got enough hair for two women and then some."

She dug her elbow into his side as she forced her hand free, checking to be sure she still had hair in that spot. She rubbed the sting. "Well, you may not have that concern for much longer." She ran her hand through her hair and got stopped about one inch into the procedure by a snarl too big to be called anything less than a mat. She gave it a good hard yank, wincing when it held. "We're probably going to have to shave my head to get the snarls out."

Once again, his hands pulled hers away. "No danger of that, either."

"Because you're going to forbid me to cut my hair?"

He smoothed his hand over her head, stroking from crown to end, smoothing down the wild tangle, lifting his hand halfway down when a snarl caught on his index finger. Men always loved her hair. There was something about the pale blond color and curl that had them always staring at it with a combination of fascination and awe. His gaze met hers, the smile still tugging at his mouth. "Pretty much."

Nothing was more galling than his assurance that his forbidding would be enough. "I hate you."

"You don't know me well enough to hate me."

"Trust me. I've built a real good case in the short time we've been acquainted."

He didn't look devastated by the statement. But the crinkles by the sides of his eyes deepened. "Then I guess I'll just have to work at changing your opinion."

Oh, wonderful. He'd taken her comment as a challenge. "Why can't you just act predictably?"

He lifted her up and scooted her down, a maneuver that would have left her a lot more comfortable if it also hadn't left her pressed intimately against him. "If you knew me better, you'd know I am being predictable."

When she tried to wiggle away, he merely curled in the arm she was lying on. The other hand went to her hip, slipped under the coat and rode down to her thigh, hitching it up. Panic immediately chased anger. The only thing that preserved her modesty were the long folds of her new skirt.

"Lift up for a minute."

"I'm comfortable just as I am."

"No, you're not."

She wasn't but that wasn't important. She tilted her head back and strained for dignity. "I am not sprawling across you. It's improper."

And if he said one word about the incongruity of a whore worrying about propriety she'd bite the end of his nose off.

"Gypsy, if both of us are going to keep from freezing our butts off tonight, seeing as our wedding night has us way over here in the hollow, we're going to have to get closer than your sense of propriety deems fit."

"I'll chance freezing."

"Well, I won't."

And that settled that. In the time it took her to draw the breath for a retort, Caine had her kneeling. As fast as she batted at his hands, he was tugging her skirts out from under her knees. God, he was fast. She had just reached around to slap his hands from her rear when he lifted her again by her shoulder and pulled her across his lap and lay down. Gravity took care of her defiance. Her body naturally flowed into the planes of his. Her thigh fell over his and her breasts pressed into his side. Before she could pull her leg back, he took her skirts and draped them over his thighs and tucked them beneath, effectively pinning her with her own clothing.

He met her glare with a raised brow and a smile.

"Pretty slick, eh?"

Did he expect her to praise his trickery?

"Taking advantage through your greater strength is what I'd call it." Two yanks on the material proved the futility of that effort.

Caine shrugged. "Whatever gets the job done is good for me." With his free hand he adjusted his hat forward as he braced his shoulders against the saddle. "Grab the blankets would you?"

She was tempted to ignore the order, but the thought of what he would do to get that job done had her reconsidering. That and the next wind that sent the dried grass rustling. It was going to be a cold night and while Caine might be big and arrogant, he was warm. She leaned toward the blankets, forgetting her injuries. Stiff muscles and her bruised rib immediately protested.

"Shoot. I forgot about that." The blankets were removed from her grasp. A broad palm rubbed small circles on her back as if the thought to absorb her pain through his touch. "You just take your time getting comfortable, and I'll take care of the covering."

He said that as if he were being perfectly reasonable, but no matter how he couched it, it was an order and it drove home the fact that he expected her to obey. The knowledge that there was nothing she could do about it ate at her defiance, because once all the settling was done, he'd want to be getting on to other things. Intimate, unpleasant things that were now her duty. God help her.

He tucked the blanket over her shoulder. "Now, what thought just made you stiffen up?"

If he didn't know, she wasn't telling him. "Nothing."

His sigh blew over the top of her head. "Are you back to worrying that I'm ornery in bed?"

"I don't want to talk about it."

He pulled her forearm up, dislodging her elbow from his bicep. "Doesn't appear to me that either of us are going to get comfortable enough to sleep without it."

A muffled chuckle from across the fire alerted her to how that low drawl of his carried. "Hush."

"I'll hush if you'll talk."

"Fine. What do you want to know?"

"I want to know what has you scared."

Her shiver had nothing to do with the wind as memories swamped her. "I just don't like being with a man."

"Because it goes against your beliefs, or because of what you've been taught?"

"We're married, it can't be against my beliefs."

"I got news for you, Gypsy, many a woman feels it's wrong to enjoy her husband."

"I can understand that."

His finger under her chin tipped her face up. "I can see where you'd have reason to fear a man who's hurt you, but, Gypsy, I've never hurt you."

Yet. The immediate tag to his assertion lingered in her mind. She just barely kept it from her lips. His hand tilted. Instead of letting her go like she expected, he swapped his fingers for his thumb, the latter brought to rest against her lips, brushing lightly. The fire had died down to the point it was just a small flicker. The faint light wasn't strong enough to penetrate where they lay.

"And that's the hitch in your git-along, isn't it, Desi? You don't have any idea who I am, or what to expect, so your mind's just leaping from one awful possibility to the next."

"You're a man."

"And you're a woman, that should make us more compatible rather than less."

"Maybe I just need more time."

His thumb made another of those lazy passes that tickled the edges of her lips and sent little tingles radiating outward. "Time can be a funny thing, Gypsy. You think it's your friend, but when it comes to fears, it's your worst enemy. You leave a scare to time's tending, and rather than making it go away, time turns it bigger and meaner and meaner than reality could ever be."

"So you say."

His thumb made another pass across her lips, following the swells and dips as if testing the shape of her words. "I know what it's like to be scared, Desi."

The "Huh?" escaped before she could contain it. The man was as big as a mountain, had more muscle than a blacksmith and had a reputation that would terrify a hardened gunslinger. What did he know of fear?

"I wasn't always this big, and there was a time I knew so little about fighting, you could probably have whupped me with one hand tied behind your back."

"I can't imagine that."

"Then you're just going to have to take my word for it the same way you're going to have to accept I have a reason to start as I mean to go on."

Because he didn't see any reason to wait. Because he wanted her. Because she was his and men liked to stake their claims. There wasn't anything she could do about it, and he was right, she was darned sick of dreading it.

Desi hauled her skirt out from under his thigh and threw herself onto her back. Yanking her skirts up, she spread her legs. Every bit of rage she felt at being, yet again, at a man's mercy ripped out, along with her snarl. "Then get it over with."

He came over her, a large black shadow, deeper than the night, scarier, more intense. Her breath caught in her lungs. A fine tremble started in her gut and spread outward, consuming her limbs, ending in her fingers and toes. Dear God, what had she invited?

"Is that what they wanted, Desi? For you to lie there like a doll for them to play with?"

His whisper was scarier than his looming. His whisper wanted to delve, ferret out her past, her weaknesses. "It doesn't matter."

There was a long pause. Something touched her cheek, and she shrieked. She was wound so tightly she couldn't contain it.

A voice intruded into their private battle.

"Just so you know, Desi, I don't hold the bond between man and wife sacred."

Sam's low, cold drawl reached across the fire and the implication had the blood rushing from her head so fast she felt as if she were falling. Except she couldn't because she was already down. She worked her hand out of the confines of the blanket, grabbing Caine's wrist. "Please."

Caine's snarl was as chilling as the wind. "Shut the hell up, Sam."

"The lady needs to know she has options."

Oh, God, she didn't want any more options. One man to deal with was more than enough.

It grated, but if begging saved her from being passed around, even for one night, she'd take it. There were times when pride wasn't worth the price to keep it. "Please. I'll do what you want," she whispered to Caine. She glanced across the clearing to the shadow that was Sam. "Don't call him over. Don't make me…"

"Fuck."

The epithet tore through her like a shot. She clung tighter, wishing it were lighter so she could see whether her begging was having any effect. "Please—"

Caine's hand came over her mouth, cutting off the plea. She could feel his stare as clear as a touch. "My wife doesn't beg, got it?" She nodded slowly. His hand left her mouth slowly.

"Sam, if you don't elaborate in the next two seconds, I'm coming over there and kicking your ass."

Desi ran her tongue across her lips, tasting the salt of his skin and the bitterness of her fear.

"Just saying the lady doesn't have to suffer thinking there isn't anyone here who won't stand for her if she wants it."

He couldn't mean what she thought.

But he did. Caine confirmed it. "Sam's offered you his protection, do you want to take it?"

Was it a trick?

"You'd just let me go?"

"Hell, no, but you're free to take him up on his offer."

Some choice. Caine or Sam. Wife or whore. "You'd fight your friend?"

"What's mine stays mine, Gypsy."

Oh, yes, he'd fight. Not because he loved her or wanted her, but because his pride was involved. And he considered her his. She understood that.

"So what's it going to be?"

She didn't know Sam. She didn't really know Caine, either, but she knew this one thing. A possessive man wasn't a sharing man. That made the devil she knew a better choice. "I don't want his protection," she whispered.

"Good." The tense muscles against her relaxed subtly.

"She make a decision?" Sam called.

"Yup. She's decided I'm the more attractive one."

"Shit. On top of needing to gain weight, the woman needs spectacles."

Sam didn't sound serious or even disappointed.

"You were joking?" she asked Caine.

"No."

She didn't know what to do with that flat pronouncement. "I don't understand you."

"You might find it easier if you didn't keep comparing me to cow shit."

She let go of his wrist. Weariness rolled over her in a debilitating wave, spawning a ripple of defeat. "I can't help it. I don't have anything else to compare you to."

6

I don't have anything else to compare you to. Caine had never heard so much hopelessness contained in simple truth. The tension left her body. Ah, hell.

He slipped his hand under her head, the wealth of hair acting as a cushion between her skull and his palm, and dropped his forehead to hers. For sure he liked her better when she was fighting. This lack of passion left him fumbling for a way to restore it. His kept his whisper so low, the words didn't drift farther than her ear. "I think I mentioned before, that's your whole problem."

A stick popped in the fire. She jumped. He pulled her closer, the length of her feeling too fragile to him, the surrender in her body there for all the wrong reasons. He brushed his lips across her cheek. Her muscles grew tighter. "Easy, Gypsy."

She didn't move, didn't respond, just held herself there as if waiting for a death blow...which in her mind, maybe she was. He slid his hands between them, found the bunched mess of her skirts. A soft whimper broke past her lips. He tugged the skirt down as a second whimper joined the first. "It's all right, Gypsy. No one's going to hurt you."

Least of all him.

The kiss he dropped on the corner of her mouth spurred the confession from her throat. Her knee drew up with the tension he could feel growing tighter and tighter. "I don't like this."

"I know." He ran his hand down her arm, under the bump of her elbow and back up. Resentment for the coat that kept his hand from her skin was his uppermost emotion until he got to her wrist. The flesh was cool. He circled the narrow joint and slid his fingers lower, meshing his fingers with hers. Her hand was like an icicle in his. "Jesus Christ."

She was freezing.

"What?"

"I'm not doing a very good job taking care of you."

He was so used to living on the trail, the discomfort of sleeping on the cold ground hadn't even registered with him. He had the muscle and mass to withstand the cold, but there wasn't anything to Desi. Just delicate flesh and fragile bone. Son of a bitch, no wonder she was freezing. He went to work on the remaining buttons on the coat, opening them with neat efficiency, ignoring the way she seemed to stop breathing as he did. When he had it open, he slid his hand inside. Where he expected to feel the warmth of her skin he found a coldness that alarmed him more. Building the fire wasn't an option as it would draw attention and wouldn't warm her nearly fast enough anyway, which only left one other option.

"Hold on a minute."

He reached into his boot and drew his knife from its scabbard. The blade winked in the faint light. Her big eyes went round with horror as he said, "I'll have you all taken care of in just a moment."

He slit the front of the poncho to make room.

She frowned up at him. "What are you doing?"

He turned the poncho around and put the knife back. She was cold and scared and almost out of fight, but she kept her head. A man had to admire that. She was something. "Making you a nest." He held out his hand. "Kneel up."

She grimaced as she did and he felt like a heel for making her move at all. He steadied her the last two feet with a hand on her ribs just under her breasts. Christ, his hand about swallowed the widest part of her bone structure. Compared to him, there really was nothing to her.

He lifted the poncho and dropped it over her head. A tug and her head popped through the opening. Her hands came up against his chest as he worked his fingers under her hair and lifted the mass free of the neck. She leaned forward as he got the last foot free and he decided he liked her like this, giving him her weight and the illusion of her trust. Someday, it would be for real.

He glanced over his shoulder, shifted them a couple of inches to the left and then with only a "hold on" to warn her, hooked an arm under her buttocks and leaned back. Her short nails scraped his chest as he caught their combined weights on his elbow, and a quick glance determined her little gasps were from fear, not pain, as he took them down the last couple feet, not stopping until he was resting supine to the ground, his head supported by the leather saddle, her weight a welcome warmth atop him. Her head rested just above his breastbone, her legs falling naturally between his.

"Better?" he asked.

The shake of her head was immediate. "No."

He frowned. "You hurting anywhere?" "No."

"No, but I liked it better before."

"You were cold."

He said that as if it mattered. Desi lifted her hips as he yanked the coat out from under her, wincing as a button scraped her inner thigh. Tracker had fetched her a dress but with only one layer of petticoats, it wasn't much protection from anything.

Caine patted her back. "Sorry about that."

"What are you doing?"

"Getting you comfortable."

On top of him? "You intend for me to sleep this way?"

"You got a better plan?"

"The ground was working just fine."

She could hear his hair swish across the leather as he shook his head. "The cold would sap the life from your bones."

"You're on the ground."

"I'm a lot bigger with a lot more muscle to take the cold." His hands slid up her thighs under the coat. "You're just a little bit of a thing."

He was right about one thing. He was warm, very warm, and if his hands weren't gathering up her skirts as she lay there, she might have been able to enjoy the heat radiating off him. "Why can't you let this go?"

"Because you're afraid of what I'm going to do, which is loco, seeing as I'd cut off my arm rather than hurt you."

"So you intend…"

She just couldn't put into words what he intended to do. "I intend to let you experience my touch so you can stop dreading it."

"The others—"

"Can't see a thing, which means they won't have any

idea anything is going on over here other than sleep unless you make a fuss."

The thought was little consolation. She pressed her face into his chest as his palms curled around her thighs with only the pantaloons to protect her modesty. He pulled and her thighs separated on either side of his thighs. She could feel his cock—hard and hotter than the rest of him—pressing up into her groin. She shifted to the side to relieve the pressure. "I don't want this."

"But I do, and unless my ears were playing tricks on me five hours ago, I believe you promised to love, honor and obey."

"I didn't have a choice." Those hands inched higher, those fingers dipped lower.

"Neither did I, but you don't see me reneging."

She couldn't see a thing of his expression with what little light there was obscured by his hat, but the glitter of his eyes reached out to her.

"That's because all the advantages are on your side," she managed to say.

"What advantages?"

"You get a woman you can have anytime you want, a woman you can vent on, order around, and it's all perfectly legal."

His fingers hit the beginning of her buttocks, lingered under the rise, tracing the crease beneath each as if fascinated by the separation. "That's how you see it, huh?"

"Yes." And she hated it. Almost as much as she hated the tickling sensation his caress was inspiring. She tried to hold still, but it was impossible. She shifted her hips away. A soft "Hmm" and a slowly drawled "I like that" were her punishment.

She didn't want him enjoying her rape. She didn't want him enjoying anything, but another lesson she'd learned in the past year was that there was nothing she could do to stop a man's pleasure. Whatever she did, lying there, fighting, it all thrilled them. The only thing she could do was battle for her own survival during every instance. She drew her hands into fists against his chest and lowered her head, notching her forehead between his pectorals, pushing against his breastbone. She could do this. She knew how to do this. Concentration and one breath at a time, following her heartbeat deep into her center until she could all but ignore what was happening to her body.

Caine's fingers tickled again. She shivered.

"Cold?"

"No."

"Good." His palms rode the rise of her buttocks, conforming to her shape while his fingers dipped between, following gravity down to the slit in her pantaloons. She held her breath. Maybe he wouldn't...

He did. His fingers slid between the whisper-light pieces of fabric, brushing gently along her pubic hair, exploring her shape with a barely there sensation that tickled. She tried to twist away, wrenching her ribs. One hand immediately came out from under her to press in the small of her back, holding her still for his pleasure. "Easy."

She shook her head. She couldn't be easy.

"Is this what you fear?" he asked as those fingers explored. "My fingers here?"

"Yes."

"Why?"

Because it hurt, but he wasn't hurting her, just touching her with butterfly-light caresses that tickled in the oddest way.

"Does it embarrass you?" he asked as his middle finger skimmed the crease of her lips.

"Yes."

With a wiggle, he separated the plump outer lips. "It shouldn't. I'm your husband. Our loving each other is right."

Right. She couldn't wrap her mind around it, but she knew what he meant. "It's not a sin now...."

"No."

And that was supposed to make everything all right? "But it's still against my will."

The finger dipping deeper into her folds stopped. "Is it?"

The low, drawled question hung between them, full of expectation. The immediate "Yes" caught on her tongue.

"Husbands and wives make love. You knew that when we married."

"Yes."

"And still you married me."

"Yes." She had.

"So you're saying you didn't mean the promises you made?"

"Did you?"

"I don't make promises lightly."

"Father Gerard made you marry me."

"He offered me a way to pay off a debt, but nothing forced me to make the promise."

"Then why did you marry me?"

"I liked what I saw."

"I'm a whore."

His hand snaked out from under the poncho so fast she never registered the change, but she felt the tug on her hair that had her head wrenching back, staring through the dark at an expression she couldn't see. "You're my wife."

She dug her nails into the front of his shirt. "It doesn't change what I was."

"It changes who you can be."

The truth hung between them. Her lip slipped between her teeth. It was so much more complicated than that.

"I can't promise you a soft life, Desi, and I can't say that I'm an easy man, but I can promise you this. I'll care for you, protect you and honor you as my wife and the mother of my children."

"Why?"

"I made a promise a long time ago not to hurt the innocent."

"And you think I'm innocent."

"Sometimes a body can't help what happens to them. The best they can do is make something of what's left."

And he was offering the status of his wife, the protection of his big body, the comfort of his home. What did he want in exchange? She bit down hard on her lip. She didn't really know what he wanted from her. "That all sounds good, but—"

"But what?"

With his hand in her hair and his fingers parting her woman's flesh it was hard to miss the aggression in the question. He could sense her weakening and like the predator he reminded her of, he was going in for the kill.

"What do you want in exchange?"

He didn't even hesitate. "I want your trust, your obedience when it's called for and a chance."

Of the three, the last was the one she sensed that mattered. "A chance for what?"

"A chance to prove I'm not what you're used to."

His fingers moved, probed, slid. Tingles shot up her spine. Panic thrummed along with her heartbeat, and above it all, the tiniest flutter of hope. That maybe he meant it. That maybe things didn't have to be an unrelenting hell from here on out. That she didn't have to endure being passed from man to man, that maybe her dreams of a home and family were not dead.

Taking a deep breath, feeling like she was stepping off a ledge, glad for the cover of darkness that hid her terror at the step she was taking, Desi said, "Yes."

"Yes' what?"

"I want to be your wife."

"And you'll give me your trust?"

Promises mattered to her, too, so she couldn't just give a blanket statement. "I'll do my best."

He released her hair. She dropped her cheek back to his chest, breathing in the scent of hard-worked man, horse and leather. She should have been offended, but she wasn't. Unlike the stinking cologne James and the others favored, there was a cleanliness about the smell that went far deeper than a bath could ever deliver.

"You're talking an honest try?" he asked.

She'd longed for so many months for someone to help her, prayed while James and his cronies had hurt her for their amusement, that a white knight from one of her fairy tales would come along and sweep her away to safety. And now someone had. He wasn't well dressed and he was definitely rough around the edges, but he seemed to have something she'd learned was a lot more important. He seemed to have integrity. She licked her lips and then answered his question. "Yes."

"Guess a man can't ask for more than that."

Some could but he wouldn't and she was grateful

for that. His hand slipped back under the blanket and poncho, finding the soft skin of her calf. Her instinct was to flinch away. She controlled it, but she couldn't control her gasp.

"Easy, Gypsy."

To give herself something to do besides focus on the way he was handling her, she asked, "Why do you call me that?"

He tucked his fingers on the back of her knee. "Because you're wild and sweet, and no matter what those SOBs did to you, you're still fiery and proud."

"Oh." It was so different than what she'd expected, so different than how she saw herself that she didn't know what else to say.

"That's all you've got to say?"

"Pretty much."

His chuckle wafted over her cheek. His breath smelled of coffee, without the rancid undertones of rotted teeth she'd gotten accustomed to. Her husband really was a different breed of man. And he was still holding her intimately, waiting for...permission? "What do you want me to do?"

"Try to relax and let me learn you."

"Learn me?"

The question ended on a gasp as his finger glided down the seam of her pussy to dip into the well of her vagina.

"Yes."

Her breath stuttered out as he pressed.

His sigh first lifted and then dropped her. "You're a small-built woman, Desi."

"Is that a problem?"

"Nope. Just a useful fact for a husband to know."

He was still whispering, the dark still encased them

in privacy, but she couldn't forget the men just across the fire. His hand moved, his fingers worked lower, sliding down the not-so-dry slit to the apex of her mound. They wiggled and probed, searching for something. She bit her lip and glanced across the way.

"Desi?"

"What?"

"They don't matter."

"They know."

"They can't hear or see, and if they're imagining anything, it's what a damn lucky man I was to see you first."

She did her best to disregard his intimate touch. "You make me sound like a prize."

He grunted and shifted beneath her, gaining a bit more reach. "Just goes to show how unbalanced your view is if you can't see that you are."

His middle finger stretched and touched a spot that made her flinch. He stilled. "You felt that?"

Her face bloomed with heat. Even if she hadn't been choking on embarrassment, she wouldn't have answered him.

He did it again. This time the sensation was sharper. Not pain, but definitely sensitive. She couldn't control her twitch.

"So, that's your sweet spot." He started circling his finger over the area, the callus dragging and bunching her flesh. Flashes of sensation came at odd moments, not unpleasant, not really anything, just ethereal streaks that made her shift and anticipate something more. She took a stab at suppressing the next one. A soft rustle indicated the shake of his head. "No, just relax and sort out how it feels."

She didn't want to.

As she curled her hips away on the next one, he whispered in her ear, "Son of a bitch, my hands are too rough."

"You're not hurting me."

"I'm not pleasuring you, either."

That was what he was looking for? Her pleasure. "My mother said relations are for a man's pleasure."

"That it is." He narrowed the circles of that finger, rasping it delicately over her moist flesh. "But I bet if I put my tongue here, you'd be screaming yours."

Oh, God, she didn't want his mouth, his teeth, there. "I don't like that."

The tension from her body communicated itself to his. His hand stilled. His other opened over her back and patted her comfortingly. "I don't imagine there's any chance you can forget, but I would appreciate it if you hold the thought that every man loves a woman differently."

"I know that."

"I don't think you do." The tug on her braid had her tilting her head back again. "No matter how scared you get, remember this one thing, the only way you'll scream in my bed is from pleasure." Another tug kept her looking toward the faint outline of his face. "Your pleasure."

"Thank you." What else could she say? Whether she believed him or not was immaterial. The thing was, he believed it.

"I can hear the doubt in your voice."

"I'm sorry."

"No need to be sorry. I don't mind a challenge."

But she minded disappointing him. He seemed willing to let their marriage start on equal ground, but sex was important to a man. If she failed him there, it would show in the relationship. She knew enough about men to know that.

His finger was back to brushing and probing, lingering longer with every flinch of her flesh, lingering so long she felt herself swell, even though she didn't feel irritation.

"Oh, yeah, that's my girl." His hand left the space between her legs. "No, don't close them."

She lay there, sprawled on his chest, her legs splayed on either side of his hips, trying to assimilate the warm, tingly sensation his touch left behind and what it meant. A scandalous woman ruining her only chance left at respectability.

The parting of his lips was audible. The gleam of his teeth barely visible as he put his finger in his mouth. The same finger that had been between her legs.

She blinked. He wouldn't. He did. His tongue curled around the digit.

"You didn't just—" She bit off the stupid question and dropped her head to his chest. When was she going to learn to keep her mouth shut?

He hummed in his throat. "I definitely did." His hand worked back under the blankets, letting in cold air as they blossomed up. "I don't think I've ever tasted anything as sweet as you."

"Have you no shame?"

"Not much." She could hear the smile in his voice.

"Men don't do that to women."

"Who the hell told you that?"

Sheer frustration had her swatting his shoulder. "Everyone knows that."

His thumb grazed her buttock through the cotton of her pantaloons, riding the seam to the gaping slit. "Then you and everyone are going to have to swap out your ideas because after that little taste I promise I'm going to be spending a lot of time with my mouth between your legs."

Her "Oh, God" ended on a high squeak as his finger returned with unerring accuracy. Smoothed by the wetness of his saliva, it drifted over that spot, finding the tingling that had died, sparking it into something she didn't recognize. Something that tightened her breath, her nipples, her fear. Leather creaked from across the fire. Dried leaves rustled as someone changed positions. Were the other men listening? Thinking of coming over?

Caine's fingers spread out over her back. Holding her to him. "There's nothing to be afraid of, Desi."

"I'm not afraid."

His fingers stilled but the feeling continued to hum, almost seemed to build. "Now, that I won't tolerate."

"What?"

"You're lying to me."

"I wasn't—"

"Unless you want me turning you over my knee right now, you won't finish that sentence."

The threat snuffed out the tingling as if it had never been.

"Ah, hell."

Three fingers joined the one pressing so intimately, cupping her mound almost protectively. "I ruined it, didn't I?"

"There wasn't anything to ruin."

She could feel him staring at her. "You're joshing, right?"

Vividly aware of his strength and his threat, she forced the truth from her throat. "I think I've forgotten how to joke."

There was a long pause and then the tension dissolved from his muscles. "Now, that's a damn shame."

Yes, it was. And the fact that he understood cracked the wall of her defenses. He wasn't supposed to notice things like that. Tears burned.

"My father always said women were made for laughter and pleasure," Caine offered as his free hand rubbed her back.

She blinked faster. "Your father said that?"

"Yup, and he apparently meant it because I never saw him smile bigger than when my mom was happy."

She couldn't imagine that. In her family, and the families of her friends, the men and women lived in different circles, coming together for meals and an occasional outing, but she couldn't remember a sense of togetherness. "That must be a nice memory."

His fingertips pressed into her spine. "It is."

The tears disappeared as she imagined a home life like that. "Do you miss them?"

It was an intimate question, but surely not too intimate to ask a man with his hands cupping her privates on her wedding night.

"Yeah." His hand slid free of her privates to spread over her buttocks. "You warm enough?"

"Yes."

"Good." He turned them, his hands holding her as he settled her carefully beneath him, taking the bumps of the maneuver on his elbows and forearms so she felt more leviated than moved. His weight came over her in a fresh blast of heat. She braced for the crush. His thighs aligned between hers. She moved them as far as she could to the side until the material of her skirt pulled her up short. His cock touched her first—it was solid, big, uncompromising in its demand, a bit painful in its pressure against her pubic bone. He shifted down so it notched between her thighs. His pants and her skirts did nothing to diminish the blunt impact. She sucked in her breath. The past blurred into the present. Faces flashed before her mind's eye. So many faces, the features interchanging until they became a visual cacophony, swallowing reason, feeding the memories of pain... *No. No. No.*

Caine's stomach lowered to hers, and then his chest. Lastly his head. The brush of his lips made her whimper.

"What's wrong, Gypsy?"

She couldn't answer. Her breaths were coming too hard, but she couldn't get enough air. She closed her eyes. Her breath came faster, shorter.

"Gypsy?"

Desi shook her head, her nose bumping his. She squeezed her eyes shut, fighting the panic. The press of his weight, the force of his male parts pushing into her, she couldn't stand it. He caught her face in his hands. Holding her still. "Breathe, Desi."

She couldn't. No matter how hard she tried, nothing was coming in. She couldn't focus on anything beyond the weight of his body and the howl of memories.

"Tracker!"

"Coming."

She tried to shake her head. She didn't want anyone seeing her like this, didn't want Tracker seeing her lying under Caine. She didn't need another man with ideas.

The crunch of moccasined feet across the dried grass sounded like thunder. Caine's body slid from hers. The blankets whipped down.

"What's the matter?"

"She can't breathe."

Other hands joined Caine's. There were always more hands. More demands. More humiliation.

"What brought this on?" she heard Tracker say in a voice that sounded hollow and distant.

"I did." Caine's answer wasn't any clearer.

"Figured that, but how?"

"I didn't hurt her."

Two hands lifted her arms, felt along the contracted muscle, while others held her down, defying her struggle for air. Just like before.

"You're sure?"

Caine was absolutely sure. He lifted Desi as she wheezed for air, her face pale in the faint light, eyes squeezed shut, hands pulled back against her chest, so terrified she couldn't breathe. "Not physically."

"Then it's fear stealing her air."

"Know anything to do about it?"

Caine propped Desi's back against his thigh. High-pitched squeaks punctuated every jerk of her ribs against his thigh.

Tracker sat back on his heels. "I might. Cup your hands over her nose and mouth like a tent."

"Hell, she needs more air not less."

"So it would seem, but I saw a kid with this issue once and the healer put a sack over her face."

"We don't have a sack."

"So maybe your hands will do."

"They'd better." He couldn't take her gasping for each breath and getting nowhere. He cupped his hands over her face. They covered the whole thing, reminding him what a little bit of a woman she was. He tucked his thumbs down out of her eyes. "Breathe, Desi. Just relax and breathe."

If anything she seemed to tense up more.

"Nothing's going to happen, sweetheart," he said. "You're just going to relax and breathe and then we're going to sleep." The whites of her eyes flashed as she looked at him. "I swear."

She arched her neck so hard the muscles in her neck trembled. "Just sleep, sweetheart."

"Tracker?" he asked as her next two breaths seemed deeper.

The big man pushed her hair off her cheek. His lips quirked in a faint smile. "She's getting her breath back now."

She tried to turn her head. Caine shook his. "Just hold still and breathe." Her fingers caught at his forearms. "Don't waste your strength giving orders. Until Tracker says my hands come off your face, they're staying put."

Tracker leaned over into her field of vision. "Just relax and let Caine do all the work, Mrs. Allen. That's what husbands are for, and I know for a fact Caine's been storing up a lifetime of pampering to wrap around his woman, so there's not much sense trying to talk him out of it."

She shook in his arms. Caine grabbed the blanket and wrapped it around her.

"See?" Tracker continued. "The man just can't help spoiling women. Whether they want it or not."

He could see she was too tired to argue.

"It's the truth, sweetheart. If Tracker's to be believed, I'm all plucked and primed to be henpecked."

Desi shook her head and took a normal breath. He'd never felt so relieved. "Good girl."

He didn't take his hands away until she managed four more and then only after Tracker gave the okay.

She shivered again. And no wonder, she was sitting on

the cold ground in an open coat. "Damn, I'm not shining as a husband here."

"It's fine."

Not by a long shot she wasn't. He lifted her into his lap, bracing his back against the saddle and tree, hitching her up against him. The utter laxity of her muscles told him more than words. "Been a rough day for you, huh?"

Her reply was softer than a man's breath. He lifted his poncho over her head and pulled her against his chest. He could hardly feel her under the bulk of his coat, but it didn't matter. He could feel her weight, feel her breath. He knew she was his. It was enough. "We've got to work on your fear reactions, sweetheart."

"There's nothing to work on."

The rasp to her voice had him pulling her closer. They had a hell of a lot to work on. "We sure do. For starters, I can tell you right now I'm going to have trouble in the future with the way you get upset."

"I can't help that."

"You're going to have to try, and for the record, I'm putting in my preferences right now. Next time you get worked up, remember screaming is good. Hollering is good. Fighting is good. Suffocating is way down at the bottom of options."

"I don't like it, either."

He nestled her head under his chin. At least the shivers had stopped. "Then we're agreed. You come up with something else to trot out when you get to feeling scared and I'll learn to like it."

"What would you suggest?"

"I made my suggestions. You just take your pick and start practicing on them."

The shake of her head was a tiny movement. As tiny as her sigh. "I don't understand you."

"We'll work on that, too, but right now, you need sleep."

"I couldn't."

"We've got a ten-hour ride tomorrow. You'd better get rest, or you'll never make it."

He could feel her determination gathering. "I'll make it."

"Good." All the determination in the world wasn't going to keep her awake, but he wasn't going to argue the point when waiting her out would work just as well. It took roughly five minutes before she went slack against him. He slid down, being careful not to wake her. Desi's head lolled to the right as he worked his shoulder down. He caught it in his palm. She turned her face into his touch with a relieved sigh. Her cheek fit perfectly into the hollow of his hand. Her fingers curled into his chest. She didn't have to worry. He wasn't going to let her go.

S he didn't make it. Six hours into the ride, as the flat-lands gave way to the rocky canyons, Desi slumped forward in the saddle.

Sam came up alongside as Caine reached for the paint's reins, pulling it up short. He clucked his tongue, eyeing Desi with disappointment.

"I had a gold piece bet on her making it."

"With Tracker?"

Sam brought the paint even with Chaser. "Yup."

"You should know better than to bet against Tracker. He's got a sixth sense when it comes to a body's endurance." A trait that had stood them all in good stead over the years. Desi listed to the left as the pony stopped. Caine slipped his arm around her narrow waist and lifted her up and over. She jerked at the shift in her balance, but she didn't come fully awake.

Sam ground his smoke out on his boot. The paint shied as Desi's legs slid down its side. Sam held it put. "I was banking on that grit of hers to make up the difference."

Caine eased Desi's weight across his saddle, tucking her shoulder under his as she settled. "She does have more than her fair share of that, but she's not at full strength."

After an initial protest, she rested against him. He tugged the coat from the twist it had gotten into around her hips. She'd have a crick for sure if she had to ride like that. Sam pulled the paint around and looped his reins over his horn. It was impossible to see his expression with his hat pulled down low like that.

"She sure has been hard used the last year."

"That is a fact." Caine adjusted Desi's thighs around the pommel. Beyond a whimper at the pain the maneuver caused her muscles, she didn't waken. As he worked the poncho up between them he asked, "So, you going to tell me what you found in her room?"

"Nothing."

Caine dropped the heavy wool over Desi's head. "What kind of nothing."

"Just that. Nothing. No clothes, no books, no geegaws, just a length of thin chain, and a bed."

Caine thought on that, picturing the significance of the chain and the lack of clothing. Pictured Desi chained there, waiting hour after hour for visits that had to scar her soul. He turned his head and spat in a useless attempt to rid his mouth of the bad taste the images left. "Bet the bed was comfortable though."

"Looked well stuffed."

It figured. The bastards wouldn't want their fun marred by a too-hard mattress.

Sam pushed his hat back. "The sheriff seemed to consider her position with James a step up from her previous position as a Comanche whore."

"I just bet he did." Men would say anything to justify their actions, and it was a real easy thing to do, abusing a woman with nothing but hell at her back. "Bet he'll squeal a whole different tune when Desi's menfolk come to call."

"Any idea when that might be?"

Caine glanced down their back trail. "I was thinking in a couple weeks after I get her settled, a visit might be in order."

"Tracker and I would be happy to tag along."

"That's not necessary."

Sam's cold gaze cut to Desi as she moaned in her sleep, lingering on her pale cheeks. "But it'd be damn enjoyable."

Caine scooted back in the saddle, giving her more room. "In that case, when the time comes, I'd appreciate the company."

Something flashed in Sam's eyes as he took his gaze off Desi. "You know you're one lucky son of a bitch, don't you?"

"I know."

Sam motioned with the reins. "Women like her, they don't come along every day."

Caine was well aware that Desi had been slated for a lot better than him.

"Especially not for men like us," Sam continued. Knowing it didn't mean he liked the sound of it being pointed out. "What are you getting at, Sam?"

"Whatever she's been through this last year, it shouldn't be held against her."

"Is that a suggestion or a threat?"

Sam straightened in that deceptively lazy way he had. The hairs on Caine's neck lifted. Nothing was deadlier than Sam when he decided on a cause. "It's whatever it needs to be."

"I know damn well she's innocent."

The sun shone on Sam's face, illuminating the rigid

set of his expression and the simmering rage darkening his blue eyes to slate gray. "Do you?" His reply was all the more lethal for the quiet way it was delivered.

Sam was remembering that day so long ago when they'd lost everything. The same memories ripped through Caine. They'd lay in the dirt together, beaten and bound, and watched man after man abuse Sam's mother. Watched the life drain from her eyes long before the renegades slit her throat. The only bright spot Caine could find in that day was that his own mother had died of a bullet before they could rape her. It was poor consolation. "I was there with you, Sam. I watched just like you did."

And when the time came, he'd hunted the sons of bitches down right alongside Sam and the rest of Hell's Eight. Not one word had been said about the way Sam had taken his revenge. No one had stayed his hand, because the same rage had simmered for years in them all, finally boiling over as one by one they tracked down the men who had massacred their families.

They'd set their reputations at the age of fifteen, terrorizing the badlands, and when every account had been settled but one, when they'd ridden into San Antonio to put paid on the last debt, they'd found a Ranger waiting for them. He'd blinked at their ages, but that hadn't stopped him from giving them an ultimatum. Join the Texas Rangers and do their hunting within the bounds of the law or hang for murder. It hadn't been much of a choice, but by then they were ready for a change. They'd taken the badges, sworn their oath and the last account had been settled the following spring, all nice and tight and legal.

"A man can see things differently when it's his wife," Sam pointed out.

"Maybe." But Caine couldn't. Not with Desi. He'd seen her pride, her pain and that incredible courage that shone through it all. It didn't matter how many men had forced themselves on her. All that mattered was that she was his and no one but he would ever touch her again. "But I'm thinking marriage gives us both a fresh start."

And he was ready to try his hand at something other than killing. Right after he settled accounts with the men who'd hurt Desi. One by one, for as long as it took until all of them knew the pain and humiliation his wife had experienced. It wouldn't heal her scars, but—he straightened the poncho—she'd be able to sleep nights not worrying that the bastards were coming back for seconds. Peace of mind was the least of things a husband should give his wife.

"Seeing as Desi is Hell's Eight now, they'll be expecting us to come after them. They might have split town."

Caine wasn't so sure. There had been something different about the Easterners he didn't trust. "Or they might be so arrogant, they think they're above justice."

"Now, that would be convenient."

The anticipation in Sam's voice gave Caine pause.

"No one does anything until I get names," he warned.

"And then?" Sam asked.

Desi snuggled into his heat. She was damn sensitive to the cold, and no wonder, seeing as there wasn't a spare pound to be found on her. Caine pulled her closer, meeting Sam's steady gaze with his own. "Then we try out a few of the more interesting techniques Tracker says his kinfolk are fond of."

Tracker's horse drew up on the other side of Desi's.

"You all talking 'bout me?"

"Just the knowledge you harbor about killing."

"Anything in particular?"

"Just the best ways to make a man ponder his actions."

Tracker's dark gaze flicked over the blond of Desi's hair, which was all that was visible above the coat. "Be happy to oblige. Any time in particular we're going to be needing the information?"

"Two weeks," Sam offered.

Tracker rested his forearm across his saddle horn. "I'll make a note to be around."

Caine nodded. "Thanks."

Tracker jerked his chin at Desi. "Beyond tired and sore, she all right?"

"Best I can tell, yes."

"She's got scars, Caine. Not all of them ones you can see."

Did everyone think he'd suddenly lost his intellect? "Desi's got grit, and a real die-hard spirit, too." And he was counting on that to carry her through.

"Just making sure you noticed."

"Why, you planning on threatening me, too?"

"Nope." Tracker straightened, his dark eyes oddly hungry as they stared at Desi. "But if she wants to leave, I won't be denying her a safe place to stay."

Sam swore. Caine merely nodded, understanding the hunger that drove the other man. His mother had been trapped by her choice of love. Her life and Tracker's had been hell. With his mixed blood, just finding a prostitute willing to serve him was an issue. A good woman of any race was probably not in his future. But a hell of a lot of loneliness was. Which was a shame. Tracker was a strong man with a real penchant for caretaking and no place to set it loose. "Then I guess it will be up to me to give her a reason to stay."

Tracker straightened, still watching Desi. "See that you do."

He looked up and the rare smile that creased his cheeks took Caine by surprise, the way it always did because of the way it took the man from killer to human with just a few shifts of muscle. "She sure did put the fear of his maker into that gambler man when she drew a bead on his balls, didn't she?"

The memory tugged Caine's own grin to the fore. "That she did."

"Should have let her plug him," Sam growled.

He wished he could have. He shrugged. "Couldn't risk them trumping up charges."

But the temptation had been there, yet even then he had been aware of the need to keep Desi safe. He brushed his lips across her hair.

"She'll be safe at Hell's Eight," Sam said, putting the used smoke in the small leather bag strapped to his saddle for that purpose. "And you know Tia's going to fall in love with her the first time she takes a swing at you."

Caine smiled at the mental image of his tiny woman taking a swing at him. No doubt Desi would think she could do damage. "What makes you think I'm going to rile her?"

Sam snorted. "Pretty much the natural contrariness of your nature."

"That and the fact you have a tendency to hand out orders rather than requests," Tracker added.

Caine shrugged. He was what he was. "It's a woman's place to take her husband's instructions."

Both men glanced at Desi and back at him, not saying a word, but their expressions were eloquent.

"She'll learn to adapt," he countered.

Sam chuckled and rode ahead. "You just keep thinking that."

Tracker eyed Desi again, then tugged his hat down, putting his smile in shadow. "I wouldn't get too comfortable based on how she's acting now. I've got a feeling when she rests up, she's going to start finding her feet."

Caine brushed the hair back from Desi's cheek, taking in the very feminine line of her profile, the delicacy of her bones, the stubbornness of that small, pointed chin and the spirit etched into every tired angle. "I'm looking forward to it."

"WAKE UP, DESI. We're home."

The words slid on that deep drawl through the warmth surrounding her. Desi shook her head, caught between being asleep and awake, resisting the call. She was safe where she was. She turned her cheek into the warmth beneath it. "Not yet."

Something gentle, yet oddly rough, touched her cheek. "Wake up for just a minute and you can go back to sleep in a warm bed."

She shook her head. She didn't want a bed. She had what she wanted. She curled her fingers deeper into the rough sheet. It'd been so long since she'd slept without fear. "Safe here."

"You'll be safe inside, too."

The rumble echoed under her ear. She frowned wondering how that was so. "No."

Fingers threaded through her hair, snapping her into alertness as they tilted her head back. Desi lifted her lids to find Caine staring down at her, his eyes shining darkly from under the brim of his hat. Around them the gloom of twilight deepened the shadows.

"Evening."

She lifted her hand to push her hair out of her face, ran into the barrier of the poncho and blinked. Last she remembered she'd been riding her own horse. A glance around revealed the paint standing to the left of Sam's horse. "I fell asleep?"

"Yes."

She worked her hand free. The cold evening air was a shock after the warmth of the poncho. "I'm sorry."

"I'm not."

She was smart enough not to ask why. "We're here?"

"Yup."

"Here" was a clearing in the woods at the foot of a high wall. At first glance, no house was in sight, but when she squinted against the gloom toward the golden spill of light she thought was just a lantern, she realized there was a house built into the canyon wall. Made of stone and adobe, it blended with the environment. It wasn't a large structure but it also wasn't the only structure she noticed now that she knew what to look for. There were several spread out across the canyon face, all looking solid and indomitable. Like the men coming at her from the shadows.

She tried to sit up straighter, but the poncho strangled her back into submission. Caine made no move to lift it up. And when she tried, his hands stilled hers.

"Might as well wait until we get the greetings done. No sense catching a chill before you meet everyone."

Anything she might have said to the contrary was snuffed by "everyone" arriving. Everyone was four men, hard-eyed men to the last, their expressions giving no indication of their thoughts as they surveyed her perched in front of Caine on the horse.

"Have a good time in town?" a man with a square jaw, dark skin and the muscular build of a blacksmith asked.

"Good enough." Caine angled the horse around. "Tucker McCade, this is my wife, Desi." The pride in his voice as he made the announcement gave her a start. "Over there's Ed Hayden and Caden Steele, and lurking under that tree is Shadow."

Tucker touched his hand to his hat. The movement pushed the brim back, adding high cheekbones, a hawk-like nose and almond-shaped eyes that cut through pretense like the blade of a knife to the list of features that comprised his brutally handsome face. "Ma'am." His gaze swung back to Caine. "Tia know you came back riding double with a wife?"

"Not yet."

"Thought not. Otherwise she'd be out here spouting orders."

"She's sure going to have something to say about it."

"Yeah," a voice said out of the shadows. "I think her bet was on Sam marrying first, seeing as he's the ladies' man."

No matter how she squinted, Desi couldn't make out the features of the owner of that voice. Shadow was well named.

"Welcome to Hell's Eight, ma'am."

Like a ripple, the greeting spread through the men. Flat and unemotional, giving her no clue as to how they felt about her or the marriage. She knew they were all wondering where she'd come from, speculating on how Caine had hitched up with her. As she forced the proper

"Thank you" from her throat, the front door opened. More light poured into the yard, illuminating the porch and a woman's voice called, "You are home, *hijos?*"

A feminine silhouette stood backlit in the doorway. Desi had the impression of full skirts and slender shoulders wrapped in a blanket, before the woman walked into the darkness of the porch. "You have come back to me in one piece, yes?"

"Hale and hearty, Tia."

This was the indomitable Tia. The woman Caine and the others so respected. Desi squinted to get a look at her.

She stepped into the twilight. Desi could see she was an older woman, maybe in her fifties, her black hair drawn back in a smooth chignon. The temples were salt-and-pepper above her surprisingly youthful face. She carried herself with a grace and dignity that suggested aristocracy. Her dark gaze snapped with unerring accuracy to Desi. "And this young woman is…?"

Dirty. Soiled. A whore. The words leapt to Desi's mind, pounded there by experience and her own sense of right and wrong. She'd been hoping Tia would be a simple woman, but she wasn't. She had the cultured ways of the world Desi had left. Every society had its levels, with those on top looking down on those below. And nothing was lower than where she'd fallen. Caine's hand spread over her stomach, pressing against the butterflies there. "My wife."

Again there was that note of pride.

The woman took a step closer and put her hands on her hips. "What kind of wife do you bring me looking like the devil dragged her through the bush backward?"

"The one I chose."

Desi could have kissed him for the lie.

"And this was a happy choice?"

"Absolutely." Pride and satisfaction laced the statement. Desi glanced at Caine over her shoulder. He was a good liar.

With a flick of her wrist Tia made her desire known. "Then put her down and let us meet."

Desi took a breath. This was it. Caine tugged the poncho over her head. Tia's gaze flicked over her too-big clothing. More shame burned as the part of her that always wanted to be liked, cringed. It wouldn't take much conversation for the woman to put two and two together and all of Caine's pride would wither under the screech of humiliation.

Tia took a step closer. Desi was surprised to see she was only of medium height. It was the way she carried herself that gave her the illusion of being bigger. That and the expectation of being obeyed that surrounded her. She had pretty eyes. Large and brown and sharp.

"You have fallen on hard times?"

Desi glanced over her shoulder at Caine. What did he want her to say. He didn't give her a clue, just stared back with none of the distress she felt inside. Desi finally settled on a "Yes."

"And my boys saved you?"

Boys? The woman called these battle-scarred warriors boys? "Yes."

"Saved? My ass. You should have seen her, Tia," Sam called over from where he was unpacking his saddlebag. "She held off three *bandoleros* with nothing more than temper and grit."

Tia's eyebrows went up. "This is true?"

"Barely left a thing for me to beat on," Caine added, with...more pride?

Tia gave a sharp nod of her head. "Good. Men should not think a woman is so easily defeated."

"Now there's a story I wouldn't mind hearing," a good-looking older man with red hair said to Caine as he came up to the group.

"And I won't mind telling it, Ed," Caine answered. "Just as soon as I get Desi warmed and settled. It's been a rough ride for her."

"How long have you been on the trail?"

"Pretty much all day."

"Are you loco? She is not a Ranger in a skirt!" Tia gasped. "You do not treat a wife this way!"

Tia turned to the men around her and clapped her hands. "Shadow, you get the big tub out and set it up in the kitchen." She made shooing motions with her hands toward the others. "Ed, you get a fire going and heat up water. We will need plenty. Tucker and Caden, you come take care of the horses."

Desi blinked as the men didn't hesitate, just scattered to do as ordered.

"Shadow," Caine said, cutting into the lull in orders. "We might have been followed."

Shadow didn't step into the light. "I'll check on it."

"I'll ride with him," Sam offered, shaking his head when Tucker walked over. "There's something I want to check in town."

Desi wrapped her arms around her waist, dreading what came next.

Tia waited until the men dispersed before putting her hands on her hips and turning back to Caine. "I am not happy with you. New wives require better care than this."

"Heck, Tia, she rode in my lap for most of the way."

"Like this made things much better."

Caine shifted. Desi looked between Tia and Caine and then back at Tia. "Actually, it did."

"Not as much as taking an easier pace would have."

It was wrong, but a devil got her tail and pulled it with the temptation to get a bit of her own back. Even if it was only playing Tia to give Caine an uncomfortable moment. Desi ducked her head and said softly, demurely, "I tried to get him to stop."

Which wasn't a lie, but it also wasn't the truth.

"I am not surprised he did not listen. He thinks every woman is as strong as a man."

"I never said that!"

Tia slapped Caine's thigh. "You behave as if it is so. What if she is with child?"

Desi felt the vibration in his chest that was his chuckle. "We've only been married one day, Tia."

"And you are telling me she is still a virgin?"

The fun went out of Desi's game. Caine's hand patted her stomach. A warning or comfort?

"No, I'm not saying that."

"Then there is hope."

"I wouldn't give it up just yet." Desi looked into her husband's face. There was no stiffness to his expression. He seemed genuinely amused. Optimistic even.

"It has been a long time since I've held a baby in my arms."

The words were underlaid with a profound sadness that dragged Desi's head around. She didn't want to like the woman or feel empathy for her, but she did. She'd lost her sister. Losing a child would be so much worse and it was clear from the haunted expression on Tia's face that she'd lost one.

"You let me get my wife settled, and I promise to

do my best to get Desi in the family way as soon as possible."

Heat flamed up Desi's neck and into her cheeks.

Tia shook her head, clearly exasperated. "Not with talk like that you won't. Embarrassing your new wife like that will have you sleeping in the barn and there will never be babies. Now——" she motioned with her hands "——you tell me why you dragged this poor girl across the territory with no rest."

"It was too dangerous to dally."

Tia snapped straight. "There is trouble?"

"Just a couple suitors that aren't happy to have been cut out of the running."

Even Desi could see Tia didn't buy that. Her gaze searched Caine's. "But you have it under control?"

"Yes."

"Good, now hand your wife over before she becomes part of that devil horse."

"Chaser's not a devil. He's just high-spirited."

"Only you would think this is a good thing." She motioned with her hands again. "Give."

Caine laughed. "It's a good thing I like high-spirited, or I would have put you out on your ear years ago."

"You maybe would have tried."

"Not likely." He grabbed the woman's hand and practically hauled her up to kiss the fingers. "You're the best thing that ever happened to us."

"This is very true." Tia stepped back and waited, hands on hips.

"Swing your leg over, Desi," Caine ordered. "So I can set you down."

Desi was stiff, and getting her leg over wasn't as easy as it should be, but she finally did it. The resulting position left her feeling as if she were on the verge of tumbling off. Chaser shifted. Tia stepped back. Desi clutched Caine's forearm as she lost her balance. The rock-hard muscle under her hands flexed as he used the momentum to ease her down the side of the horse.

It was awkward and the instant her butt left Caine's thigh, she knew she was going to fall. She twisted about. The horse sidestepped. She dug her nails into Caine's forearms and held on for dear life.

"Desi?" His drawl was low and patient and demonstrated none of the terror snapping through her.

"What?"

"Your feet are about six inches off the ground."

A glance confirmed his statement. She closed her eyes. She let go of his hands and dropped. Pain knifed up from her feet. She stumbled and caught the edge of the saddle.

A hand wrapped around her arm. She gasped and whirled. "Easy, ma'am."

Trapped. The one word ricocheted through her mind as she stared up into the hawklike features of the man holding her. Dark, like the ones who'd killed her parents, and possessing the same cruel set to the mouth. And his eyes, she couldn't look away from his eyes. They were eerily light gray, almost silver… She took a step back. Tucker's mouth jerked at the corner as he let her go. She rubbed her arm where he'd touched and took another step back, aware of how it all looked, gasping as the cuts on her feet split open with the move.

"I'm sorry."

Tucker's expression didn't change. "For what?"

For being a coward. For jumping at shadows. For always expecting the worst when she used to see the possibilities. "You just startled me."

The corner of his mouth twitched again. "Next you'll be saying you didn't know I was Indian." Sarcasm packed every one of those ten clipped words.

She didn't know what to say. Part of her reaction *had* been because he was Indian.

"Let it go, Tucker," Caine ordered.

"Why should I?"

"Because if you don't, you're going to feel like a total ass later."

Desi licked her lips and leaned back as Tucker's anger rode her nerves like the blade of a knife. His strange silver gaze flicked to Caine and then to her.

"You don't say."

"I do."

Desi reached for Caine, finding the rough leather of his boot with her palm. She couldn't look away from Tucker. She also couldn't stop herself from trying to explain. "I don't do well when startled."

It wasn't much of an explanation. This time when those eyes ran over her, they did it more slowly, coming back to her face to linger with disturbing intensity. "Neither do I."

Was he warning her? She licked her lips again. "I'll remember."

"Desi?"

She didn't take her eyes off Tucker as she answered Caine. "What?"

"Look at me."

Keeping her eyes on Tucker as much as possible, she tilted her head. Tucker's hand flashed in her periphery vision. She gasped and leapt back, throwing up her arms to protect her face. Curses rang around her. A low, rumbling growl rose above them. Caine's hand grabbed hers, the rough calluses abrading with comforting familiarity.

"Son of a bitch, Boone, if you don't straighten up I'm going to take you out back and shoot you," Tucker said.

She opened her eyes. A dog—a very big dog, with a smooth red coat, long ears and a fully raised ruff—stood between her and Tucker and it was snarling—at *Tucker.*

She couldn't see the dog's face, but Tucker was giving him a heck of a glare.

"You can't kill Boone, Tucker," Caine drawled. "He's Hell's Eight."

Tucker didn't look convinced. "The damn dog is so lazy he's worthless. Won't track, won't hunt and is afraid of his own shadow."

"He doesn't look too afraid right now."

Desi had to agree. He looked very intimidating, snarling at Tucker. She glanced over at Tia. She was observing the scenario with a strange expression on her face.

"If he doesn't shut up soon, I'm going to slit his throat."

Desi couldn't let that happen. Not when the dog was protecting her. She reached out and touched the hound's tail. He glanced at her over his shoulder. He had the biggest eyes, with lots of bags underneath. His tail wagged and then he resumed his threatening stance.

"Call him off, Desi," Caine ordered.

Was he crazy? "He's not my dog."

Tucker was the one who answered. "Looks like he's decided he is."

"Boone?" She took the way the dog stilled to mean he was listening. She tapped her thigh with her free hand. "Come here."

For a split second she didn't think he was going to respond, then with a short, grunting growl, he spun around, took the two steps to reach her side and collapsed against her pinning her to the horse, long ears falling back. She petted his head tentatively. The wrinkles in his face sagged almost smooth with bliss. "Good boy."

"Welcome to Hell's Eight, ma'am."

The tension was gone from Tucker's face. "You're not mad at me anymore."

"No."

"Why?"

He pointed to the dog. "Boone's a particular hound. He's never cozied up to anyone before."

"You're forgiving me because your dog likes me?"

"He's your dog. I'm giving him to you. And yes." He touched his hat in a small salute. "I think I can find my way to forgiving our misunderstanding."

Saddle leather creaked as Caine swung down beside her. His arm came around her shoulder immediately. "You flirting with my wife, Tucker?"

Desi couldn't imagine the big, dark man doing something as lighthearted as flirting.

"What would you do if I was?"

Unbelievably, Caine laughed. "Teach you how to do it right. That was a damn pathetic attempt."

Tucker smiled at Caine. "I wasn't trying." His gaze dropped back to her. "You should see me when I try."

She didn't want to see that. It would be like watching a wolf cozy up to a bunny. Way too much potential danger for her. From here on out, she wanted the placid life. No more adventure. No more excitement. Just one day predictably flowing into the next.

Caine tucked her into his side. She snuck a glance at his face. The shadows were no kinder to the harsh planes of his face than the light. If Tucker was a wolf, Caine was a cougar—lean, lethal and pure predator.

His green eyes flicked to hers, male possession in the depths. A shudder ran up her spine. She quickly quelled it. A wife was different than a whore. And Caine, at least, looked to be a man who valued his possessions. She forced herself to lean into his side as he clearly wanted. She might have done stupid things in the past, but she was smart enough to know a strong man to protect her was not something a woman should sneeze at. Not out here where the size of a man's muscle counted more than the size of his bank account. She rubbed the hound's ears, and for the first time she really began to accept she was Caine's wife.

Something brushed her hair. Caine's chin or his lips? There was no way to tell and, truthfully, she didn't know if she wanted to know. She was playing a game of survival. If she started worrying now about who got hurt being fooled, she'd never make it to tomorrow. She brought her weight down on her right foot. She winced. Tucker frowned and Tia asked, "Are you injured?"

Caine's reply overrode hers His hands slid behind her knees. "Her feet are shredded."

Tucker went still. "From what?"

Caine swung her up into his arms. Her weight didn't even put a dent in his calm. "Running barefoot."

"Why was she running?" Tia asked. Desi looped her arms around Caine's neck, burying her face in his throat. Once he answered, they would all know what she was. "Because I scared her."

It wasn't what that she had expected him to say.

"Why would you do that?" Tucker asked.

Caine's hand opened on her back beneath her shoulder blades, taking the pressure off her arms. "It's been so long since I dealt with a decent woman, I lost my head."

"Uh-huh."

It didn't sound like Tucker believed that lie, but Desi didn't care. She wanted to believe it.

"Unless you've got something else we need to talk about, I want to get my wife in out of the cold."

Desi was beginning to get used to the way Caine said *wife*. She let her hands slip down his chest and rested her cheek on his shoulder. It had a nice solid *real* sound when he said it.

"I'm done." Tucker touched his finger to his hat brim. "Evening, ma'am."

"Evening." She barely had the time to get the word out before Caine was moving. He closed the distance to the house in long, sure strides, none of the weariness dragging her down apparent in anything he did.

As his boot hit the first step of the porch he said, "You can owe me for that."

"What?"

"That doubt back there, thinking I wouldn't shield you."

"I had no reason to think you would."

"You're my wife. Of course, I would."

She could feel him looking at her, willing her to look at him. She didn't. Not because she was afraid, but because it required too much energy to lift her head. "What do I owe you?"

Two thuds of his boot heels and they were on the wide porch. "An apology."

"Why?"

He stopped just inside the door. His sigh was big enough to lift her up. "Because, Desi girl, you're my wife, humiliating you humiliates me, and because as my wife, you should know that."

She didn't know anything of the sort. "Pretending I'm not what I am isn't going to change anything."

"And what are you, *niña?*" Tia asked from somewhere to her right.

Damn the too big jacket! The way it bunched up, she might as well be wearing blinders. Desi didn't know why she hesitated to answer. It wasn't like the truth wasn't going to come out anyway.

"Spoiled, very spoiled."

Caine snorted. "Hardly."

But she had been. Before James, before the Comancheros, she'd been pampered and indulged. Anything she'd wanted had been given to her with a smile and a pat on the head. Anything to keep her quiet and out of the way, she was beginning to understand. "I was a very spoiled child."

Tia came into her line of vision, her head tilted to the side and those beautiful eyes seemed to see a lot of what Desi wanted hidden. This was not a dumb woman. "And now a very tired woman, I am thinking."

"Definitely."

Tia waved in the direction of the doorway to the right. "I have started your bath."

That brought her head up. She hadn't had a real bath in forever. "There hasn't been time to heat the water."

Back home, indoor plumbing was becoming common for the wealthy, but she couldn't see it existing here.

With an elegant gesture that indicated they should precede her, Tia said, "I keep the reservoir on the stove filled for whenever the men come in."

Caine headed for the door. Tia fell into step behind.

"The tub is not completely filled, but the men have the fire started and will add more hot water as time goes."

Desi felt a light tug on her hair.

"I am thinking it will take much to get your hair clean."

Desi put her hand to the side of her head, feeling the mats. "I think it might be easier just to cut it all off."

Caine's "No" was immediate. Tia's wasn't far behind.

"It's just hair. It'll grow back."

Tia headed for the cupboard back by the door they'd just come in. "A woman's hair is her glory."

Caine set her in a chair and lifted a skein off her shoulder. The knotted curls twisted around his fingers.

"And a man's pride and joy," Tia added, glancing fondly at Caine as she grabbed a jar. "Men love a woman's hair."

Desi eyed the mess Caine was holding out of the corner of her eye. It fell in a matted lump when he dropped it.

"You really may not have a choice."

Caine squatted beside Desi and started untying the moccasins he'd laced her into. "I keep telling you, Gypsy, there's always a choice."

8

If Desi had been expecting privacy, she was doomed to disappointment. As the last binding came off her feet, Tia gasped. "Your feet are a mess." She cast a look at Caine. "How again did it happen?"

Desi turned her foot and looked at the angry abrasions. "I didn't run fast enough."

The brim of Caine's hat blocked her view of his face, but from the jerk of his shoulders, he might have chuckled. She had an insane urge to knock that hat off his head. It was as much of a shield as the carefully blank expression he often wore.

"From what?"

Again, Caine didn't deny his part in her downfall. "Me."

He pressed to the sides of the deep cut down the middle of her right foot. Blood welled. "You opened this up again."

Tia halted on the way to the tub and headed back the way she'd just come. "I will get the salve." As she walked by, she clapped Caine on the head, knocking his hat askew. "And you—I taught you better on how to treat a wife."

Caine straightened his hat. "She wasn't my wife at the time."

Tia spun around and came back, swatted his hat again and put her hands on her hips. "And this makes it better how?"

"Guess it doesn't." That seemed to be the answer Tia was looking for.

"I will get the salve." She waved one elegant hand toward Desi. "You make your apologies to your wife."

Caine straightened his hat as Tia marched from the room, the heels of her shoes rapping out a staccato rhythm gradually fading away. He pushed the brim back as he gently set Desi's foot against his thigh. Instead of the anger she expected to see in his eyes, she saw laughter. He picked up her other foot.

"If I make my apologies, you planning on accepting them?"

Her ankle looked ridiculously fragile in his large hands. As out of place as she felt. "If I don't, will you get in trouble?"

"Uh-huh." He traced the sole of her foot, his finger lifting and dipping in abstract patterns. "This one's not so bad." He looked up and caught her studying him.

"What?"

"Why aren't you mad?"

"At Tia?"

"Yes."

He shrugged. "It's hard to be mad at Tia. Especially when she's right."

"It wasn't your fault. You couldn't know I would run."

"Sweetheart, an idiot could see you were intent on running." He shrugged. "I just misjudged the when." Tia was coming back with the same speed with which she'd left. Caine arched a brow at her. "So, you going to watch Tia whale on me some more or accept my apology?"

As if on cue, Tia called. "Did you apologize, *m'hijo?*"

"Yes."

Tia came around the back of the chair with an arch of her brow that reminded Desi so much of Caine, even though she knew they weren't related by blood. "And did she accept?"

Caine's smile didn't flicker. "I'm waiting to find out."

Tia glanced between Caine and Desi. "If you are waiting, you did not do it right."

"Guess I'll have to polish up my shine."

"Until you do, there will be no food for you at my table."

"Hell, Desi, make up your mind quick."

Desi ignored Caine and focused on Tia. The woman apparently had a lot of power here. "You'd make him miss supper?"

Tia shrugged. "It will not be the first time. Your husband can be stubborn sometimes."

She eyed the brim of Caine's hat. It was covered with dust and would need a brushing off. As his wife, that was probably one of her new duties. "So I've discovered."

The corner of Caine's mouth twitched. Desi looked at the other woman, then at Caine. "Will she really ban you from the table?"

He shrugged and put her foot down. "Tia is one tough cookie."

For a minute Desi was tempted. It would feel so good to make someone suffer, and Caine had done more than his share to aggravate her. Then she remembered the chocolate. And the way he'd kept her warm. But mostly she remembered that pride in his voice. *Wife.*

"He's pulling your leg," she told Tia. "I accepted his apology."

Tia snorted. "Already she lies for you." She handed Caine a glass jar.

"But it counts," he pointed out smoothly.

Tia shook her head. This time when she cuffed his head, it was much gentler. "At least you had the sense to marry up with a woman with a soft heart."

Over his head Tia's gaze met Desi's. "But it is not good you keep your heart too soft. He is the type to take advantage."

She'd already figured that out. "I'll keep it in mind."

"This, you do."

It was hot in the coat in the warm kitchen. Desi blew her hair off her forehead.

Tia gave her one assessing look and then turned back to Caine. "Bath first and then bandages."

"I was thinking the same thing."

Tia waved at her clothes. "She cannot bathe fully dressed."

"I'm working on that."

"The water is not getting any hotter."

This time there was no mistaking the twitch of Caine's lips for anything other than amusement.

"Understood."

Desi grabbed the edge of the coat. "I'm not getting undressed with you here."

Caine shrugged as if apologizing to Tia. "She's shy."

"Then I will leave."

"No." Tia was not the one Desi wanted to leave.

As if she didn't hear, Tia checked the pot on the stove. "The stew still needs to cook down so there is no hurry." She pulled a jar out of her pocket and handed it to Desi. "This should help with your snarls. Much better than scissors. Brush it through before you rinse it out."

She curled her fingers around the jar. It was surprisingly heavy. "Thank you."

Tia nodded and patted her shoulder. "You are Hell's Eight now. There are no more worries for you. We take care of our own."

DESI HAD TO DIG her fingers into the base of the chair to keep herself from kicking Caine out of her way and plunging into that tub. She hadn't had a real soak-in-a-tub bath in more than a year, and she wasn't letting this opportunity pass her by. A light touch on her calf brought her gaze down. Caine was looking at her again, the stupid brim of that hat blocking the expression in his eyes.

"Anyone tell you you think too much?"

"No."

"It's a bad habit."

He carefully placed her foot down. With the same care he reached for the coat sleeves, slow and easy, as if he were approaching a wild animal. And maybe he was right to treat her that way, because inside she felt anything but stable. She'd been bouncing between fight and surrender for so long, she wasn't sure she knew what to do with anything in between.

Accepting the slightest consideration apparently threw her into a panic. Like now. She knew Caine was helping her out of her coat because she couldn't take a bath with it on, and because she was beginning to sweat in the warm kitchen, but inside, every muscle, every nerve

ending coiled into a taut expectancy of pain. And all he
did was slide the coat off her shoulders and toss it over
a chair.

She caught his hand as he reached for the buttons at
the collar of her dress. "I can do this myself."

"But that wouldn't be as much fun."

Stupidity had her asking, "For who?"

That definitely was another grin. "For me."

She wrapped both her hands around his. "Please, let
me do it."

He paused. His head cocked to the side as if he were
considering it. His fingers touched her cheek. "I've had
it in my head for years how this night would go."

"Why?"

He shrugged. "Women dream about the wedding day.
Men plan the night."

"But you don't love me, and this isn't our wedding
night."

"I'm not counting the night on the trail, and you're
still my wife. While, sure enough, parts of tonight aren't
going to be what I imagined, this part can be."

Despite her tugging, his fingers were back to working
on those buttons. She really didn't want to know, but that
same stupid part of her that had her asking who now had
her asking, "What part?"

Four buttons surrendered in rapid succession. "Readying you."

The blush shot up from her toes in a torrid heat. She
glanced at the windows. As dark as it was getting outside
and with the lamps lit inside, the slightest crack in the
curtains would allow people outside to look in. "That
wouldn't be anything like 'learning me,' would it?"

His glance followed hers. He took her hands and held
them against the open placket. "Keep my place."

He got to his feet in that smooth way that always focused her attention. There was something in the way he moved that drew the eye, started speculation. Was he that coordinated in everything he did? He crossed the room, the muscles flexed beneath the pliable cotton of his pants, smoothing the soft material, emphasizing the power that was so much a part of him. As he reached the window to close the first shutter, that power was thrown into sharp relief. The stretch of his arms emphasized the breadth of those wide shoulders, delineated the expanse of his back beneath the simple blue cotton of his shirt, highlighted the narrowness of his hips and the long lean length of his legs.

Caine, she realized, was a man who would stop any woman in her tracks. And he was her husband. That was going to take some getting used to. One by one, the shutters closed. Each time that quiet click of the latch fell into place, she started. And each time the hint of fear died, her confusion grew, because she should be terrified.

Like the first Comancheros who'd captured her, there was a wildness about Caine. A primitive I-take-what-I-want attitude that made it ludicrous to think of him as her safe haven. Yet she did, deep down where instinct ruled. However, even if equating Caine with safety provided a false sense of security, it was all she had, and she wanted to cling to it. To him.

The feeling was irrational and could be suicidal when he turned on her, which he would—he wouldn't have any choice if he wanted to keep his pride. And to a man, pride was everything. But still, when she watched him, a sense of peace flowed over her. She wrapped her fingers in the front of her dress. She might just be losing her mind.

Caine turned, studying her as always. His gaze

dropped to her hand and then back to her face. "What are you thinking, Gypsy girl, that has those pretty eyes so big?"

"That I don't know what to think."

He came toward her with his slow, even stride. "Then maybe you should just stop thinking."

"I'm not good at that."

Caine just bet she wasn't. The woman was clever and inventive. She was also worn to a nub, physically and mentally. And as determined as she was to make herself into an island, he'd never seen a woman more in need of someone to lean on. If only until she got back on her feet. On the next step he could see the pulse pounding in her throat. Fast. Frantic.

Guilt for what he was going to demand from her stabbed through him until he thought on it. Most brides came to their wedding nights unknowing of what was going to happen. Their nerves tight with imagining and embarrassment. Desi was no different. She just had different fears, but the result, for him, was the same. He had to calm her, gentle her. Ease her into the reality of their life together. He slid his fingers under hers, pressing until she relinquished the lapel. He aligned his palm around hers. "Well, in that case, maybe you should just follow my lead."

"And maybe I shouldn't do anything until I can think clearly."

He'd have been disappointed if she'd just gone along with the suggestion, he realized. He liked that spirit in her. Hooking his pinkie around her forefinger, he pulled, stepping back as he did, drawing her hand away from her dress. The front fell open, revealing the plain white linen of her camisole. He'd never been more aroused by the sight of anything in his life. His cock throbbed with a wild ache as he said, "Now, Gypsy, where would the fun be in that?"

The thin cotton fluttered as she took a shuddering breath. "Not much, I'm hoping."

Her sass tickled him deep inside where he'd long thought he'd lost sensation. He chucked her under the chin with his thumb. "Now right there is the weak spot in your thinking. A man and wife should have lots of fun together."

Those big blue eyes narrowed. "My mother spent years educating me on what to expect as a wife. She never mentioned a word about fun."

Caine brought that small hand to his mouth, brushing his lips across the faintly grubby back. "Well, now that we know where the hole in your thinking got started, we can patch it up."

"The only one who thinks it's a problem is you."

"Lucky for you, you have a knowledgeable husband to spare you from a future of yawning boredom."

He placed her palm on his shoulder, skimming the back of his fingers over her wrist, down the feminine roundness until he reached the softness of her upper arm. If he did a shift over to the left, he could be holding her breast. His palm burned with the urge. It would be so easy. He took a breath. Under the scent of horse, wool and feminine sweat came the sweet scent of Desi herself.

The urge to touch her grew stronger. He suppressed it. In the end, he'd have her breast and her pleasure, but getting there was going to be a longer trip than he was used to. Good thing he was a patient man.

"Your bath is getting cold."

Her breath sucked in slow and steady, as if she intended to balance her nerves with the perfection of the measure. When she answered, her tone was just as even, just as careful. "If you'd leave I could get on with it."

"You can't walk."

"It's only a little ways."

"There's no need to suffer at all. Not when I'm here."

"But that's the whole point. I don't want you here."

"Tough."

"You are an incredibly stubborn man."

He dodged the swat of her free hand and unbuttoned the last few buttons over her abdomen. "You just catching on to that?"

"No."

He spread the wool front until it slid off her shoulders.

"Didn't think you were short on brains."

The compliment seemed to fly over her head. She grabbed at the front of her dress. He caught her hand and put it with the other, on his shoulders. On a "Grab hold, sweetheart," he swung her up. The squeal she made sparked his smile as she lurched for his neck. He winced as her jagged nails scratched his nape. Turning, he sat down on the chair by the tub with her on his lap.

For a second, she was as stiff as a board, but then she relaxed into him as she had on the horse, waiting for him to show her the next move. He didn't make her wait long. Just started easing the far sleeve off her shoulder. As it slid an inch down her arm, he leaned her away, just far enough to encourage the other sleeve in the same downward slide.

As the dress dropped, her color rose. He'd never been with a woman who blushed before. It was intriguing, charming and incredibly arousing. He leaned in, catching the heat on his tongue as he found her collarbone, tracing its path with his lips until he could switch easily to her neck, up to the line of her jaw, the softness of her cheek. "Damn."

"What?"

She didn't need to sound so scared. There wasn't a single thing wrong with her. He turned his head, finding the corner of her mouth. "You're sweet, Gypsy. Just very, very sweet."

She didn't move, just sat there absorbing his words, or maybe dreading his kiss. He didn't like that thought. He turned her face to his. There were a lot of emotions in her eyes, but none of them repugnance. "Don't you want to know how I kiss?"

Her lips disappeared between her teeth and then slowly, so slowly, reappeared, then pursed. Just a little.

Deep inside his chest, something twisted painfully. He absorbed the sensations—tenderness, caring—before brushing his mouth over hers. Desi's lips parted immediately in a stiff little move. Beneath his hand, the muscles in her neck contracted.

"No, sweetheart. Don't tighten up. It's just a kiss."

He took her gasp the way she took his words. Completely, letting the sound flow through him, sink into his blood, find his pulse and kick it up. He kissed her gently, ignoring the invite of her parted lips, learning the outer curves, her reactions. It worried her when he covered her mouth with his, but as he backed off and just nibbled on the edges, she relaxed, maybe even responded. It was hard to tell. She was so nervous.

He touched the tip of his tongue to the bow of her upper lip, riding the swell of the high arch, flicking lightly down the middle. This time her gasp was harder. He supported her head on his hand, stroking her cheek with his thumb.

Desi swallowed hard. "See, nothing to worry about."

Caine smiled, keeping his mouth close to hers. "A husband is no competition for a bath, eh?"

She shook her head. The rub of her soft lips against his harder ones was a sultry temptation. He curled his fingers into her skull with the need to drag her harder against him, but he had three days' growth of beard on his face. Her tender skin wouldn't survive that. "Then maybe we'd better get you into that water."

He pushed the dress the rest of the way off her shoulders. It pooled at her waist, trapping her hands and exposing her torso. The blush he thought so charmingly pink before raged a fiery red.

"No need to be embarrassed, I've seen you naked before."

She tugged at her arms. "But I was too busy to care then."

The image of her running nude through that meadow was seared into his mind. If he disregarded the cause, it made for a very pleasant memory. He smiled. "That you were."

He unbuttoned the cuffs of the dress. Then he went for the ties of the camisole. Beyond a twitching of her fingers, she let him. It might be fear or trust or scheming, but for whatever reason she'd decided on the path of least resistance tonight. And for that he was grateful. The camisole followed the path of her dress. The lighter material caught on the tips of her breasts, requiring the merest touch of his fingers to get it on its way. "You've got very pretty breasts, Desi."

And she did. Small, with delicate pink nipples that would nestle his palm. He touched a bruise on the inner curve of the left breast. When Desi turned her face away, he brought it right back. "Don't you hide your face, Desi girl. You've got nothing to be ashamed of, but the bastard who did this, he's got a lot to answer for."

As always, when he mentioned her previous life, she froze up like a cornered fox, weighing her options, debating which way to dart. What lie to present. "You already killed them. They can't pay twice."

He shook his head at her. Did she think he'd been born yesterday? "I've had enough bruises to recognize new from old, and this bruise is at least a week old, which means you got it before you were kidnapped."

Color left her skin so fast she swayed. "I—"

She got hung up there, mouth working, eyes closed, no sound coming out.

"Gypsy, you can stop dancing around the fact you had a life before we married. I've made my peace with it." He lifted her off his lap. "Put your weight on your heels for just a second."

As fast as he could, he unbuttoned, untied and pushed until her dress, camisole, petticoats and pantaloons fell in one tangled pool to the floor. He tucked his arm behind her knees and stood. He never thought he'd be glad to see the fear on a woman's face, but the start she gave when he lifted her up was a step up from the mortification she'd been struggling with before. He strode over to the tub. "This is going to sting those feet at first, but then it'll feel good. If you need to, you can sink those pretty teeth into my arm."

Desi didn't make a sound as he lowered her into the water, but he thought it would have been easier if she'd screamed. Jesus, he couldn't stand to see her suffer. He leaned over the tub, pulling her face into his chest as her breath came in hard pants. He wanted to yank her out of the tub, out of reality, just carry her to someplace where he could take all the bad things from her memory, all the pain from her body. Some place she'd be safe and happy.

The scent of lavender rose to surround them, blocking out the scents of the cooking meal, of sweat, of horses and spread with soothing calm over his emotions. Caine kept Desi's face pressed to his chest until the tension left her body. "You all right now?"

She squirmed in his hold. He realized he was holding her too tightly. "Shit."

"This is fine."

He let her go, staying close in case she felt faint. She huddled there, knees drawn up and arms crossed over her chest, looking so fragile it gouged his heart. The knobs of her vertebrae poked in sharp relief along her spine while she waited on what he would do next. He dipped his fingers in the water by her side. It barely cleared her hips. "Guess Tia underestimated how big you were."

No, it wasn't. When he imagined this moment, he'd imagined her luxuriating in hot water up to her shoulders the way women did, relishing the luxury of a full bath and scented water. He knew how good it felt when he sat in the huge tub, and he knew how often he'd wished the water could be deeper and just surround him in warmth. For her it could.

"I think we can do better." He stood. "I'll get more water."

"No!" He spun around. At the prompt of his ached brow she explained, "Tia doesn't have to bring more water."

She thought… He chuckled. "There isn't a man on Hell's Eight who would let any woman lug water, let alone Tia." Just the thought made him chuckle harder. "And you don't want to hear what Tia would have to say about it if any man tried."

"Oh."

If possible she hunched tighter into a ball. The impression of fragility increased. There just wasn't that much of her and in the soft glow from the oil lamp, what there was appeared more feminine than ever. More dainty. More in need of a man's protection. He sighed. "How about we make a deal?"

"What?"

"You start working on accepting that you're mine, and I'll keep my back turned while you soak in that tub."

She was a wary thing, but obviously smart enough to know to take what she could when she could. "All right."

He headed for the back door. When his hand touched the knob, she started so badly he could hear the water slosh. It was easy to guess why. He didn't turn as he asked, "Desi?"

"What?"

"Do you think I'm a possessive man?"

There was no hesitation in her answer. "Yes."

"Do you think I'm a man who knows how to protect his own?"

Again no hesitation. "Yes."

"And do you know you're mine?"

This time a small hesitation and a flicker of something he couldn't define before, "Yes."

"Then I think you can trust that I can fetch water for your bath without another man so much as getting a hint of a peek at the room my wife's bathing in, let alone my wife."

Water sloshed again and then there came the softest of whispers. So soft it took him a moment to realize it was a "Sorry." He turned the knob.

"Apology accepted."

6

Twenty minutes soaking in a full-to-the-brim tub of hot water could do a lot for a woman. It could steal the tension from her bones, the cold from her soul. It could even make her forget that her husband was in the same room. Make her forget everything except that one brief taste of heaven, one Desi was determined to savor. Lord knew when it would come back again. Floorboards creaked. Caine was on the move. Her haven was about to be invaded.

She felt him before he even touched her. Lassitude from the bath delayed her reaction. Two thunks punctuated his kneeling behind the high-back tub. Low and deep, his drawl slid into the calm of her bath.

"Time to get that hair washed, Gypsy."

Tension in her skull let her know he'd lifted the heavy mass up. She took a breath and sank beneath the scented water. Around her waves marked the swishing of his hands in the water while tugs on her scalp marked his progress. A tap on her shoulder directed her to rise up on her knees. A dry cloth immediately wiped her face. The man thought of everything.

She took it from him, pressing it to her eyes. A sweet aroma blended with the scent of lavender and then his strong fingers were on her scalp, massaging gently, working a different soap through her hair. She reached up.

"No. Just lean back and let me do this."

She didn't focus on the edge to his drawl, didn't focus on what he could see poised above her. She just settled back against the tub again and clung to her languor. Time enough to worry about everything later.

No one had washed her hair since she was a child. She'd always been too impatient to wait on a maid, and quite frankly, had considered another's hands on her an intrusion, but Caine's touch was different. Firm and gentle, it seemed more like a caress than a functional act, and the places his fingers lingered seemed to find the last corded bits of tension within her and unraveled them one slow circle at a time. He pressed gently at her temples and she groaned. How could such a big man be so gentle?

"Lean forward and close your eyes." She did, knowing what was coming and resenting it because it would mean the end to the moment. The thought was strange enough to break the spell. Since when did she have moments with a man?

Warm water poured over her head, sluicing down her shoulders and into the water around her, the waterfall another soothing break in a hellish day. Again a towel was placed in her hands. As she wiped her face, Caine gathered up the weight of her hair. "Your hair is beautiful."

"It's a chore."

"No way in hell are you cutting it," he informed her as he squeezed out the moisture.

"I don't see where there's much choice. It's matted."

"I'll take care of the knots."

A glance up showed the stubborn set of his jaw and

the broad stretch of his shoulders. She blinked. He wasn't wearing a shirt. She took a breath and wrestled with that reality as Caine reached for another bucket. Shirtless didn't mean naked. It didn't even mean lustful. If she thought about it, it actually meant practical, as there was no way he could wash her hair without getting a shirt soaked. She put the cloth over her eyes. Definitely practical.

The floorboard creaked a warning. There was the sound of the metal hinge being released and then more of that honeyed scent. Stronger this time. And then Caine's hands were back on her hair, rubbing something into the mats, working beneath to massage her scalp, finding again all those spots that just melted her bones. She decided to ignore his shirtless state. The pleasure was too unique to throw away in order to worry about something that couldn't be helped or prevented.

Caine's hand on her shoulder brought her back against the tub. She lifted the edge of the cloth. Out of the corner of her eye she could see the wide expanse of his shoulders and the puckered slash of a scar on the left one. He must be kneeling. His lips brushed her hair. "Relax. This is going to take a while."

His fingers drifted to the hollow just below her ears and behind her jaw. Subtle pressure there sent bliss shuddering through her entire body. She dropped her hands to her sides and gave up fighting him, just letting them float in the water. Her legs couldn't float bent as they were, but her thighs relaxed, falling to the sides as it just became too hard to keep them upright. And best yet, her feet didn't hurt anymore. The water numbed them.

Caine's thumbs brushed her earlobes before withdrawing. Another shiver skipped along her pleasure center and settled, along with the rest in her core.

"That's my girl."

She'd be anything he wanted as long as he didn't disturb this moment, this contentment. From the tugs on her hair she knew he was working on the snarls, but no hard yanks indicated impatience. After what she guessed was five minutes, she suggested again, "It really would be easier to cut off the worst."

"No."

His response was immediate, deep and hoarse.

The man definitely liked her hair. She cracked her right lid. The homey kitchen that had been so alien and scary an hour ago seemed intimate and comfortable now. The knowledge that something about her pleased him gave her hope, because based on his ability to resist falling on her with the urge to rut, there wasn't much about her that did appeal to him. The comb reached her scalp. He'd worked that far already? "That cream of Tia's must be a miracle."

"Tracker and Tucker swear by it."

The image of the two men came to mind. Both men had long thick hair, not all dry and shaggy like she was used to seeing men's hair. "I hope Tia scents it differently for them."

That vibration in Caine's touch must be laughter. "After the first time, when they came out smelling as pretty as a spinster at a social, she saw the necessity."

There was more to the story than he was telling.

"Why?"

"Because the rest of us couldn't help teasing, and they couldn't help responding."

"You fought?"

She tried to imagine all those men fighting and couldn't. It was too violent an image. Caine ran the comb through her hair one last time. There was a soft click of something being placed on the floor and then his hands were on her shoulders, kneading at the tension that had gathered there. "More play than real, but when we broke one of Tia's tables, she'd had enough."

"You think a lot of Tia, don't you?"

"Yes. Though she wasn't in the best shape when we met her, she opened her home to us."

"She'd been hurt?"

"Seems like back then everyone had been hurt. Tia'd lost her husband, her baby and other things she's never talked about, and yet when she saw us, she just started over, making a new family of us all." He shrugged. "There isn't anything any of us wouldn't do for her."

And no wonder. Desi rocked her head from side to side. "Don't you have to rinse this stuff out?"

"In a minute."

His drawl was as lazy as she felt. Her lids drifted down. His stroke grew longer as her limbs grew heavier. God, he had wonderful hands. "All right."

"A husband likes to know his efforts are appreciated."

He kept hammering that term as if she were a stubborn nail and if he just found the right angle, she'd cooperate with his plans. And if her body wasn't so strangely tingly and heavy, and if she wasn't so close to sleep, she'd probably come up with all sorts of reasons why it wasn't going to happen, but right now she was just too incapacitated to do anything but yawn.

His chuckle seemed to come from afar. His hands continued to stroke, the movements getting slower, broader, stretching over her collarbone down to the tops of her breasts in slow easy circles, the abrasion of the hard calluses on his fingers smoothed by the water.

Another scent blended with the lavender. It took three

heartbeats to identify it. Caine. She took a deep breath, experimenting. Instead of disturbing her calm, knowing he was there—that he wouldn't let anyone burst in on her—just increased her sense of security. There was something to be said for a possessive husband.

His hands lifted off her shoulders, riding up the arch of her neck, pressing her head back against the flat ridge of the tub into the cushion of his chest by stroking along the underside of her chin with his fingertips. They trailed back down the same lazy path, lightly grazing her skin, skimming over her collarbone and then the tops of her breasts. The fingers opened and stretched, extending until they reached the plump middle of her breasts, holding there a heartbeat before retracing their course. Over and over, he did the same thing, keeping her cocooned within the arc of his shoulders, within the lure of safety he presented. His hands felt so good she didn't complain as he took the massage further, extending the touch as she sank deeper into the cotton-soft well of pleasure he created so effortlessly. He compelled her into the hard cushion of his chest. She couldn't suppress a moan when on the next pass his fingertips reached the edge of her areola.

The shock of her own voice making that sound popped her eyes open. She looked down. His hands were shockingly dark against the white of her sin. Big and callused, the backs crisscrossed with scars, they dwarfed her chest. And below, her nipples strained, hard and puckered as if from cold. Except she wasn't. As she watched, those fingers slid farther, grazing the hard peaks in a rasp of sensation. She jerked away.

"No, Gypsy." Caine's forearms hooking over her shoulder kept her put for the next caress. His chest shifted behind her as he bent to whisper in her ear. "This is just another way to make you feel good."

The husky announcement slid along her nerves with the same finesse his fingertips slid over her nipples. Smooth and sure, sending little shocks outward that seemed to blend into the heaviness in her core. She'd had many men touch her breasts. No one had ever made her feel like this. As if another person had taken over her body, she sat there and let Caine touch her.

"Good, sweetheart. You just lie there and let me do everything."

As if she had a choice. Not only was he her husband, he was apparently a warlock with the ability to steal a person's will. Over and over he perpetuated the broad caress, starting at her shoulders before slowly sweeping down to her nipples, circling them with his fingertips before retreating. And with every pass, the tingling grew, and along with it, a sense of impatience. She wanted more.

On the next pass, she arched. To no avail. He had her pinned. She was treated to another aggravatingly light, barely there grazing of her nipples. Water sloshed as she twisted her hips, and the waves bathed her woman's place with little pulses of sensation. That fast, the tingling in her breast found a new place to make its presence known. Her knees fell all the way to the side, her legs too heavy to support. More ripples of warm water slid through the swollen folds, picking up the heat of her flesh and reflecting it back.

As if hearing the call, Caine's right hand slid over her nipple and kept on going, the rough palm startling a bolt of sensation as it caught on the tender tip. Her gasp prompted the hiss of his breath. A hiss she echoed as she watched his large hand graze her stomach, the fingers spreading and arching until only the middle one road her skin, sliding through the water-darkened patch of curls covering her mound, hesitating a second before it dipped down the center.

"I—"

She never got to finish the thought because his left hand, still at her breast, turned, cupped and contracted. A sharp ache surged in her womb. Before she could get her breath back from that, Caine had her nipple between his fingers and her sweet spot under his control. He rubbed gently while his fingers squeezed, every move a delicate coaxing rather than the rough demand she'd expect of a man of his size and reputation.

Maybe it was the confusion of that very thing that had her lying there accepting it, or maybe it was the novelty of the achy tingling his touch engendered that had her staying so still. Whatever it was, she didn't fight, and didn't resist. Just sat there, a helpless victim of the magic Caine wielded so calmly.

After a few minutes the magic began to ebb, and she was left with just the sensation of his fingers delicately pinching the swollen nubs and his finger rubbing between her legs. It wasn't enough. She needed more. She lifted herself into his touch.

A hoarse whisper approved her response. "That's my Gypsy girl."

And the pressure increased. She'd never felt anything like the sharp stab that went through her at the deeper pressure.

"Oh…"

"Like that, do you?"

"I've never felt—" Thank God she bit her lip before she finished that scandalous statement.

"Now that's a pure shame. Every woman should know how this feels."

She twisted into the pinch of his fingers on her nipple, losing the sensation on her clit as she did.

"Now look what you did," Caine murmured against her ear, his deep drawl as seductive as his touch. "You messed with my rhythm." Pressure on her right shoulder dropped her back into place. "No moving. Your job is to just sit there and feel good."

"I can't." Everything in her gathered into a foreign demand to move, to entice.

"You will."

She tried, she really did, but every time he milked her nipple and then rubbed her clit, bouncing her from one sensation to the other, it got harder and harder.

His hand stilled on her clit.

She shook her head. "Don't stop." She didn't want this to go away. It had never felt good before. She hadn't known it could.

"Shh, sweetheart. You're going to like this."

"This," was his fingertips closing around her swollen clit the same way they embraced her nipple. The roughness was more evident there, more welcome, and as he drew them up the short distension, she had to bite her lips to keep from crying out.

"No." His tongue flicked the corner of her lips, slipped between, eased down the crease, forcing her lip free of her teeth. "Let me hear you, Gypsy girl. Feel you."

He nuzzled her cheek as he pinched her nipple stronger the before. The hot little ache had her whimpering. The heat that followed had her grinding her hips into his hand for the echo of pleasure he'd trained her to expect. He gave it to her in a short pump. She twisted her head, unsure of what she was feeling, how to react. Was it pain?

Pleasure? He did it again and she didn't care what it was as long as he did it longer. Harder.

"Caine."

"Right here."

He kept up the steady rhythm and after a couple minutes, she knew what she needed. Her hips twisted and rose. Water sloshed. Her face muscles ached from the grinding effort to keep her shameful needs under control. Tears burned down her face. Caine's hands stilled. A sob broke past her control.

"Shit." The unrelenting pressure on her nipple and clit eased. "Am I hurting you, Desi?"

She couldn't form words, so she just shook her head as more frustrated tears welled.

There was a pause and then the flick of his nail across her clit. Fire seared her nerve endings and a high-pitched cry broke from her control.

"Ah." His cheek pressed against her as she felt his smile. "You're a hot little thing, aren't you?"

The shame of that burned right along with passion, but it wasn't enough to stop the growing hunger. Especially when he flicked her clit again. The sensation wasn't as sharp this time, but it fed the humming expectation of more. And the tension that held her enthralled now had more to do with hope than dread.

He gave it to her, milking her clit and her breast, encouraging her gasps and cries with husky grunts of approval, keeping her torso pinned with his forearms but allowing her hips to arch into his touch, answering her demands with harder strokes, longer pinches, laughing when she thrashed beneath him. Oh, God, she couldn't stand this.

She turned her head and bit into his biceps, primitive satisfaction welling through her as his shout rose above her moans, barely restraining herself from savaging his arm as he clamped down on her nipple with restrained force. The ensuing delight dug deeper into the ache in her womb, amplifying it.

"Son of a bitch, scoot forward."

She did, her attention mindlessly focused on the fingers holding her clit. Would he do the same to her there?

The shock of his big body sliding down behind her in the tub was a splash of reality. His grip switched to her waist. Her nipple ached in the cool air as he lifted her up. Water spilled over the side in a violent wave as Caine worked his legs between hers. "Straddle me."

She scooted her feet forward.

"No. Kneel."

She did, wiggling her feet under his ribs, bracing her hands on his knees for leverage as she wedged her knees between his hips and the side of the tub. His hand slipped between them from the front, the hairs on his wrist teasing her sensitive clit as he pulled his cock through.

"Now bring yourself down."

More water splashed. "The floor—"

"Will clean, now bring yourself down on me."

She did, straight on the wide plane of his cock. She caught her breath at the sheer size of him.

"This is going to feel so good." His fingers parted her pussy lips. Spreading them, finding her sweet spot and aligning it with the center of the thick column. "Oh, yeah." He circled the turgid nub, bringing it smartly to attention at the familiar caress. "That's what I want."

His left hand came back to her breast, enfolding it in heat and pressure. Once again he began the game, light pressure that teased and tormented, that called up the demand, but didn't answer it until she couldn't stand the lack any longer. When she was twisting on him, grinding down on his hard shaft, he tipped her forward with a forefinger between her shoulder blades. He kept pressing until the angle of her body held her swollen clit against the hot length of his cock.

She caught her breath as his hissed in. His left hand maintained its presence at her nipple while his right cupped her buttock. His thumb dipped between the crack to rest on a place no one had ever touched and gave her one command. "Move."

In a shock of sensation, her entire focus centered on that thumb. When he punctuated the order with a slow pressure, she rose up on her knees, dragging her clit along his cock. His thumb was with her all the way, circling and pressing, distracting her from the pleasure riding his cock gave her. She reached her knees but not the end of his cock. He was massive.

"Back down now."

Going back meant meeting the challenge of his thumb. She hesitated. The throb in her clit demanded she move, that she give back the delicious pleasure it craved. A firm pinch on her nipple took the decision out of her hands. Her instinctive jerk sent sizzles of pleasure outward from her clit while the pressure against her anus only added a darker, more forbidden element. There was no pain, no forced entry, just that pressure that teased and taunted. Until she got to that last inch. Then the pressure changed. She stopped.

"All the way, sweetheart."

She squeezed her eyes shut and pressed. The invasion she expected didn't come. Just more pleasure. The way it always seemed to when she followed his orders, whether it be with food, clothing, warmth or—she rose again—this.

His hand left her breast to gather up her hair and move it over her shoulder. She could feel his eyes on her back, hear his satisfied low growl, feel the way his cock jumped against her.

"You like the way I look."

"Definitely."

"I'm not too scrawny?"

In a tight voice he said, "Sweetheart, if you'd get back to moving, I'd even give you a whopping perfect."

He was hungry, needing to come, his big body vibrating under hers and he could still find humor? "You're so strange."

"Strange good or bad?"

She slid up slowly, savoring the sensation and the reality of what she was about to confess. "Strange good."

"That being the case, any chance I can get you to pick up the pace?"

Another thrust of his hips. She shook her head, he was so different than anything she'd ever experienced. This was so different. She did what he asked, trusting him. He was her husband after all. Riding his thick cock, she took pleasure from his hands, his shaft, the knowledge that maybe it wasn't going to be so bad, if all he needed was this.

The tip of her clit caught on the edge of his cock. Her head fell back. Oh, God, *this!* Her hips bucked convulsively. Her chest snapped into the support of his hands. Caine steadied her, keeping her at the angle they both needed, pushing her to the foreign well of pleasure, keeping her on the edge, taunting her to take the final step over the edge into the unknown that terrified her as much as it called to her.

"Let go, Desi. I've got you."

She shook her head even as she twisted in his arms,

too afraid to reach forward for that little something more that would release her from this agony.

"Yes!"

His palm grazed her hip. His thumb worked between her mound and her belly, catching on the puffy flesh, driving a cry from her throat as it searched, found and centered, and then pressed, elongating her clit with the pressure against his hot cock. The coiled tension shattered. She smothered her scream against his upper arm as ecstasy exploded outward, biting down as his cock jerked in heated demand against her throbbing pussy, creating aftershocks that doubled her over. His hoarse shout rose above the slosh of the water, her moans, the hiss of the oil lamp.

She collapsed against his thighs, her pussy clenching in echo with his pulse. He released her breast and clit. She shuddered as even the change in pressure seemed suddenly too much. He murmured something soft and stroked her back, pulling her up and against him. She caught her weight on his knees as he lifted her higher, only belatedly thinking to use her leg muscles. Water droplets landed in the bath with tiny splats as his breath caressed her buttocks.

She blinked. He was looking at her. If she didn't die of embarrassment now, it absolutely wasn't possible. She didn't die but she did jump when he pressed his face into the crease.

He wouldn't.

He did. Softly, lightly, he flicked her anus with his tongue, lapping tenderly at the tight bud. "Oh, heavens."

Desi reached behind and swatted at Caine's head with the last of her strength, amazed at both her daring and the utter weakness of her muscles.

His chuckle vibrated against her. Her womb clenched at the darkly forbidden sensation. Then he lifted her higher, his elbows spreading her thighs. Even though she knew what was coming, nothing could have prepared her for the sheer bliss of his tongue on her still convulsing flesh.

Another of those hums and he went to town, probing, licking, lapping, tapping her too sensitive clit with his tongue, holding her in place while he did it again. Ignoring her protests, suckling as she cried out and thrashed and pounded at his thighs, too sensitive to withstand the near pain, screaming when another orgasm wrenched over her, banging her head on his arm as she jackknifed into the sharp bliss, riding his mouth through the pleasure, her breath coming in soft moans as he turned her.

His mouth found her aching nipple as he brought her down on the fat head of his cock, snuggling it into the tiny well of her pussy, suckling her through the aftermath, keeping her from crashing by feeding the intimacy.

The tension in him built as her muscles contracted on his cock. She dropped her head on his shoulder, and bore down, unable to fight him anymore. Quivering muscles began to spread and the burn began. His hand on her hip kept her still. "Just like this, sweetheart. Make me come like this."

She did. Rocking on him gently, caught on the edge of terror, she wanted to give him what he'd given her, not knowing how to, more afraid of the voice inside her that demanded she surrender to him than the sex act itself.

"That's it," he murmured as something inside her relaxed and delicate muscles parted enough to take the tip. "Just like that. Nice and sweet."

She must be insane. He must be a warlock, because

despite the burn, despite the ache, despite the sheer impossibility of something that huge fitting where it was probing, a dark forbidden voice was whispering, "More."

She pressed, he jerked, his teeth nipping her nipple and once again it was his hand staying her. "No. Just this, Squeeze me. Desi. Milk me. Make me want to give you my seed."

His seed. Yes. That's what she wanted. She could imagine how good it would feel flowing over the burn in a potent balm. The aftershocks of her orgasm were still pulsing within her. She gave them to him, caressing the tip of his cock in intimate little hugs, sharing the pleasure he'd taught her, giving back until his head dropped back and his hands clamped her hips like vises, sealing her to him as the first hot jet hit her nerve endings in a searing brand, scalding the reality of the situation into her brain as he groaned her name. He was her husband, and he'd given her pleasure.

His eyes opened, as if hearing her thoughts. His grip tightened. His hips arched up. Anxiety flared through her pleasure as he tunneled a short span into her tight channel, his seed easing the entry.

She felt overstretched, overwhelmed. She needed a reprieve. He didn't give it to her. Just held her gaze as his cock jerked and swelled, depositing another scalding burst of silky moisture within her. His thumb found her clit and stroked. This time she was the one who pressed down, the demand for more overriding her survival instincts.

Joy wove through the pain, catching the edge and dragging it with her as she took a fraction more. Caine cupped her buttocks in his hands, denying them what they both wanted. She met his gaze, all the confusion and conflicting emotion inside centering on the resolution in his as he said simply, "Mine."

The knock at the door ruptured the intimacy.

Caine steadied Desi as she jumped, not letting her lift that tight pussy from the tip of his cock. Not yet.

"What is it?" he called, stroking Desi's back, moving under her wet hair, cupping her slender shoulders and savoring her soft skin.

"Supper will burn if you do not hurry," Tia warned.

"All right."

From the way Desi was trying to burrow into his chest, her arms crossed over her breasts, Caine could tell the intimacy he'd worked so hard to create was gone. A pity. She was a hot little bundle of passion when a man got past her guard. He caught her hands in his and pulled them away from her chest, tucking them behind her back, arching her spine and thrusting those breasts out. His cock hardened again as if he hadn't just come twice, nudging its way deeper into the snug little channel that he wanted to fuck until they were both raw and sated and completely lost in each other.

Desi flinched and shifted to the side.

"Easy." She didn't have to worry. He recognized when he'd reached a woman's limits. And he'd about reached

Desi's. But in a good way. Finding out men could be fun must really be exploding her concepts of what was proper.

"Caine?"

Her voice splintered on his name. "I know, sweetheart. Just trust me and stand up."

She did, her flesh releasing him with a reluctant kiss of regret. Her soft cry as the fat head slipped was rich with loss. He also stood, ignoring the water sloshing onto the floor, and spanned her buttocks with his hand, dropping his middle finger between and finding her vagina with unerring accuracy.

She was swollen and slick with his seed, her opening still spasming with the aftershocks of his possession. He capped it, keeping more in her. Primitive satisfaction at the mark of possession welled in his chest. She shifted uneasily, but at the end of the movement, settled into his touch.

"That's another thing I like, sweetheart. The way you respond to me."

"It's indecent."

"It's arousing as all get out." He picked her up and carried her over to the chair, shaking his head as she clung. One of these days she'd learn to trust him to not let her fall.

The way her eyes sprang wide as her sore rear made contact with the hard surface reminded him how new she was to this life. The soak in the tub might have loosened her up, but it hadn't taken away all her discomfort. He handed her a towel to wrap around herself and caressed her cheek as she clutched it to her. He gathered up the salve Tia had left and the strips of bandages.

Desi shifted again.

"Rear a little tender?"

The blush that overtook her face was bright enough that she should have caught fire on the spot. Her gaze dropped to his now hard cock. She made a strangled sound in her throat, and her chin snapped up before her hands folded in her lap with ladylike perfection. If one disregarded the white-knuckled clenching.

"I'll take that as a yes." He knelt in front of her and picked up her feet. The cuts were clean, slightly pruned from their time in the tub, but not angry with infection. "These look good."

She murmured something. A quick glance showed her wrestling with the towel. He left her to it as he dressed her feet. By the time he had them bandaged her color was down to pink and the towel was wrapped so tightly across her chest it cut grooves under her arms. "They should be fine in a couple days." He stood.

She eyed him warily, her gaze locked in the safe zone above his shoulders. "Thank you."

He held out his hand. She placed hers in it. As soon as she got upright he tugged. She gasped and tumbled against him, her fingers opening over his pectorals as he took her weight. Another gasp had him looking down. She was staring to the side of his chest. He tracked her gaze to his upper arm. A perfect set of teeth marks, red with dark settling around the edges, decorated his right bicep.

"I'm so sorry."

He turned her around and pushed her down over the table before she could think to stiffen. "Nothing to apologize for."

She slung her hair off her face as she propped herself up on her elbows, her gaze clinging to the mark. "I bit you."

"And I came when you did. Seems that worked out well all around."

He lifted the edge of her towel. The cool air on her privates brought her out of her shock. "What are you doing?"

"Taking care of that other soreness."

He placed his palm in the middle of her shoulders to keep her still. It took more effort than he expected. For all her frailty, Desi had surprising strength. Dishes rattled on the table as she kicked out. He dipped his fingers in the salve. "You keep that up and you'll have everyone in here watching me treat your fanny."

Her hips stilled but her head turned in the direction of the door and her "Hush" was as imperious an order as Tia had ever given. If he discounted the frantic edge.

"Then hold still."

She had a gorgeous ass. Surprisingly full for all her slenderness, soft and white with a definite heart shape. He smoothed the salve into her white skin. First one cheek then the other. It melted immediately, making the surface shiny and slick. She flinched as he placed both palms on her buttocks and squeezed gently. Above her head her nails dug into the table. Damn, she was a suspicious one.

"Easy, sweetheart. Just a few minutes and I'll have you feeling like new."

He massaged the salve in gently, gathering more when he'd spread all he could, working her stiff muscles in long smooth glides. Her struggles stilled. Little by little, she began to relax. Her head lowered to the table, her fingers spread wide and a soft moan sighed from her lips.

"Where did you learn to do that?"

He'd learned this trick from a Chinese woman he'd

spent time with, but a man didn't tell his wife something like that. "A body picks things up here and there."

"It's scandalous, but . . ." Another of those sighs simmered in his blood like the most potent of whiskey.

"But what?"

"Do you think everyone will mind waiting on supper?"

His chuckle took him by surprise. "I expect they'll find a way to survive until I get your rear in sitting order."

"I don't think that's possible."

"Oh, you of little faith."

He balanced his fingertips in the hollow of her spine before drawing them up the lush rise of her buttocks, pressing slightly into the crease between as he followed the womanly contours down, pausing only when his thumbs snubbed on the tight crinkle of her anus.

Slick with salve, they slid easily over the puckered opening. Her gasp drew him back over the same spot as he palmed his way back up, only to center his fingers and come back down again. This time, however, when he reached that spot, he paused for a more lingering touch. She gasped again and in the aftermath the subtlest of tension entered her muscles.

He lowered his back over hers, letting her absorb a heavier touch as he covered her. "Did you like that, Gypsy?"

She didn't answer, but her breath caught. He kept circling while he waited for her answer, his fingers working into the swollen flesh beneath. Finally, she nodded.

He tapped the tightly clenched opening. Dishes rattled as she jumped. Her ass flexed in a little kiss. A bead of come dampened his fingers. His come, which he'd given her as she'd orgasmed around him. "Can you feel that, baby? My seed in you?"

A tiny squeak followed quickly by a barely audible "Yes."

"Do you know how much it arouses me to know part of me is in you here?" He anchored his thumb against her anus, pressing the tight center, just enough to give her the taste of another desire pulsing within him as he pushed two fingers into her tight sheath.

"Caine?"

While she wrestled with her breathing, every muscle in her body shuddering in rhythm with her pulsing channel, he stepped back and lifted his aching cock to the tiny hole, letting his weight maintain the contact. Giving her just enough to tempt.

"Just a little tease, baby. Something to hold on to for later."

He didn't know if he was going to make it to later. Just the promise of that crinkled little opening had his balls pulling up snug and lust boiling over. He parted her buttocks, giving himself a better view of his big cock pressing against her, of the tight flesh starting to flatten and give…

"Supper," she gasped.

She was right. They didn't have time for this. Caine let his cock slide up the tempting crevice and his thighs cradle her soft ass for a heartbeat before leaning forward so his lips grazed her ear as he whispered, "But after supper, baby. I'll have all night to pleasure you."

He swatted the left globe playfully, enjoying the residual jiggle and her surprise. She was such a delightful mix of contradictions, it'd probably take his whole lifetime to sort them out.

"Just like I promised. All in sitting order."

She reached back cautiously with her hand. "I don't know if I can move."

He drew her into his arms, his smile spreading inside as he scooped her up.

"Now there, Gypsy, is just another way having a husband comes in handy."

DINNER WAS ORGANIZED CHAOS. Big bowls of stew, beans, biscuits, slabs of steak and greens ladened the surface of the long trestle table. Tia appointed Sam to say the blessing. As if the "Amen" were the signal everyone was waiting on, the men launched in to conversation as they dug in. Jokes were exchanged and business was discussed, all in a discordant yet somehow cheerful overlay of noise Desi was content to hide beneath. She took a dab of a couple things, enough to give her something to play with. She was so nervous, her throat so tight, there was just no way she could get food past the knot in her throat to her stomach. She couldn't believe how she'd been with him, earlier. The things he'd made her feel. No decent woman would have let him do what she had, would have responded as she had. And now Caine expected her to go upstairs and do more. With the same freedom. Her stomach heaved. She chipped off a piece of the flaky biscuit she'd been playing with. Cut it again, and again.

Around her, conversation flowed. As she'd been taught in her former life, she smiled at the appropriate moments, made polite input to keep the momentum flowing. And just like in her younger days, no one paid her a bit of mind. She could have been a bowl of flowers on the table, pretty decoration with no further purpose required.

She sighed and nipped off another section of biscuit

with precision. Lovely. There wasn't much difference in her previous life than her present one.

She mashed the bit of biscuit with her fork tines and brought it to her mouth, pretending to eat the crumbs off the tip. The only difference was, in her previous life she'd been too ignorant to see the truth of her worth, and now her eyes were open.

The sudden silence penetrated her reverie. She looked up. Everyone was staring at her. And everyone was frowning. She wiped her mouth with her napkin before resettling it onto her lap. "I'm sorry, did I miss a question?"

"Nah, we've all been too busy eating to chat much," Sam called down the table.

A glance showed the truth of that. The big bowls were almost empty, the men's plates wiped clean. She blinked. They did know how to put away food.

They were still staring at her. She glanced at Tia, who was frowning at her plate.

"The boys are waiting to have seconds."

She pretended an understanding she didn't have.
"Oh."

And still they stared.

"With this pack of vultures, it's best to get your preferences in early or there won't be anything left to scavenge later," Tracker offered.

"I would like another biscuit," Tia said, holding out her plate. The plate traveled the length of the table going from hand to hand until it reached the other end and before coming back the same way, and on the surface were two biscuits. Tia took the plate and raised her brow at the second biscuit.

"Just in case you get the urge to nibble later," an older man, who'd greeted Desi but whose name she couldn't remember, called down the length of the table. Tia's blush as she took the plate was telling. Though that extra biscuit got a lot of covetous looks, no one grumbled out loud. Tia fussed with her napkin a second, and then, in that dignified way she had, said, "Thank you."

With Tia's preferences stated, the men were back to looking at Desi. As hard as it was to believe that the men could still be hungry after the huge amount of food already consumed, there was no mistaking the hum of impatience. They were waiting for her to make a claim on the items remaining before diving in. This she could handle. Desi put on her best company smile and waved them on. "You go right ahead. I couldn't eat another bite."

The response was immediate.

"Hell, to take another bite she'd have to have taken a first."

"You mean she wasn't just checking the lay of the land before digging in?"

"Shit, a strong wind could take her out and she's done."

"A body can't function without a decent meal to balance them out."

"Your wife needs to eat, Caine."

As if the last comment gave the men something to grab onto, they stared at Caine, who sat across the table from her. He scooped the last bit of honey off his plate with his biscuit. Those warlock eyes of his briefly touched her plate and then her face. "I figure if we give her nerves time to settle, her stomach will be back to talking with her backbone."

"And when that happens, ma'am, what kind of thing would you be liking?" Tucker took her plate from in front of her.

She didn't have an answer for him.

"Stew's always better after setting a spell," Tucker offered.

A murmur of agreement and a ladle of stew went onto her plate and then passed to the next man. They make a body bilious."

"Hell, Sam, don't go putting beans on there. They make a body bilious."

She blinked.

"Tortillas go down easy." A tortilla took up a position on the edge.

"Greens are good for the constitution."

"They get soggy," someone protested.

"They're healthy," someone else countered. Ten pairs of eyes fastened on her, and with a nod, greens went onto the plate.

"Red meat's good for the blood."

She hated red meat. Caine nodded. Steak hit the plate. Her plate passed to Tucker.

"The biscuits *were* darned good," Tucker said with a glance at Tracker, the underlying humor in his voice not lost on Desi. There was a pregnant pause. All eyes went to the few remaining biscuits. A muscle worked in Tracker's jaw.

"She can have this one of mine," Tia offered.

Another hesitation and then Tracker shook his head, his long hair catching blue streaks from the lamp light. A biscuit hit her plate with grudging care. She felt guilty because whereas she didn't want it, biscuits were obviously Tucker's favorite. The plate was passed back up the other side of the table. When it came to Caine, it stopped, nearly groaning from the weight of the food on it. He inspected it and then set it in front of him. "That should do."

Desi played with her knife and fork, waiting. The plate

didn't budge. Without the food she had nothing to do with her hands. "Are you going to give my plate back?"

He flicked an eyebrow at her. "No sense tempting you to mash it up before your stomach gets to growling."

Before she could come up with a suitable response, preferably a cutting one, Sam made a lunge for the stew bowl that Tucker attempted to pass by him. "I'll take that."

Caine snagged it with a smile. "After me."

"Hell, there's nothing left after you."

Caine ladled stew onto his plate. "As it should be."

Sam snatched the huge bowl out of his hands and glanced at the contents. "Did you even leave me a sweet potato?"

"Not on purpose."

Sam put the big earthenware bowl in front of him and grabbed the ladle, swishing it around. "You watch out for him, Desi. The man has a sweet tooth and he's not exactly scrupulous about feeding it. Ha!" Sam brandished a scoop of stew, an orange chunk of potato sitting proudly on top. "Eat my dust," he crowed to the rest of the table before passing the bowl on down.

It was the same all around the table, men making bold claims, grabbing at bowls, but no matter how closely she watched, no one took more than their fair share. The competition seemed to be more who could blame the loudest, accuse the most inventively, than to actually take more food than was fair. With a start, she realized they really were a family.

"It is always this way," Tia sighed. "No matter how much I lecture, they can only be serious for the grace, and then they play."

"They're having fun."

Tia smiled. "Yes, but I can see from your face you

are not used to such behavior. It was different in your home."

The last was a statement and not a question.

"Very different."

"No frivolity?"

"No." Frivolity wasn't encouraged in women who were intended as wives for important businessmen. Though she and her twin had managed to find some fun, it had never been at the dinner table.

Tia looked down the table to where Tracker and the older gentleman were wrestling over the last biscuit.

"I think it would be easier for you to adapt than for us to get them to change."

Their good humor was infectious. A smile twitched her lips. "I think so, too."

Tracker emerged victorious with the biscuit. "Ed will pout now."

She didn't want diner to end on a sad note. "I can give him mine."

Tia shook her head. "That one needs to learn not everything he wants will be his."

Desi frowned. It seemed a strange lesson to leave to a biscuit. Fingers touched hers.

"Tia's sweet on Ed," Caine explained as soon as her eyes met his.

Tia's chair scraped back. She stood to her full height, her chin coming up. She looked down her elegant nose at Caine. "It is not your place to speculate on my life."

"I don't mind," Ed called. "Speculate away."

Tia glared at him, her hands fisted at her sides. "You have no say in this."

"Don't rightly see how that works as I'm half the discussion."

Tia picked up a biscuit and threw it at him. Ed caught

it deftly, a smile on his face, as Tia turned and left the room not one bit diminished by her anger. He wrapped the biscuit in a napkin. "I do believe she's beginning to soften up, boys."

"Yup, at this rate you might work up to courting level by the time you're ninety," Sam put in.

"Hell, just goes to show what you know, boy. I passed courting about a year ago. I'm now working up to stating my intentions."

"Well hurry and get 'round to it," Sam countered.

"When Tia gets testy, her cooking suffers."

Ed shrugged. "Seeing as Caine brought in backup, I don't think we need to worry about that anymore."

The satisfied ripple that went thought the men as they turned and smiled at her demanded a response.

"I can't cook."

The announcement dropped like a bomb into the banter. Everyone, including Caine, gaped at her as if she'd sprouted a second head. What could she say? That she'd been trained to instruct cooks, not to actually cook? She didn't think that would have much relevance here.

"But you can learn, right?"

How hard could it be? "I suppose so."

"Damn straight she can learn."

"A woman who can't cook is about as useful as tits on a boar hog."

"Watch your language, Ed," Caine snapped.

"Sorry, ma'am."

Again the touch of Caine's fingers. Again the demand she look at him. When she did, she found laughter lurked around his eyes and mouth. "You really might want to get on my good side now."

"Why?"

"Unless you want to spend day and night in the kitchen, you'll need an excuse to get out."

"And you're it?"

"No man's going to argue with a newly married husband who wants his wife's time."

"So it's be nice to you, or be a slave in the kitchen?"

His hand closed over hers. "Yup."

She didn't protest. "There's always a third option."

His eyebrow cocked up as he drew his fingertips along her knuckle in a slow tease. "What?"

"I could just be a lousy cook."

The smile that had been lurking sprang to the fore. "Sweetheart, that won't get you off the hook now."

"Why ever not?"

"There's a saying that hope springs eternal, and when that hope involves an empty stomach, it's pretty much a bottomless pit."

"There's also the truth if you don't cook, one of us will have to."

She'd already reached that conclusion before Tucker pointed it out. She sighed. "Guess I'll have to learn to cook."

"Or just cozy up to your husband."

She cut Caine a glare as the men immediately around them chuckled, understanding why Tia had stormed from the room. Men could be so frustrating. She pulled her hand from under Caine's. "I'll learn to cook."

The snub didn't even put a dent in Caine's smile. He threaded his fingers through hers. "Well, I guess that just means I win all the way around."

Desi expected Caine to jump on her right after dinner. She didn't expect him to bundle her up in a quilt and carry her to the door.

"I can walk, you know."

"We already covered that ground earlier."

"I think we should go over it again."

"Why?"

"Because if I think hard enough I can come up with a reason you'll accept."

"Sweetheart, you sure are grass-green when it comes to men."

"I am not."

He turned sideways to get them through the door. "Are you, if you think there's any amount of logic that would have a man passing up the opportunity to hold a pretty woman in his arms."

The way he said things actually made her want to go back to believing in fairy tales. "Why are we going outside?"

"Because there's something I want you to see."

"Can't I see it in daylight?" She pulled the quilt closer as the cold air hit her cheeks. And in case he didn't understand her complaint because of the bright moon illuminating the landscape in an ethereal white light she added, "When it's warmer."

"Nope."

A nicker caught her attention. Two horses stood hitched to the rail. Beside them sat Boone. Other dogs stirred on the porch, hopeful expressions on their faces. Apparently everyone but Desi was looking forward to this.

"Oh, no. I'm not getting on another horse." Her inner thighs still ached from the last two days.

"You don't have to get on. I'll lift you."

She shook her head. The soothing effects of the bath had worn off. Just the thought of straddling a horse had her wincing.

"No."

Caine paused at the horse's side. Boone whined and thumped his tail on the hard ground. "Because you don't want to go with me or because you're still hurting in sensitive places?"

"What happens if I say both?"

"Nothing other than if you say different."

Which meant she was still going. "Okay. The latter. I can't ride, Caine."

He set her down on the edge of the porch. "I took that into account." He glanced toward the horses. "Tracker?"

"You all finally ready?"

"Yup."

Tracker stepped out of the shadows and unwrapped the reins from the post.

She glared at Caine. "You said I wouldn't have to ride!"

"Uh-huh." Caine took the reins from Tracker and swung up into the saddle. "So I did."

"Ma'am."

Tracker was standing as if waiting for permission. She looked between him and Caine and then the impatient horse. If the porch wasn't behind her she would have stepped back, her feet be damned. "I'm not riding that horse."

"Sure enough you're not." Tracker caught her about the waist and swung her up and around, straight into Caine's arms.

As he settled her in front of him, she tucked herself into a stiff ball of hostility. "You tricked me."

Tracker chuckled. His teeth were very white in the moonlight. "You made it so easy, thinking the worst."

Yes, she had. "Well that doesn't mean you had to exploit my tendency."

Caine pulled the thick quilt up from where it had slipped off her shoulder. "Out here any weakness is likely to get exploited, one way or another."

Tracker swung up on his bay. "That is the truth." He pulled his rifle out of the scabbard and rested it across the saddle horn. "Ready?"

Behind her, Caine nodded, the exaggerated shadow of his Stetson obliterating her view of the trail.

After commanding the dogs to stay, he set the horse in motion.

Desi had never ridden for pleasure at night. Even a night that was lit by a big Comanche moon. It made her nervous, but after a few minutes of Chaser following Tracker's sure-footed bay, she started to relax. This wasn't the first time these horses had taken this path up the mountain.

"Where are we going?"

"It's a surprise."

"I don't care much for surprises."

"Now that's a shame." Caine leaned forward, reaching to brush a branch out of their way.

"So why don't you tell me where we're going?"

"Because I happen to like surprises."

"When you're the one handing them out." She hadn't meant to say that aloud.

A glance up showed she'd dislodged another of his smiles. "That is the truth."

Caine let the branch go once they were past. His hand dropped to her hip. "You okay?"

"I'm comfortable."

"Are you still sore?"

The blush rose from her toes. She was going to kill

him. Just as soon as she got over her mortification, she was going to kill him. She cut a glance at Tracker. She didn't think he'd overheard. "Hush!"

Caine's fingers curled around her thigh. "Are you...?"

If she didn't burst into flames in the next two seconds it was going to be a miracle. "I'm fine."

"That doesn't answer my question."

Just the asking of it made the intimate ache surge to the forefront of her mind. She ducked her head into the quilt and whispered, "A little."

The fingers squeezed. "A little more salve will help with that."

"No."

His chuckle vibrated against her side. "I won't mind."

She was sure he wouldn't. "I would."

"Why?"

"Because it's not respectable."

"And you're a respectable wife now?"

"Yes."

"And that means I don't get to have any fun?"

"Not like that."

Chaser lunged up an incline. She grabbed at Caine's chest, though his arm around her waist remained as immovable as always, holding her secure. When the horse settled back into a steady rhythm he said, "I can see I'm going to have to work on your definition of respectable."

"My definition is fine. It's your wants that are scandalous."

"I'm a good man."

"And you deserve a good woman."

"Hell, where's the fair in that?"

She relaxed a little as the horse fell back into a normal gait. "What do you mean?"

"Seems to me a man who spends his days being good deserves a scandalous woman in his bed."

"You are so confusing."

"And here I thought I was being about as plainspoken as a man can get."

"Every man wants a proper woman to rear his children and care for his home."

"Sounds dull as mud."

"What?" She couldn't have heard him right.

"I said, it sounds as dull as mud. No man in his right mind wants to come home to a saint."

"You're wrong."

His right brow disappeared up into the shadow thrown by his hat. "Seeing as how I'm a man, I think I have the right of it, and I'm telling you right now, Desi Allen, the one man who deserves to come home to a scandalous woman is a good man. There's just no better reward."

She yanked the quilt around her shoulders, anger burning deep. Just because she was his wife didn't give him the right to make fun of her. The conviction grew with every hard clop of the horses hooves' over the rock and dirt.

"I'll be over yonder keeping an eye on things," Tracker called, wheeling his horse around, pointing to the edge of the trees.

Desi watched him go with equal parts dismay and relief. The former because no one knew better than her that this was a dangerous land and the reminder that they were away from the house made her nervous, and the latter because no matter how this marriage came about, she couldn't help feeling that her fights with Caine were private and some distance allowed her to keep them that way.

"Desi?"

"What?"

"Look up."

"Why?" She seemed to be always asking him that.

"Because you're going to regret it forever if you don't."

She only did so because she couldn't handle another regret in her life. And then she gasped, resentment crushed beneath wonder. They were on the edge of a cliff and before them, seeming to spread outward from their very feet was...the universe. The star-studded carpet stretched out in front of her, endlessly embracing the moonlit landscape below. Dark hollows wove between swells of granite that glowed with a ghostly edge above the single, sparkling ribbon of light that rippled through it all. It was timeless, breathtakingly beautiful. Overwhelming.

"See that?" She followed the point of Caine's finger to the ribbon way off in the distance. "That's the San Antonio River. Everything between here and there, for as far as you can see, is Hell's Eight land."

She blinked. That was a lot of land to hold. The men were nothing if not ambitious. "Why are you showing me this?"

"Because you're part of Hell's Eight now, and I wanted you to know what that meant."

As far as she could tell, it meant she was smack-dab in the middle of Indian land, living amidst a bunch of men tough enough to think they could actually make something of this wilderness. The knowledge left her not knowing which angle to address. She settled for the obvious.

"This is Indian land."

"There are a few tribes that lay claim to it."

She could hear the "but" in his voice. She brought it out into the open. "And they don't object to you being here?"

"We don't bother them if they don't bother us."

She was not naive enough to know there weren't skirmishes. "And when they do?"

"We settle it."

There was nothing in the inflection of his voice to infer anything. "You fight."

"If it comes to that."

She considered the magnificent expanse. No wonder Caine had refused to let her ride off on her own that first day. Desperation had blinded her to the reality of its vastness. It was a very dangerous place. "You would think there would be enough for everyone."

"There is."

"Then why do you fight?"

"Because some men can't rest easy unless they have it all."

But not him? She glanced at Caine from beneath her lashes. He was looking over the land, his gaze narrowed and his mouth set into a straight line. "And you're satisfied with what you have?"

He shook his head before looking down. His eyes were almost black in the shadow of his hat brim. "Not by a long shot. We've got a start here, planted our roots, but before we're done, Hell's Eight will be known."

"You already are."

With a wave of his hand, he dismissed the legend that followed the men wherever they went. "For more than killing."

She didn't see how that was possible. The men of Hell's Eight were bigger than life. The bogeyman took a backseat to them when a mother wanted to scare the mischief out of her kids. "What do you want to be known for?"

Caine patted the shoulder of the horse they sat on. "Horses."

"Horses?"

His eyebrow cocked. "That expression on your face mean you never considered I'd like to do something besides survive?"

"Honestly, I hadn't given the subject any thought one way or another." Which, after she'd said it, didn't sound any better than a blunt "no."

"I'll allow you might have had other things on your mind."

He didn't say anything more, just surveyed the land before them with a determination that was tangible.

"What made you decide on horses?"

"My pa raised the best horses in the territory. Guess the need just rides in the blood."

He'd lost his parents as a boy. Lost his home. His childhood. His future. But he hadn't given up. She had to wonder how much of the determination to make Hell's Eight a name to be reckoned with was a need to get his life back and how much was to make something of himself. "But you're a Texas Ranger."

"Most men are more than one thing."

"Women, too."

"That is a fact." She had his attention once again. "What do you want to be?"

She didn't have to think twice on it. "Useful."

That sent both his brows up. "What makes you think you're not already?"

"I grew up very spoiled by your standards. Whatever I wanted was handed to me."

"Seems to me that's about perfect."

"It was fun as a child, but as I got older, it became irritating."

"Felt the urge to kick over the traces, did you?"

Caine didn't sound as shocked as her parents had been. Probably because he'd never seen her proper. She was very good at proper when she put her mind to it.

"Yes. I got a little outrageous."

"That how you landed out here?"

"No." The summoning of the memory called up the pain. It was hard to keep her voice even. "My father fell in love with the West. He read about it in his newspaper."

Though she tried to push it back, Desi recalled her father's face as it had been then—animated, cheeks slightly flushed as he talked about the opportunity and adventure waiting for them west of the Mississippi. And then she remembered how his face had been the last time she'd seen it. A bloody hole oozing gore. She dug her fingers into the quilt, holding back her grief and rage through sheer force of will. "He saw it as a place of opportunity and adventure."

"Uh-huh." She didn't look as Caine pushed the quilt down off her face. "And he thought it was a good idea to bring your ma and you with him?"

"And my brother and sister, too."

"Goddamn fool."

She studied the way the moonlight played across the folds of the quilt. The immediate agreement that swelled in her throat was a betrayal she couldn't suppress.

"Yes."

"What happened to your family?"

"They killed everyone but me and my sister."

"Where's your sister?"

"I don't know." Her face went rigid with the effort

to keep the agony of how she'd last seen Ari out of her voice. It actually hurt. She would never forget. Ari's eyes, swollen from tears and blows, lip bleeding, kneeling in the dirt as the Comancheros bared her body to the men who'd bought Desi, trying to get them to go double on the price. "The men who saved me were too cheap to ransom us both."

"Ransom?" His finger traced the angle of her cheekbone. "Is that what they were calling it?"

She bit her lip, refusing to let Caine drag her into the truth of what it was. Part of her couldn't bear it, as irrational as it was. She didn't want to discuss how stupid she'd been thinking the white men had come to save her. How naively she'd gone with them, how confident she'd been that she could convince her rescuers to save Ari, too. "Yes."

"So the Comancheros took your sister on south?"

"Yes."

"How long has it been?"

"Three hundred and fifty-six days."

"You ever hear from her?"

"No."

"She might be dead."

She wrenched around in his arms, her hands curling into claws with the need to rip the possibility from his lips. "Don't you ever say that again."

"Desi…"

Rage screamed out along with her, "Shut up!"

Rather than argue her into accepting what she wouldn't, his arm went around her shoulders and pulled her into his chest. "I'm sorry."

So was she. It didn't change anything.

Her sister was still lost, suffering God knew what, hoping with the same desperation as Desi had that she'd be found, saved. And Desi couldn't do anything to save her because she didn't know where she was.

The weight of that crushed the air from her lungs. She let Caine hold her. And when he released her hands she didn't fight.

"You can't say it and make it true," she whispered, staring at the stretch of night sky. Somewhere maybe, Ari was staring at the same sky, wondering where she was, if she was all right.

"I won't."

"She's my twin."

"Damn."

"I'd know if she was dead." She wrapped her fingers around her wrist and rubbed. "Deep inside, I'd know."

"I'm sure you would."

She looked up, knowing it was stupid to ask for comfort but needing it anyway. "Do you think she thinks I abandoned her?"

Ah, hell, why didn't she just take a knife and gut him? It would have the same effect as looking at him with those big blue eyes brimming with sadness but no tears. Just bottomless pain that Caine didn't know how in hell to ease. He played with a curl that fell across his chest. "I think she knows the truth. That you would have helped her if you could, but you were both helpless and neither of you could have done anything."

"I could have tried harder when they bought me."

"How?" He'd seen the condition the Comancheros left women in. "You were beaten, raped, half-starved, in shock and exhausted. Imprisoned by men with no conscience—what exactly could you have done?"

"I could have convinced them twins were twice the pleasure."

The way she said that told him she'd heard it often

enough to convince herself that it had actually been an option.

"If they'd wanted both of you, they would have taken both of you."

"I could have——"

Shit, she couldn't have done anything. Caine caught Desi's chin and yanked her gaze away from her hands. "They would have just fucked you both in the dirt, had the experience and a laugh and then still walked away with only one."

She jerked her chin. "You don't know that."

He didn't let go. "Yes, I do."

"I could have at least made them take Ari." The hot, burning desperation in her gaze worried him. She'd thought about this a long time. To the point she wasn't rational. He'd brought her up here to give her the sense of place it always gave him and all he'd managed to do was open a snake pit of memories.

"Ari? Is that your sister's name?"

She blinked. "Yes."

"Whatever happened to her, I'm sure she was just as worried about you being dragged off by James and his crew."

She shook her head. An awful blankness came over her face. "No."

"There's no way, being your twin, she didn't feel the same way about you as you do about her."

Her tongue licked her lips, but it didn't leave any moisture behind. "They lied."

"How."

"They said they could only save one of us. We had to choose."

"And you won."

A shake of her head denied his assumption. "I lost, but they took something I said wrong."

On purpose he bet. "And?"

"They took me."

He might as well have it all. She'd already about cut his heart out of his chest. No sense leaving the job half-done. "And?"

"I couldn't convince them they'd made a mistake. I tried, but they wouldn't listen."

"Ari understood."

Again, the shake of her head. "I heard Ari scream, when I looked back they had her on her knees. She was naked and fighting. Her face was all bloody."

The fingers around her wrist were going to leave bruises they were clenched so tightly. Caine pried them open, knowing he was opening a chasm in her control as he did. Not caring. Needing her to let go. To let him take this pain from her.

"They were laughing."

Son of a bitch. The bastards could have at least waited.

"You couldn't have done anything."

"I could have insisted on staying."

As fast as he broke her grip she replaced it. "To what end? It wasn't like you walked into a picnic."

"You don't understand," she whispered in a cry that ripped layers from his soul. "There were eleven of them. And with me gone, there was just her."

Tracker's "Son of a bitch" whipped out of the darkness, echoing the frustrated anger roiling within Caine. What had her father been thinking, bringing two sheltered young women out here? And once he had, why hadn't he hired enough protection to keep them safe? Caine drew the rage up short. No amount of might-have-beens were going to help Desi deal with the horror. What she needed was something to hang her sanity on. A hope. "You said yourself, Ari survived. That's all that matters."

She blinked, guilt and desperation taking second place to the need to believe. Where her fingers bit into her wrist, the skin glowed an eerie white. "Yes. She survived."

He was never so glad to see tears in all his born days as the ones that flooded Desi's eyes. A crying woman was a sane one. "So all that needs to be done is to find her and then you two can talk it all out, right?"

A branch snapped from Tracker's direction, along with another curse. Caine knew what prompted it. Chances were, Ari was dead or so bad off she might as well be, but Desi didn't need to hear that. She needed something to carry her through, and he was going to give it to her, no matter how unlikely the possibility was. "As long as she's alive, there's hope."

"You think she can be found?"

"Yes." If she was alive, she could be found. It was the "if" that had him troubled. The fragile width of Desi's ribs expanded and then jerked to a halt. About the time he got concerned she was going to have another attack, she released her breath in a whisper so full of pain and hope he felt cut up inside.

"Do you think you could bring my sister back to me?"

Caine couldn't get his lips around the promise. If Ari wasn't dead, her mind probably was as far gone as her body would be from disease and abuse. White whores got little rest in the Mexican-dominated territory. And as much as he wanted to make Desi the promise she needed, he couldn't promise to bring her the sister she remembered. Explaining that would require some fancy phrasing.

A shadow separated from the trees. "I'll bring her back to you, ma'am."

Over Desi's head, Caine raised his brow at Tracker. The man just sat there on horseback, a black silhouette, nothing in his stance to indicate why he was offering.

Desi sat up against him as Tracker urged his horse out of the trees, his shadow expanding in the moonlight, reaching them before the light reached his face, revealing the hard set of his mouth and the coldness of his gaze.

"You promise?"

"Yes."

Desi shifted in Caine's lap, leaning back to see his face, her fingers digging into his wrist hard enough that he'd be wearing bruises to match hers come morning. They were nothing compared to the bruises her pain left on his soul as she asked, "Can I believe him?"

"If anyone can find your sister, it will be Tracker."

Her searching gaze held his. He didn't flinch. He had nothing to hide. It was the truth. The last of the bleakness fled her expression and was replaced by a determination that would be scary if he didn't recognize what drove it. She turned back to Tracker. Her "Find her" was the snarl of a woman who'd never give up.

Tracker reined his horse as it responded to the aggression radiating off Desi. His expression didn't change as he asked, "And when I find her, if she doesn't want to come?"

"Why wouldn't she want to come?"

"Sometimes a woman can let what happens to her shape the way she sees herself."

"You're saying she might feel I won't want to claim her as my sister after all she's been through?"

"She might be bad, Desi," Caine warned. "Physically

and mentally, there might not be much left of the sister you remember."

Desi's expression hardened to the stone of Tracker's. Her head came up and she shook with the emotion burning within her. "You bring her home to me, no matter what you find, do you understand?"

Tracker nodded and picked up his reins. It wasn't enough for Desi. Caine could feel the impatience building in her, the need, as she practically growled, "No matter what, you bring her home."

Tracker nodded. "I'll bring her."

It still wasn't enough. Leather creaked as Desi shifted again to pin Caine with her glare. "You'll make him do it?"

No one could make Tracker do anything. Caine held Desi's gaze, feeling as if he held together the remnants of her soul as he promised, "I'll gut-shoot him if he even tries to back out."

That did the trick. As Desi calmed, Caine didn't know whether to be flattered or appalled she thought him capable of gut-shooting his friend over a broken promise, but at least she'd settled down.

Tracker motioned to the right with his rifle. "We need to head back."

Caine followed the direction of his point. Orange light almost too small to be noticed flickered among the rocks about ten miles east of the ranch. "Uh-huh."

He turned Chaser with pressure from his knee, anticipation coiling in his gut. Desi's past was coming calling.

11

She didn't stay settled for long. As soon as they got back to the house, Desi started twitching. It was all Caine could do to keep her on the horse once they reached the barn. "Hold on a minute," he ordered as she squirmed to get down.

"I want to get to the house."

So did he, but probably not for the same reasons. "And I don't want you opening up those feet again."

Desi twisted in his lap, moonlight painting her hair an ethereal white. "I'll be careful."

He let her flip over on her belly, then placed his palm in the middle of her back, pressing her into his thighs. The little squeal and kick she gave when she realized she couldn't get away made him chuckle. "I intend for you to be very careful."

"Let me down."

Tracker looked back over his shoulder and smiled. "Need any help?"

"I've got it under control."

No sooner had the words left his mouth than Desi sank her teeth into his thigh, which made him jump and Chaser crow-hop and Desi squeal again. For a minute, it was all Caine could do to control Desi's squirming and Chaser's crow-hopping.

Tracker's "So I can see" was more than a little dry as he dismounted and came over.

"Unless you have a hankering to land in that pile of manure, Gypsy girl, you'll hold still," Caine advised his wife as he turned Chaser in small circles, getting him back under control. On the third spin, Desi relented and held still, though he wouldn't say she relaxed as tension hummed through her muscles like bees in a hive. He took his hand off her back, shaking his head. "And you call me stubborn."

Desi propped herself on her elbows. Her hair hung in a long braid toward the ground. The braid he'd put there. He liked knowing that.

"You are."

"Uh-huh. Now, why are you in such a hurry?"

"I want to draw Mr. Tracker a picture."

He wondered how Tracker was taking to the handle of "Mister." "Of your sister?"

"Yes."

"Doesn't she look like you?"

"Yes." She wiggled. "But softer."

Caine grabbed her hands and eased her down. Tracker caught her weight, keeping it off her feet. "I find that mighty hard to believe."

Desi was the softest thing he'd ever seen.

She glanced over her shoulder, her torso arching to see his face. Tracker took a step forward, balancing her weight. A strand of his long black hair fell over her chest. Caine had a violent urge to cut it off.

"She's very gentle," Desi explained.

Caine dismounted and ducked under Chaser's neck, reaching for her. Tracker handed her over without a sound. Desi's weight settled into him and a little of the hot aggression that had flared at seeing her in Tracker's arms faded as Desi turned to him for reassurance. "She's never hurt anyone in her life."

"And you're a wildcat."

He only had a moment to absorb the blue of her gaze before her attention was back on Tracker. "I've always protected her."

And it about killed her when her last attempt had failed. Caine understood that.

Tracker inclined his head. "I'll keep it in mind when I find her."

Desi's elbow collided with Caine's throat as she twisted to maintain eye contact with the big man. "But you will find her?"

Tracker didn't answer, just picked up the reins and led the horses out of the lamplight into the darkness. The likelihood of Tracker finding her sister wasn't high. It was a big country and a white woman was a prize to be kept hidden. Desi strained against him, reaching for the promise that no one could give her. It was up to him to balance the truth. "It's not his way to promise what he can't keep, Desi."

She twisted so hard on that reality, he almost dropped her.

"But you'll try?" she called, straining after Tracker. Tracker disappeared into the dark interior as Desi quivered in Caine's arms, muscles stretched taut as she strained for the hope she couldn't let go.

Deep and low, the promise reached back. "I'll do my best."

"He has to find her."

Caine wasn't sure if Desi's soft whisper was to convince herself, him or God. He gave Desi a little toss up to a more comfortable position in his arms and headed for the house. "Tracker's got a real sense for finding things."

"My sister is not a thing."

"That she's not. But you've got a promise from Tracker and that's about as close to gold as you'll ever see."

"What makes him so different?"

He'd be jealous of her fascination with his friend if it weren't for the reasons behind it. She needed reassurance.

"Tracker never had it easy. His ma was a Mexican wh——" He caught himself in time. "A loose woman and his pa, Indian. A bad combination for a kid out here and it was made worse by the fact his pa was a mean drunk. It wasn't so bad when his ma was alive, but after she died, hell, grown men used to kick him and Shadow around just for the fun of it."

"Shadow, too?"

"Shadow and Tracker are brothers."

"I didn't know that."

"They don't advertise it," Caine remembered back to the hell of those days, when Tracker and Shadow would show up at his back door, always sporting empty stomachs and new bruises. How his father would curse and his mother wring her hands before setting down huge plates of food in front of the two boys, which they would polish off in seconds.

"Pa tried to shield them, and Mom tried to make up for it, but it was never enough. The only thing that saved them was they grew early, fought dirty and learned to hug the shadows."

"How awful!"

It had been pretty awful when he looked back at it as an adult. He wished he had understood as a youngster.

"It sure as shoot was for those raiders. When they hit our town, no one saw Tracker or Shadow, but we knew where they were by the screams of those men."

"They must have been so young."

"In years, but they had a hell of a lot of hate stored up, and when that self-proclaimed general rode into town, they just let it loose. One renegade at a time."

Sometimes he thought they still were.

"Dear God."

Memories he didn't want rolled over him, memories of women screaming for children, children screaming for parents, the thunder of horses' hooves, the war and the blood... Hell, everywhere the stench of blood. Of his family, his friends, his community.

"I don't understand how that could happen."

Neither did he. "War isn't pretty."

Her hand covered his. Soft and warm, delicate. Too delicate for this land. "I'm sorry you suffered that."

He shrugged and buried the screams to the place where he couldn't hear them. "It's a hard land, Gypsy, but there's a lot of reward for those that can tame it."

Her stomach rumbled, planting him firmly back in the present. More than Desi needed to hear about Hell's Eight, she needed food. "How about we get that dinner plate of yours, and I tell you a happier story?"

Even in the moonlight he could see the pink rising on her cheeks. Even an empty stomach could get that reaction out of her. He grinned, and when the blush deepened to rose and her gaze scooted from his, he chuckled. "Have I ever mentioned how much I like the way you blush?"

"No."

"Well, I do." The night air frosted his breath. "It's sweet, innocent and sexy."

"I'm not innocent."

Her grip tightened on his neck as he took the first step of the porch, releasing more of that lavender scent that reminded him of all the lush softness of her body. "You arguing with me?"

No answer.

"Because if you are, I've got to say it's a darn foolish thing to be taking up arms about, trying to convince me I'm seeing you wrong."

"But you are."

He made his sigh evident as he shook his head. "You just had to wander there, huh?"

"Where?"

"To the proving ground." He opened the front door and angled them through. It wasn't hard. She wasn't very big. The parlor, which normally would have boasted a few people, was empty. In consideration, no doubt, to the privacy the newlyweds were expected to need at the end of a moonlit ride.

"What's the proving ground?"

He headed on through to the kitchen. She was right to be suspicious. "That place where I get to prove to you I'm right, and you're wrong." He dipped her down when they got close to the drawer beside the stove. "Grab that salve out of there, would you?"

She made no move to do as he requested. Rather, just kind of pulled herself into a ball. Funny how she could do that, make herself invisible while sitting in plain sight. It was damn effective for shutting off a conversation without saying a word. "No, huh?"

Her chin set. "No."

"No problem. I'll just get it later."

She came out of hiding on that one. And she came

out swinging. "I think, as your wife, I'm entitled to some respect."

He set her on the chair and straightened, pushing his hat back. "You do?"

"Yes."

"And you feel I haven't been treating you that way?"

"No."

"Any particular reason, or is that a general insult you're handing out?"

That warning elicited no evidence of caution, just a kind of mental digging in that surfaced in the tight set of her lips and the narrowing of her eyes. "I wasn't always a wh—"

He placed his hand over her mouth. "You might want to take a moment before you finish out that thought."

That chin of hers notched higher. He took his hand away.

"Why? Because if I do, you'll paddle my butt?"

He did enjoy that sass she let loose when she wasn't worried about being proper. "Sweetheart, I intend to get around to doing that anyway."

Her bravado stuttered under shock. Her mouth worked and then her lips set. "That is exactly what I'm talking about. You can't say such things to me."

"Even if they're true?"

"Especially if they're true."

She wasn't making a lick of sense, but since he'd fetched her out of that stream, this was the first bit of true fire he'd seen from her, so she could snap at him all she wanted and he'd allow it. She was sexy as hell when angry. He stood up straight. "You just want to go around in a daze of make believe?"

She nodded. "If I have to."

"Because you think what I say to you is a sign of disrespect?"

"I don't think it, I know it."

This he had to hear. "How?"

"Before I met up with…unfortunate circumstances, I was a proper young woman, raised to be the perfect wife."

"Seriously? Perfect?"

Her hand balled into a fist on the brown-and-red quilt. He wondered, if he kept prodding her, would she take a swing at him? She nodded and the thick braid he'd put in her hair half looped over her shoulder. "Yes."

It was more a hiss than a word. He tugged the braid free of the quilt. It fell across his hand, connecting them. "And it was important to you to be perfect?"

"I wanted to make my parents happy."

"And your future husband?"

She shrugged. "Not so much. He didn't exist, after all."

"But if he had?" He wound her braid around his hand. "You would have tried to please him?"

Her eyes narrowed. She untangled her hair and pulled it away from his toying. "Yes."

"Ah."

He turned and put his hat on the counter and took her supper plate out of the warmer.

"Ah, what?"

He set the food on the table beside her, getting a knife and fork out of the drawer. He put them beside the plate. "Ah, I understand." He motioned to the plate. "Eat."

"I'm not hungry."

He hooked the adjacent chair with his boot and dragged it kitty corner. With a twist, he turned it so he could straddle it. He rested his arms across the back and motioned toward her stomach. "You might want to tell your stomach that."

"I would know if I were hungry."

At that moment, her stomach chose to rumble again. Color heated her cheeks, but he wouldn't say embarrassment loosened her up.

"If you don't keep your strength up, opportunities might pass you by."

"Opportunities to escape?"

He let the jab slide. "Likely. Along with opportunities to find what you're looking for."

"I'm looking for my sister."

"And today you found someone who can find her." Her lip slipped between her teeth. There was a pause.

"And yesterday I found you."

"I believe the right of that is that I was the one who did the finding." He motioned to the plate. "Eat before your food gets cold."

She eased sideways in the chair. A dainty, elegant movement that even he could see spoke of breeding. Desi removed the napkin and placed it on her lap. Her fingers curled around the fork. "When will Tracker start looking for Ari?"

"A couple weeks. We've got some things to settle around here first."

She picked up the knife and fork and with a smooth movement that was almost too pretty, scooped a bit of stew onto the tines. In a slow, measured move, the food traveled to her mouth. Her lips parted, surrounded the morsel and slid it off the fork. The utensil returned to hover at the side of her plate. With equal care she chewed. The whole process was so innately feminine his cock went hard in a rush.

"Damn, sweetheart, mealtimes are going to be embarrassing."

She stopped chewing. Her eyebrows rose in query. No doubt it was impolite to speak with food in her mouth. He took the napkin out of her lap and wiped a nonexistent smear from the corner for the simple reason that he wanted to touch her. "You make eating a peep show."

She blinked, but she didn't get angry, and her cheeks didn't flush. She had no idea what he was talking about. "You eat very prettily."

A tinge of pink did dust her cheeks at that. She swallowed, and he watched the fragile muscles in her throat work. He even found that seductive.

Caine put the napkin back in her lap. She dipped that fork again. He sat back in his chair and just let the ache spread through him as she repeated the seductive process. Bite after bite. Swallow after swallow. When she started on the tortilla he had to take a break. "I'll get you some water."

"Thank you."

He was halfway to the back door before he thought to offer her anything else. "Unless you'd rather have coffee." There was always coffee simmering somewhere on the ranch.

A little shudder went through her. "No, thank you."

He grabbed the pitcher off the edge of the counter. "I'll get you fresh."

If he didn't get to a place where he could adjust his shaft, the damn thing was going to break in two. No doubt she'd consider it another sign of disrespect. As soon as he was clear of the door, he let out the breath he'd been holding and adjusted himself. Neither the cold air nor the extra room did anything to cool his lust. If Desi always ate like that, he was never making it through a meal with her without sporting a hard-on. No doubt, he thought with a wry smile, she'd consider that a sign of disrespect, too.

He tossed the water into the yard and went to the pump. As he primed the mechanism, he looked around. Everywhere he looked there was evidence of the plans he and the others had, of what they intended this place to be. The Hell's Eight stronghold was a fortress and built to last. The houses, set against the cliff wall as they were, could take an attack without crumbling. Made of rock and adobe, they couldn't be burned out. The only luxuries the place sported were the barns, the well pump and the escape tunnel that cut back through the canyons. That might have to change. With two women on the place and maybe children down the road, more softness was going to be needed.

Especially for a woman who'd apparently grown up with everything. He didn't doubt Desi's claim that she came from a much better background. If her speech and manners weren't enough to give a clue, the way she ate cinched the deal. Class was in every gesture. Worry about appearances steeped in every measured chew. Only those with nothing better to do had time to worry about inconsequential things like that. He sighed.

Her past meant he might have to adjust the way he dealt with her. He didn't doubt Desi's claim that she way she'd burned for him earlier. Maybe.

When he went back inside, Desi was wiping her mouth and the plate was shoved aside. She'd eaten half. As she set the napkin by her plate, she flicked the corner of her mouth with her tongue. The flash of tempting pink made mincemeat of his efforts to cool off. Caine snagged a cup from the hook on the wall and placed it before her. Standing as he was and sitting as she was, there was no way to hide the effect she had on him. Her cheeks flamed as red as a woodpecker's head and her thanks was strangled.

Caine leaned his hip against the table. "While I was outside I got to thinking about what you said."

"And?"

Game as always, she took her drink in small sips that had her swallowing in even pulses, the way she would if she were taking his seed. Caine ground his teeth. Son of a bitch. She was burning him from the inside out and she didn't even know.

"I've decided you're just going to have to adjust to the husband you have."

She blinked in that way she had when absorbing information. "Why?"

He hitched his hip up on the table. If they were more settled, she more comfortable, it would have been easy to draw her mouth to his cock, let her lips play over him in a soft caress through his pants, teasing them both with the sensual prelude. The blush on her cheeks burned brighter, but she didn't back away or down. He cradled her blush into the palm of his hand. "Because you have a very strong effect on me, and I'm too old to be trying to hide it like a green kid catching peeks through the door of a bordello."

"But I'm your wife."

"And considering that means you're the only woman I'll be coming for over the next fifty years, I don't see where that's a complication."

"I wouldn't mind."

"What?"

"If you felt that way with other women." A little wave of her hand filled in the blanks.

She was telling him he could have other women with

her blessing. Caine laughed. Who did she think she was fooling? "Yes, you would. You'd be mad enough to chew lead and spit bullets. Fortunately, I wasn't raised that way. One man cleaving unto one woman until death do you part."

Her grip on the metal cup turned white-knuckled, but her voice remained calm. She pulled her cheek away from his hand. "But that's for couples who love each other. There are no illusions between us."

He followed the heat of her skin. "Just the ones born of your imaginings."

Blue eyes flashed a wary exasperation. "Which would be?"

Damn, he liked it when she challenged him. "The ones that say I'm going to disappoint you."

"I never said that." She took a sip of her water. "I don't have any expectations of you at all."

He gave her chin the shelf of his hand to rest on. Not that she needed it. Annoyance was doing a pretty good job of keeping the elevation of that particular body part just so. He tapped her nose with his thumb, smiling when her eyes crossed trying to follow the movement. "Now that lie you're going to have to make up to me."

"It's not a lie. I don't expect anything of you at all."

He stroked his thumb across her lips, watching the frown form between her brows and the tension take up residence in her gaze. "You expect me to turn on you every second of the day like some rabid skunk. You expect me to throw in your face the events of the last year every time I get close. You expect me to use it as a license to hurt you, to humiliate you whenever you let down your guard."

He touched his fingertip to her ear, letting his thumb

slide down the ultrasoft skin of her cheek. "It's just not going to happen, Desi."

"Bull."

So much mistrust fed by so much pain.

He bypassed the temptation of her ear to cup her skull in his palm. "I get that it's my job to prove it, but it's also your job to keep open to the possibility that I'm not the skunk you're afraid of finding."

She cocked her head back, challenged him eye to eye. "So things will be easier for you?"

"I was thinking on it being easier for you."

"I just bet."

He blew out a breath and considered the wall she'd built around her trust. He bet it rivaled Hell's Eight for impenetrability. "I can see you're pretty set in your beliefs."

She didn't answer. She didn't need to. Her expression said it all. "So here's the deal. It's not my way to hide things or wrap things up fancy. You're pretty as a picture and the fire in you calls to me. I wanted you earlier. I want you now. And I'm going to want you later. I wasn't taught the right and wrongs of pleasuring a wife. That being the case, there's no disrespect meant when I let you know how you make me burn. It's just how I am, and you could consider the fact that at least you'll always know where you stand with me."

"Even if I don't like it?"

"It's my job to ensure you like it."

"It's not fair."

He shrugged. "Life rarely is, but the fact is, there's nothing you or I could ever do together that's not right, so when I ask you for something just hold that thought tight."

"What about what I want?"

"There's nothing I won't give you in bed. You just tell me what it is, and you've got it."

"I want to be left alone."

Quiet and despairing, the statement drifted between them. He sighed and stroked her cheek twice with his thumb before killing off the remnant of hope. "Except that."

It didn't take much pressure from his fingers to turn her head. As soon as she caught a gander of the bulge in his pants, he met resistance. He had more strength in his wrist than she had in her neck. He turned her head until she was flush with his cock head.

"That's what you do to me, sweetheart. Just watching you eat gets me hard."

"I don't do it on purpose."

"That just makes it all the more special." He hitched his hips forward, every nerve ending centering on the tip of his cock, every sense tuned to bridging the gap between her full lips and his body. "Put your mouth on me."

She jumped. He didn't know if it was because of his word choice or what he required. Pressure from his fingertips on her nape got her moving. Barely. She stopped a hairsbreadth from contact. Hot, moist breath seeped through the cotton of his pants, searing his flesh in sensual blows. "That's it, just like that." He rubbed his fingers through her hair. "Let me feel those sweet lips, Gypsy girl. Just give me this one little kiss...."

He held there for an instant as her lashes fluttered down on her cheeks, her mouth parted, her breasts rose and fell. With a nudge, he closed the gap. Agonizing pleasure shot up his spine as his shaft absorbed the softness of her mouth. Her lips parted farther, stretching the material against his sensitized flesh, her mouth moving, manipulating...

Biting. Agony lanced up his spine.

"Son of a bitch!" Caine dug his fingers into Desi's jaw, releasing her teeth from his shaft, holding her in place as he rode the hurt out, clenching his teeth as nausea pitched in his gut. When the first wave of blackness receded, he opened his eyes. She was staring at him, her cheeks bulging around his grip, mutiny and terror identical twins in her eyes. It took everything he had to loosen his grip as another sick wave passed over him. When he could trust his voice he said, "I don't recall asking for a bite."

"I improvised." The taunt was muted by her inability to shape her mouth around the words.

He unbuttoned the flap of his pants, watching her eyes follow every move of his hands, watching her swallow. She damn well better be nervous, pulling a stunt like that. There was many a man who would have killed her for it.

"And now you'll make it up to me."

He took out his near flaccid cock and pulled her forward. Her eyes widened at the sight. He was used to that. He was a big man, even soft. Then they narrowed and the smile she shot was a teeth-baring event. She leaned in.

"Don't even think about biting me again."

Three short breaths slid over the sensitive crest like moist silk and then she nodded. He lifted his cock and drew her in. Her glance flicked to the windows. The shutters were drawn back. Anyone could see in. He was pissed enough not to care. "What are you waiting for?"

Tears welled in her eyes. He steeled himself not to

care. He was her husband. She was his wife. And only one of them was the boss.

She leaned forward. A sob lurched through her, catching on his conscience, dragging it forward.

Still, he might have held on to his anger if she hadn't widened his perception to take in the whole picture—her fists clenched in her lap as she prepared to take him in her mouth, the tears in her eyes and the flicker of acceptance in her gaze.

Ah, hell! He was an ass. The woman expected to be treated like this. The bite had been a test. And he was failing it. Failing her. His wife. The one woman who should never have to fear him. Son of a bitch. Caine slid out of her mouth, off the table. His cock throbbed in the cool air, not caring about honor or pain, just wanting more of Desi's incredible mouth.

And Desi; she just sat there staring at him, all emotion drained from her face except for blank acceptance. Caine cursed and shoved his penis back into his pants. He expected an abused horse to test his leadership, why the hell hadn't he expected it from her?

Desi didn't resist when he pulled her into his arms. Didn't scream or fight. Just let him do what he wanted. He tugged her face into his chest, his reasons purely selfish. He didn't want to see the pain in her eyes, or worse, the knowledge that he'd proven himself to be the son of a bitch she had expected. "I'm sorry, sweetheart."

She didn't fight him; just stood there stiffly in his arms, her slight body trembling with nearly imperceptible shivers that gnawed at his conscience. "Sure enough, I've got a dark side."

No answer. He held her until her breath slowed and the tension left her muscles. He brushed his lips across her hair. "From here on out, you have my word, I'll do my best to control it."

If it killed him, he'd control it. A log popped in the stove. She jumped.

"This is not how I pictured my wedding night, you know."

Still no response. "I figured there'd be a big celebration, and I'd have to steal my bride away." He stroked his hand down her back, slipping his fingers under the braid, finding the hollow in her spine and nestling into the curve. "She'd be nervous, but eager. I'd be eager and nervous."

His description wasn't that far off from what had happened. He cupped her head in his palm as she drew a shuddering breath.

"You were right about one thing, though." She didn't look up, as he expected. "I did let your previous experience color my thinking. It wasn't disrespect, but I did move faster than I should, because I figured it was familiar territory for both of us."

So he hadn't stressed finesse; hadn't given her what every woman deserved. A night to remember. The guilt of that would haunt him forever. He kissed the top of her head.

"You had a right to bite, sweetheart. Every woman deserves to see the tender side of her husband when he comes to her."

The shudder that ran through her on her next breath lashed him raw. A fine husband he'd turned out to be. "I'm not sure how much tender I have left in me, Gypsy, but I promise you, from here on out, you're going to experience it."

The tension seeped from her muscles in increments. He didn't know if the relaxation came from exhaustion or surrender. He could force her to look at him, but there'd been enough force between them. She could have knocked him down with a feather when her hands touched his hips and then his waist, before wrapping around his back.

"I don't want to wait."

She didn't make a lick of sense. "Look at me, Desi."

When she did, there was nothing in her expression to soothe his nerves. Just layers and layers of pain. Older, old and new. And no denying the newest level was his creation.

He touched the trail of tears on her cheek. He'd made her cry. "Goddamn, I'm sorry."

She shook her head and bit her lip. "It's my fault."

"How do you figure that?"

She didn't meet his gaze. "I shouldn't have bitten you."

"I shouldn't have pushed you."

Her knuckles pressed into his back. "You were only taking what was yours."

Taking. Yeah, he'd been doing that. "As out of line as I was, I'm lucky you just bit me."

She stilled. "You're not angry?"

"Only at myself."

She braced her hand on his chest, placing her fingers one by one against his shirt, as if the proper alignment were critical to making her point. "I don't want to fight anymore."

"Then you won't have to."

"I can't promise not to anger you though. Sometimes…"

Her nails bit through his shirt. He touched her shoulder, her back, the thick quilt keeping him from the contact he desired. "What?"

It came out on a hoarse whisper. "I'm just so afraid. All the time, I'm afraid. I can't sleep for nightmares, can't be awake without remembering, reliving…" She shrugged. "I can't do anything without the past closing in."

He hadn't helped, expecting their marriage to put it all behind them, for her past experiences to give him a pass on all the niceties a man gave his wife. "Desi—"

The shake of her head cut him off. "This is my last chance. I know what I have to do. It's just—"

He cut her off. "Hard."

She didn't act as though she heard him. "I just need you to understand—things happen inside me sometimes."

She'd been abused, no matter how well she covered it, she was off balance and afraid and his pushing was just throwing her back into the helpless fear. "I understand."

She took a deep breath and moved those fingers a fraction wider, once again focusing on the precise alignment. "I want this marriage."

He wrapped the thick braid of her hair around his fist, keeping her gaze locked to his. "And you think I don't?"

She shook her head, whether negating his interruption or his wanting of the marriage, he didn't know. Her other hand came to join the first, pressing against his chest. "I understand what you want from me. I just need a little time."

He didn't think she understood anything beyond the reality as a married woman, she had more status than a whore, even if her husband, in her eyes, still treated her as one. To her, that was still better than the alternative. It took him a minute to find an argument for the certainty she held dear—that it was all up to her.

"Desi, did your mother teach you that your husband is responsible for caring for his wife?"

Wariness entered her gaze. "Yes."

"Then it follows what went wrong tonight is my fault."

"You just wanted a kiss. I've done it a hundred times—" She slapped her hand over her mouth.

He didn't let his rage at the thought flow. "The difference was tonight you felt safe enough with me to put up a protest." He tucked a stray tendril behind her ear, smiling as it immediately popped out, doing what it wanted, despite his wishes. "That's not a bad foot to start a marriage on."

Her gaze flicked his. "I hurt you."

"I deserved it for being an ass."

Her mouth opened and closed. Her hands fisted. "You weren't trying to hurt me."

"Doesn't matter what I was trying for, it only matters what I accomplished." He let the hair go where it wanted. "And, sweetheart, I get the impression I've been hurting you pretty regular like." She didn't deny it. "Haven't I?"

She shrugged. "It's nothing I can't adjust to."

"Now there's a statement to make a man wince."

"You asked." She pushed against his chest.

"No need to get your feathers in a twist. That was directed at me, not you." It was amazingly easy to keep her put. "Tell me something though, why'd you do it?"

"I wanted to hurt you."

He leaned back to get a look at her face. "That was your way of fighting?"

"Yes."

Everything about her was tiny and small, delicate, and her idea of getting an edge on a man was to get close enough to bite his cock? "Gypsy, we have got to teach you to fight."

"I told you, I don't want to fight with you."

"I don't particularly want to fight with you, either, but I suspect I'm not going to get a wink of sleep until I know you have a better way of dealing should there ever be a need."

"My way works fine."

"Your way keeps you too close." He circled her arm with his fingers. "There's not enough muscle on you to go up against any man over the age of eight."

She jerked out of his embrace, coming down on her left foot and wincing. "I am not weak."

He steadied her with a hand to her arm. "It wasn't an insult."

"It wasn't a compliment."

"I wasn't aware you were looking for pretty words."

"You don't seem to be aware of anything except rutting when it comes to me."

She had him there. "You're right."

He let her go, allowing her arm to feed through his grip until he could catch her hand. Her gaze jerked to his, apprehension shadowing every nuance of her posture. He wanted to pull her close and tell her she never had to be afraid again. Except that this time, he was the one who'd instilled the fear. He settled for rubbing his thumb over the back of her hand, and then sighed. "Which is why, starting now, we're going to start this marriage over."

12

"**Y**our husband wants you."

She wished. Desi pushed the hair out of her face with the back of her hand. She gave the shirts in the laundry kettle another stir with the wooden paddle, suppressing a moan as her overworked muscles burned at the exertion. "For what?"

Tia held out her hand for the paddle. "You will have to ask him."

She would if she wasn't afraid of the answer. Since the evening of their fight over a week ago, Caine hadn't wanted her physically, and she couldn't shake the feeling that she'd somehow ruined things. If Caine threw her out, she had nowhere to go, and Tracker probably wouldn't look for her sister. She couldn't let that happen. Ari depended on her.

Desi tightened her grip on the paddle. "Caine wants me to learn to do this."

"He does not expect you to try to learn everything at once."

Probably not. The man didn't seem to have very high expectations regarding her. Since the night he'd said they were going to start over, he'd been distant; watching her but not approaching. As if he knew it was only a matter of time until she disappointed him again. And that bothered her almost as much as the thought of disappointing her sister. "I can work a bit longer."

Tia's hand didn't drop, but she did point. "Maybe, but your husband wants you now for other things."

She turned to see Caine leading a placid-looking horse to the hitching post in front of the house. There couldn't have been a bigger study in contrasts. Caine, who moved with that fluid grace so innate to the Hell's Eight men, and the horse that plodded along as if courting sleep with every step.

There was only one reason Caine would be dragging hundreds of pounds of lazy horseflesh to the hitching post. "So I see."

Desi wanted nothing more than to fall into bed and sleep for a week, but instead she was going to walk over to that huge horse, grit her teeth and try to prove to the world that the animal didn't terrify her, that she could do the simplest thing like swing her leg over the horse's back and get in the saddle without needing a mounting block or a leg up—Caine's first goal for her.

She'd rather be nibbled to death by ducks.

She grabbed her coat and pulled it on. The wet hem of her skirt slapped against her calves as she crossed the yard. Sweat chilled on her skin as the cool wind blew across her temples. Caine watched her the whole way. She couldn't see his eyes because of the hat, but she could feel the intensity. Men stopped their work to watch. Instead of earning respect with her continued efforts, she was becoming a source of entertainment as the men bet on how long it would take her to mount on her own, and how long it would take her to give up. She was not giving up.

As soon as she got close enough, she asked, "Anyone betting on me making it today?"

Caine didn't answer immediately, just ran his gaze over her. She didn't think he missed a thing, from the unhooked button on her boots to the sweat at her temples. She was a mess, inside and out. Her mother would have been appalled, but there was an odd sort of balance in her outside matching her inside for once, so he'd just have to take her as she was.

"Just one."

She stopped ten feet from the horse. She didn't like the way its ear twitched. "I guess that's a step up from zero."

"You're wearing them down."

Her back spasmed in a rolling wave. She took a breath and held it until the pain passed. "Just not in the way I'd imagined."

His posture changed infinitesimally. A tip of his head and then she caught the glitter of green.

"You feeling poorly?"

Not for all the tea in China would she admit she was on her last leg. "I'm fine."

If she kept saying it, eventually it would be true.

"Uh-huh." Another of those pauses that made her uncomfortable, and then Caine motioned to the horse. "You can't mount from over there."

"I'm aware of that." She just couldn't get her feet to move forward.

"Lily's getting impatient."

Lily hadn't done a thing but twitch her ear since arriving at the post, which should have eased her mind, but she didn't trust the horse and couldn't get rid of the impression that it was just waiting for the opportunity to send her tumbling. "She'll get past it."

"There's no need to be afraid."

"I'm not afraid."

"No need to lie, either."

Since she couldn't deny lying, she settled for glaring.

"You rode that paint easy enough," Caine pointed out.

She'd been in an "I'm dead anyway" state of mind then, terrified and desperate, running on fear and half-baked notions, but now, if she could convince Caine she wasn't worthless, she might have something to live for and might have a chance to find her sister. That was a heck of a lot to lose. She eyed the mare's one blue eye. "He didn't have a mean eye."

He patted the horse's neck. "Ah, Lily's watch-eyed, but she doesn't have a mean bone in her body."

Just then Lily stomped her foot and snorted. "So you say."

"She's the most placid horse on Hell's Eight."

That statement, as far as Desi could see, didn't mean much. Most of the animals here were wild terrors of flashing hooves and snapping teeth. How Caine expected to turn them into cavalry mounts she had no idea, but he hadn't batted an eye when he'd told her his intent. She cut him another glare as he observed her approach, no expression on his face. Part of his training techniques probably involved staring them into submission.

The stirrup, as always, was a long way off the ground. The amount of leg she'd have to show just to get her foot up there was scandalous, but the least of her concerns. Just lifting her leg that high was going to cripple her. If she wasn't already overworked into being too sore to make it happen. She took a breath, and another step. She grabbed the wooden stirrup. Just the thought of lifting it exhausted her. Getting herself into the saddle was going to be impossible. "You say someone placed a bet on me making it today?"

"Yes."

Bless that someone's soul for believing in her. "Then someone's going to be happy tonight."

She grabbed the apron of the saddle in her left hand and leaned back farther and farther as she raised her foot. Lily sidestepped away. Desi stumbled, falling against the horse. She didn't pull away, didn't even care when the horse brought its head around to her butt. Let it take a chunk out of her. Right now exhaustion and muscle pain commanded the moment.

A hand touched her shoulder. "Gypsy?"

He hadn't called her that in a week. It didn't sound so good now, with his voice full of pity. She waved him away. "I'm fine. Just taking a rest."

"We can let this go to another day."

And not measure up in his eyes again? She didn't think so. Caine might have gotten the worst of a bad bargain with her as a wife, but she could learn to be as strong as any western woman. "I can't disappoint my only believer."

"He'll survive."

She looked at him over her shoulder, eyeing with pure envy all that heavy muscle sitting so gracefully on his big-boned frame. She shook her head and pushed away from the horse. "Maybe, but I'm not sure I will."

"You've had your back up for the last week."

She bounced on her toes, stretching her muscles, tears burning with the agony. "I don't know what you're talking about."

Caine pushed his hat back, and she had a clear view

of his eyes and the concern within. "Whatever you're trying to prove, it's unnecessary."

The patient set of his mouth, that small smile that could mean anything—oh, it was very necessary. "Maybe not to you."

"Who else matters?"

She grabbed the saddle and the stirrup. "Me."

As soon as she had her weight off balance on one leg, the horse crowded her and snapped its head around. She yanked up and away from those teeth. The mare snorted and tossed its head. Two crow hops that had her whimpering with pain, and she was dangling off the saddle. Lily gave a little buck. Desi screamed and hung on.

Out of the corner of her eye, she saw Caine reaching for her. She kicked out with her free leg. "Get away from me."

"Damn it, you're going to get hurt."

She hung on for dear life, dragging herself up with muscles that screamed. "You said she was gentle."

"Nothing's that gentle."

The damn horse better be because she wasn't failing again. "I…can…do…this!"

For once, luck was on her side. The next half buck tossed her up. She made a wild grab, hooking the saddle horn with her elbow. Metal bit into bone, her squeal was half victory and half pain. It was easier to get up now that her weight was against the horse rather than dangling off it. The next minute wasn't pretty, but little by little, eyes closed tightly, scrabbling with fingers and toes, she got herself onto the saddle. Knee, calf, hip, then total collapse over the horse's neck.

Desi sucked in a deep breath that reeked of horse and leather. Her back screamed in relief or rebellion, she wasn't sure, but she did know if the horse would just stay still, she could fall asleep right there. Just snore her way through the terror.

Boots crunched on the hard ground. Desi didn't have to open her eyes to know who was crooning to the horse. Only one man stayed that unflappably possessed when wrestling with demons. And Lily was definitely a demon. A big, hairy, smelly, four-legged, hay-munching demon.

"You planning on taking a nap now that you're up there?"

"I was thinking about it."

A pause and then, "It'd be a shame to waste all that work by getting right off. Might as well get a lesson in while you're up there."

Getting a lesson meant bending over and turning the right stirrup so she could get her foot in. "No."

There was a longer pause. Caine probably hadn't expected that, but she didn't think he'd ever dealt with a completely exhausted, nothing-left-to-lose woman before.

"You're too sensible to waste all that effort."

He thought she was sensible? She cracked an eye as he came around the right side of the horse. "What makes you think that?"

"I've been watching you, Gypsy."

"You always watch me."

He picked up the stirrup and turned it. His hand around her ankle was firm through the too-big boots she'd borrowed from Tia. He gently turned her foot and put her toe in the stirrup. "You make a damn pretty view."

She shouldn't be warmed when he said things like that. Men always said things like that to women. It meant nothing. But she was. "You are so stubborn."

"Just a mite."

She opened her other eye. His hands were tanned and lean, appealing in a masculine way as he gathered up the reins. "Sit up straight." His command didn't come as a surprise. He was relentless.

With a silent groan she sat straight in the saddle. "I did just fine riding when we first met."

"You couldn't tack out the horse and had to escape on foot, which led to me capturing you. If Sam hadn't snatched you out of the saddle when you put your heels to that paint, you'd have broken your neck on the next break in stride."

He didn't have to make it sound so much like a fact. "That is supposition on your part."

"I know a fact when I'm looking at it." His big hand came down on her thigh, the heat permeating her skirt. "Tuck your heels down."

"Bastard," she hissed under her breath, grimacing as she did as he asked.

He walked beside the horse, green eyes alert, measuring every inch of her posture. A touch on her knee and she forced her foot down a bit more. "That's better."

Under the guise of a sigh, she breathed, "Sadist."

His head canted to the left, revealing the smile tugging at his firm mouth. "If you keep calling me names, I won't haul water for a bath for you tonight."

That was a serious bargaining chip. She'd been making do with basin baths for the last two days, too tired to even contemplate hauling even one bucket of hot water to warm that, let alone what it would take for a bath.

"What kind of bath?" If he was talking a little hip bath, she had a few more names she wanted to toss out.

"A full soak in the tub for as long as you want." His fingers squeezed her thigh, absorbing her wince.

She narrowed her gaze. "Why?"

"Because you've been working hard, and I think you deserve it."

So he had noticed. A kernel of warmth bloomed inside.

Lily's head came up and her sluglike pace perked with sudden energy.

"Keep those reins taut," Caine ordered as he headed toward the barn.

Desi gasped and did more than pull them tight. She hauled them back. Lily sat back on her haunches, which had Desi grasping the horn for dear life. Caine grabbed the reins and soothed the horse. "Easy. You hurt her mouth."

The horse buried her head in Caine's chest and cast Desi the most soulful look from her big brown eyes. Despite everything, Desi felt a stab of guilt. And envy. The only peace she'd known for years had been found in her husband's arms. And it'd been denied her lately.

"She scared me."

"She's just eager for her oats."

And she was eager for her bath. Caine pulled the horse up at the barn door. He tugged at the reins. Desi let them go gladly. As he looped them over the hitching post with a flick of his wrists, she braced herself for the effort to get down. "That's all for today?"

He patted the mare's neck. "I think you've both been through enough."

Guilt flicked along her conscience again. "I didn't mean to hurt her."

His hands came around her hips. "She knows that." Desi closed her eyes. His touch felt so good. Something soft brushed her hand. Had he kissed her?

A glance down revealed Caine wearing that half amused, half something else smile on his face. And he was looking at her in a way that made her feel flustered for reasons she couldn't define. For something to say she asked, "Who was the one who believed in me?"

He took his hat off and put it on her head, seating it with a little tap, protecting her eyes from the sun. "Me."

She blinked, not only because the sun was in her eyes, but because of the way he said it. As if he knew a secret no one else did, as if he knew *her* the way no one else could. The smile started deep inside. Caine Allen believed in her.

She kicked her feet free of the stirrups and reached for him. As she twisted, something whined past. Lily screamed a horrible sound and her head snapped back, slamming into Desi's nose. Lights streaked out from behind her eyes. She grabbed the rearing horse's neck. Something hot and wet seeped into the front of her dress. Blood. Oh, God, Lily had been shot. Rawhide slapped the backs of her fingers as the reins snapped, while the report of a gun rebounded off the canyon walls.

The horse reared and spun, tearing her away from Caine. Terror laced the normally placid animal's shrill scream. An answering terror ripped along Desi's nerve endings as the ground fell away. For an instant Lily teetered between falling backward and landing on four feet.

"Jump, Desi!"

She heard the order but couldn't obey. The mare bunched her powerful muscles and plunged forward, racing away from the ranch. Away from safety.

Behind her Caine cursed and Tia yelled. Desi blinked the tears from her eyes and looked over her shoulder.

Caine's hat blew off. She grabbed for it in a purely reflexive move, overbalancing as a result. Stupid! So stupid. She scrambled for the stirrup with her foot as everything listed to the left. The overused muscles in her arms and thighs burned as she pulled herself back up. If Lily hadn't veered sharply to the left around the barn, she never would have made it. As soon as she got upright again, Desi buried her face dead center of Lily's neck and clenched every muscle she had. If she fell at this speed, on this rocky terrain, she'd break her neck for sure.

Damn it! This was all Caine's fault. She stretched for the dangling bit of rein. He'd made her get on this horse and now it was carrying her away. A shout yanked her head up. At the edge of the rocks a man stood waving his arms. She couldn't make out his features because his hat was pulled low. She closed her eyes as Lily bore down on him. At the last possible second the horse veered to the side. The man lunged for the mare's head. Lily squealed and snapped her head back. This time Desi avoided getting her nose smashed.

The stranger called her name. Desi didn't recognize the voice, didn't recognize the man. He lunged again for the horse's head, or for her, she wasn't sure. She kicked out. Her foot grazed his cheek as his hand clutched her ankle. She kicked again, terror clinging to her as tightly as she clung to the mare. The boot slipped off her foot. She had just one moment to savor her freedom before Lily plunged down an embankment. She was too far over the horse's neck to counter the downward force.

Oh, Lord, oh, Lord. Lily didn't slow on the uneven ground, just ran, weaving here, leaping there, giving Desi no chance to recover her balance. Trees rushed past in a blur. Her heart thundered in her ears. With every stretch of the powerful animal's stride she listed farther and farther. A fall was inevitable, but Desi refused to accept it. She clutched the horn and Lily's mane, sure deep in her heart that Caine would save her if she just held on.

A glance ahead and she groaned. A creek. Surely too wide for the horse to jump. She tightened her grip. Lily gathered her weight onto her haunches and with a lurch, soared across the creek. Desi soared right along with her, time stilling as she parted from the saddle, drifted on air… A surreal moment of peace in the middle of chaos. She landed with a splash. Frigid water flew up her nose, poured down her neck. She couldn't move, couldn't breathe, couldn't assimilate anything beyond the bone-numbing shock of the temperature. From the far bank came the sound of Lily's fading hoofbeats. And on the path she'd just traveled, the sound of another horse coming fast. One horse. Just one.

Her heart skipped a beat. Fear clogged her throat. Caine wouldn't come alone. Not with a threat out there. He'd come with an army of Hell's Eight. Desi crabbed her way backward through the water, frantically scanning the sides of the creek for a place to hide. Her hand dipped into a hole. Her elbow buckled. She went down hard. Water filled her ears. She couldn't hear him coming, couldn't tell where he was. It had to be the man who'd tried to stop her.

She rolled over onto her stomach, gasping as the cold hit her breasts and abdomen, shaking her hair out of her eyes as she scanned the bank. Twenty feet ahead on the right, a tangle of tree roots stretched down into the creek like a fortress. It wasn't much and it wouldn't hide her completely, but if she could lie behind it, maybe her brown dress and wet hair would make her blend with the shadow of the frozen bank. If the stranger didn't look too hard, it might do. Desi couldn't feel her hands. Her feet were uncooperative blocks. Her thighs were painfully stiff. She couldn't keep her teeth from chattering, couldn't stop the raw explosions of terror from bursting past her lips in harsh gasps. She wanted to jump and run. She forced herself to stay low and crawl.

He was almost upon her. She lay flat in the water and wiggled under the thick roots. One snagged on her dress. She drowned her scream in the water, inhaling liquid on the next uncontrollable gasp. The need to cough strangled in her chest. She buried her face in her arm, trying to control her breathing, her panic, utterly convinced that this time James would win, because it had to be James who'd sent whomever had fired that shot.

The splash of his horse's hooves hitting the creek jerked a yelp to her throat. She bit her tongue until the coppery taste of blood filled her mouth. Soundlessly she maneuvered herself into the undercut along the bank. There was another splash and another. Hoofbeats. He was looking for her. Her heart thundered in her ears. Her body quaked as if with fever, and her teeth... Oh, God! Her molars were chattering loud enough anyone could hear. She shoved the base of her thumb between her teeth, submerged everything but her head in deeper water. She had no weapon, no defenses. She was so cold she doubted she could run even if she needed to. The splashes came closer, a shade faster. Did he see her? Did he know where she hid?

The next splash was just to the right of her spot. There wasn't another. He was waiting there. Why? She strained, but the only discernible sound was the pounding of her heart and the rush of the water.

Wind blew ripples over the slower eddy where she lay. Something slid across leather. The familiar sound of a rifle clearing its scabbard. She cringed waiting on the bullet. Would it hurt? Then she heard what he must have—the rapid tattoo of hoofbeats coming fast. Caine.

She willed the man to flee. *Run! Run, damn you!*

The horse shifted but didn't move. Again, why? She forced herself to concentrate, trying to remember the lay of the land. The bank was high on this side. Maybe high enough to hide a man with a gun. Maybe high enough to give him a shot. This time Caine's name screamed in her mind for a different reason. She felt around with her hand in the water and found a stone. She bit her lip as she gouged it free of its bed. Tears poured down her cheeks as agony shot up her arm. Staying low, she drifted with the current to the far side of the root system.

Please, give me enough time.

She didn't know why she prayed. She'd long since stopped believing God heard her. She knelt in the stream, her muscles sluggish with cold. The man was between her and the setting sun, nothing more than a black silhouette. A target. The thunder of hoofbeats throbbed in her ears, in her blood, finding her rage, bringing it to the fore. The silhouette brought up its arm. The long line of the rifle barrel lifted, pointed.

Desi drew a deep breath, held it and then released it on a bloodcurdling scream. "Caine, watch out!"

She threw the rock, hitting the horse on the hindquarters. The man swore as he brought the startled horse under control. He turned and brought the rifle up again, pointing it at her. She stumbled on the uneven streambed and fell. Rifle shots exploded in a cacophony of death as a Comanche yell tore through the air. Another followed. More shots. Little plunks of water sprayed up around her as she lay in the creek. And then…nothing.

She collapsed, waiting for one of the bullets to find

her, not really caring anymore, her energy sapped, her bravery gone. She was just so damn tired of trying. Something heavy landed in the water ahead. The stranger. She tried to push to her feet, got as far as her hands and knees, but could go no farther. All she could do was kneel there and sway. More splashes, curses, and then boots hit the water in front of her, splashing her face with an icy spray. She was too far gone to flinch.

"Desi?"

Arms came around her, lifted her. Her name came more urgently. "Desi!"

She just hung there and shook. Her body aching, her soul withering, James would never let her go. She'd never be free. There was no place she'd be safe.

Caine swung her up in his arms, carrying her past Tracker, who was preparing to drag the dead man out of the creek. Her attacker didn't look so big lying there in the water, bloody trails flowing outward from his corpse, gathering on the edges of the lingering ice before slipping beneath. She couldn't take her eyes from the sight as shudders shook her from head to toe, coming so fast and hard they rocked her like convulsions. Caine lay her on the cold ground. She wanted to reach for him but her arms wouldn't work. He ran his hands down her arms, her ribs, her legs, efficiently probing her flesh, looking for broken bones.

"She hurt?" Sam asked, shrugging out of his coat. Caine's expression was grim as he gently rotated her ankle. "I don't know. There's blood on her dress."

There was? She had to think on that. It took her four tries to get the words out. "L...Lily."

"Ed's gone after her." Tucker dropped his coat beside her as Caine stripped hers off.

The wind cut through her like a knife.

"Goddamn it!" Caine grabbed the neck of her dress, tore it down the middle. He touched a bruise on her shoulder as Tucker turned his back. Face still grim, mouth pressed tight, Caine wrapped her in Sam's coat. It cocooned her. Before she could thank him, he was shrugging out of his, wrapping it tightly around her legs, immobilizing her. She worked her arm into a sleeve. There was no hope for the second one. She couldn't find the armhole and she was too stiff from cold to twist and search for it.

"Caine?"

"Don't fucking say a word."

If she could have, she would slapped him. She hadn't asked for this. "You're...the one...who insisted...I...learn to ride."

His mouth twisted. "So I did."

"I think what Caine's trying to say right now is he just had the shit scared out of him and he needs a few minutes."

Desi glanced at Tracker as he strode over, sliding his gun back into its holster.

"Like hell," Caine grunted, lifting her. "I'm pissed as hell that she risked herself like that."

She worked her hand out of the coat and patted his hand. "Would have...shot you."

The set of his jaw got even harder. "Better me than you."

Not in her book. Tracker looked between the two of them. The corner of his mouth twitched.

"You all can settle this little tiff when you get home." He jerked his thumb over his shoulder. "Right now, I need to know what you want me to do with our friend."

"Anything on him?"

"Nothing."

"Do you recognize him?"

"Yeah. He's one of our newer hands, Drake Carpenter."

Caine hefted her up into the saddle. "Son of a bitch."

Desi clutched the horn, terror rising anew as the horse stomped his foot. In a second Caine was behind her. "I've got you, Gypsy."

His arm came around her waist and the fear that had been eating her alive started to fade. He did have her. Hard and secure. She felt his shiver as the wind kicked up. More guilt piled onto the load she already felt.

"How'd he get hired on?" Caine asked, hitching her up so she half sat on his thighs.

"He was a recommend of the padre. Said his family had fallen on hard times."

"When Ed brings his body in, have it sent home to his family." A few seconds passed. Caine pulled her tighter against him. "How many more do we have like that?"

"Three or four," Tucker said, vaulting into his saddle with that easy way he had. He glanced at her and then Caine. "I'll see them off Hell's Eight land come morning."

"Do that."

Despite herself, Desi's gaze was drawn to the body lying facedown on the bank.

"Do you know him?" Caine asked.

"No." But she bet James knew a hundred more he could send after her. Another shudder took her. Caine mistook its cause.

"We'll be home in a bit."

"No...rush."

"Not too anxious to try galloping again?" Tracker asked, bringing his horse up alongside.

without a film of soap, which not only meant Desi had fallen asleep before she could clean up, but that he also had an undisturbed view of her body.

Those high-tipped, small but lush breasts with their soft nipples played peekaboo with the surface of the water. Farther down her stomach the points of her hipbones were visible—too visible—above the darker shadow of her woman's mound. She was so small, she could stretch her legs out with just the slight bend of those cute knees necessary to accommodate her size, which pretty much left them lifted and spread as if she were thinking of tempting a lover. He dipped his fingers in the water. It was cooling. He picked up the bucket, careful not to bump the rim, and poured hot water down by her feet. Her head lolled to the other side as the stream of water disturbed her sleep. He stopped pouring immediately. He didn't want to wake her. For the first time, she actually looked at peace.

I dream in my sleep.

He put the bucket down. He just bet she did. He knelt beside the tub and took the washcloth from her relaxed hand. It slid into the water with a ripple. He scooped up some of the soft scented soap Tia had given Desi. The smell of lilacs intensified. A fresh, delicate scent that made him think of spring and flowers strong enough to flourish in this harsh land. And Desi.

He worked the soap into the washcloth and then picked up her arm, keeping his touch light. Desi was a lot like a lilac flower. She looked all fine and fragile, but she had that inner strength that mattered more than outward muscle. No matter how big the storm that hit her, she'd just bend with it until it was over, then sink those roots deeper and grow stronger.

Caine lathered the soap over her skin, massaging sore

This shiver had nothing to do with the cold. "No." Tucker laughed. "Can't say that I blame you, but you sure did stick like a burr there for a bit."

Desi pulled the collar of the too big jacket down so she could see him. "I did...good, didn't I?"

"Right up until you came out of hiding, you did damn good." Caine's hand opened over her stomach, pressing her back against him. "Used your head and stayed safe until help came." His fingers curled into her abdomen with unconscious strength. "But then you went and lost all common sense."

The collar poked her in the eye when she tilted her head back. She shoved it aside to find him frowning down at her. "I didn't think...you saw him."

At least the shudders were beginning to abate.

"I'm a Texas Ranger."

"What does that have to do with...anything?"

"It means I didn't need to see him. I know a bad situation when I see it."

So did she and this was a very bad situation. Tucker and Tracker took up positions on either side, rifle butts braced on either side of their thighs. She wrapped her fingers around the saddle horn and let the lapel bunch back up, holding the shivers back so no one could mistake how serious she was. "And this is very bad."

"What is?"

"I can't stay here anymore."

Caine's grip tightened. "You've got nowhere else to go."

It didn't matter. "James can get to me here."

"He won't catch us with our pants down again," Tracker interjected.

The sick fear didn't leave her gut. "He shot Lily."

"Ed will take care of her," Caine soothed.

She thought of the way the soft-eyed mare had snuggled her head so trustingly into Caine's chest, her terror and pain at being shot. How easily she could have been killed. Desi licked her lips, and found the courage to say the right thing. "Next time it might not be a horse, it might be one of you."

And she couldn't have lived with that.

"There won't be a next time."

Yes, there would. *He* would never give her up. And if he didn't give up, James wouldn't. She held Caine's gaze, searching it for a weakness she could exploit. For his own protection. "You don't know them."

"True." His hand cupped her cheek, his thumb stroked across her lips in an incredibly tender caress. "But I'm damn eager to make their acquaintance."

13

He had her running scared. She'd taken the ... tempted kidnapping in stride, but he had her running scared. Caine set the bucket inside the kitche... door and leaned against the jamb, watching Desi in th... bath. That hadn't been his intention when he'd given her time, but it seemed to be what he'd accomplished. Instead of learning to trust him and appreciating th... courting he was doing, she was just getting edgier an... edgier. And while he couldn't fault Desi for the eff... she was putting in to being helpful, there was a desp... ate edge to her behavior that he didn't like. He wan... her settled, not wearing herself out in exhaustion p... ing something that didn't matter.

Her head lolled to the side against the high back o... copper tub. She was asleep. He shook his head. It w... right that with the sun still shining, she was exha... He grabbed the bucket and carried it over to the ... the tub. Her hair was piled on top of her head, rut... contained with an abundance of metal hairpins.

He touched a finger to a curl. As if anythin... tame that wild mass. He followed the trail of t... down her cheek. Her eyes were closed, and her... flushed from the heat of the water. The water...

muscles through the cloth when he got to a place that made her frown, working gently at her sore body, wanting to give her a small part of that peace. He moved up to her shoulder, smiling at the little moue of disappointment that shaped her lips when he stopped massaging. She was a very sensual woman. If he played his cards right and eased her into being comfortable with that sensuality, he'd be a damn lucky man.

There was a bruise on her shoulder. Old, nearly faded, but still discernible. It was a thumbprint. He placed his thumb over it. The man who'd made it was smaller than him. He moved the washcloth over the spot, covering it as cold rage burgeoned. Waiting didn't set well with him. Every second the bastards who marked her spent on this earth was an affront he couldn't stomach. The bastards needed to die and they needed to die hard. A soft grunt from Desi alerted him to the fact he was scrubbing at her flesh too hard.

Damn it, he would contain the emotions clawing at him long enough to give her the bath she needed and then carry her to bed and give her the rest she craved. Caine wiped at the column of her throat. She had a long neck. Elegant. A neck meant for jewels, not the faint line of sunburn that came from working outside. Guilt settled alongside Caine's rage. She was meant for better things than he could give her.

The stubborn self-serving side of him didn't give a shit. Desi was his. The soft men who populated that fancy world she'd come from had failed her, left her to die a slow, lingering death of the soul in a way she never would have.

Caine brought the cloth under her arms and then over her breasts, being careful of her skin, whiter than the cloth, so fine he could see the faint tracery of veins beneath. If she'd been his woman and been stolen, he never would have stopped looking for her. No matter how many years passed. And no matter what state he found her in, he'd have wanted her back.

He worked the cloth lower, ignoring the throb of his cock as he skimmed her woman's mound and then tucked under her thigh and lifted. Not too high, he didn't want her slipping down in the bath. Her moan drew him up short. He massaged the tense muscle, smiling when she moaned again and her leg relaxed. Desi followed a man's lead easily enough when that mind of hers wasn't charging ahead, supposing the worst.

He inched his way down her thigh to her knee and then to her calf. His hand naturally wrapped around her ankle. It was as delicate as the rest of her. He marveled at the strength in such a fragile joint. She was a thoroughbred for sure. All speed and spirit, yet in need of careful handling because that high spirit could lead her where her body just couldn't keep up. His fingers snagged on a ridge of flesh that shouldn't be there. He frowned, exploring the ridge that wrapped the same path as his fingers. A closer look revealed flesh whiter than the flesh of her skin. Scar tissue. He only knew one thing that left a mark like that.

Nothing in the room but a chain and a bed.

He closed his grip, chaining her with flesh instead of metal. The last of his guilt disappeared as the heat of her skin blended with the heat of his. "Never again, Gypsy."

He might be a hard man without the fancy she was used to, but he knew how to protect what was his. "You can count on that."

Common sense said she was too asleep to hear him, but he liked to think the slight frown left her face because she understood. He checked her feet. The wounds were healed. He eased her leg back into the water. Scooping up more soap, he mirrored the same ritual on the other side, paying more attention as he went, finding more sore spots, more bruises and more scars. And every one he discovered lashed at his rage, whipping it up into a vicious fury that solidified in his gut. With calm efficiency he washed between her legs and buttocks, using his fingers rather than the cloth, keeping his touch as impersonal as he could while his mind logged every fold, every indent. He debated washing her hair, but it would take hours to dry and she needed sleep more than she needed clean hair.

He balanced her chin on his finger, touching his thumb to her damp, flushed countenance. "Gypsy, love."

She frowned but didn't wake. He smoothed the soap into her right cheek, wiping it gently away before wiping at the other cheek. Three more swipes and he had her face done. He dropped the cloth in the water. Rolling up his sleeves, he eased his hands under her arms and around her back.

"I need you to stand."

Her eyelashes fluttered. "Huh?"

"Stand up."

Her effort was disjointed and clumsy, but it was enough. He stood and she lolled against him. Clearly, keeping her that way was his responsibility. He grabbed the towel off the back of the chair and wrapped it around her. He didn't need her getting a chill. Through the thin veil of his now wet shirt he felt the lift of her lashes and the poke of her nipples. He tucked the towel between them as her head fell back, and she blinked at him.

"I finished my bath?"

"Yup."

She frowned, clearly not remembering. She took over the arranging of the towel, transforming his haphazard stuffing to efficient tucks.

"All set?"

She blinked again at the question, only half awake.

"To go to bed," he clarified.

She nodded. "I'm so tired."

"I know, sweetheart." The endearment came naturally as he lifted her. She didn't fight, just tucked her head into the hollow of his shoulder and placed her palm against his neck. It was an act of trust.

It just took a minute to get to the bedroom. He nodded to Tia and Ed in the hall.

Tia nodded to the closed parlor door, and with an eye on Desi, who was dozing against his chest, whispered, "Sam is back. He, Tracker and Tucker are waiting in the parlor to talk to you."

"Thanks. I'll head down after I get Desi settled."

Ed smiled and put his arm around Tia's waist. To Caine's surprise, she didn't shake it off. Ed nodded to Desi. "She is a good woman. Just the right amount of stubborn like Tia here. You were smart to snatch her up."

That was quite a compliment coming from Ed. "I thought so. Could you tell Sam I'll be right down?"

"Will do."

"Thanks."

The heat when he opened the door hit him like a punch. He might have stoked the little parlor stove too heavily earlier, but Desi was so sensitive to cold, he didn't want to take chances. He fished her nightgown from under the pillow and tugged it over her head before laying her on the bed. Her hands clung to his shoulders. He caught them in his, brushing a kiss across the back before letting them go. The sheets rustled as she turned on her side and tucked them under the pillow. Caine eased her legs to the side, straightened her gown and lifted the covers over her.

She sighed and snuggled into the bed. He took the pins out of her hair, spreading the long thick curls over the bed before separating them into sections and braiding them. He tied the braid with ribbon from the bed stand. It wasn't the best, but it would do.

Caine touched the end of the braid. He liked having cleaned and cared for her, liked knowing she was sleeping comfortably because of the ease he gave her. Liked even more knowing when he came back after meeting with the others, she'd be here in his bed, and as soon as he slid in beside her, that smooth, silky body would curve naturally into the shelter of his.

He turned down the light and prepared to leave.

"Caine?"

The sheets rustled as Desi reached across the mattress. Caine caught her hand in his.

"What is it? Are you cold?"

Desi nodded and tugged at his hand. "Always cold without you."

The half-sleepy declaration did queer things to his chest. She tugged again.

He leaned over and kissed her cheek, freeing his hand and pulling the quilt over her shoulders, tucking it around her so no draft could sneak under. He couldn't get into bed with her. His clothes were too wet and his cock too hard. "I'll be back in a bit, after I talk to Sam."

"Promise?"

"I promise."

Her eyes closed and she huddled deeper. "Okay."

He paused for a minute at the door. The lamplight

caught on her hair, coloring it a deep yellow. Desi looked damn good in his bed. Right.

He drew the door closed.

Sam, Tracker and Tucker were waiting for him in the parlor.

Tucker took one look at his clothes and asked, "You decide to go for a swim in the tub?"

Caine crossed to the sideboard and poured himself a finger of whiskey. "Desi fell asleep in the bath."

Tracker grunted. "More like you wore her out. You can't keep at her like this."

Caine glared at Tracker before spreading his displeasure about. "What I do or don't do with my wife is none of your business."

"We're just saying, you might want to lay off her a bit and let her settle," Sam interjected. "That's all."

Caine dropped into the chair by the door. He took a long pull on his whiskey. "For your information, I've laid off her since the first night."

"Then why the hell is she so on edge?" Sam demanded.

"Must be she's waiting on him to pounce," Tracker said, grabbing the whiskey bottle and bringing it over. At Caine's raised brow, he clarified, "For the strain on your nerves."

He poured more in the glass than Caine ever allowed himself on any given night.

"Thanks."

"Whatever she's waiting for," Sam said, "you'd better deliver it because the woman can't afford to lose another pound."

"True enough," Tracker agreed. "As it is, if we get

a stiff wind up here, we're going to have to tie her down."

Caine ground his back teeth. "I'm working on it."

"Working on what?" Tia asked, stopping by the door with a stack of folded clothes.

"Desi."

"Work on her eating."

That was from Tucker. The man had a real problem with anyone or anything going hungry.

"She is not going to eat unless her nerves settle."

Caine ran his hand through his hair. "I know, Tia."

"Her nerves will not settle unless she feels she has a place."

"She's my wife, how much more sense of place does she need?"

"Men leave their wives all the time."

Wonderful. Caine took another sip of his whiskey. "Any man worth his salt does not abandon his wife."

"We know that, *hijo*, but she doesn't." Tia shrugged.

"It is why she works so hard. So you will notice."

"I came to that conclusion myself." Just that evening.

Tia nodded. "Good, then you can fix it."

And pigs flew daily. He cocked a brow at Tia. "Got any ideas as to how?"

Tia shifted the pile of clothes in her arms. "I would not think of interfering between a husband and a wife."

That got a chuckle all around. Tia was chock-full of opinions and not one was she shy about sharing. "Since when?"

Her gaze didn't leave his. "Since now. You created the problem, you must fix it."

Caine ran his hands around the back of his neck and

finished off his whiskey. "This isn't like when I was a kid, and I landed the buckboard in a mud hole."

"No, it isn't. It is much more important."

"Desi's been raised fine."

"You bring this up why?"

"I don't know shit about women, let alone one like her."

Tia's lips quirked. "You know enough to have the ones in town fighting over your visits."

Heat burned the back of his neck. He hadn't realized Tia knew about that side of his life. "It's not the same."

The look she gave him was pitying. "Women are women everywhere. It is only in men's minds there is created a difference."

Before he could counter that, she moved on, leaving him with an empty whiskey glass, the expectant stares of the others and no clue as to how to handle any of it.

"So how long do you intend to keep letting her go on like this?" Tracker asked.

Caine shrugged and motioned for the whiskey to be passed down. "Until she wears out, or learns."

"Getting drunk isn't going to help anything."

"It might help my headache."

Sam snatched the bottle, keeping it away. "Until morning, and then Desi would just have to deal with your surliness."

Tracker took the bottle back. "And that would just make matters worse."

"How much worse can they get?"

Sam sighed and again took the bottle from Tracker. "A lot."

Shit. Every sense came to high alert. "You find out something in town?"

Sam had no hesitation in refilling his own glass. "They're not letting her go."

"They?"

"On the surface, it looks like James is pressing his claim, but if you hang out a bit in the shadows, you discover it's the bankers who want her."

As Sam was very good at drifting through the shadowy areas of life, Caine didn't doubt his word for a moment. "Any idea why?"

"No, but I've put feelers out."

Which probably meant he'd coaxed some woman into spying. With his angelic good looks and natural persuasiveness, Sam could get women to do anything and think it was their idea from the get-go. "How badly do they want her back?"

"They've put out a reward for her return."

Shit. A big enough reward would mean every *bandolero* in the territory would be on their asses. "I don't suppose they were their usual cheap asses when they put out the reward?"

"They offered one thousand in gold, which explains Carpenter's efforts."

"Fuck!" Tucker muttered.

That about said it all.

"But why the hell shoot her?"

Sam set his glass on the table beside his wing-back chair. "The answer to that isn't going to make you happy."

Caine held up his hand. "Wait."

He didn't want to hear this without something to take off the edge. With a flick of his fingers he demanded the bottle back. Tracker walked it over, naturally blending with the shadows. As Tracker poured, Sam released the rest of his news.

"They don't care if she's dead or alive when she comes in, just identifiable."

That information explained Carpenter's trigger-happy efforts. "Shit, we should have just slit their throats and been done with it the minute we saw them," Caine muttered.

Tracker's hand didn't even twitch. "I've been wondering what to get you as a wedding present." He jammed the cork back into the whiskey bottle. The smile that spread his lips was feral, primitive and promised someone's death. "Looks like I just found the perfect gift."

"The bankers have definitely outlived their right to exist," Caine agreed, "but until we know why they put a bounty on Desi, they're going to get to live."

Tracker fingered the blade strapped to his ankle. "But not James?"

Caine raised his glass and let the raw burn blend with the razor edge of his rage. He recalled James's arrogance. The way he'd shot terror through Desi with a look. The satisfaction on his face when he'd seen her reaction. Caine twirled the whiskey in his glass, watching as it caught the light. "No, not James."

"Good."

Caine looked up, pinning Tucker with his gaze. "It's my woman he touched. My woman he hurt. My woman he threatens, so it'll be my hand that ends his miserable life."

"Damn it, she's Hell's Eight, Caine," Tucker argued. "We should all get a piece of the bastards."

The fury flowed through Caine, so cold it burned, so complete it took over the calm behind which he tucked all emotion, ruling that out. "He's mine."

Sam dropped back into his chair. "Tell me at least you're not going to make it quick and clean."

"No." There'd be nothing clean about it. The bastard would suffer. "The punishment will fit the crime."

"Good."

"We still don't know why. It doesn't make sense they'd go to this much trouble to replace a whore."

Caine placed his glass on the table with a soft click and got to his feet. Tucker arched his brow. "I'm not insulting your woman, just talking from their view."

Caine didn't care. "Find another way to put it."

"Lay off, both of you," Sam said. "We need brains, not temper right now."

Caine sat down and took another pull of whiskey. The burn did nothing to settle his rage. His wife was working herself into the grave trying to prove something he didn't understand, people were trying to kill her for reasons he didn't know and, until he figured out the why of it all, he had to lay low and do nothing. He wasn't used to laying low. "So, what's everyone thinking?"

"There's money involved somewhere." Tracker resumed his seat.

"Always is when there are bankers involved," Sam agreed.

"But why not care if she's dead?"

That was the part that bothered Caine. "It could be inheritance. Desi all but said she came from money. Her folks are dead, but she has a sister."

"Think she's involved?"

"No."

"She any place we can ask?"

Tracker shook his head, his long hair falling in his face, emphasizing the harsh planes of his cheekbones, reflecting off the wicked scar on his cheek. "No."

"Hell."

"It doesn't make sense," Sam groused. "Money is inherited. If Desi and her sister are wealthy, why wouldn't one of the bankers just marry up with her and take control of her portion?"

"Maybe the will forbids it?" Tucker suggested

"Don't see how it could." Sam shrugged. "A man automatically takes control of everything his wife has the day he says 'I do.'"

Caine sighed. "Which would mean it would make more sense for the bankers to dispute the legality of my marriage to Desi than to kill her off."

"Could be they haven't tried that 'cause everyone knows what a possessive, stubborn son of a bitch you are and knows any move to court action would end in you eliminating the source," Tucker suggested.

"Maybe." But it wasn't likely. "I want everyone who we're not sure of escorted off Hell's Eight, and I want the others called back."

"It'll take me a few days to find them and get them here."

Caine nodded at Tucker. "You handle that."

He put his whiskey aside. "I'll leave immediately."

"Sam, you still got relatives back east?"

"A few."

"Any chance you can wire them and ask them a favor?"

"Uncle Mark has connections. You tell me what we need, and he might be able to get the information."

"Good, but hold off finding a telegraph until the others get here."

"Wouldn't think of missing the fun."

"Good. And one more thing."

As one, they looked at him. "No mention of this to Desi. At least until we've got some facts. She's got enough on her plate."

"It'll be hard to keep her safe without her knowing."

"We'll just make out I'm in the habit of worrying."

"Won't be a lie in that."

Caine flipped Sam an obscene gesture. "And in the interim, I'll try to find out discreetly if Desi has any more information that can help."

Tracker's bark of laughter wasn't appreciated. "Now that I've got to hang around to see. Caine Allen practicing subtle."

"A stampede would have a better shot at it," Sam chuckled.

Caine snarled a "fuck off" and polished off his whiskey. The warm glow took the edge off his need to act, but did nothing to mute his anger. A nod from Tucker caught his attention. He glanced over his shoulder. Through he door he saw a flash of white. "Desi?"

No response. He turned, and she appeared in the doorway, the thin nightgown doing nothing to hide her shape beneath, considering the lantern on the hall table was right behind her. "Is something wrong?"

Her head turned. She stared vaguely in his direction and started walking. He made it halfway to his feet before she slid into his lap. Her arms went around his neck as she snuggled in on a sigh.

"Gypsy?"

"She awake?" Tracker asked.

Caine tipped her chin up. Her eyes were open but unfocused. "I don't think so."

"She's wandering in her sleep?" Tucker asked.

"Yup."

"Why?" Sam always wanted to know why.

Caine sighed. "I don't know." He eased her away. Desi shook her head, wrapped her arms around his neck. Her nails dug into his nape as she clung.

"No."

He let her pull herself back in. Her cheek rubbed against his chest. Her whispered "Safe" came out on another sigh.

The next little sigh she gave heated his skin. Caine cupped her head and tested her cheek with his thumb. Her skin was cool. She was getting chilled again. "Pass me that throw, would you?" he asked Tucker.

The blanket was tossed over. Caine wrapped it around Desi and stood. "So we're agreed on what we're doing?"

The other men nodded, their hard gazes locked on Desi. The set to their mouths reflected the same seething anger he felt inside. "Good. As soon as I get Desi back in bed, we'll hammer out the details."

He brushed his lips over her hair, breathing in the scent of sweet lilac and soft woman, pulling her a little closer as he did, and whispering, "I've got you, Gypsy."

And he was never letting her go.

14

One of them was coming. Desi eased the hairpin out from the lock. She got to her feet, holding the chain so it wouldn't rattle, inching away from the sliver of light and back to the bed. With the utmost care, she tucked the hairpin into a tiny slit in the mattress, smoothing it down so there was no evidence of the hiding place. With almost desperate panic, she checked the lock in the shackle around her ankle. There was the barest of scratches on the surface, but unless he looked closely, suspected something, he'd never attribute it to anything more than normal wear and tear.

Desi stroked the lock. Hope battling with despair. She was close to figuring out how the mechanism worked. If she could only do it before they tired of her or things changed, she'd be free. She just had to figure it out in time. The footsteps got closer. For a moment she didn't recognize them. Were they sending someone new?

And then she heard it, that slight drag on the other step. Oh, God, it was him.

She'd thought he'd forgotten about her, maybe moved on. Her heartbeat drummed in her ears. The door handle lifted. The latch clicked. She made it to the appropriate spot beside the bed just in time. She dropped to her knees and bowed her head just as the door creaked on its hinges.

He was in the room. She could feel his presence, but unless she lifted her head, she couldn't see him. She wasn't lifting her head. If she lifted her head, he'd kill her. He'd told her so and she believed him. She'd never met anyone so lacking in human warmth. Whenever he entered the room the temperature dropped. Like now. Several moments passed with the only sound her terrified breaths. A sulfur scratched and light flared. The stench of kerosene stung her nostrils. Light filled the room.

"This is how you greet me?"

The question was delivered in a quiet voice, rich in culture but devoid of inflection.

Was he pleased? Displeased? She mentally ran a list of what she was supposed to do. Her head was down, her hands on the floor, her knees spread. He had to be pleased. She was doing everything right. A chill that had nothing to do with the temperature in the room and her naked state shook her from head to toe. Three steps and he was in front of her. The black, polished tips of his fine leather shoes filled her vision. They didn't move, just rested there. After a minute, he sighed. A quick glance up revealed no bulge in his pants. Maybe he hadn't come for that.

"I can see your training has been neglected."

He'd caught her looking. She snapped her gaze back down. Nausea gathered in her stomach, and deep within, the shaking started but hope hung on. Maybe it was something else that had upset him. Maybe he really hadn't caught her breaking her position.

His foot moved forward. The hard sole of his shoe covered her fingers, pressed on the knuckles and bore down. Pain exploded up her arm. She bit her lip on the cry that welled. Noise was a protest. Protesting was not allowed. If she wanted to save herself from further pain she had to be quiet. No matter what, she had to be quiet.

His foot lifted. Her hand throbbed. Had he broken her fingers? She didn't dare move to find out. Maybe, if she was very lucky, he'd consider that punishment enough.

He reached over her head, his shadow stretched with the move, encasing her in darkness. Icy terror swelled deep inside. All of her senses strained for a sign of what he intended. The soft rustle of cloth sliding across wood was as loud as a scream. Not the hood. Oh, please, she thought. Not the hood. Heavy cloth fell over her head. Three tugs and it was fastened and her world turned utterly black. Her breath grew more labored as she struggled to get air through the material. She was suffocating.

"Please." The useless plea broke from her lips.

Retaliation was swift. A hand fastened on the hood and yanked her up, wrenching her spine as she was thrown facedown on the bed. She turned her head to the side, struggling for breath through the fabric of her pain and terror.

She measured time in the pounding of her heart. One, two, three, four, five…on six, her arm was jerked above her head. On seven she felt his shirt against her back, his pants against her thighs and his semihard cock against her pussy.

"I can see they've been too soft with you." His grip shifted to either side of her right wrist. The mattress dipped as he took his weight on his elbows. "You need another lesson."

The statement was as straightforward and as calm as

his twisting on her wrist. Each hand going in a different direction, straining the joint, slowly, steadily.

And she began to measure time in her ability to withstand the agony. It wasn't long before helpless whimpers slipped past her determination. His cock hardened with each cry she couldn't control until she was openly sobbing, and he was penetrating her. And still he twisted, delivering his lesson with the methodical precision he always used, until she was screaming without end, mindless from the agony. Screaming and screaming, drowning out his orders, his perversion, with the sound of her own voice, holding on to her sanity because of that tiny, fragile hope she'd secreted away. Holding on because there wasn't any other choice. He'd never break her.

"Desi?"

The male voice broke into her dream. Light flooded the mask, making her blink. She shook her head, confusion wrestling with memory.

"You feeling okay?"

Caine, not *him*. Desi took a shuddering breath, her hand going to her wrist. It was just a nightmare. She pushed the sheet off her face and sat up, still rubbing her wrist. Caine stood in the doorway. Light from the hall spilled into the room. "I'm fine."

"Uh-huh." Light flowed into the room as Caine lit an oil lamp. He put the glass chimney back down on the base and straightened. His gaze flicked down and then back to her face. "Nightmare come calling?"

"I have them sometimes."

He rested his shoulder against the doorjamb. His shirt fell open, exposing his chest. "I'm thinking this one might be my fault."

"It's not."

"After today's events and the way I've been confusing you, it's a wonder you're not screaming when awake."

He rubbed his palm over his chest. She flicked her gaze down over the muscle slabbing his abdomen, before looking back up. She tightened her grip on the covers.

"I'll get the hang of things."

"Not if you keep looking to me for direction, and I keep changing the game."

Game? He saw this as a game? That explained a lot. "I'm fine."

"No, you're not, but you will be. I've decided we need to get this marriage back on the right footing."

There was only one thing he could mean by that. She glanced at the window. The moon was low in the sky. It was late. And he was at the bedroom door half-dressed. That could mean only one thing. "You've decided to bed me again."

His eyebrow went up. "Among other things. Does that scare you?"

Not as much as the unlimited potential of "other things." She had a feeling that her experiences, which she had thought so vast, were woefully inadequate to what Caine wanted from her. She licked her dry lips and rubbed her wrist. "No."

"Good. That'll make things easier."

She couldn't believe how nervous she was. How scandalously excited. The lamp sputtered. Caine leaned down and adjusted the wick.

Muted lamplight, she decided as he straightened, was kinder than the sun to the violence etched into his large frame, the soft light mellowing the random network of scars slashed into the tanned skin of his torso. Some of those scars small, others long and deep, cutting into the powerful swell of his pectorals or across the rippled strength of his abdomen. There wasn't a spare ounce on the man. Not an inch of softness she could pin her hopes to. Just well-developed muscle flowing over solid bone in a silent testament to the fact that this was a man in his prime. Confident, strong. Intimidating.

She took a slow breath through her nose, stilling the welling panic as the lamp on the table cast his shadow high up the wall behind him when he stepped into the room. Very intimidating. So much like her nightmare except she could look at him, which only seemed to make things worse. Nausea welled. She swallowed once, twice and, on the third try, managed to get her stomach down where it belonged.

She buried her fingers into the fold of the thick quilt that covered her legs, leaning back into the headboard, needing its support, uncaring of how the carvings cut into her skin through the thin linen nightgown. He was just a man, she told the panicked part of her soul. Just a man like any other. What was going to happen tonight wasn't going to be any different than what she'd endured over the last three hundred seventy-eight nights. He'd make his demands, she'd meet them and then he'd be happy. Simple. Easy. Straightforward. It didn't have to affect her any more than that.

Except it would. She knew it would because Caine wasn't a stranger claiming what she didn't willingly give. She'd made promises to him. Promises given under duress, but there was still enough of her old life in her that she felt compelled to try to honor them. As he neared the bed, those green eyes of his burned into her skin as if he saw every hesitation, every vulnerability. She searched his face for some sign of what he was thinking.

The lamplight that eased the violence of his past did nothing to mellow the harshness of his features, highlighting the sharp planes and deepening the hollows, enhancing the aggressive masculinity he wore so easily. The flickering light also played hide-and-seek with the signs she'd come to look for. Those subtle indentations around his eyes or mouth that told her whether he was amused, angry or biding his time. She sat up straighter in the bed.

The shadow from the canopy fell over the upper half of his face as he reached her side, cutting off even that venue from her search, leaving only the set of his mouth to give her a hint as to what he was thinking. And the slight quirk-up on the right side did nothing to throw the brake on her imagination of what a man like him would want in the bedroom from a woman like her.

"Nervous?"

She watched his lips part, saw them shape around the word; a heartbeat later processed the sound, and still she jumped as if he'd sneaked up behind her and shouted "boo." In the wake of that, her automatic "Not really" sounded as foolish as she felt.

The previous quirk spread to a smile.

"Glad to hear it."

The muscles in his chest flexed as his hands dropped to the waistband of his pants. She followed the gather and swell of muscle as it rippled under his skin, over his shoulders, down his arms, the biceps bunching before flattening into the sinewy strength of his forearms. His hands were large, the flesh on the back tanned darker than his chest. The first button on the pants gave, and then the next, exposing the thin line of hair that narrowed down toward the thick bulge below. As he worked on the third, she couldn't shake the feeling that she'd jumped from the frying pan into the fire. With James and his cronies, she'd at least known they wanted her alive as a continued source for their pleasure. Even with *him*, she'd understood her role.

With Caine, she knew what he wanted, she just wasn't sure she could deliver. It was a very strange position to be in. She licked her dry lips and concentrated on the ugly scar rising from beneath the waistband of his denims to arc over the jut of his hipbone, relying on the contrast of light-to-dark too stark to distract her from what he was. A man paid to hunt the worst of the worst. A man who lived and breathed the violence of this territory. A man she didn't have a prayer of escaping. Her husband.

The man she trusted.

The knowledge spread through her. She trusted Caine, and in light of that, sitting here like a scared virgin was the most ludicrous thing she'd ever done. She smoothed the quilt, squared her shoulders and shook the fear from her posture with a toss of her head. Caine wanted her. He knew how to make her feel good, and if she just followed that to its natural conclusion, she could be what he wanted, because it was what she wanted, too.

The mattress dipped as he sat beside her, rolling her hip into his. She caught herself on her elbow, maintaining distance between them, focusing harder as her mouth went bone-dry and the power of speech deserted her. Weakness seeped in behind the cold, a warning that she only had a few minutes to regain control. She narrowed her attention to the rhythm of his pulse, focusing on the count as if her sanity depended on it. Which it did. This was the scariest thing she'd ever done.

One. Two. Three. Four. The silence dragged on as he sat there watching her swallow and choke because she didn't have enough saliva left to complete the process. His expression told her nothing. Said nothing, leaving plenty of room for her to take herself to task for hoping.

This land chewed up and spit out those who hoped. It had taken her father, her mother, her brother and her sister, but it wasn't going to take her. Or so she had decided back when she'd given up hope, but now in this room, she found it was back. Because of her husband. The man who spun practical, everyday things into fairy tales. And now it was her turn, to either go for the hope or turn her back on it.

Caine's shoulder slid between her and the light, taking her into darkness in one smooth move. The bed dipped the other way as he braced his palm beside her hip, jostling her concentration. She blinked, straining to see. Was that beat number six or seven? His fingers pressed hers through the quilt. The scent of pine soap and man surrounded her, reminding her that Caine had expectations that she had just disappointed with her blunt declaration. Where was her common sense? But she knew where it was—buried beneath the fear that had become her constant companion. Fear of being disappointed. Fear of disappointing. The loss of control. Fear could make people do the craziest things. Herself included.

She needed to regain ground. Her mouth worked twice before she found her voice. When it came out, it was a rasp of what she wanted, but at least each word was clearly spoken and evenly spaced. "I can pretend for you."

Above her, Caine stilled. "What?"

The tendons in his neck constricted, telling her he was looking at her, but she wasn't looking back. She could do a lot of things, but looking at a man while she proposed sex games was way down on the bottom of her list. "I can pretend to not know anything about this."

"That's darned obliging of you."

Nothing in his voice let on what he was thinking. She

shook her hair back over her shoulder and tracked the thrust of his collarbone, mentally estimating its length, breaking that down into halves and then quarters. Anything to keep herself from thinking about what she was doing. She shrugged. "I've done it before." It was a favorite game of James's. One she hated. "You just have to tell me how you want me to be."

Another of those pauses that bothered her and then he asked, "Do you want me to guess or do you have options you can trot out?"

Two. She had exactly two. Neither of which she liked, but one was physically preferable to the other. "I'm real good at pretending I like it."

That was a lie. Up until him, she hadn't had a clue how a pleasured woman reacted and always failed to achieve it in the past. But this time, if necessary, she could probably fake it no matter what he wanted.

His "What else you got?" sent her heart to her toes. She took a breath and gathered her courage. If he was one of those who liked to prove his power by conquering a virgin, she was in for a long night.

"I can scream like it hurts while you're taking me."

"Shit."

Just that, one low curse that told her absolutely nothing, and then he shut up.

But he didn't go still. His hand came around her head, his thumb resting under her chin—dry, warm and rough. He had defeated her efforts to hide with frightening ease. The words came out of nowhere as her gaze reluctantly climbed the column of his throat under the force of his will, babbling like a brook over the well of her reserve, terror of disappointing him the driving force. If only he would tell her what he liked, she could make him happy.

Her fingers instinctively rubbed her wrist, feeling the slight ridge where the bone had mended.

"I can scream like a banshee for as long as you need." The set of his mouth wasn't encouraging. "You won't even have to make it seem more real."

She had plenty of memories to draw on and she'd long ago learned this was one place where pride gained her nothing. She caught his wrist in her hand, holding tight, as if, through the force of her grip, she could sway the outcome. She wanted to please him. "Honestly."

Another nudge of his thumb and there was no more hiding. She had to look into his eyes. It was hard to see in the dim light, but she was reasonably sure the glitter there was anger. James had never liked it, either, when she'd tried to "manipulate" him. Her voice faded to a whisper. "I promise you won't be disappointed."

The words hung between them, suspended on the intangible thread of hope that refused to die. The thumb under her chin rubbed lightly back and forth.

"What if I don't want you pretending?"

"I don't understand."

"What if I want the real thing?"

He couldn't mean what she thought. "You want me to actually *be* a virgin again?"

The faint lines beside his eyes fanned out with his amusement. "Now, Gypsy, I think that's beyond both our reaches."

It took her a moment, but she finally understood. "You're playing with me."

"Nah, just tweaking your funny bone."

"I don't find it funny."

"I can see that."

His fingers opened around the back of her skull. At the same time, he leaned in, crowding her into the waiting cushion of his palm. His breath hit her forehead in even puffs that smelled of baking soda and something pleasant. Mint?

He'd brushed his teeth before coming to her. The small consideration wormed under her resolve, lodging in the growing bubble of hope. She gripped the quilt harder, the pain in her knuckles joining the pain in her neck.

"Why don't you just tell me what you want?"

"Because maybe I don't want anything except what happens."

He couldn't be more difficult. "You don't make sense."

"I've been told that a time or two."

He had to care about something. "Doesn't it bother you?"

"Nope. Contrary suits my nature."

That she did believe. His eyes searched hers before sliding down over her face, her chin, then lower. "If you'd relax those neck muscles, sweetheart, you'd be a whole lot more comfortable."

"I'm fine."

He shook his head and the amusement in his eyes migrated to the creases beside his mouth. "Much more fine and you're going to get a permanent charley horse right...about...here."

His index finger pressed on the spot where she felt the strain the most, sending a sharp stab of sensation shooting down her spine. Her gasp faded to a moan as that finger rubbed, soothed. Pleasure chased the pain. Before she realized it, she was leaning into his hand, accepting his support. How did he do that to her?

One quick jerk showed there was no going back.

While she'd been wallowing, he'd moved into her space. As she absorbed that fact he pressed his chest along hers, the heat from his body seeping through her nightgown, warming her skin before sinking deeper, driving home the truth she'd been skirting. More than she feared disappointing Caine, she feared the mysterious power he had that made her want to crawl under his skin and curl up next to his strength. He made her want to depend on him, and that would never do.

She cut a glance to the side. The floor was only eight inches away. If she couldn't go up, maybe she could go over. As if he'd read her mind, the mattress dipped and his leg straddled hers, fencing her in. Against her hip, his cock throbbed. For all his easygoing claims, part of him was serious. His mouth brushed her temple. A kiss or an accident?

"Just stay there, Desi, and let me take care of you."

A kiss, she decided as he did it again—definitely a kiss. And from a man who saw her as needy rather than strong. She shoved at his chest. "I don't need taking care of."

Her hardest shove merely dislodged his smile, which wasn't what she was going for.

"That's too bad, because I have a need to care for you."

His mouth moved down the side of her face, as soft as his drawl, reflecting the slow easy rhythm of his speech, grazing her skin in a butterfly caress that raised goose bumps and shivers she couldn't explain, luring her into relaxing. She stiffened her spine. He made everything seem so easy. "Too bad for you."

His chuckle wafted over the curve of her ear. A sharp sensation shot straight to her groin, riding the shiver that started between her shoulder blades and lodged in her pussy, so foreign it took her three seconds to realize it was pleasure. He was making her feel good, when she was supposed to be making him feel good. She turned her head away.

"No, baby. Let me pleasure you. That's all I want."

His thigh slid between her, and his chin nudged her gown aside as his mouth tasted the skin between her neck and shoulder.

That would be all he wanted until he got mad or frustrated with her response. The familiar surge of anger wove through the spell he was casting like a lifeline. Familiar, dark and cold, it countered his heat, his temptation, with the brutal reality she understood. He'd be satisfied only as long as she gave him the response he was looking for, but as soon as she read him wrong, he'd strike, and she'd be defenseless. Vulnerable. Her fingers went instinctively to her wrist, finding and pressing into the ridge. Did he think she was too stupid to understand how it would be? She wanted to hit him, hurt him, rage at him, anything but sit here suffering feelings she didn't understand. "Fine."

He drew back, his smile fading as he looked at her face. Her heart took another plunge toward her toes.

Caine didn't know what meaning Desi had attached to his words, but he was reasonably sure it wasn't the one he'd meant. Anger, resentment and fear were written all over her as she lay in the big bed, dwarfed by its size, face as white as the sheets, fingers rubbing a spot on her wrist, fighting like hell for a poker face she didn't have a prayer of achieving. The only hint of the emotion he sensed coursing through her was revealed by the flickering of her eyelids as he moved his hand.

"Easy, Desi."

He didn't really expect her to settle, but the way she

jumped and then went board-stiff when he shifted his grip pissed him off. "Look at me."

She did, her blue eyes huge in her pale face, her expression waffling between resentment and anger.

"You need to get used to the fact that I like spoiling you."

"But you'll get bored."

She said it as if it were the worst thing ever. "That will never happen."

She didn't look convinced. He tried to imagine how she felt faced with a man's strength and determination. She was just a bit of a thing, the size of her spirit dwarfing the reality of her build, but not replacing it. No matter how hard she fought, if a man wanted her down, she'd go. If he wanted her legs spread, they'd spread. He wrapped his hand over hers, tucking his thumb under hers, feeling the betraying ridge. And if a man wanted her bones to break, they'd snap.

You won't even have to hurt me to make it seem more real.

Anger roughened his voice. "How'd your wrist get broken?"

Her tongue licked at her lips, but by the second pass it was clear she didn't have the spit to do the job. She finally gave up and shrugged. "I was careless."

She didn't have a careless bone in her body, but she had pride, a lot of it, and she had it running full out now. Chin up, shoulders square, she met his gaze dead-on, daring him to believe her, daring him to call her a liar. Son of a bitch.

Caine stood, bent and scooped her up, quilt and all. Her startled gasp burrowed into the hollow of his shoulder as he yanked the folds free of the foot of the mattress. Her nails clung to his neck as he sat back down on the bed with her in his lap, a stiff unyielding weight. He held her like that, rubbing his hand in light circular motions over her shoulder, the circles decreasing in size until his palm nestled into the curve of her spine like it was made to be there.

The hiss of the oil lamp blended with the ragged rasps of her breath as she fought for the control that was so important to her. Her lashes fluttered as she took sneak peeks at his face, no doubt waiting for him to pounce.

He didn't break the silence with words. What would be the point? Some realizations a person just had to work out in their own way. She took a breath, her ribs pressing against his chest, the bones feeling about as substantial as a bird's wing. He closed his fingers around her upper arm. They met easily. He remembered her face as she'd fought off the outlaws, the expression fierce and primitive, determined to fight to the end. She'd be a hell of an asset to any man out here. And she was his. The sense of pride took him by surprise. "You did good out there with those outlaws."

She let her breath out on a controlled exhalation as she followed his leap of subject.

"Thank you."

He released her arm. "If those other women had jumped in and fought with the same determination, you would have had those boys running for cover."

She was back to staring at his chest. "They were waiting for rescue."

Whereas she hadn't expected anyone to come after her. Had been banking on it, he bet. Admiration cozied up to pride. "Whereas you had the good sense to know the best bet is to always help yourself."

A log popped in the small potbellied stove. Caine absorbed her start into his palm, keeping her put, resuming his rubbing because it seemed to relax her.

"What are you doing?"

He stroked his fingers down her arm, the heat of her skin seeping through the linen gown. "Making conversation."

"Why?" Her question packed more wariness than a preacher opening the door to a soiled dove.

"Because I figure it'll make you more comfortable."

She looked at him, opened her mouth, closed it and then shook her head. He'd give his last dollar to know what went on behind those big blue eyes.

"What?"

She didn't answer immediately. She just became still in that way that told him she was building to something, coiling into herself, bracing herself. He held her wrist, his thumb on the old break, his finger on her pulse.

"I'm not a child."

He curled his fingers under on the next pass, letting his nails drag down the sleeve of her nightgown in a slow caress, eyeing the thrust of her breasts beneath the white material. "I'm aware of that."

"I don't need to be soothed before I get fucked."

Caine had no doubt the crudity was deliberate. He didn't have to apply pressure to get her to look at him. She did that of her own volition, her eyes narrowed, her expression set, her spine braced. He tugged her lower lip free of the upper, slipping his thumb along the inner lining, the dryness belying the militant set of her chin. She was scared spitless, but not of him. Which only meant what she feared was herself. Or how he made her feel. Either of which he could work with.

He bent his head, running his tongue along the soft expanse, moistening the flesh before taking it between his teeth, accepting her gasp, her fear, her suspicion, holding it as he held her, gently, firmly until the tension between them arced to the breaking point. He allowed her to pull back a hairsbreadth before cutting off her retreat by the simple act of curving his fingertips into the back of her neck. He released her lip. Her hand came between them, fingers touching the spot where they'd been joined, staring at him as he ran his tongue over his lips, searching for her taste, finding it, sweet, tangy and salty. Totally feminine. He drew her closer, needing to feel her curves against him. "I told you before, you're my wife."

She curled her fingers into a fist. "So?"

He had to admire the way she so foolishly stood her ground, tossing out invites to battles she didn't have a prayer of winning. She had guts. He leaned in, holding her gaze, taking the rapid puffs of her breath as his, pressing his hand into her hips, holding her close to his strength. "So my wife doesn't get fucked."

Desi blinked, her pupils dilating with shock, her full lips parting on a gasp before that chin went up, those gorgeous eyes narrowed and she was back to her fighting self. "What does she get then?"

He brushed a kiss over the part in her hair, feeling the quiver go through her, admiring her more for the guts that kept her put when she obviously wanted to run. "Me."

Someday, he meant for her to see that as a good thing.

The shake of her head was almost imperceptible. "Why are you doing this?"

"What?"

"Pretending we're married. Pretending that this is

real." A sweep of her hand encompassed the entirety of their situation. "That it matters."

A tug on her hair had her head tilting back and her gaze meeting his. "It does."

"Why?"

"Because you want it to."

She blinked rapidly. If she cried, he was going to put his fist through the wall.

She didn't cry. Her palm flattened on his chest. "Please don't."

He covered her hand with his. It was cold and trembling, imperceptibly belying the calm she projected. "What?"

"Don't dress it up in pretty words. Just leave it like it is. No pretense. No hope for more. We got married because we had to. I'm comfortable with that."

"That's a damn bleak way of looking at things."

"I'm realistic."

That wouldn't be what he'd call it. He turned, lowering her to the mattress, bracing himself above her, being careful to keep his weight to the side. She was so damn fragile he felt like he'd squash her flat if he wasn't careful. "So I take it you just want me to get on with it?"

"Please."

"Now that, wife, is a word a man likes to hear in bed."

15

How could a man so hard, so dangerous, kiss so softly? Desi lay beneath Caine, surrounded by his heat, his power, holding her breath as the mattress creaked when he leaned in, releasing it on a startled gasp as he fitted his mouth to hers, edge to edge, exerting the slighted pressure, holding himself there, seeming in no hurry, though she could feel his cock pressing into her side through his denims. His lips—so different from hers...firmer, wider—touched the other corner of her mouth in a caress similar to the one he'd just finished.

"What do you want from me?"

His mouth left her ear, drifted downward. "Right now, or just in general?"

His lips found a spot they seemed to like, just under her ear. Instead of moving on, they pressed, opened, sucked. Another streak of sensation followed the first, racing down the now familiar path, making her jerk as it landed hard on the first, the repercussions reverberating outward in a wave of tingles that had no mercy. It spread to her breasts, her thighs, her lungs, making her "Now...what do you want from me, now" more gasp than demand. Her determination was buried under a wave of heat.

He didn't take his mouth from her skin as he answered, just let his words bleed into the caress, fortifying the tingles and creating an ache in her pussy that pushed her hips up into the power of his. Searching for more.

"I want whatever you feel, good or bad, no pretending and no faking." Another kiss—longer—followed by a strong suction that ended in an acute sting that had her gasping and arching. Then the soothing pass of his tongue over the spot. Once, twice and then again. Every stroke finding that sweet spot that magnified all pleasure and made it more than it was, more than she could bear lying still. Her heels dug into the mattress. His hand came under her hips, opening over the curve of her buttock, each finger imprinting demand into her flesh like a brand. Up. She needed to move up. She followed his lead, canting her neck into the press of his lips. His cock brushed her mound and in a splinter of feeling, she found the cure for the aimless aching hunger writhing inside.

That was what she needed, what she wanted. But harder. Much harder. A shift of her thighs centered his cock. Oh, God, that felt good. She grabbed his shoulders as reality tilted, cotton and linen doing nothing to mute the satisfaction she could sense waiting for her if she could just get it right. Her hips bounced to the left, away from the restraint of his hand. The tug on the delicate skin between her buttocks froze her in place, caught between sensation and need. His grip shifted and his fingers rode the deep crease between her cheeks, slipping lower, gliding along the material, the smooth linen barrier amplifying sensation. His fingers bumped over the ridge of her anus, pausing when she gasped as the dark sensation shot inward, centering, pressing as she arched and shuddered, anchoring her between the promise of his cock and the darker glide of his finger.

She closed her eyes, unable to move. Shadows played over her eyelids as he changed positions. The mattress bounced as he shifted his weight to his elbow, sending tiny, potent vibrations outward from the pinpoint heat of their joining. His hand squeezed between them and his wrist pressed into her stomach just above her pubic bone, drawing the tight skin up to align her clit with the seam of his pants—rubbing it up and down the sensual roughness as he worked the buttons until she thought she'd explode. Then, unbelievably, he levered up, depriving her of his weight and that intriguing sensation.

"Look at me."

She twisted, wanting it back, bearing down when all that met her search was his fingertip, moaning when the tip entered that tiniest bit. She cried out as the heavy weight of his cock dropped onto her engorged clit in a voluptuous culmination, searing it with smooth heat as his drawl rolled over her in a tense growl, lifting the hairs on her arms, tightening her nipples, readying her.

She did, raising her lids with difficulty. His expression was chiseled with the force of his need, his eyes slitted and intent as he watched her. Beneath her, his finger insinuated itself deeper with a rhythmic thrust. She gasped, arching away as the edge of pain blended with the cusp of pleasure, finding nowhere to go that felt as good, coming back as he centered her with a dual pulse of his finger and his hips, desire ripping at her simultaneously from front and back, demanding satisfaction.

"Has anyone taken you here yet?"

The question hovered in the heat between them, shimmering with possibilities.

She shook her head, torn between intrigue and fear.

It would hurt, had to hurt, but her body ignored logic, weeping with anticipation, following his lead as he maintained the pressure, her pussy twitching with anticipation as her ass flowered to his attention.

"It won't fit," she gasped.

The smile that touched his mouth was knowing as she clenched around him, hungry for whatever he would give.

"Yes, it will. Slow and easy, little by little until you want to explode from the pleasure."

His head dipped, blocking out the light, leaving only the impression of his satisfaction. The sheets rustled a protest as he smoothed his hand over her ass, away from the ache he'd created, leaving her bereft. "But not today."

Despair battled with relief, releasing from her in a high-pitched whimper that flowed into his chuckle as he fitted his lips to hers, rubbing lightly, teasing her with the heat of his breath and a ghost of sensation. He stroked first one corner of her mouth and then the other. She dug her nails into his shoulders, drawing him to her. Another chuckle and then his tongue smoothed along the seam of her lips, tickling unbearably.

A shake of his head punctuated his "Uh-uh" when she would have pulled away. His thumb and forefinger caught her chin, keeping her put as a bolt of pure lust drove deep into her core where it coiled and grew, magnifying the anticipation. "Open."

With an incoherent cry, she opened her mouth for his possession, taking his thrust deep, bracing herself for the choking roughness she'd been taught by others, finding instead a controlled wildness that called up an equally wild response from within. His fingertips pressed between her shoulder blades, arching her up as he kissed his way down, nibbling at her lips, her chin, her throat. His other hand tugged the buttons on her nightgown. The next kiss nestled into the hollow of her throat, finding the frantic tattoo of her pulse, measuring it, encouraging it until the rapid beat became part of the moment, throbbing under her skin, echoing in her ears.

He moved lower still, riding the curve of her torso until his chin rested in the valley between her breasts, the rasp of his evening beard was one more stimulus in an overcharged moment. His hand slid under the placket of her nightgown, his skin impossibly dark as he pushed the material aside, not stopping until the soft linen cupped beneath her breast, pressing it in and up, toward his mouth.

"Now, there's a pretty sight."

She looked. Her nipple was taut and red, the white flesh beneath plump and lush in the golden lamplight. His gaze caught hers. "Just one thing missing."

She wasn't stupid enough to ask what, even if she could have found her voice. It didn't matter. His lips parted and she caught a glimpse of his tongue, his teeth. Heaven and hell. She pushed against his shoulder, uncertainty blending with anticipation. "Caine?"

"Right here."

"Here" was a fraction of an inch away from the vulnerable tip. He caught her hands, manacling them with one of his, separating from his goal long enough to drag them over her head and press them to the mattress. She tugged. He didn't let go. Just smiled.

"Stay put, darling."

She didn't have a choice. The thigh he threw over hers pinned her legs. A quick kiss on her lips and he was moving back down. She strained to see, morbidly obsessed with watching it happen. All she could see was the top of his head getting closer to her chest. She squeezed her eyes shut as her fingers found the ridge in her wrist and rubbed it like a talisman, remembering too late what she'd invited. Pleasure and pride disappeared in a torrent of dread. "Oh, God. Please. Don't. Don't."

She couldn't bear it.

Caine stilled. Against her thigh his cock stretched and throbbed in an offbeat echo to her own racing pulse. One second stretched to the next. He didn't move. Didn't even seem to breathe. Hope rose and then he bent. From one heartbeat to the next she went from hope to terror. His mouth closed over her nipple. She screamed, anticipating the agony of the bite, drowning in the horror, yanking at her arms, twisting in his grip. She had to get free.

"Jesus, Mary and Joseph!" The curse sliced into her terror, splitting it into two entities—one that demanded fight and the other that craved flight. Neither was possible. He was too strong. She couldn't get away. She flinched as he rose, ducking the blow that was coming.

Another curse and then her name rapped out in a sharp imperative. She struggled harder.

She got her hands free, but he grabbed them again when she went for his eyes with her nails, pressing the backs into the mattress. He held her until exhaustion took the strength from her resolve, the sounds he was making slowly shaping into syllables as she panted for breath, and finally comprehensible words. "Easy, Desi girl."

It wasn't what he said, but the way he said it that gave her pause. She'd heard men talk to wild horses that way, gentling them. She'd never heard a man use that tone on a woman.

She opened her eyes, blinking against the hair tangled over them. He was watching her, his expression inscrutable. His mouth was a tight, straight line in his face. His grip on her wrists loosened. "All done?"

She nodded, drained by the futility of effort. She'd been kidding herself by thinking she could win against him.

He released her left wrist, bracing his weight on his right forearm as he brushed the hair away from her cheek. His finger skimmed her temple, oddly enough making her think of the kiss he'd placed there earlier.

"I'm your husband, Desi."

"I know." Her voice was hoarse from her screams.

"I'm thinking that doesn't mean much to you yet, but to me that means it's my job to stand between you and anyone or anything that would hurt you."

She didn't know what to say so she just lay there, drawing air into her burning lungs.

"Even my own base urges."

He brought her right wrist up to his mouth, pressing his lips against the reddened area hard enough that she knew he felt the evidence of the break. The cold, deadly rage in his gaze belied the gentleness of his drawl as he said, "Now, why don't you tell me about the man who liked to hear you scream."

"Please…"

"Please what?"

Please fuck her, hurt her, ignore her, anything but make her remember him. "Don't bring him into this."

"He's been in this since the first day we met, and I'm damn sick and tired of it."

"I'm sorry."

"I don't want you sorry. I want you honest so I know where the fears are lurking to ambush me."

"I'm not doing it on purpose."

His hand tightened on her head, the other tucked

behind her back. "Never said you were, but you've got to admit, we've had some problems."

Problems he wouldn't have had if he'd married a woman without her history. Problems he wouldn't have had if he weren't an honorable man who kept his promises. She curled her fingers into fists. "I'll do better."

If it killed her, she'd do better.

Caine sighed and rolled onto his back, draping her over him, tucking her knees up. His palm kept her face pressed to his chest. Beneath her ear, she could hear the beat of his heart, faster than normal but steady. Between her legs, his cock. Equally steady. She scooted down, pressing him closer. She'd much rather have him make love to her than question her. The small smack on her butt scooted her right back up. But strangely, not with fear. That spank had seemed more play than anger.

"None of that now. We need to talk."

She was half tempted to try it again to see what happened. She inched down. "There's nothing to talk about."

His hand cupped her rear, halting her efforts. "I might not be an expert on women, Gypsy, but even I know this isn't something you can do better at. Not with you having so many open wounds inside where I can't see, and me unknowingly bringing the salt to rub in them."

She rested her cheek on her hands. "Why do you always have to be right?"

"Because it beats the heck out of being wrong?"

She bet it did. "Someday, I'm going to be the one who's right."

"You going to make me eat shoe leather when you are?"

It took her a moment to figure out what the little tugs in her hair were. He was playing with the ends. Lazily, as if his body wasn't throbbing under hers. As if he wasn't waiting on an answer to a question that was important to him. He was giving her time to work up her courage. She didn't kid herself that he'd let her get away without answering, but he understood she needed time. She rubbed her finger over the scar beneath her palm. "No."

"What are you going to do?"

"Just be shocked by the novelty of it."

His laugh jostled her up and down. "I bet you'll think of a way to rub my nose in it."

"Maybe." But she couldn't see herself wanting to. No one had ever made her feel as Caine did. As if she mattered for herself. As if her happiness mattered to him on a level she couldn't see. A level she didn't trust. To him, she seemed to be more than disposable. And she owed him. More than the truth, but that was all he was asking for. She took a breath. And then another. And another. Each one shorter than the last, each one not giving her what she needed.

"Breathe, sweetheart."

She shook her head. "I...just...want...it...over... with."

Both hands moved to her back, the surfaces of his fingers were rough, but the sweeps of his hands gentle. "So do I, but I don't want you losing air on the way. You need the sack?"

He'd kept one handy since that first attack.

She shook her head. She was not going to breathe into a bag in front of him. "Just...allow...me...a...minute."

"I've got all night."

The night was almost gone and he hadn't slept any of it. Yet she knew he'd be up at first light working. And then he'd be tired. She closed her eyes, willing the panic away. One minute stretched to two and then five. Her breathing eased.

"I gather this was one bad character."

She nodded.

"He yell a lot?"

She shook her head and cleared her throat. "The others always yelled and blustered, but he always spoke in a very clear, cultured voice. Even when he was hurting me, he never raised it."

His hand stroked her hair from crown to ends. "Guess we don't have to worry about you mixing me up with him that way. I can kick up a fuss when the occasion warrants it."

"No."

"So, how do you mix us up?"

"It's important to you that I do things right."

"Right in as how I want it?"

"Yes."

His hand paused at her shoulders. "So when I give you orders, you start hearing someone else."

It wasn't that easy. She shrugged, not knowing how to explain it.

"I'm not counting that as an answer."

"Sometimes I just get confused in my mind between what I want to do and what parts of me scream for me to do. Sometimes I can't even tell what's real and what's not."

His hand resumed stroking. "Like when I went to kiss your breasts just now. You wanted it at first."

She nodded, heat flooding her cheeks, her chest tightening. "Yes."

"Then what happened?"

"I saw your teeth."

"Shit."

No wonder she'd gone loco. Caine slid his hand under her hair, needing the contact with her skin. A man could do a lot of damage to a woman with his teeth. "I'm bossy, sweetheart, but I don't hurt women."

"I know." That hint of a nod. "But sometimes you forget."

Again that tension preceding that little nod. "This bastard that hurt you, can you describe him for me?"

"Just his shoes."

He didn't think he'd ever been with a woman who could only describe his shoes after the encounter. "Nothing more?"

She squirmed, and then in a thread of sound said, "And his privates."

Now, there was a picture for a wanted poster. Shoes, balls and a dick. "No face?"

Her fingers wrapped around her wrist and rubbed. "He didn't come that often and when he did, I wasn't allowed to look at him."

"Ever?"

"No."

He rolled them over, easing her back onto the bed. He couldn't get the thought of a man biting her breasts out of his head. She let go of her wrist and grabbed the sheet.

He stilled the attempt. "No. I want to see."

It just took a little tug and the white sheet slipped from her fingers. "And just so we're clear, I don't want to see to humiliate you or embarrass you. I just want to see that you're all right."

"I'm fine."

He kissed her wrist where it lay against her shoulder before taking each hand and laying them up by her head. "Keep them there."

She did, but her lips slipped between her teeth. The light wasn't good enough to tell much. Her skin was so white it'd be hard to find a scar short of sunlight but her nipples were a bright pink, still semipuckered from his earlier attention. He touched his finger to the tip. She gave a light gasp.

"Did he bite you here?"

Her face flushed brighter, if that were possible. "Why can't you let it go?"

He looked up. Damn, she was serious. "You're my wife."

"But I wasn't then."

"You're not thinking that just because someone took advantage of you before we met that he gets to just walk away now that you have a man to stand for you, are you?"

It was clear as day from the widening of her eyes and the lack of verbal response that she did. He kept his voice normal as he set her to rights.

"No one, but no one, gets to hurt you and then walk away."

"You can't go back and find them all."

He touched the faint line that could be a scar on her areola. "Like hell I can't."

Her hand covered his despite his order to keep them put. As if taking the scar from his sight would do anything to settle his determination. "It's over with."

It wouldn't be over with until every one of the bastards were buzzard food. Caine met her gaze, letting her see the determination rolling through him. "I've spent my whole life kicking ass and it'll be a cold day in hell before I change my ways when my wife's the one hurt."

"They'll kill you."

"They're welcome to try."

Her fingers wrapped around his. "No, they're not." It was his turn to blink. She could change moods faster than a cutting horse could turn.

"You have to understand, Caine, these are very dangerous men."

She was worried about him. He dropped a kiss on her lips.

"Sweetheart, you aren't exactly married to an angel."

"But you haven't met them."

"That'll be set to rights soon."

She squeezed the feeling right out of his fingers. "They've taken everything from me, I'm not letting them take you, too."

If he wasn't mistaken, she'd just told him she cared for him. Damn she could pick her moments. "It isn't a matter of letting, sweetheart, it's a matter of setting things right."

"No, it's a matter of common sense, and if you aren't going to exercise any, then I'll just have to exercise some for you."

He braced himself on his elbow. "Damn, if you don't mean that."

"Of course I mean it."

If her frown got any bigger she was going to have permanent creases. "Would you, by any chance, be ordering me to let it go?"

She folded her arms across her chest and eyed him suspiciously. "Would that work?"

"No. But I'd be touched that you tried."

"Then I'm just going to have to try something else, and you'll have to be touched by that."

His smile caught him by surprise. He was used to cajoling a woman in bed but he couldn't ever remember a time when he'd sparred with one between the sheets. He touched his finger to the vein at her temple. "You're welcome to give it a shot."

"You don't think I can do it?"

"I think you can do a lot of things, Gypsy girl, but getting me to forget about the son of a bitch who broke your wrist so he could get off isn't one of them." He kissed her gently, being careful to keep his weight off her because he knew for sure that triggered memories. "In that, you don't have a prayer in hell."

Her mouth flowered beneath his, kissing him back, clinging with near desperation, telling him what she couldn't say. She needed him.

When he came up for air he whispered, "I'm not walking away, Desi, and no one's taking me away, so relax and let this marriage happen."

"You promise?"

Even though they both knew it wasn't a promise he could keep, he gave it to her for the simple reason she needed it. "I promise."

Her hands spread over his back, pulling him to her, "Then make me feel good, Caine."

16

"How good? 'Like a lady' good or 'like a woman' good?"

"What's the difference?"

"One's a hell of a lot more fun."

If Caine thought to throw her off with straight talk, he was mistaken. She pursed her lips and cocked her head to the side. "I was a lady for a lot of years and never had much fun, so I'm thinking, 'like a woman' good."

"Damn, I love it when you bring your wild side out to play."

"You think I have a wild side?"

"I think you're wild, passionate and everything else a man could want."

"You're a very strange man."

"Now is that any way to go talking about your husband?"

Her arms linked around his neck, pulling him toward her.

He braced his arm on the other side of her. "No."

"But—"

He shook his head. "No reminders."

Her gaze skated over his. "That's going to be hard to accomplish."

"You thinking you know all there is to know about lovemaking because of what they did to you?"

That was a definite "yes" in her eyes. He rolled them back to the middle of the bed, stopping with her on top. Her little gasp as she ended up straddling his cock, along with the lowering of her lids, was as sexy as hell.

She was clearly unfamiliar with this position. Probably because it gave her freedom, and a sense of freedom was something her captors wouldn't have wanted to encourage in her. He tugged the blankets from beneath them and then freed her from the nightgown. He wanted her as wild as he could get her. "Lift up."

A little smack on her right buttock had her moving with an alacrity that had those breasts shimmying. Her legs were just long enough for her hips to clear his, making it a tricky process to get his pants down, but once he got going, he could see the benefits. With every push, the damp, silky-soft heat of her pussy caressed the back of his hands.

He shoved his pants past his knees and kicked them free of his bare feet. His cock throbbed, jerked up, seeking her heat. He put his hands on her hips, holding her gaze.

"Sink down now, sweetheart. Bring that petal-soft pussy down over me."

She did, biting her lips, fear and temptation in those big blue eyes. Her muscles clenched, locking him out.

He brought his hand up to her cheek. "Tonight I want you to hold on to one thought. What happens between us is happening between a husband and a wife. And it's for *our* pleasure."

She blushed and her gaze ducked his.

"What?" He touched his thumb to the corner of her mouth.

"I'm worried I'm not going to do this right."

"So am I, so that's just one more thing we have in common."

That pulled her up short. "You're worried?"

"Sure. Why wouldn't I be? Every woman's different and a man who can't please his wife has a lot to lose."

"You expect to please me?"

"Definitely." He slid his cock up along the warm nest she'd created, tilting her hips with his hand until he felt the little tip of her clit stroke him, too. "Do you like that?"

"It's fine."

"Fine" seemed to be the adjective she applied to anything that didn't hurt. Except she was enjoying this. The proof was in the spill of her cream around him.

"Do you want me to do it again?"

"If you like."

Oh, he liked. He liked the way she shuddered on the upstroke, and the way her breath broke on the down, suspending in her lungs in an agony of anticipation until he returned to the rhythm. The way her fingers dug into his shoulders as she pushed back, seeking more. Oh, yes. He definitely liked.

He did it again, and again, sliding her along his cock, bathing himself in the liquid fire, watching as, all the while, she fought it. The pleasure. The surrender. Her lip slid between her teeth as the cream slid from her body. Her muscles contracted in a rhythmic prelude to release, but there wasn't any anticipation in her eyes, just that same breathless struggle between what her body wanted and what she couldn't accept.

He pulled her face to his, kissing her lips, taking her little squeaks into his mouth, smiling at the pitch of her last.

"Stay with me now," he whispered, before bringing his

mouth toward her breast, stopping an inch away, giving her a chance to adjust. She went stiff as a board. Fear or anticipation?

The answer came as Desi closed that distance, bridging that gap in a leap of faith that humbled him. He opened his mouth and accepted the fragile gift, curling his tongue around the hard peak in a gentle hug. Her gasp was his reward, along with a soft "Oh, yes" as he began to suck. Her hand came to his cheek, holding his mouth to the angle that pleased, shyness fading under passion. Damn, he loved her like this.

Urgency gathered in the base of his spine, different than before, hotter, laden with potent embers of emotion he'd identify if passion weren't riding him so hard. Releasing her breast, he lifted her forward and up. "I need you, Desi. Don't hold back."

Her lashes flickered under the lash of truth, but he didn't see distaste in her expression, just a deepening of the confusion as he coaxed her up. He took his hand off her hip and grasped his cock, pushing it back along that slick temptation, his breath hissing in a harsh rasp as all that heat and wetness tore at his control.

Her hair slid free of her braid and tumbled around them. The scent of lilacs and Desi filled his next breath.

He held her gaze and let her see his excitement, his restraint, his passion. A slow blink heralded the arrival of his cock at its destination. The delicate muscles clenched in an intimate kiss. The pressure in his balls built. He wanted her to go with him. Wanted this to be more than a fulfilling of an obligation for her.

He rubbed the petal-soft skin of her cheek. "What's going through that head of yours, Desi girl?"

"I don't know who you are."

"I'm your husband."

"But what does that mean?"

He pressed up while urging her down, keeping it slow and steady, watching her face for signs of discomfort. "It means you're not alone anymore."

Her frown got deeper. Pain?

"Am I hurting you?"

Her hair whipped across his chest in taunting little flicks of sensation as she shook her head.

He had to exert more pressure to keep her face to his.

"Then what's wrong."

"I…"

Her muscles gave up the unequal battle. His cock popped the first inch into that tight inferno.

"Oh!"

Her eyes closed. So did his. The white-hot pleasure whipped through him, summoning the threads of passion and spinning them into a blistering need for satisfaction. She was as tight as he remembered. Hot, sweet and melting around him, the inner muscles rippling in tiny repercussions to his possession.

He tested the point of their joining. The delicate skin felt paper-thin. He gritted his teeth against the instinctive urge to plunge deep. To claim her hard and fast. He gave a tentative pulse of his hips. The skin pulled in with his cock. Desi gave a soft little cry.

Pain? Pleasure? He couldn't be sure. Son of a bitch, he should have prepared her better. He'd never been with a woman so small before. The fan of her lashes against her cheeks emphasized the slightly exotic cast to her face.

"Am I hurting you, Desi?"

Another small shake of her head that coincided with the ripple that went through her body. He pulled back, her soft cry cutting his withdrawal short.

"Are you all right?"

Another shake of the head. He needed to see her expression. "Open your eyes."

A sharp squeeze of her chin punctuated the order. Her lashes lifted slowly, languorously, revealing the eyes of a woman confused by the response of her own body.

"There's my wild Gypsy." The smile started deep inside. "Now, let's see if I can find that sweet spot that makes you feel so good."

He stretched his thumb inward, sifting through the damp curls, finding her sensitive little clit, watching her eyes the whole time. She flinched at his first touch and those inner muscles fluttered along the head of his cock. His balls burned and cramped in response, eager to give her what she wanted. The second touch didn't get a reaction at all. Neither did the third. The hesitantly eager glow of anticipation began to fade from her expression. Worry took its place.

He wasn't worried. "Easy, sweetheart."

"It's not working anymore."

"Everything's working fine." She just needed a stronger touch now that he had her attention. The next pass had a little more force, enough so the callus on his thumb grazed her harder. She jerked and gasped and took a bit more. "See?"

He didn't expect a response and he didn't get one. All her attention was inward, concentrating on the whip of pleasure he was sending her with his thumb. He made his next pass slower, incrementally harder. Her moan was the sweetest music. "That's it, Gypsy. Let me hear you, see you. Let me know how much you enjoy everything I do to you."

Her hips rocked over him. She strained for more. His cock throbbed with the same rhythm and the same need.

He waited for her to take him deeper with every pass of his thumb, but it didn't happen. It was almost as if she didn't connect the pleasure he was giving her with his hand, with the pleasure he could give her with his cock.

"Desi," he gasped as she clenched desperately around him, her hot little cries ringing in his ears. "Take me inside you this time. Every time you feel that spike that feels so good, work yourself down on me."

For an instant, her gaze focused, and in that brief span of time he saw lust, confusion and a desperate hope. Damn, he wanted to fill that hope, fill her with pleasure, confidence, security. This time when he touched her, he lingered and pressed, urging her back and down even as she shuddered and took him.

"That's it. Just like that. Again."

He gave and she took, working herself down on him inch by erotic inch, her body first fighting and then welcoming his possession until she finally had everything he had to give and there was no telling where he ended and she began. He took her clit between his thumb and forefinger and tugged at the same instant he thrust up, lifting her off the bed with his need, driving hard and sure, milking her as she milked him. Pleasure so intense as to be painful held him in its relentless grip until he couldn't hold back. But he had to. She came first. Always.

"Come with me, Desi. Let yourself go, sweetheart. Let go."

He wanted to hear that soft little cry of his name again as she came, hear that feminine acknowledgment that she knew who he was, who gave her this. The next caress should have brought her to the edge, left her teetering as she was, but instead she tightened around him, against him, and he felt it—her distancing herself from the magic surrounding them. He felt it, but was helpless to stop it. Not when she lifted off him and then came back down—hard, fast, riding him in a way guaranteed to steal a man's patience—and she stole his in three strong pulses of her hips, her eyes echoing the sadness he felt inside as his orgasm rushed over him.

He shook his head at her, gritting his teeth as he came, pulling her down, sealing their bodies together, flooding her with his seed, giving her his pleasure, not letting her escape that, at least.

17

That damn rooster was going to meet its maker.

Desi scattered a bit more grain on the ground, coaxing the hens out of the house. From the edge of the enclosure, the rooster watched, head canted to the right, comb flopped over, staring balefully at her out of one small beady eye. She threw some more corn to the side, trying to lure him away from the edge of the pen. He didn't move, but the fluff of his feathers meant business. So did she.

Desi gripped the basket handle in both hands. The damn bird—she repeated the curse because it felt so good—had forced her to stay up late last night sewing the gashes he'd put in her clothes. And when Caine had asked her why, she'd been forced to lie. He already saw her as a useless bit of fluff in need of pampering. She was not confirming it by admitting that a ten-pound rooster had defeated her. If Tia didn't swear the hens wouldn't lay without the rooster around, she would have gladly wrung his neck. Not that she'd worked up to that skill yet, but for him, the bald-eyed bully, she'd give it a try.

The rooster strutted forward, wings twitching, tail feathers spread. There was a definite attitude to his approach, a confidence that shouldn't be there considering the differences in their size and the fact that she was setting his feathered butt in the stew pot as soon as a new rooster came up. A confidence that was only there because he'd won yesterday's skirmish.

She jerked her sleeves down over her hands, grateful the men had bought her a dress that was too big. She needed armor to deal with his cocky ass.

Again she got that little thrill from using the profanity. Ladies did not use profanity. She'd been told that all her life. Neither did respectable wives, and lately she'd discovered why. Once a woman started, there wasn't any stopping, and why would she want to? Being able to vent anger so succinctly was wonderful. No swallowing it back, no lingering taste of bitterness, no polite smiles, just the releasing of an invective that was just...liberating.

In a much smaller way, it was almost as good as that first afternoon with Caine in the bath. But not as frightening. The way Caine could steal her will, her purpose, was the scariest thing she'd ever felt because if she let go she'd lose herself in him and nothing would be the same again. She'd never be the same, so while she didn't deny him his husbandly rights, she kept herself separate at the last.

She tightened her grip on the egg basket. It was getting harder to do that all the time, though. She might have a chance of resisting him forever, but it was getting harder and harder to fight herself. But she was strong, and she had a plan. Besides, nowhere in any book on comportment or in any salon conversation had she heard anyone say it was a woman's responsibility to enjoy it. Quite the opposite in fact. Only loose women enjoyed physical relations. And she was not loose.

She took a step toward the rooster. The hens around her feet clucked and shuffled away, diving back into the feed as soon as she was clear. Now, she just needed to convince Caine of that. It shouldn't be so hard, seeing as he saw her as a bit of fluff and was quite ready to believe all sorts of silly things about her. Like she couldn't do the same work as Tia. But in this area he had a blind spot. He was going to have to work on that, along with his expectations of how it should be between them. But seeing as how that wasn't going to happen for a long time, for now she'd just deal with the rooster.

It gave a cluck. She growled. It squawked. She approached. The wings came out. She raised the basket. When it reared its head, she snarled, "Not this time."

It screeched. She stood her ground.

"Those eggs are mine."

That put him in a tizzy. A god-awful racket came from its beak as it flew at her feet first. She swung the basket, knocking it aside. It hit the ground in a ball of huff and fluff, but she knew it'd be back. Yesterday had taught her that. It flew at her. She kicked out. It bounced up, spurring for her face.

If she could get into the henhouse, she could close the door and get the eggs. And if she didn't drop them like yesterday, she could learn to bake Caine's favorite cake. Yet another challenge to add to her repertoire. Desi was three steps from the door when she heard the flap of wings and the air fanning her hair. She spun, wielding the basket. She missed. Apparently she wasn't the only one who'd learned something. The rooster was right there, in her face. She screeched and ducked. He landed on her back, claws digging, beak pecking. A snarl came from the left and she went down under a heavy weight. Boone.

She jumped up. With a scream of rage, the rooster jumped off. With a snarl, Boone was after him. Desi slapped at her skirt and rubbed the bruises to her skull from the demon bird's beak. "Get him, Boone."

Boone had the advantage for about five feet, but the rooster jumped straight up, catching the hound by surprise. Before Boone could gather his feet under him, the rooster was on his shoulders, wings flapping, looking like the devil sprouting from his back. Boone's snarls turned to howls. With a yip he spun and headed back toward her, jowls flapping, big brown eyes wide with terror. And the rooster sticking to him like a burr.

"Oh, no." She grabbed the basket off the ground and sprinted for the henhouse. She yanked the door open. Behind her Boone howled. She debated, but she couldn't just leave him like that. Especially as he'd saved her.

She held the door open. "Come on, Boone."

He cleared the rickety ramp with one leap. Holding the basket like a shield she knocked the rooster off and then shut the door. Boone whined and looked around. Clearly he knew he wasn't supposed to be in here just as clearly as he knew what waited on them both outside that door. One angry, victorious rooster.

Desi gave him a pet and then went for the eggs. "We have got to do better than this in the future, Boone."

She put eggs in the basket as she went down the array of nests. No sense wasting the opportunity. "Otherwise Caine will be putting us both up for trade."

Boone whined and licked at a scratch on his shoulder.

She knew exactly how he felt. The pecks on the back of her head hurt like heck, and if she wasn't clever tonight, her husband would see the scratches stinging the back of her neck and ask questions she did not want to answer. The last roost was empty. She bit her lip. A bad layer became dinner. She glared at the door on the other side of which she could hear the rooster cackling. "Oh, sure, you've got all the time in the world to bother me, but when it comes to doing the rest of the job, pfft!"

There were no more eggs, which meant it was time to go back out. This is where she had run into trouble yesterday. Of course, yesterday, she hadn't had Boone with her. She patted his head. "You distract him while I get away with the eggs, all right?"

He looked at the door and then at her. His lower lids sagged down his cheeks.

"I'll save you an extra bone after dinner."

The end of his tail wagged.

"A big one."

He got to his feet. She grabbed the latch. "Ready?" His ears pricked forward. She listened, too. There wasn't any noise. Maybe the randy featherbrain had gone to fornicate with one of the hens. She lifted the latch. "Go, Boone!"

On a whine he burst out the door. She was right behind him for all of one step before he cut to the left, little more than a red streak, leaving her behind to face the red-feathered demon bird at the base of the ramp. Deserter! She was moving too fast to stop. She swore the rooster grinned as it sprang.

She swung the basket, wincing as the eggs rattled, throwing her hand up to guard her eyes, not slowing down, because for all his aggressiveness, the rooster had a territory and wouldn't leave it. She just needed to get outside it. "Get off me."

She shook her arm. He latched on to the basket rim. The rooster dug its claws in the basket, beating at her with his wings. She swatted at him. "I just need six eggs," you selfish bastard." He flapped and gained purchase. His beady little eyes fixed on her hand. "You can spare six!"

Tia said Caine loved spice cake and she'd already told him she was going to try her hand at making one. From the way he squawked and worked up toward her arm, there wasn't a selfless bone in the rooster's horrid body.

She swung and ran. He clung and pecked. Her hand was on fire. By sheer luck she hit his head. He fell off. But he bounced back. There was no way she'd make the last ten feet. She grabbed an egg and threw it at him. It missed. He came at her, talons spread. She landed the next egg right on his arrogant beak.

She ran and threw, he squawked and attacked, and when he hit that invisible line that was his territory, she whooped and shouted with victory. She'd made it. She looked in the basket, six eggs left. Just enough.

"Next time, I'll get them all!" she called, glaring at the bird now strutting across the yard. She turned, tripped on a rock and went down. There was no mistaking the sound of eggs breaking for anything other than what it was. Nor the sound of male laughter as she pushed to her feet.

Three men she didn't know were standing with Tucker and Ed, watching her, big grins on their beard-stubbled faces. Humiliation rose fast and furious as they touched the brims of their hats in greeting, fueling her anger, giving her something to latch her pride on to. She got to her feet, put her chin in the air and asked Tucker, "Where's Caine?"

He nodded toward the barn. "Working with that stallion we finally caught."

"Thank you." She dusted off her hands, nodded to the men and turned on her heel.

"I don't think he wants you in there," Ed added.

"Tough."

"When you catch up to him," one of the new men said, "tell him we found some of those wolves he was worried about."

She looked the man over. He was a touch shorter than Caine, whipcord lean with an aura of toughness that reached out in clear warning. "Who are you?"

He removed his smoke from the corner of his surprisingly sensual mouth. "Caden Steele, ma'am."

She looked to Tucker. "Is he Hell's Eight?"

"Yes."

"Then I'll deliver the message."

Right after she delivered one of her own.

The barn door was closed. From inside came the sound of nervous prancing and snorts, along with a steady, low murmur. Apparently Caine's day was going much better than hers. Desi shoved the door open so hard it slammed against the wall with a loud bang. "Caine Allen."

Snorts exploded into screams. Something hard pounded on wood in a rapid tattoo. Caine's curse was right behind. She headed toward the source of the commotion. "Caine!"

The door two stalls ahead exploded open as a body came flying out. It hit the floor with an "oof" and a cloud of dust.

It was Caine. She marched up to him. "Caine Allen!" He blinked up at her, a dazed expression on his face. She leaned over and picked a piece of hay out of his hair and then held out her hand to help him up. As he stood, she told him, "You are going to teach me to fight."

He was going to paddle her ass. It took only two steps to reach her side. Two completely normal steps to reach his extraordinary wife. He caught her arm as she swiped at her skirt. As always the delicacy of her amazed him. She was so different from him. Different even than Tia. She'd been born in softness, raised in gentleness, yet there wasn't an ounce of give to her resolve. As proud as any man on Hell's Eight, and able to give all of them a run for their money when it came to sheer grit. Ignoring her huff, he turned her and brushed the dirt and debris off her back. There was blood on the neck of her dress. And feathers caught in her hair. He had a good idea of what had gotten her dander up.

He let her spin back around, but not out of his grip. He tucked his finger under her chin, not just because he wanted her to understand how important this was, but because he liked to feel the softness of her skin. There wasn't anything else like it in the world.

"Don't you ever burst into the barn yelling when I'm working with a horse. You could get hurt."

Her eyebrows rose. "You were the one on your posterior in the dirt."

"Because you came in screeching."

"Go to hell."

The curse sent his eyebrows up. "You've been doing a lot of that lately."

"What?"

"Swearing."

She blinked and set her shoulders. "So?"

"I don't like it."

"Then plug your ears, because I've decided it's not fair you have all the benefits."

The retort made him want to smile again. He was going to have to take her in hand soon, but not yet. She was just finding her feet, testing limits. He'd give her enough room to play out the rough edges, then he'd rein her in. Maybe. Truth was, he liked watching the fire in her spark.

He stroked his thumb over her lips. "What's that supposed to mean?"

"It's just that I don't think it's fair that men have the release of swearing the moment they are mad while women don't."

"You ever think maybe you wouldn't need that release if you'd just let yourself go in bed?"

He dropped his hand to her arm and guided her toward the door. Her head turned right and left. It wasn't hard to figure out why. "There's no one in here but me and you."

She stopped and faced him. "Stop doing that!"

"What?"

She stamped her foot. "Knowing what I'm thinking before I say it."

"It's not like I have to work too hard. You don't exactly have a poker face."

Her mouth worked. Her arm muscles tightened and, to his horror, a sheen of tears glistened on the edges of her glare.

"Go to hell."

He'd take umbrage with that order if he didn't think it would shatter the last of her control. He sighed and let go of her arm. "I've already been there and have never had a hankering to go back."

She stepped back, rubbing the spot where he'd held her. "It might be time for a revisit. It could be you'll find you fit in there just fine now."

He shook his head and motioned to her arm. "Did I hurt you?"

He thought he'd been careful, but there was no telling. Skin like hers probably bruised easily.

Her jaw worked. "No. I'm not so delicate that your hand on my arm left a mark."

He'd have her pull the shoulder of her dress down to prove it if those tears weren't hovering. He made a mental note to check her arm tonight in bed. "Uh-huh." He motioned to the wide-open door. "So what brought you barging in here?"

Her chin came up. "I want you to teach me to fight."

"Now?"

"Right now."

He looked over at her. "Any particular reason?"

Her arms crossed. "I'm sick of being at the mercy of everyone on this ranch."

Anger slid neatly between weariness and the pleasure he got from just being around her. "Has someone been bothering you?"

He couldn't think of a single person on Hell's Eight who would show his wife anything but proper respect, but sometimes, a man's lust overrode his common sense and Desi was the type of woman to put a lot of lust into a man.

Her nod of acknowledgment solidified his rage to a cold hard knot. He had promised her she'd be safe here. "Who?"

"You're hurting me."

He hadn't even realized he'd moved, but he had her shoulders in his hands and he was almost lifting her off the floor. Damn, she made mincemeat of his self-control. "Give me the bastard's name." He'd be dead before sundown.

"That demon rooster."

It took a second for the information to work through to his brain. "Cantankerous?"

"Yes, he's cantankerous, and mean and vicious and he's standing between me and my cooking lesson."

"You want me to teach you to fight Cantankerous?"

"That's his name?"

"Yes."

She nodded. "Then yes, I want you to teach me to fight Cantankerous and James and anything else that comes my way."

"Why?" He needed the why. This was the first time she'd come to him for something for herself, and he needed her to tell him why. Needed her to trust him that much.

"Because I'm damn tired of always losing."

He could understand that. "So is there a time limit on how fast I need to teach you to take on all comers?"

"As fast as possible."

He motioned to the small white feather clinging to her hair. "So how many rounds did you go with Cantankerous?"

"Four."

He raised his eyebrows. She had guts. "Did you win any?"

Her mouth set in a disgusted purse. "Not once."

But she'd kept coming back. "You ever think of just asking for help?"

Her fingers dug into her forearms. "No."

He shook his head and settled his hat. "You are stubborn."

"I'm persistent when necessary."

Heck, he even liked the way she talked, in short clipped words with enunciated vowels. So different than the slow drawls or singsong accents he was used to. "It would have been easier to ask for help."

"I'm not incompetent."

"Uh-huh." He caught her hand and tugged her in. When he pushed her sleeve up, he saw the peck marks. Red punctures surrounded by the start of bruising. His gut twisted and something hard and hot like anger rose. "Didn't Tia tell you about the pacifier?"

"The what?"

"Corn." He caught her hand. "C'mon."

He didn't give her a choice, just tugged her along behind him until they got to the feed bin. Beside it sat a crudely shaped, red-cloth silhouette of a chicken that had been stuffed with husks. It rustled as he picked it up. "This is the pacifier."

"A stuffed toy?"

"Yup." He headed back out of the gloom of the shed into the sun. As soon as he got to the hen yard, he tossed the toy to the left. Cantankerous was on it in a second, squawking, hollering, pecking and then humping.

"He's, he's…" Desi seemed stuck for words. A blush rose up her cheeks. She yanked her hand from his. "You bribe him with relations?"

He shrugged, waiting for her to make a connection. "It works."

"You think—" a wave of her hand indicated the happy rooster "—that solves everything."

"It does simplify things."

Her eyes narrowed. "They're just animals."

"Last I checked, so is a man."

Her hands landed on her hips. "You do not want me to try and seduce you to get my way."

"What makes you so sure?"

"Because…"

She didn't seem to have a ready answer. He plucked a feather off her sleeve. He let it drift to the ground. She watched it float and then land. Her shoulders squared. "Because that would be scandalous!"

"And you being scandalous would be a problem for me?" He had no idea where she got her ideas, but they were normally ass backward. And this one wasn't a bit different.

"Of course."

"Why?" His cock was hard just at the thought of her thinking about being scandalous.

She darted a gaze around the open yard. "This is not the place to discuss this."

He'd ask why again, but he knew. Because she worried someone would overhear. She worried that someone would think the worst. She apparently spent a good part of her day worrying. And her night fighting. Him. He sighed and grabbed her hand, calling across the yard, "Tucker?"

"Yeah."

"Could you check on Devil?"

"I'll get him settled."

"Thanks."

He spun on his heel.

"Where are we going?"

"To someplace private."

"Why?"

"To talk."

Desi braced her feet. "About what?"

He barely felt the resistance. The kitchen door came into his line of sight. Coffee sounded good. "About your hurting yourself for no reason."

Her feet slipped. He pulled her into his side, switching his grip to her waist. "I didn't want to bother you."

"You don't want to bother me, love me, enjoy me, which makes me wonder why you're so damn determined to please me." He clasped her waist in his hands and popped her up onto the porch. "Everywhere but the one place it matters."

She spun around as if he'd put a bullet in her butt. "In bed?"

Two steps and he was beside her, working with her natural tendency to keep his face in view, he kissed her lips as he leaned across and opened the door. He pushed her through. "Yes."

Tia took one look at the fury on Desi's face as they came into the kitchen and stopped stirring the contents of the pot bubbling on the stove. Her second glance encompassed his groin. Her lips twitched. She placed the lid on the pot. "I am going to take a nap."

Caine nodded. His "I'd appreciate it" easily overrode Desi's "There's no need."

Tia disappeared through the door on an echo of laughter while Caine dropped the bar on the outside door. Desi spun around so fast her skirts belled out and then wrapped around her legs. Her gaze locked on his groin. He could see the pulse pounding in her throat. "There's definitely a need."

He sat her in the closest chair. When she would have sprung back to her feet, he pushed her down. "Just sit."

He grabbed two mugs and a towel. Coffee was always sitting on the stove. He wrapped the towel around the handle of the pot and filled the cups—hers only halfway because she preferred it diluted with sugar and cream. He brought the cups over to the table. Reaching into the sugar bowl he grabbed three chunks and dropped them into her mug. The splash of hot coffee stung his hand.

The small pain barely penetrated his anger. He was not pleased with her and he saw no reason to pretend otherwise.

She popped up. "I'll get the cream."

"Sit."

She subsided back in the chair, watching him warily for the short time it took him to get a spoon and to skim a cup of that morning's cream from the milk bucket. And he got the salve. He brought the items back and set them on the table in front of her. She jumped as the spoon clattered on the table.

His frustration boiled over. "Goddamn it, that's enough!"

Desi started so badly her chair rattled, but that chin came up and those gorgeous say-everything eyes didn't flinch from his.

"I've given you no cause to fear me. You're my wife."

She shrugged. "For however long you want."

Jesus H. Christ, was that what she thought? "If that's the case, how come you haven't been working harder at keeping me happy."

"I've never told you no."

"But you've never welcomed me, either."

Except for that first night. He couldn't get the memory of that first night out of his head, which went a long way to adding to his frustration.

She stared at him for a full minute, all the emotion churning inside visible in those big blue eyes. Fear, want, fear, frustration, fear, hunger and then that blank, protective nothing that she thought fooled everyone. "I can't be the woman you want me to be."

"You already are. You just need to accept it." He reached for the salve.

"What's that?"

He didn't miss the way her eyes flicked to his cock before her lips slipped between her teeth. He sighed. "Salve for the cuts Cantankerous left, Gypsy, nothing more."

Her shoulders visibly slumped with relief. And that ticked him off. She'd enjoyed her time with him. Why would she think the next would be different? "Don't worry. When I get around to claiming your ass, you'll get plenty of notice."

He grabbed the jar and stood as she gasped at the crudity of his flat statement. All the color had leeched from her face, and her eyes were huge. He refused to feel guilty for it. "Don't look so shocked. Underneath, all men are the same—just waiting to pounce."

The small shake of her head disturbed the current of his rage. "Not you."

"You have a strange way of showing it if you really believe that." He directed her with of flick of his finger. "Move your hair out of the way."

She pulled her braid over her shoulder. There was an angry scratch on her neck. He stopped himself a second before he touched her skin. As mad as he was, he didn't want to inadvertently hurt her. "He got you good here."

And that pissed him off more. She'd suffered because she wouldn't come to him. "Next time you ask me when something doesn't seem to be going right."

Her whispered "I'm sorry" barely penetrated the anger hazing his thoughts.

"I'm spending altogether too much time making you safe for you to put yourself at risk out of nothing more than sheer stubbornness."

The muscles under his fingertips tensed. Over Desi's head, he could see her fingers curl around the spoon.

This time her tone wasn't so soft. "I was doing what you told me to do."

"Which was?"

"You told me to learn."

"And that means you can't ask for help when you need it?"

The salve melted into the heat of her skin, the light shine enhancing the vulnerability to her nape and the vivid red cut that marred it.

The answer rapped out short and sweet. "I did."

"When?"

"In the barn."

When she'd burst in hollering, scaring the bejeezus out of him and the stallion had busted loose and almost gotten to her. After she'd been cut up by Cantankerous. He touched an older scar just to the right. More than once. Nothing she did made sense. "Desi girl, this place you come from, what exactly did you do there?"

The fingers clenching the spoon tightened. "Nothing important."

Judging from where Cantankerous had sunk his claws, she had to have been pecked on her head. Caine sifted through her hair with his fingertips, finding the spots easily. Tank had nailed her five times. He put the salve on the table and parted her hair. "Care to elaborate?"

"No." The set of her chin was as mulish as her tone. He smoothed the salve into the small puncture. "If I hazard a guess, will you be mad?"

Her immediate agreement stirred his humor into the crazy mix of his emotions. "Well, prepare yourself for a temper tantrum."

She didn't look up as she asked, just grasped that spoon. "Why do you do this?"

"Do what?"

"Push and pry at things better left alone?"

He placed salve on the last three peck marks. "Maybe because I don't think they're best left alone."

"Because you're not happy?"

He wiped his hand on the towel. "I admit the fact that you're not making me happy has something to do with it."

She turned and glared at him. "You're not making me happy, either."

He eyed the spoon she held in her hand like a dagger. There was a whole lot of rage in that tight grip. "There's also that. Which would be why I'm always poking and prying, as you call it. And—" he poured the cream into her coffee "—why I'm going to hazard a guess that your main job was looking pretty."

The spoon twisted and then speared into the coffee cup. "I did it very well."

He replaced the mug of cream on the table. "Seeing as I could spend all day looking at you without wearing out my eyes, I'm going to bet you did, but that might have been something for you to tell me earlier."

"Why? So you can convince yourself I'm even more useless?"

He turned his chair around and straddled it, resting his arm across the back as he studied her. There was a light flush on her creamy cheeks and her pulse was pounding in her throat twice normal speed. She was agitated, but damn if he could tell whether it was from fear, anger or desire. She took a sip of her coffee. The rapid blinking of her eyes could have been from the heat of the beverage, or it could have been tears.

He hooked his finger under her chin and lifted her face to his. Sure enough, her eyes were wet and this close, there was no missing the lines of strain radiating outward from the edges. "Ah, hell."

She was upset.

Her eyes narrowed and her lips flattened to a straight line, and that fast, all signs of vulnerability fled her expression.

"Just because my family had a lot of money doesn't mean I'm useless. I can learn."

He just wanted to snatch her up and hold her close, but as prickly as she was, she'd probably slap his head off for the attempt. "I've never considered you useless, Desi."

"But you've never considered me useful, either."

She had him there. "And you need me to think of you as useful?"

"Yes."

"So I won't send you away when the time comes?" She nodded as if that clarified everything.

"And this coming time, when is it?"

She didn't answer immediately, and he didn't let her hide from him by ducking her head. Which actually, beyond one little attempt, didn't seem to be her main inclination. The spoon hit the table with a thud. "When they come for me."

"You're expecting them to come?"

"He won't let me go."

"*He* already has. We're married."

The look she gave him was pitying, as if he didn't understand something basic. "That won't matter to him."

"Sweetheart, in your mind he might be the biggest, baddest hombre to cross the San Antonio, but in reality, he's just a man."

If she'd argued, he would have felt better. Instead, she

just stared at him. Clearly, she felt the mystery man was invulnerable. He tucked a tendril of hair off her cheek and came at her from another angle.

"What makes you so sure, even if he comes, that I'll let you go?"

She didn't flinch from the question, didn't flinch from his stare. She just watched him in that unnaturally quiet way and said, "Because he'll hurt those you love until you do."

He could see she believed that to the bottom of her soul. He let the knowledge sink in, sorted through it, weighed it. Tried to imagine how such terrifying certainty would color the way he saw things. How he did things. The decisions he made.

He picked up her coffee and handed it to her. "He'll come after Tia and the others?"

She blinked, as if just realizing he was there. After staring at it for a second, she took it. He waited two sips for her comeback, and when it came, it about broke his heart with the courage it displayed. "It would probably be better if you sent me back now."

The "so no one else gets hurt" went unspoken, but he heard it nonetheless. He digested that. She was willing to sacrifice herself so Tia and the others didn't get hurt. She'd tried to sacrifice herself so her sister could get away. He stood. And every night she sacrificed herself in his bed. The reason for that he wasn't sure of yet, but he had a feeling he wasn't going to like the answer when he got it.

"I think I'll hold off on that, though I do appreciate the offer." He slid his chair back under the table, took the cup from her hand and placed it beside his. "Give me your hand."

"Why?"

"I've a need to hold you without giving myself a crick."

She placed her palm in his. "I don't need to be held."

He pulled her to her feet. "I didn't say you needed to be."

As soon as she was tucked against him, the violent waves subsided, coalesced and he could think. "You've been wrestling with some pretty big monsters, haven't you, Gypsy?"

No response. "Monsters you've been afraid to tell me about for fear of who might get hurt."

Still no response.

"And maybe fear of what you might lose?"

The warmth of her breath stuttered to a halt. Her ribs pressed against his arms as she went rigid. If it wasn't for the nails digging into his chest, he might have thought she'd had a fit. But those nails were pressing deep, spasming with the fear shuddering through her.

He brushed a kiss over the top of her head. "I bet you couldn't believe your lucky stars when you married up with me. A man with my reputation would certainly give any threat pause, and with my connections, had a lot to offer in your hunt for your sister."

"It wasn't like that." The whisper rushed out on the breath she'd been holding.

"What was it then?"

She shrugged. "Things just happened."

He nipped her attempt to push out of his embrace in the bud.

"And you took advantage of them."

"I didn't know what else to do."

He opened his hand across her back, centering his palm between her shoulder blades, the delicacy of her build reinforcing the narrowness of her options. She was a resourceful woman. "So you did the best you could. You used me."

She cringed as if that were a bad thing. "I'm sorry."

He tipped her face up. Her eyes were dark with worry. "You fretting my feelings are hurt?"

"Yes."

"Well, don't. People have tried to use me before for a whole lot less reason."

"But I never wanted to be one of them."

"But you were, and now you owe me."

He let the "again" hang unspoken between them.

"What do you want?"

"Five minutes of honesty."

18

What did he think five minutes would gain? Desi stared up at him as he rubbed her back. He was always touching her, tempting her, caring for her, and it always made her feel so bad, because she didn't deserve it.

He was a good man. Hard enough to survive in this land, but good. He deserved better than to be used; better than what she'd become. He deserved a woman like she used to be. Innocent, uncorrupted. Unknowing. Considering all that, the least she could give him was honesty.

"I can spare five minutes."

She pulled out a chair. He didn't say a word as she sat. Just watched her in that way he had, assessing every inhale and exhale, probably every involuntary twitch of her muscles, cataloging it all so he'd know if she lied. Unreasoning resentment flowed through her at the suspicion in his look.

"I can tell the truth, you know."

He reached across her for his coffee, his scent and strength enfolding her, making her want to reach up and cling. "I don't recall saying you couldn't."

"You didn't have to. Your stare said it all."

His lips quirked as he straightened. "That'll save on

conversation in the future, but today, just in case I'm reading you wrong, like you have a habit of reading me wrong…" He took a sip of coffee. "I think I'll take advantage of my five minutes."

"There's only four now."

"You had the clock running while negotiating?"

"Yes." She wasn't big on inquisitions.

Caine leaned his hip against the table. "You don't play fair."

He didn't say it like it was a bad thing, which made her more suspicious. "I never said I did. You're the one who keeps making me out to be more than I am."

"So you keep telling me."

The brush of his thumb on her cheek was soft, even comforting. She wanted to push it away, but to do so would lead him to look for the reason, and she didn't want him looking any deeper than the surface, because truth be told, she was too vulnerable to him and the fairy tale he liked to paint that the past didn't matter, that he could keep her safe, that he would even want to once the newness wore off and he started thinking about what he'd truly been shackled to. After a couple seconds, his lips quirked.

"Did you come from back east?"

"Yes."

"Did your people come from money?"

She thought of the house, the conveniences, the servants, the ease of having everything she wanted without any worries. "A lot of it."

"With your parents dead, who's in line for it?"

"My sister and I." She frowned. "Maybe." At least she'd always assumed that, but something in the way his gaze sharpened made her rethink. She bit her lip as reality sank in. "Actually, I don't know."

"Damn, you sure?"

Dear God, she wasn't. How could she be so ignorant about something as basic as her inheritance? She gave her coffee a sharp stir. "I was supposed to look pretty, remember?"

He nodded. "Just checking."

She couldn't let it go. She'd given up all hope of returning to her old life, word of what had happened would keep her and her sister ostracized, but she'd been counting on the money to make a new beginning. "Doesn't inheritance always come to the children?"

"Sometimes." Caine shrugged and sipped some more coffee. "Sometimes it can have conditions. You ever remember your pa or ma talking about your inheritance or maybe your money in relation to your marriage."

"Only that everything was in place and that it should be brilliant." And she'd let it go at that because it should be brilliant. And she'd let it go at that because it never occurred to her that she needed to know more, or that her perfect life could fall apart.

"Brilliant, huh?" Caine took another sip of coffee. The width of the cup did nothing to hide his smile. "You were that good at being pretty?"

"I was the best." Her own smile was rueful. She'd taken such pride in being the best, too. "Though to be fair, being the perfect ornament doesn't take much skill."

"Seems to me it would take a hell of a lot of control. I've met eastern men, and they tend to have a need to exaggerate their own importance."

Desi took a sip of her coffee, eyeing him over the brim. "In my experience, that need isn't limited to the east."

His only nod to her sarcasm was an amused "Ouch." And then nothing. She waited while he took a leisurely sip of his coffee and focused on a point over her shoulder. And then another. And with each second that passed, she was aware of time slipping away, of the deadline looming. She looked at the clock by the dining room door. He only had two minutes left. It shouldn't matter to her, but when he went for a third sip, she couldn't help blurting out, "You're running out of time."

Caine didn't even glance at the clock. "I appreciate you keeping track."

She resisted the urge to turn and look at what held his attention, but only because she knew what he really was doing was thinking. For all his lazy talking ways, the man's mind never settled. And that was making her nervous. She clenched her fingers around the warm cup.

He motioned with the cup. "The other man, the one who liked to hurt you, are you still worried he'll get you back?"

Horror, terror and rebellion twisted together inside as they always did at the mention of *him*. She glanced at the clock. She still owed him ninety more seconds of honesty. "Yes."

His hand settled on her shoulder. "He won't, you know."

The statement was made with the same nonchalance with which someone talked about the weather, but while Desi didn't share Caine's confidence, she wasn't fool enough to irritate him by saying so.

His fingertips rubbed up and down her neck in tiny increments. So soft she had to strain to feel them.

"Did you marry me to escape him?"

Oh, God, why was he making her say these things out loud? "Yes."

"Do you expect this marriage to last?"

Pain in her knuckles alerted her to the fact she was

squeezing the mug too hard. She relaxed her grip but she couldn't do anything about the tightness in her throat.

"No."

Caine rested his foot on the rung of her chair, imprisoning her between his hard thigh and the side of the table. The wood offered a subtle protest that echoed the silent chant ripping through her. No. No. No.

Desi glanced at his leg and then his face. Did he think she was going to run? Could he sense how much she wanted to?

"Because he'll come for you?"

It would be so easy to just say yes, and let it go. She glanced into his eyes, something she'd been avoiding doing until now. The irises were green with dark shadows flickering at the edges.

People have tried to use me before for a whole lot less reason.

Lying to him now would truly make her one of them. She didn't want to hurt him like that, didn't want to hurt him at all. He deserved better. There was still a minute on the clock. "No."

Caine cocked his eyebrow at her. "You wouldn't be trying to run out my time by drawing out your answers would you?"

She bit her lip. "No."

But she might have if she'd thought of it earlier.

"Then answer me right."

"When the novelty wears off, you're going to feel differently about me."

But she wasn't going to feel differently about him, and she wouldn't go any deeper into that hell than she had to.

"The novelty being the way I desire you?"

She nodded, her attention instinctively falling to the thick, tempting outline of his manhood that stretched down his thigh.

"And you figure the easiest way for me to be shed of an unwanted wife is to let the bastard take you."

"It would be the easiest."

"And therefore the most logical."

She nodded.

"That's a hell of an opinion you have of me."

There was something in his voice that struck her wrong. She glanced at his face. She found nothing obvious, just that cool measuring assessment, but she couldn't shake the inner sense that he was upset. She touched his left knee, driven by that irrational inner urge to comfort him. Beneath the cotton of his pants, his cock flexed. Her fingers strayed higher, stroking softly.

Even though she knew there was no way she could have hurt him, she said, "I'm sorry."

His knee bent, shortening the distance between her hand and its destination. "You should be."

Her mouth went dry as his shaft jumped again. He truly was a warlock and the proof was in how much she wanted to unbutton his pants and take out that big cock, ease him into her mouth and bring him the softness of release. Just nurse him gently until he came, taking the stress from his big frame and that darkness from his gaze. Even if only for a few seconds.

Seconds... She looked at the clock. "Your time is almost up."

His fingers on her neck stopped that imperceptible caressing and just rested against her. "It's all right. I've only got one more question."

She waited. He didn't seem in any hurry to get to it.

Her fingers strayed higher. His hand cupped her head. His thumb under her chin brought her gaze up. She hoped her thoughts didn't show in her face.

"What is it?"

"Are you holding back with me in bed?"

She blinked. "How am I supposed to answer that?"

"With the truth."

Dear God, had she said that out loud? From the way he was watching her, she must have. And from the razor sharpness of his gaze, this was the only question he'd ever intended to have an answer to all along. "Maybe."

"Maybe is a hedge, not an answer."

Anger flared out of nowhere, resentment holding it up with a steady support. She leaned back against his hand, straining against his hold. "Well, maybe 'maybe' is the best I can do."

He held her where he wanted her with aggravating ease. "I don't think so."

She glared at him. "And what do you know?"

"That you promised to answer me honestly."

His weight shifted forward as he settled into a better position, bringing that hard cock to the forefront of her attention. All she needed to do was slide her palm up the solid muscle of his thigh and she could touch it, make it leap and throb, give him pleasure. All he had to do was press on her neck and give her a command and she wouldn't have any choice. Why didn't he just do it?

His fingertips caressed the nape of her neck but didn't pull away, which meant she didn't have any choice but to answer the question she'd promised to.

"It just feels wrong to enjoy it."

"Going to hell' wrong?"

She wished it were that simple.

She licked her lips. "Wrong because of my past, how we married, wrong because of how this will all turn out. Wrong because I'm me and you're you and you deserve so much better."

"So you're protecting me?"

She shook her head, her gaze locked on his cock. Was it her imagination or had it really gotten bigger? She'd promised him honesty. She glanced at the clock. Five seconds left. "I'm protecting myself."

His thumb tipped her chin up before moving to the corner of her mouth. "And now, sweetheart? Who are you protecting now?"

"I don't know what you mean."

His thumb pressed, parting her lips, and she had a sinking feeling she hadn't concealed her thoughts at all. His next words convinced her.

"Denying yourself my cock? Who is that protecting? Me or you?"

Humiliation swamped her in a deluge of heat. He knew, knew how her mouth watered to taste him; knew how she wanted to make him come. She closed her eyes, unable to watch the confirmation change his expression from intent to smug. She forced the small whisper out. "I don't know."

"Look at me."

She opened her eyes, expecting smug victory. Instead, she found something else. Emotion. It was pure, unadulterated emotion that tightened the harsh planes of his face to an utterly masculine edge of demand. A demand everything inside her that was feminine clamored to appease. She couldn't breathe, couldn't move. All she could do was stare helplessly at him as he asked, "What were you thinking when you were looking at my cock?"

Oh, Lord. He was going to make her say it. "You said only one more question."

"I lied." Without any remorse he ordered, "Tell me, Desi."

His tone brooked no denial. And truth was, she was tired of maintaining the pretense. She allowed her hand to travel those few critical inches to cuddle the broad head of his shaft, letting it settle into the cup of her palm. What did it matter now?

"I was thinking how nice it would be to make you happy."

He cut to the chase with his usual efficiency. "By taking me in your mouth?"

The only time she ever saw him relaxed was after he came. "Yes."

His cock leapt beneath her palm.

"How?"

She focused on her hand on his cock, on fitting the ridge precisely into her palm so she didn't have to focus on the humiliation, hoping he would let it go before her control snapped. "Gently."

"Why?"

The wildness welled. She lashed out with her hand, aiming for his face. He caught it in his, curtailing the impulse, controlling it.

"What does it matter?" It was almost a wail.

"Because I want to know."

"I just wanted to give you some softness. All right? That's all."

"Why?"

She rested her cheek against his thigh, giving up. "It doesn't matter."

"I think it does."

Then he was just going to have to stew right along with her. "I don't know."

His thumb tipped her chin up, no doubt because he wanted to read the truth in her eyes. She raised her lids, letting him see whatever he wanted there. It wouldn't change anything. "Ah, Desi girl, you really don't know, do you?"

And he did? "I told you I wouldn't lie."

"So you did."

There was something different about his expression now, too subtle to define, but her body responded to it. Softening, peaking, yearning. A tickling sensation shot up from her palm. She looked down. She was stroking his cock through the rough cotton of his pants. When she glanced back up, Caine was smiling, but it wasn't a mocking smile. His thumb touched the corner of her mouth.

"Don't ever think I don't want your softness, Gypsy, or that I don't value it."

"You like it?"

"Yes."

"Why?"

"It's natural, sweet and rare."

He wasn't lying. Some of his confidence flowed into her. She cocked her head to the side. "That's not what my mother told me."

His harshly beautiful face lit up with genuine amusement. "I seriously doubt your mother brought up that particular delight at all."

"No," she admitted with a small smile. "She didn't."

But she wished she had. Then maybe she'd be able to sort out the feelings inside.

"Do you still want to make me happy?" Caine asked.

Heat shot through her, not all of it from embarrassment. Desi measured his length with her fingers. He was a big man all over. It would be so easy for him to hurt her, but he never did. She remembered how hard he'd struggled to please her while she fought him, remembered the bliss of his mouth on her privates. How the flick of his tongue could shatter her defences and leave her open and vulnerable. Replete. She stroked him softly before sliding her hand higher, toward the buttons. "You won't be upset?"

"Sweetheart, you can take my cock into that sweet mouth anytime you want and all you'll find under your ministrations is a very happy man."

She hoped that was true. She opened the first button. "James said relieving a man this way was a whore's job."

He helped her with the second button. "James is a weak-minded fool who wouldn't know right from wrong if it came up and bit him on the ass."

When he went for the third, she brushed his hands away. This was her gift. She turned her face into the pulse of his cock, biting gently, smiling at his hiss of pleasure. His fingers threaded through her hair, pulling her in.

"And you do?"

"Yes."

"And this is right?" She needed to hear him say it. "Between us, Desi, whatever we want is right." His palms curved around her skull. "Now give me that softness you've been teasing me with."

19

She unbuttoned the last button. The material gaped in invitation. He brought his leg down as she slid her hands into the welcoming hollow, palming the hard curve of his buttocks before sliding his pants down. They fell six inches and stopped as he leaned back against the table. She looked up at him.

"In case I have to get dressed in a hurry," he explained.

The possibility teased her awareness. Someone might come in, might catch her tempting Caine with her mouth, might see her giving him pleasure. A hot bolt of lust shuddered through her, tightening her nipples. His hands in her hair steadied her as she sank to her knees in front of him.

"Does that excite you, sweetheart? Worrying that someone might see me enjoying your mouth?"

It scared and excited her in equal parts. She nodded.

"It excites me, too."

Her breath caught, trapped in her throat by the temptation that he'd want to explore that excitement. That he'd let others watch.

"Gypsy?" Caine's thumbs rubbed over her cheeks in

small measured circles, waiting on her obedience to the unspoken order. She struggled to contain her breathing, her insecurity. Success came in three heartbeats. She made her expression blank.

His wasn't. It was hard with desire, soft with understanding, chiseled with intent, as complex as he was. "What's between us is private, and you can trust me to keep it that way."

She hesitated, her hands on his pants. "I'm trying."

"I know you are but, next time you get to second-guessing, try reminding yourself who I am."

Ranger, gunslinger, killer. "My husband?"

"You can take the question mark off the end."

She bit her tongue on another "sorry." He was right. She had to stop thinking that way.

"Do you know what that means?" he asked.

"You'll always be there for me."

"And?"

"You'll always protect me."

"And?"

She didn't have another statement to throw into the void. "You're going to have to help me with the last."

He smiled. "Figures you'd blank on that one." Pressure on the back of her skull prompted her forward. "I'm the man who will always put you first."

DESI KNELT THERE WITHIN the embrace of his thighs, absorbing the reality, feeling the encouragement in his hand behind her head, his power, and waited. He just sat there, hips propped against the edge of the table, cock hard, pants open, waiting. On her. Despite the fact that Caine was hungry and needed satisfaction, he patiently waited to see what she wanted to do. She glanced up. "I can do this my way and you won't interfere?"

He cocked that eyebrow at her. "Are you planning on letting that wild side loose?"

The familiar gesture caught on her smile and brought it forward. She massaged tiny circles into his thighs with her fingertips. "Maybe."

The right corner of his mouth kicked up. "Then definitely."

"What if I do it wrong?"

He shrugged. "As this is your show, I don't see how you can."

Her show. Desi opened her hands, feeling the muscles jump and twitch against her palms, absorbing the tension radiating through him and the reality of what this meant. She was in charge. She could take it easy or make it hard. She could bring him off fast or not at all. And he would let her. The knowledge swept over her in a thrilling rush that blended with her desire to please him in the most interesting way, increasing her desire while increasing her sense of…herself? It didn't make sense but she liked knowing that she could control a man for a change.

"You planning on thinking me into coming or actually doing something to get me there?"

Desi shook her head at him and looked at him from under her lashes. "I thought you said I was in control?"

His thighs pressed into her hands, his fingers stirred in her hair. "I was just wondering."

Understanding slid alongside the sharp bite of passion, cushioning it in softness. He was trusting her to take care of him. Desi let the knowledge sink in. This time when she took Caine in her mouth it wouldn't be because she was scared or because he was forcing it, but because she wanted to please him. And this time when he gave her his cock it would be because he wanted to please her. They were giving. To each other. The way she'd always thought a husband and wife should. The smile on her face spread to her soul. The smile on her thigh muscles convulsed under the stroke of her fingers.

His thigh muscles convulsed under the stroke of her fingers.

"I like that," she whispered.

"What?"

"The way you respond to my touch."

"I can't help it. You have the hottest, sweetest hands."

She cast him another glance from under her lashes, letting her gaze link with his, her smile flirt with his.

"But not as hot as my mouth."

His chuckle was as raw as her desire to do this right. To please him. She slid her fingers up to that tantalizing separation of material that revealed the intimate thatch of male hair, darker than on his head. Wiry. Tough. Appealing. He drew in a long breath.

"Then no, I wasn't planning on thinking you to the finish."

She twined her fingers in that line of hair, smiling wider as the tight curls wrapped around her knuckles. They were so like the man himself. Take charge to the core. And yet he'd surrendered that control to her. It gave her such hope.

Caine's fingers snagged at the base of her braid. Did he think she was going to give up this moment now that she had it? She reached behind her and caught his wrist.

"I'm in charge."

"I know, sweetheart, just bracing myself."

Desi tugged his pants down farther, revealing the bottom slab of his abdominal muscles, the thick base of his imprisoned penis and the arch of where the shaft doubled under the pressure of confinement.

She touched the hard, satiny-smooth surface with

her pinkie, absorbing its heat. It pressed back, straining toward her, throbbing with a solid pulse that echoed her own. With gentle encouragement, she eased him up and out, inch by delicious inch, until the thick shaft fell into the cradle of her hands, heavy and full of life. For her.

"Damn," he moaned, "that's good."

"And just think, I'm just getting started."

"I may not make it to the finish."

"I wasn't planning on giving you a choice."

His "hot damn" made her smile. The man was always making her smile. Scooting forward on her knees, she found a more comfortable position. Caine's fingers twitched and that big chest jerked under a sharp breath when her fingertips feathered along his length. She met his gaze and licked her lips as she eased his cock head down.

"Not as good as this is going to feel."

"Have I mentioned how I love your wild side?"

She wished he'd love her. The thought flashed in her mind. She suppressed it just as quickly.

"I'd rather you show me."

His hard mouth relaxed into a grin. "You bring that mouth a little closer, and I will."

Desi shook her head. He really couldn't quit giving orders. She forgave him though. She could feel the tension driving him. The want. Could see it in the way the green of his eyes deepened to near black, and the way his fingers trembled with tension. He was giving her what she wanted, but it was costing him.

She brought his cock closer, so close her breath teased over the slit in the plump crest. He shuddered. Oh, he wanted her mouth, but she wasn't giving it to him. Not just yet. She touched her tongue to the middle of her lower lip, flicking it forward and back until the surface was wet and slick. Caine's groan was the sweetest music.

"I should warn you," he drawled as if she didn't know he was burning for her from the inside out, "I don't take well to teasing."

She raised her eyebrows, wishing she could isolate the movement to one brow like he did because it was so much more eloquent. "Is that a threat?"

"Just making conversation."

While he rubbed and pressed on the back of her head? It was more in the line of influencing. He was such a cheater.

"I think that was a threat." She blew across the broad tip of his shaft, smiling when the little hole in the center winked at her. She acknowledged the salute with a tiny flick of her tongue. "So maybe before I go further, you should spell out the repercussions for me."

He didn't answer immediately. It didn't take much to figure out why. He was struggling to control his breathing. She took advantage of his hesitation to press on. "Or better yet, maybe I should just discover them for myself."

This time she let her tongue flatten and linger, swirling across as much of the convex area as she could cover, searching for all the sensitive spots, cataloging them, holding his gaze as she did, cataloging also the subtle shift of emotion within. Emotion that didn't show in his face, but she was beginning to learn to read him through the almost invisible clues he did give off.

Like the way his nostrils flared as she nudged her tongue into that tiny slit. He liked that. The carefully even tension of his fingertips on her head was a clue he was hoping for more. She could give him that. She could give him a lot of things if he'd let her. Desi stroked her hands along the side of Caine's cock as she drew back. He was wet from her ministrations, hard with anticipation and need. She blew another breath over the moist surface as she squeezed with her hands. Just once, just enough to tempt him to want more.

The jerk of his hips was as involuntary as was the drop of pre-come that followed. The bead balanced on the tip, perfectly round, perfectly clear. Growing as she ghosted her fingers along his shaft in deliberately easy motions. Stretching under the weight of his desire.

Desi rested her cheek against Caine's thigh, giving him responsibility for some of her weight as she tipped his cock up, reached out with her tongue and took that reward for her own, letting the salty sweet taste of victory spread through her mouth, into her soul. He was hers.

Caine's curse was music, the jerk of his cock, the melting of the hardness in his eyes was exhilarating. But the way he cupped her cheek as she absorbed his shaft into the hot cavern of her mouth was the present she longed for—tenderness, acceptance. Encouragement. All she'd ever dreamed of a man giving her was in that touch.

She sipped at him, applying random tendrils of suction, ignoring the violent tension humming off him, the near angry demand for more stimulation. She didn't want to give him more violence. She wanted to give him gentleness. Holding his gaze, she nuzzled her cheek high on his thigh and took his cock a tiny bit deeper.

His fingers pressed on her cheek, forcing the sensitive inner lining against the ridge.

"I need more than this to come, baby."

She shook her head, pleasuring them both with the intimate massage. This was going to be sweet and intimate. A blending rather than a taking.

"No?"

She shook her head again and continued to suck lightly, steadily, giving him a rhythm to follow if he wanted to.

"You need this?"

Another nod wasn't necessary. She could see his understanding in his eyes. To her it was necessary. There was a moment's pause during which his eyes searched hers, in which his grip tightened. Inside, disappointment flared. He wasn't going to allow it. He was going to take over.

And then, amazingly, his head canted that fraction to the side that told her he'd reached a decision, and the "take charge" tension disappeared. His hand cradled her face rather than restrained, but against her tongue, his cock still throbbed. His expression mirrored the change inside. Gentling with the same need flowing through her. The need to please through giving.

"Then take what you need, baby."

She didn't need to take. She needed to give. Her way for once. She needed to give someone pleasure rather than have them steal it from her. She needed... She relaxed into the comfort of his hands, the cradle of his thighs. Just this.

A pulse of hot fluid spiced her tongue. She swallowed it with lazy greed. She needed this.

A second flowed into two, three and then ten, which added up to minutes and still he didn't rush her or push, just let her build the rhythm as she wanted, surprising her, and maybe himself, by how arousing it was to keep things slow and easy. She'd meant this for him. But inside her, the demand built steadily, as if they were connected by more than just flesh. As the pulse in his cock accelerated, so did the ache in her core.

She shifted, rubbing her thighs together to still the

restless need, but it wouldn't lessen. It was focused on the tension in Caine, the passion sharpening his features until it stripped away all remnants of civilization and left behind the man as he was: deadly, capable and hers. All hers.

Another pulse of fluid. His cock went rock hard. His thumb pressed in on her cheek, melding them together, cheek to cock, skin to skin.

"Desi?"

She didn't need him to tell her. He was going to come. She stopped suckling and started sucking, pulling his response from him, demanding that he give it to her the way she wanted. He gritted his teeth. His head fell back and then he was coming, not with hard thrusts and curses, but in a long, drawn-out shudder that flowed into her mouth, along with the soft, almost desperate whisper of her name. Pulse after pulse, whisper after whisper, until nothing else existed except the fragile sense of togetherness linking them for this one moment. And deep inside Desi, something shifted and crumbled.

HE DIDN'T LIKE IT. Caine held Desi to him, shuddered as his bone-dry balls tried to offer her something more, something unsubstantial. Something he'd never had, and gritted his teeth against the blissful burn. He'd never had a woman take him like that, never let a woman have control, and he didn't like the way it left him feeling. Like something was different.

Caine wrapped Desi's thick braid around his hand, pulling her into his groin, jerking at every tender kiss she pressed against him, too sensitized to bear it. Too hungry to pull away. He slid off the table, standing before her. Desi's arms came around his hips. Soft and sweet, hugging tightly, reminding him she needed him and not the other way around.

When he pulled her up, she didn't fight him, just went into his embrace. All sweet, willing woman, melting against him, melting into him. He tipped her head back. She didn't resist, just offered him her mouth with a totally feminine tilt of her head.

Caine took it. He wanted to give her back the gentleness she'd given him, but it wasn't in him. Not now, with the memory of how she'd taken him, the sweet insistence, the acceptance. It called to something primitive within him, summoned it to the surface, made it rage until all he wanted to do was throw her on the table and fuck her so hard she'd be marked forever. His.

The kiss he pressed on her lips reflected the emotions raging through him. She didn't seem to mind his violence, the absolute possession he took of her mouth—she just opened hers and accepted it. But then again, Desi had had a lot of men come at her violently. It was something she was no doubt used to.

And something he didn't want her expecting from him. Between them, it had to be different. The realization sank deep. He wanted her to see him more than a duty or a man to be obeyed. He wanted her to want him because she needed him inside, where it mattered to a woman. In that place where a woman accepted one man above all others.

He broke off the kiss. "Son of a bitch."

Desi blinked at his curse, but didn't move. Just stayed where he'd placed her. Waiting, those full lips red and swollen from taking his cock and his kiss. Taunting him with their nearness.

He smoothed his thumb over the bottom one. "Let's try that again."

Inside the beast raged. He kept it harnessed, bringing his mouth to hers with slow precision, edge to edge, center to center, sinking into the kiss rather than diving in, teasing with his tongue rather than demanding. The shudder that took her from head to toe was a revelation. He could demand from her all he wanted, and he was a good enough lover to get some response, but if he wanted the fire of that first night, he was going to have to give her something no other man ever had. Consideration.

Her tongue touched his lip and then retreated, a subtle tension entering her muscles. She expected that little touch to set him off. Take it as an invitation to conquer, but he didn't think he'd go there today. As ready as his cock was, he recognized a test when it sat in front of him. She wanted his passion, longed for his gentleness, but braced herself for lust. He rested his forehead against hers.

"I'm finding, Gypsy, that I want to give you softness, too."

She blinked and then just as quickly frowned, as if he'd said something dirty. "You don't like gentle."

As if his likes were all that mattered. He placed another kiss dead center of the pucker on her forehead. "It'd be more correct to say no woman ever inspired me to want to give it a try." He brushed a kiss on the end of her nose. "But you, Gypsy, make me want to try all sorts of new things."

With a lift and a twist he had her sitting on the edge of the table. Her thighs parted naturally as he stepped in. She was still giving him suspicious looks. "It's not a bad thing, Desi."

"Men have habits."

"That they do." He tilted her head back, barely resisting the urge to undo her braid and have that gorgeous hair falling over his hands. If someone came in, he'd need to be able to make her presentable in a flash. "But—" he captured her gaze with his "—some men are lucky enough to have wives who make them want to try new ones."

Her arms came around his neck and some of the tension left her face. "Like me."

He dropped his forehead to hers as he gathered up her skirt. "Definitely like you."

"Because I've known a lot of men?"

"If this skirt wasn't so much in the way, I'd spank your ass for that disservice."

If he hadn't been watching so closely, he would have missed the shadow of excitement that sparked in her gaze at the word *spank*. He thought back to that first day. What had made her shiver. And smiled. "Ah, we're going to have so much fun together."

"Because you don't have to worry about me?"

They were back to the too-many-men thing. His hand found the curve of her thigh. "Because we're two of the lucky ones."

He palmed the slim length and moved it higher, taking her little gasp into his mouth as he brushed the tight curls guarding her pussy. "Who have this."

Her squirming nudged his finger between the swollen lips of her labia and into the liquid heat beyond.

"And this is important?"

His smile grew at the blatant fishing. He wrapped his arm around her back, stabilizing her as he slid his fingers deeper. "You said yourself, men have their habits." She clenched around him. "And the way you respond to me is one I'm fast adding to my list of must-haves."

"And it doesn't make you wonder?"

He tested her with a second finger. A twitch and a

spill of cream rewarded his efforts. "About whether you respond to every man this way?"

She bit her lip and nodded. Her expression was one of a woman caught between bliss and the agony of doubt.

"I'm not a green kid, Desi Allen. I know what's real." He stroked his tongue over her upper lip, waiting for and enjoying her shiver when it came, along with a liquid pulse of her channel. "And you, wife, were made only for me."

She went still, her lips unresponsive beneath his as she digested what he meant. Her gaze clung to his and then she smiled, that sweet, soft, incredibly sassy smile that shot lust through him like a bolt of lightning. "You are insane."

"But I'm your insanity."

"Yes, you are."

She hugged him so hard it might have hurt if she had the muscle of a woman used to hard work, but all her squeezing did was put a knot in his gut and coax that foreign softness out of his soul. He caught her cry in his mouth as his thumb settled, feather-light, on her clit.

"So, that being the case, maybe you ought to just settle in and enjoy me?"

She pressed her lips to his throat. "Maybe I should."

He pushed slow and easy with his fingers, stretching her as his thumb rubbed; keeping it gentle, coaxing rather than demanding. "Maybe you should." Her nails stung his nape. "Because I have a whole lot of gentle to try on you."

"Now?"

The squeak was barely coherent.

"Now." He gave her another finger, holding still as she shuddered under the delicate assault. "Now, I'm going to let you come on my fingers, all soft and womanly, but tonight," he said, sliding his fingers to the hilt in the well-lubricated channel, "you're going to come in my mouth, hot and delicious."

Another squeak. "I am?"

A withdrawal and a thrust. "Yes." Her ankles hooked behind his thighs and her back arched in that subtle way he'd come to recognize. She was very close. "Sucking me off turned you on, didn't it, baby?"

She nodded.

"I want the words."

That breathless "Yes" barely counted as speech, but he accepted it mainly because the next thrust of his fingers, combined with the next pass of his thumb, took all of her breath in a high-pitched cry.

"And kissing that sweet little pussy is going to turn *me* on, so you think on that while you're going about your business today. You think on how tonight, I'm going to lick you, kiss you, suck this little clit..."

He punctuated the last with a firm brush on the swollen knot. Desi came around him in a sweet rain of pleasure, her body jerking into his. Caine pulled her closer, encouraging the way she clung with her legs, her nails.

"And then you think on how much I'm going to enjoy drinking in your pleasure. So much—" he thrust a little harder this time, prolonging the aftershocks " —I might just have to do it all again." He withdrew his fingers. "And again." He pumped his fingers deep. "And again."

Another ripple passed through her. A smaller climax than the first. He seated his fingers to the hilt and pulled her face into his throat, letting her come down gently, enjoying the fluttering contractions and the hot breath buffeting the pulse in his throat. "Just like that, baby." He rested his cheek on her hair. "It's going to be sweet and satisfying for both of us tonight."

"Promises, promises."

He kissed her head for that bit of humor and then, because he liked the feel of her hair against his lips, left them there. She smelled of lilacs and satisfied woman. "And everyone knows you can take a Hell's Eight promise to the bank."

She wiggled against him. He pulled his fingers free. Her muscles relinquished him with a reluctance as expressive as her moan. Damn, he'd like to take her to bed and do nothing but bring that sound to her lips over and over again.

"I'd rather have a promise from my husband."

Because it was more intimate. He understood that. "Definitely from your husband."

Desi leaned her head back into his shoulder, still accepting his support. "Don't think this gets you out of teaching me to fight."

"Hmm…" The kiss he gave her lingered a bit longer than the quick bussing he'd intended. She just tasted so good. "I'm thinking it should cut me some leeway."

He didn't like the thought of her in confrontations.

Her ankles unhooked from his thighs, and her feet slid down his legs.

"Not today."

"Why?"

She patted his cheek. A bit of daring she hadn't aspired to before. An indirect expression of claiming he liked. "Because tomorrow I've got to learn to milk the damn cow."

His laugh caught them both by surprise. He stepped back, smoothed her skirts down over her thighs. Her hands clung to his shoulders, the show of vulnerability at odds with the confident smile on her face. He took one of her small hands and brought it to his lips, kissing the back, holding her gaze. "Then I guess I don't have any choice."

And as much as he didn't like the thought of her having to fight, he hated more the thought of her in a situation where she needed to know how but didn't. Like what had happened to her in town.

He put his hands around her waist. It was just a three-foot drop to the floor but she clung to his arms as if he were lifting her over a chasm. "I won't drop you, Desi."

Her "I know" was as confident as her grip was tight. No doubt because she still thought it was necessary to try to control her safety. Even with him.

Her feet hit the floor. He pulled out the chair and pressed her into it. "Now, how about I fix you a snack? You're going to need your strength if you plan to learn to fight."

"You're going to teach me?"

He sighed and flipped her braid over her shoulder. The fact that she needed to reiterate her request after he'd already conceded just went to show how far they had yet to go in getting into the reality of being man and wife.

"I'll teach you."

20

Three days later, Caine decided Desi didn't have a lick of natural talent, which shouldn't surprise him, seeing as she was an easterner, but the ferocity with which she tried had made him expect…he didn't know what. Just more.

He came up behind her, reaching around to guide her. "Hold the gun like I told you."

She jerked it into position.

"Gently." He adjusted her aim. "The goal isn't to throw the gun but to let the gun throw the bullet."

"I just want it to get there."

He couldn't see her expression clearly, but he could see the creases across the top of her nose from how hard she was concentrating. "Well, when it comes to shooting, all helping it along does is ruin your shot."

She sighed and squared her shoulders.

"Now, remember the kick and brace for it."

She aimed at the bottle sitting atop the log.

"Good." He kept his hand on top of her wrist as she settled her weight. He'd seen more than one greenhorn bust his face by not preparing for the kickback. "Now, squeeze the trigger steadily and gently. Just picture that bottle as the bastard's face and go easy into the shot."

She did exactly as he said, right up until she met that last resistance of the trigger. At the precise instant she squeezed the trigger, she ducked her head. The recoil kicked the gun up into his hand. The shot went wild.

"You can't close your eyes and expect to hit your target."

She didn't look at him. "How do you know I closed my eyes?"

"Didn't you?"

She huffed and brought the gun back up. "I won't this time."

He got his hand over hers just in time. She didn't close her eyes this time. She still missed, but she managed to nick the log.

"Ha!" She spun around, eyes alight. "I told you I could do it."

He tilted the gun away. "You haven't done anything yet, but you're getting close."

Her frown was half play, half serious. "You can really be a killjoy."

"I tell you what, you hit it this time, and I'll show you how to take down a man bigger than you."

"Everyone's bigger than me."

"Then it would be a right handy skill to have, wouldn't it?"

She stared at him, pursed her lips and then frowned. "What happens if I miss?"

"Then I guess you get the booby prize."

"And that would be?"

"A kiss."

She caught her lip between her teeth for a second before releasing it slowly, deliberately, in a small smile. Holding his gaze, she pointed behind her in the general direction of the target and pulled the trigger. Caine leapt for the gun as the shot went wild, swearing and snatching it out of her hand. Sam burst out of the outhouse in a crouch, his long johns around his waist, gun in his hand, curses trailing his exit. One glance in their direction was all it took for him to assess the situation. He stood, holstered his gun and looked at the hole in the top of the outhouse.

"Goddamn it, Allen," he hollered, yanking his sleeve up his right arm. "Are you teaching that woman to shoot or redecorating?"

Desi didn't spare Sam a glance, just stared at Caine with that little smile playing on her lips. He took the gun out of her hand, not taking his eyes off that smile and all that it meant. "Both."

He emptied the bullets out and put it back in his holster.

Desi still didn't look away, didn't move, just said in all innocence, "I missed."

The corner of his mouth twitched. "So you did."

On purpose, no less.

It was such an easy thing to hook his fingers behind her neck and pull that little smile closer. To direct her with the pressure of his fingertips so when she took those two steps in, she was centered against him. Natural that her head would tip back. Right that his mouth meet hers in a reward rich with claiming, possession and...laughter. He'd never laughed through a kiss before, but he did this one, and it didn't diminish the heat at all, merely spiced it with a richer context as their breath met and mingled like their tongues.

He removed his lips a fraction from hers. "You're turning into quite a caution, Mrs. Allen."

She gave him more of her weight. "But you like it..."

There was still a touch of a question mark in that

statement, but he could work with it. A trace of moisture glistened on her lips. He covered it with his thumb. "It has its high points."

"Well, I'm not appreciating them." Sam stomped up, hauling up his left sleeve. "Next time you get a notion to aerate the outhouse, I'd appreciate notice."

Desi glanced up, but didn't step out of Caine's arms. "I'm sorry, did I hurt you?"

"No, but my hat's never going to be the same." Sam stuck his finger through a hole in the crown. "It's a shame, too. I liked this hat."

"Caine will buy you a new one."

That was news to him. "I will?"

Desi slapped—actually slapped—his shoulder. She was getting quite brave with him. "Yes."

"Well, in that case, I'm ordering up one of those expensive Stetsons I saw in the mercantile."

"You do and it's coming out of your hide," Caine growled.

"You'll have to take that up with your missus." Sam settled his hat on his head. "She promised."

"And as I'm Hell's Eight, you have to take it to the bank," Desi inserted, laughter in her voice and in her expression. The same laughter that worked in him.

"I suppose I'm going to have to." He glanced at Sam's hat. "That was a darn reckless thing to do, Desi, shooting blindly like that."

Her eyes sparkled up at him. "Then why are you laughing?"

Because she was smiling up at him with genuine humor. Because she'd done it just for a kiss. And because Sam had looked damn hilarious bursting out of that outhouse. "Hard not to with the spectacle you created."

Her expression of disbelief was almost believable. *"I created?"*

"You are the one with the gun."

"You are the one doing the teaching."

"You are the one who took the shot."

"But only because you tempted me."

He pulled her lip down. He didn't want to argue with that. A man liked to know he could tempt his wife. "I did, huh?"

Her smile softened. Sweetened. Her hand came up to his shoulder, the palm curved to fit him. "Yes."

Her lip was hot and slick as he slid his thumb along it. He rested his nail against the white of her teeth. "Still, you could have hurt someone. I wouldn't be a responsible husband if I let that go uncorrected."

"Uncorrected?"

His hand slid down her back over the slenderness of her spine. It wasn't so easy to feel the bone. She was getting up to a normal weight. She took his meaning as he patted her buttock, lingering on the plump curve.

Her brows rose. "And you take your responsibilities as a husband seriously?"

"Very much so." He squeezed her rear. "Which will give you something to look forward to tonight."

There was nothing subtle about her blush. It covered her face in a wild rush, highlighting the blueness in her gaze, the fullness of her lips, the return of life to her personality. "You think you can control me?"

He smiled and laughed out loud, causing several heads to turn in their direction. "I know I can."

"Because you're my husband?"

He kept her tucked against him, his cock pushing against her abdomen, his personality pushing against her challenge. Awareness of both flared in her eyes a moment before he said, "Because I'm your man, and you know you can trust yourself to me."

She was too strong to just give in. "Just because I can, doesn't mean I will."

He brushed her hair away from her cheek with the back of his fingers, lingering on the heat still coloring her cheek. "No, it doesn't, but you still will."

"What makes you so sure?"

That answer was written all over her face for a man who was lucky to know her well enough to see it. "Because you want to."

SHE HAD TO WAIT days for him to deliver on his promise. Days in which she had ample opportunity to stew, anticipate and then get annoyed. Those wolves that Ed mentioned had turned out to be quite a problem, creating the need for nightly patrols and daily discussions. Her body would hum every day in anticipation of the night, only to fuss with frustration when Caine either didn't come to bed or came to bed too tired for the drawn-out sex play he'd promised. And as he'd pointed out so succinctly in the yard, she wanted to experience his dominance in bed. Longed for it with a breathless need that defied description. She wanted to give herself the way he needed her to, but for her pleasure, not his. Desired to bridge that last chasm between them by giving what he needed to take. And it was completely for herself as he'd known. How did he know her so well?

Desi stood by the bed and stared at the door, anticipation and nervousness tingling through her limbs. As her nanny would have said, all her chickens were about to come home to roost. And as usual, she wasn't sure how she felt about that. Caine made her reckless, made her want to walk the edge of cliffs she'd never climbed just because there might be fun in it. He brought out that part of her that had had her mother despairing at parties, her father cutting off her allowance and suitors swarming around her at balls and gatherings.

With Caine, it was different, though. With Caine, cutting loose was exciting, comforting, fun even. Because with Caine, she knew, deep in her gut, that whatever she did, no matter how outrageous she got, he could handle it. And her.

Like with the gun the other day. She still couldn't believe she'd done that, pulled the trigger for no other reason than to feel his mouth on hers. It had been reckless in the extreme, going with the wild feeling that surged so often against the wall of caution she'd erected, but Caine had laughed. Actually laughed, and then given her the one thing no one else ever had. The comfort of limits she could live with.

So now she was up here waiting on her punishment, dressed in her nightgown but no underpinnings, body taut and expectant, aching in places no lady ever mentioned. She adjusted her position at the foot of the big bed. And still being disobedient.

She was supposed to be waiting under the covers while Caine finished his business with the three rough-looking men who'd come in last week. Not because he found the thought seductive, but because he worried she'd catch a chill. She was reasonably sure that he'd much prefer to see her as she was now, with her gown on but the front undone so it barely clung to her shoulders and gaped away from her chest and abdomen, stopping just short of revealing all. For all he was a big tough Ranger and Hell's Eight, he was a worrier. As if she could be cold with as much wood as he stuffed into the little stove.

Boot steps sounded on the stairs. A shiver of excitement went through her, followed quickly by a twinge of anxiety. This had to work. She didn't think she could make it through another day at war with herself. The top stair creaked the way it always did. It was just a few more steps to the door.

She smoothed the curls from her face, pushed her left sleeve just a little closer to disaster and leaned back against the bedpost. The door latch lifted before she decided what to do with her hands. She settled on clasping them before her in a demure, ladylike manner. Mostly because it brought her cleavage into nice display.

Caine took one step into the room, spotted her and froze. His gaze touched her face, her torso, her groin and then slowly traveled back up, picking up heat with every inch it traveled. Her flesh prickled with awareness. She licked her lips, fought back nervousness and plunged on.

"Hi."

The door closed slowly behind him. Not taking his eyes from her chest, he flipped the lock into place. His eyes met hers—hot, flickering with the wildness he kept restrained. "I thought I told you to wait in bed."

Oh, she loved it when he got that low growl in his drawl. She shifted against the post, arching her back more, presenting herself better. "I got bored."

Two steps and he was in front of her, his shadow covering her in darkness, his body bathing her in heat and temptation. One finger eased under the ribbon trim at the collar. "Did you think you'd get out of trouble this way?"

She couldn't find her voice as his eyes stared into hers,

seeming to go so much deeper than the surface, playing with the truth in her soul the way his finger played with that ribbon. She shook her head.

His right eyebrow quirked up and that touch of a smile deepened as his callused fingertip skimmed downward, following the path of the lapel but not disturbing it, crossing the ridge of her collarbone, gliding over the swell of her breast. "Were you looking to get your spanking sooner by being disobedient?"

She wrapped her fingers around his wrist, not stopping him, just holding on. As soon as she touched him, that shaking uncertainty inside died. This was Caine. She had nothing to be afraid of. The feeling welled, warming her from the inside out. And that inner wildness surged to the fore.

She teased her lips with the tip of her tongue, allowing herself a smile as he watched the movement. Teased the inside of his wrist with the rub of her fingers, bringing his hand to the point of her breast. "Maybe I was just trying to ensure you didn't change your mind."

The only change in his expression was the flicker of his lashes. No matter how she tried, she couldn't read what he was thinking, though she had an idea he saw everything she was trying to hide. "Maybe?"

"Truthfully?"

His touch skimmed her ribs, followed the concave hollow of her abdomen, before pausing at the cluster of curls below. "Always."

She hadn't expected to get into this so early in the evening but she might never get a better opportunity. "I'm never sure what to do around you."

This time he did smile. He also took a half step forward as his hand closed over the underside of her breast. His chest pressed her back, imprisoning her between his hard body and the hard post. Her shudder was pure instinct. There was something wildly arousing about being helpless before Caine.

"Your instincts are sound."

Her "How do you know?" ended on a squeak as his thumb and forefinger closed over her aching nipple.

"Because everything you think is on your face." She shook her hair out of her face. "And what am I thinking now?"

He didn't even hesitate. "You're enjoying the feeling of being helpless."

She blinked. Maybe he really could read her.

His fingers squeezed with delicate precision on her plump nipple. Sensation shot deep into her chest. Her knees buckled. He caught her on his thigh. Goose bumps chased over her skin, his laugh in hot pursuit, flowing over her throat and down her shoulder.

"You liked that?"

She dropped her head back against the pole. "Oh, yes."

"What else do you like?"

"I'm not sure."

His lips brushed her neck, then his teeth. Another shudder shook her. "But you have ideas?"

He nipped her neck. She grabbed his waist for support.

"Some."

It was a lie, she only had vague ideas of how she could be for him.

Another half step and his cock was pressing into her. "Let's hear them."

She'd started the game, and now she had to finish it. She just hadn't expected it to be so hard. "I want to be your wife tonight."

"You've been my wife for the last few weeks." She cut him a glance from under her lashes. He was watching her, measuring her emotions and whatever he could see, those vivid green eyes she'd once thought so cold, hot and dark above the harsh slash of his cheekbones, turbulent with the fires that burned within him. Fire he normally kept controlled and contained. Especially with her. And suddenly, she knew one thing for sure.

She raised her hands above her head, linking them at the wrist before pressing them back into the bedpost. "I don't want to be someone you hold back with in bed."

He accepted the invitation with a deep chuckle that shimmered through her senses, wending its way to her center. Her pussy fluttered with the same vibration. His hand clamped over her wrists, tugging her up and forward against him, into the green fire of his eyes. Her womb clenched with a desperate hunger as another chuckle wrapped her in its seductive embrace, and then she was falling through space, backward, her tumble caught by the mattress. Before the echoes of the first bounce ended, he was over her—big, dark and ready.

THE UNWELCOME PANIC started the minute he came over her, his larger hands catching hers, pinning them back above her head, stretching her torso while his legs came between hers, making room for the solid weight of his cock to wedge tight against her. Another spasm, another gasp, pleasure and terror—present and past.

She dug her nails into her palms and raised her face for his kiss, her breasts for his caress, pushing aside the other images battering the edges of reality, demanding their chance. Desi kept her eyes wide open, locked on Caine's face, refusing to give them dominance. They had no place here.

Screams whipped the edges of her mind as she rolled

her torso against his, hooking her ankles behind his hips, pulling him down. He didn't budge, just braced his arm to her side and continued to study her. His dark gaze skimmed her face, the slight tremor in her lips, the pulse in her throat.

"Kiss me, Caine."

"Why?"

"Because I need you."

"Uh-huh. What's going on, Gypsy?"

The patience in his tone was like a mile-high barricade she couldn't get over, the falter in her confidence a key to those swarming memories to unlock the door and plunge into the here and now until it was no longer clear who held her down, whether this was good or bad, whether she should plead or scream. All that came out was a whimper that broke past her control.

That fast and the weight was gone and she was no longer on her back but on her stomach with Caine as her bed. And his hand was cupping her head, holding her close. "Bad memories?"

She nodded, took one breath and then two before pushing herself up to straddle his waist. All that hard muscle nestled against her privates restored the edge of hunger. "Just for a minute."

One hand lingered on her cheek, holding her still for his perusal while the other came down on her rear in a sharp smack. The sting shot deep into the seat of her desire, warming it. "Don't lie to me."

"I'm not."

"You were afraid."

"And now I'm interested." She wiggled on him. "Which are you going to focus on?"

His hand ghosted her hip. She shivered as her womb clenched. He smiled. "Definitely the last."

"Good, because I want to be myself with you to-night."

His hand passed over her hip again, this time delivering a little pat with his fingertips. It wasn't enough, not nearly enough, but it did drive her forward with hope. "And who is that?"

A good question. She opened and closed her fingers on his shoulder, taking care to fit them precisely to the combination of bone and muscle. He was built so differently than her. So different than the men she'd known back home. Even all the padding in their suit coats hadn't bulked them up to Caine's strength. She met his gaze honestly. "I'm not sure anymore, but that soft little scared woman who you always have to be gentle around? That's not me."

"I don't have a problem being gentle with you." His thumb stroked across her cheek. "I actually like it."

There was no way around it, she was just going to have to spit it out. "But I don't like you always being gentle with me." She took a deep breath and ignored the heat creeping over her cheeks. She'd never get what she wanted if she allowed shyness to rule. She dug her nails into the hard curve of muscle. And she wanted Caine. "You've only seen me since after I was kidnapped. You didn't know me before."

"I bet you were a sweet little thing."

Good heavens, he really didn't know her. "You would lose that bet. I was an absolute hellion."

His indulgent smile irked her to no end. "I'm sure."

"There's a wildness in me, Caine. It scared my parents and a lot of the men who came to court me."

The touch of his finger to the corner of her mouth was sweet. "It doesn't scare me."

"I know." She reached behind her for the fly on

his pants, patting his cock when it leapt to her touch. "But I find, when I'm in bed with you, my old problem returns."

He immediately frowned, his gaze searching hers, no doubt looking for an imaginary dragon to slay. The man seemed to live in fear that she'd be upset. "What problem?"

"The wildness."

His eyes went from green to dark in a heartbeat. He cupped her rear in his palms. "And that is a problem?"

She bit her lip. "I'm afraid..."

"I thought you were starting to feel safe with me."

The first two buttons gave without a fight. "It's not about safe." She paused, and thought again. "Well, maybe it is, in a way."

She wasn't as afraid with Caine at her side. A woman couldn't ask for more protection than the men of Hell's Eight. Caine pushed the left sleeve off her shoulder. It joined the right down by her hips. "What's it about then?"

She shook her wrist free. "It's about how I feel when I'm with you."

"Safe?"

She shook her head. Pushing her hair back with her free hand, feeling like she was on the edge of a very high cliff, she confessed, "Wild, but trapped."

Beneath her he froze, and his face got that closed expression that could mean anything, which didn't do a thing for her nerves. She kept working at the buttons on his fly. The third button was more stubborn than the first two, just adding to the overall panic threatening to consume her.

There was no hope for it. It was too late to back out now. "I want to be what you want."

"You are."

She shook her head. "In bed you're so worried about scaring me that I can't do what I sense you want."

"And what do you think I want?"

He'd already told her. Memories burned into her mind, tempting her with the remembered freedom, and horrifying her because she had been so wanton. Memories of her and him, together that first day. "Me following your commands and my instinct."

"And I've been messing that up?"

She nodded. "You won't let me get past the fear."

He went quiet again and behind the steadiness of his gaze, she knew his mind worked, weighing what she said against what he believed. "And you want that?"

With everything in her, she nodded. "I'm so tired of being afraid."

"So you want me to let go, to love you the way I want, and if you get afraid, just press on?"

"Yes."

Caine looked up into those big blue eyes, and saw the truth of what she was asking. She'd convinced herself that the fear was worse than the reality and now she wanted him to take the choice away. He touched the blush on her cheek. It wasn't going to happen. There were a lot of things he could make himself do, but forcing a woman wasn't one of them. But maybe he could coax her. "I get to do things my way?"

Her eyes widened and her gaze locked with his. She sucked in a breath, but didn't release it. It reminded him of how she'd looked that first meeting, kneeling in the grass, eyes pleading, mouth hot and determined. Desperate beyond measure. This was mighty important to her.

"Yes."

"Then come here."

21

He enforced the order with a tug on her hips. It took another tug before she realized what he wanted. She scooted forward, unconsciously letting him support her weight on his palms in another of those betraying moments of trust.

He didn't rush her, just let his fingers sink into the lush curves as he admired the view. She had the daintiest little pussy he'd ever seen, as delicately made as the rest of her, dusted with a thin layer of blond curls that did little to hide the ripe flesh beyond.

Beautiful pink flesh just swelling with passion. Another nudge and she shuffled forward, her knees hitting the underside of his arms. She stopped, teasing him with her scent and the promise of her taste. His next nudge didn't get a response. It only took a glance to figure out why. She had no idea what he wanted, which was a crime in his book. He stroked her buttocks, soothing her because he could feel the tension building. The woman had a real problem with always wanting to get things right.

"Remember the other day when I said I wanted to kiss you here?" A graze of his thumb indicated his meaning.

The shiver that took her from head to toe indicated she got it.

"You mean before you reneged?"

"I didn't renege, I gave you an IOU, and yes, then."

He brought his thumb to the top of the seductive slit and pressed, prolonging the shiver. "What I want now is for you to bring yourself high enough so I can do it."

The flush started in her chest and swept up over her neck and cheeks, building until she was rosy from the torso up. "You want me to…?"

She couldn't seem to find the words to finish the sentence. He pulled hard enough that she didn't have a choice but to work her legs over his shoulders before finishing for her. "I want you to set this little pussy on my face and let me just enjoy myself."

The squeak she made gave birth to a smile. The eager little twitch of her feminine muscles sent a tide of lust through his body. Her scent wafted over him as she straddled his face, bathing him in moist temptation. Saliva flooded his mouth as desire rose in a relentless wave. The few seconds it took her to center herself stretched into eternity. When she made a tentative descent and then stopped, his growl was nothing short of pure frustration.

Shifting his grip to her waist, he took control from her, bringing all that lush, sweet temptation within reach. Another squeak and then an equally high-pitched "I can't watch."

His laugh took him by surprise. She was always making him smile, laugh, reevaluate what he thought was normal, disturbing the calm he was used to. He didn't mind it nearly as much as he used to. "You can do whatever you want as long as you feel."

He wanted her to feel. He wanted every kiss, every

lap, every nibble imprinted onto her soul. He pressed a soft kiss to her right labia, repeating the gesture on the left, holding that connection a heartbeat longer as she swayed above him. He steadied her with a press from his palm. That lasted until he dipped his tongue between the silken folds, lapping gently, easing her into the idea of the total possession he was intent on. He could stay there forever, surrounded by her taste, her scent, her passion. If his angle was better.

Reluctantly, he pulled his tongue away from the fragrant haven, pausing a moment to let her flavor roll through his mouth before dispersing it with speech.

"Brace your hands over my head."

After the slightest hesitation, she did, her hair swinging down, blocking out the light. He glanced up. She was watching him, a frown between her brows.

"I thought you weren't going to look?"

"I can't help it. It's like watching lightning flash."

He brought his right hand down. Skimming his fingertips over her buttocks, letting them glide into the crease between. "It gets you that hot, eh?"

The frown didn't decrease. "That nervous."

He could tell from the way she jumped when his fingertips nestled into the well of her vagina. "You afraid I'm going to bite?"

From the way her eyes widened, it obviously hadn't occurred to her. "Are you?"

"Maybe a nip here——" a touch to her labia "—and there." A quick graze of her swelling clit. "But only if you're very good and ask very nicely."

"Oh."

He smiled again. Clearly she didn't know what to make of that. "So what has you nervous?"

Her mouth worked for the duration of two anxious glances, and then a shake of her head.

"You worried I'm not going to like you this way?"

"It's not sanitary."

"It's no different than when you take me in your mouth."

She blinked and then in a carefully controlled voice said, "There's a big difference."

"On that I will agree. Men are ugly creatures, where you, Desi girl, are as pretty as a flower."

He traced her contours with his finger, letting her see the desire burning him from the inside out, capturing the pearl of fluid clinging to the baby-soft hair covering her mound. He closed his eyes as the fresh taste spread over his tongue. Sweet. He opened his eyes and met her gaze dead on. "And you taste better than any chocolate."

Her gaze darkened, her hips twitched, but the frown between her eyes deepened. "You're not ugly."

It was his turn to blink. He parted her folds, exposing the deep pink inner surface and the nub of her clitoris. "I don't have a patch on you, Gypsy girl. I'm all scarred and hard and you're just sweet perfection."

"I like your scars."

"Good thing, as I have so many." He drew lazy circles on her flesh as he worked his way to that high point.

Her hips moved in a subtle shift against his tongue, increasing the friction.

"What else do you like?" he asked, giving her mind something else to work on than fretting if she should let him do this.

He tapped her clitoris lightly, holding her steady as she flinched, flattening his tongue as she pressed down, providing a warm cushion for her to snuggle that nerve-laden nub into. He cupped her buttocks in both his palms, holding her right there.

"I like the way you look," she gasped. "I like the way your face reflects your inner strength. I just need to look at you to know I can trust you."

He rewarded her with a little rub. The restless movement of her body stopped. A quiver started in her arms and ended against his receptive tongue, leaving her muscles tense and expectant in the aftermath. She was warning up to the idea of his mouth. Caine bussed her shy, swelling clit lightly before meeting her gaze and asking, "What else do you like?"

"I like the way you can carry me if you need to."

As if that were anything special. She barely weighed enough to register. Still it was a concession, so he rewarded her with another slow, leisurely lap, glossing over the engorged nub until the flex of her knees told him she needed more. He gave it to her in a steady, gliding pass, moaning himself as her flesh swelled and moistened, encouraging her to more obvious statements of her need.

One more kiss and he asked, "Anything else?"

She didn't immediately answer, just stared at him, the conflict going on inside reflected in her expression.

"C'mon, Gypsy, let that wildness out."

Another hesitation and then a softly whispered, "I love the way you smell, the way you feel against my tongue—" The statement broke in a gasp as he laved her again. She caught her breath, pushing against his mouth as she groaned, "The way you taste."

Her shuddered "Oh, God, harder!" broke the last of his control. She was ready, more than ready for what he wanted from her. Her complete submission. "Come here."

He pulled her down onto the lash of his tongue, the

taste of her desire whipping like a forest fire through his system, her cries and pleas, just more fuel to the flames. He wanted to devour her, drive her from peak to peak, higher and higher, until she'd come at the touch of his tongue, until she was so much his she couldn't think of another man.

Her shock as she felt his teeth pulled him back from the aggressive edge. She was new to this. If he wasn't careful, he'd ruin it. "Easy, baby."

Her hair whipped across the sheets in a hiss of impatience. "I don't want easy."

"Then stop fighting me. Relax into what I'm making you feel."

"That's not—" she gasped as he caught her clit in his teeth "—as easy as you make it sound."

He let her anticipate the sweet sting before he covered his teeth with his lips and let them glide off slow and easy.

"Sweetheart, accepting pleasure from your husband should be the most natural thing going."

"And if I go wild and lose control?"

"Then I'll catch you."

She lowered herself back to him, not waiting for his coaxing. "And what happens if you lose control?"

"Then you catch me."

She cupped her mound in her hand, putting the barrier of her fingers between them. He kissed the back and slid his tongue between her fingers, inevitably finding his way back to that silky heat, smiling as she gasped and rocked against him. She didn't have a prayer of keeping him from her.

"We're partners?"

"Until the day we die."

Her eyes met his, searching. "You really believe that."

It wasn't a question. "Don't you?"

There was a long pause, and then that indefinable tension that colored all their interactions disappeared. That wonderful smile she so rarely showed him spread across her face, revealing the slightly crooked eyetooth he loved to run his tongue over. "Yes."

He kissed her fingers. "Then prove it. Move your hand."

The smile turned positively witchy. "Make me."

An answering smile started deep in his gut. "You should never challenge a Ranger, Desi girl."

"I'm not."

He raised his brow at her.

"I'm challenging my husband."

"Even worse."

He rubbed his palm over her buttock, heating the firm flesh to his hand. "Challenging a husband makes it a matter of principle."

Her hand didn't move, but her butt pressed into his palm with dark yearning. "Lucky me."

He brought his hand down on her in a sharp spank. She gasped and jerked, but not in fear. Surprise and interest darkened her gaze as the hot little sting spread.

"I think it's more like lucky me. Move your hand."

She shook her head. He didn't miss the way her breath caught and she held herself perfectly still, her back subtly arched. She was waiting for him to do it again. He did, ghosting his hand over her left cheek, watching her tremble as the anticipation crested in disappointment. Before it could settle, he spanked her again, this time hard enough to give a little sting.

"Oh, God."

"Oh, God, save me' or 'Oh, God, do it again'?"

A pregnant little pause and then, "Do it again."

Damn, she was a hot little thing. The next smack yanked a cry from her lips, and her hand out of his way. She braced herself on the bed, her spine arching, pushing her buttocks back, her pussy down. He took advantage of both invitations. Laving her silken flesh with his tongue, giving her the stinging pleasure of another smack. Against his tongue, her pussy spasmed. Cream spilled from her body, breathless cries from her lungs.

He moved his attention toward that tight little bundle of nerves that swelled, cradling it gently, rubbing her ass and her clit in time, massaging the heat into both, measuring her pleasure in the pulse of her breath, the clench of her muscles, the shudder that took her from head to toe.

"That's my girl," he whispered against her.

"Wife," she gasped.

He smiled and traced a smooth path from her anus to her vagina, teasing the entrance, tickling the nerves to life. "*That* I'm not likely to forget."

He slid his finger in that first little bit. She clenched around him, hard and tight. He rode out the spasm, waiting for her to relax before working his finger deeper. She clenched again, halting his progress. He took her clit into the heat of his mouth, and slapped her ass just a bit harder than before, delivering to them both a white-hot bolt of delight.

She rocked on his face, her breath coming in sporadic gasps. His cock throbbed with the same rhythm as he supported her weight in one hand. She gripped him tighter, he spanked her harder. Her pleasure flowed, desire roared, lust surged through him. His cock leapt and fought the confines of his pants. His muscles knotted with hunger as her body opened for his thrust. God, she was sweet.

Another spank, another ripple, another lap. Little by little, he drove her higher, increasing the pressure, the depth, the force with every other beat, letting her cries drive him on, absorbing her shock, her pleasure, keeping it up until her body was whipcord taut. He nipped her clit, once, twice, holding the sensitive flange of flesh between his teeth, letting her wonder, worry, giving her that little edge that spiked her passion higher before bearing down, ever so lightly.

Her back arched, her head, the ends of her hair lashed his stomach as she writhed above him, caught on the plane between pain and pleasure, unsure which way to go, what to do. Needing guidance. Guidance he was more than willing to give. Wanted to give. He wanted to give her everything. Every pleasure. Every desire. Everything her wild little soul desired.

"Come for me." He thrust his finger deep, settling his thumb on her clitoris, rubbing hard as he spanked her ass in a rapid cadence bringing the erotic sting to play.

"Now, Desi."

She fell into his command, into her climax and then into his arms. And he caught her as he'd promised, kissing her mouth, her breasts, the underside of her chin before going back to her mouth, taking each little gasp into himself as she slid his thigh up, pressing in, coaxing another shudder out of her. Another sigh. Her arms came around his neck as she settled against him, light as down. She whispered his name.

"What?"

"I told you I would."

Her fingers made a half-ass pat at his cheek. "You caught me."

She turned fully into his arms. "And you always keep your promises."

"I'm Hell's Eight."

"So am I."

He brushed the hair off her cheek. "Better than that."

He rolled her under him, throwing his thigh over hers. "You're mine."

She didn't argue, didn't open her eyes, just smiled that soft, enigmatic smile. "Hmm."

He propped himself up on his elbow. Her gown was bunched around her waist and gaped away from her right breast. The white mound shivered with her erratic breathing. The little tip was hard and pink and straining. He'd neglected her breasts. He'd have to make up for that. He caught the peak in his mouth. She jumped, her hands cradling his head, half holding him and half pushing him away.

He glanced up. "Sensitive?"

Her lip slipped between her teeth. She nodded.

He cupped the plump mound in his palm. Her flesh was white and smooth. His hand was dark and rough, swallowing the mound. Too rough for her. She deserved better, and if her father hadn't been a dream-fed fool she'd be living back east in a big fancy house with servants and a man like him wouldn't even get close enough to see the color of her eyes, let alone touch her breast.

Bur her father had been a fool and now she was his, and he wasn't anyone's fool. She was so small, so dainty and so damn sexy she made him ache with lust, passion and a hundred softer emotions he couldn't name. "I'll be easy, then."

That vow wasn't as simple as it sounded. While she lay replete and oversensitive from her orgasms, his own desire was riding him hard. His balls ached, his cock throbbed and every nerve in his body burned as if consumed by fire. Caine needed to be in her. He wanted nothing more than to climb on top of her, push her legs apart and fuck her hard and deep, make a place for himself in her body the way he wanted to make a place for himself in her life.

Except the latter wasn't going to happen. She was too fine for this land. Too fine to want to stay with him once she healed. But for now she was his, and he hadn't gotten where he was in life by throwing away opportunities. And he could learn to live with the guilt of denying her the life she'd been raised for. Maybe.

The turgid tip of her breast, damp from his mouth, swollen from his attentions, beckoned. He answered the call gently, ever so gently suckling the spongy nipple, beating back his selfish urges. This was his wife, the woman he'd promised to cherish. She arched up into his kiss, offering him more. Without hesitation, he took it, sucking harder, absorbing her start, holding her in place as he gave her what they both needed, forcing her to accept both the pleasure and edge of pain she craved, keeping her in place, steadying her through the shock until she reached the gratification beyond, knowing she found it when she gasped and grabbed his head.

"Harder."

The whisper whipped around him, flaying his control. He wanted to yank her beneath him, mount her, mark her, brand her as his, compel her to fit into his life. He shook his head as she gasped and her fingers feathered through his hair. He'd never felt the need to brand another woman, but with Desi, it was an overwhelming urge, maybe because he knew how unfair it was for him to have claimed her. She groaned and held him to her. Unfair or not, she was his. Contradictions and all. So delicate and sweet in looks, yet wild and demanding in her passion. Eager for the tiny bite of pain with her pleasure, pulling back from it however, even as he gave it to her. As if she feared that part of her.

He glanced at her face; the frown, the tension pleating her brow mixed with passion softening her lips, and he understood.

She feared how he would see her if she revealed it. He shook his head again, letting the edge of his teeth tease the edge of her nipple as he did so. "Desi?"

"What?"

"You're not supposed to be holding back."

"I'm trying not to."

He could see she was. He shifted up, not releasing her nipple right away, stretching it away from her body, pausing when her lids flickered and her breath caught, letting her sink into the pleasure, maximizing it with a flick of his tongue before releasing it with a little pop. He brushed a kiss over her chin, her nose and the closed lids of her eyes. High color rode the edge of her cheekbones. He hitched up until he could cup her cheek in his hand. A stroke of his thumb and she looked at him. The impact of those blue eyes hit his gut harder than a sucker punch. So much want. So much trust. "Do you really want me to take over?"

"Would you?"

It wouldn't be a hardship. It was his nature to command any situation he was in, but he had to be sure she knew what she was asking for. "Even if you get scared?"

She didn't answer right off. He respected that. It was a big deal to give a man control. Especially with her background.

"Yes."

"Why?"

"You always ask that."

"Probably because I always want to know."

Her fingers skimmed his elbow and rode up his arm, disturbing the hairs along the way. With feminine delicacy they closed around his wrist, holding him as he'd held her. "Because I think relaxing enough to enjoy what you make me feel is going to take all my concentration."

He smiled and dropped his forehead to hers. Lord help him, she was going to concentrate. "Well, if one of the things you plan on concentrating on is how to hide that you like your loving rough sometimes, you can take it off the list."

Her lips pursed in a perfect O of horror.

"You know about that?"

He didn't understand how she thought he could have missed it. "I not only know about it, I'm celebrating it."

"But you don't like to hurt me."

He was glad she didn't phrase that as a question. He kept her face turned toward his. "No, but I love making you go wild in my arms, giving you what you need to come, holding you while you shudder and scream, coming with you." He lowered his mouth until his was a hairsbreadth from hers, so close their breath intermingled. "I love giving you everything it takes to get you there, spanking your ass, your pussy, your clit."

Her high-pitched squeak hit his lip in a sharp blow, slicing straight to his cock. A quick glance showed her pulse going twice its normal rate.

"You like the sound of that, don't you, sweetheart? Your man taking away your options, commanding your pleasure? Giving him whatever he wants, that gets you humming, doesn't it?"

Her eyes closed and her tongue passed over her lips in a quick jerk. He didn't think she was going to answer, but then she tightened her grip and confessed. "God help me, yes."

Confidence flowed into him right along with lust. He kissed her lightly before tucking her under him. "Trust me, Gypsy, you don't need God right now. Giving you what you need will be my pleasure."

22

His shadow blocked out the light, fear and possibly common sense, because even though she was surrendering everything to Caine, Desi wasn't afraid. Instead, as Caine came over her, the heavy weight of his big body pressing her into the mattress, she felt free. Freer than she'd ever felt in her life. Caine didn't need her to be perfect. He liked her just the way she was, with all her unconventional thoughts and reactions. He even liked her temper.

She slid her fingers into the cool strands of his hair. He needed a haircut. The sense of right deepened as she realized, as his wife, it would be her job to give it to him. She smiled as she pulled his mouth to hers. Lord knew what he'd look like after she got done with him.

"Kiss me, Caine."

She wanted his mouth on hers, wanted to be so immersed in him. There'd be no chance for the memories to howl.

He obliged, his mouth taking hers with that barely civilized command that melted her all the way down to her toes. A press of his thumb underneath brought her chin up, improving the angle for the sure thrust of his tongue. His taste flooded her mouth. Welcome. So very welcome. She focused on the touch of his hand, his scent, his taste, blocking out everything else. Until there was just Caine.

His lips parted from hers, not going far, hovering just out of reach. The arch of her neck was instinctive. His hum of approval immediate.

"Concentrating, Gypsy?"

"Yes."

"Good."

Something tickled her ear. She was tempted to open her eyes and see what, but if she did that, she might lose the illusion she was weaving around them. That this was their first time. That there'd never been anyone else. That he loved her as much as she loved him. *Oh, God, she loved him.*

"About what?"

"About how good you feel against me, how good you smell, taste." She smiled. "Just…you."

She knew, from the way his thumb stroked her temple, that she hadn't fooled him that that was all there was. He'd be wanting her to open her eyes next. She forestalled him with a simple, "Don't."

"What?"

"Don't make me open my eyes. Just let me pretend."

The sheets rustled as he shifted, contemplating what she'd just said. "I'm not sure I like knowing my woman's got her eyes closed, wishing herself away, as I'm making love to her."

"I'm not wishing myself away." She wanted to drown herself in him. "I just want to pretend that this is the first time, that there's no past screaming at me, no disappointments between us and I'm coming to you pure."

His hoarse "Ah, shit" almost had her opening her eyes. She let go of his wrist and fumbled her way to his shoulders. Her palms molded to the hard strength with an easy familiarity. She held on as she whispered, "Let me pretend, Caine, please."

The cool slide of his hair brushed the back of her hand before she felt the firmness of his lips.

"You pretend all you want, baby, but when you decide what to add to your make-believe world, you understand this..." His lips left her. So did his weight. He turned her over, talking all the while. "I've never had a woman more pure come to my bed." The mattress sank around her as his weight came down over her back. "Things happen to a body in life. Accidents of fate that leave scars inside and out, but they don't matter." One of his hands worked between them, cotton scraping the backs of her thighs as he pushed his pants down. "Don't get me wrong, if I could go back in time, I'd kill every one of the sons of bitches before they laid a finger on you, but I don't think of your past as an imperfection any more than I think of—" he dropped his hand to her knee where a crescent scar rested "—this scar, that I bet you got playing when you were a little girl, as an imperfection."

She'd actually gotten it trying to escape, but she liked Caine's perception better, so she didn't correct him.

Desi went a second without his heat, heard a drawer open and close, a belt buckle hit the floor and then his thighs came back between hers, the hairs dusting his flesh tickling her. She dug her fingers into the sheets as his cock settled high on the crease of her buttocks, searing her flesh.

Caine's view of life might be simplistic compared to the intricacies of the society in which she'd grown up, but like the man himself, it was a philosophy that rolled with life's vagaries rather than trying to fight them. And in Caine's world, a wife was a partner to be treasured, honored, protected. And maybe if she played her cards right, loved.

She groaned as his cock slid down her rear, falling into the deep crease, dragging against the sensitive flesh until it slipped into her cream. A woman loved by Caine would never worry about his fidelity, being judged or the future, simply because a woman loved by Caine would be his world. And Caine's world was big and forgiving and full of acceptance.

His cock nuzzled in, finding the well of her vagina with ease, lingering, pressing. His hand slid downward under her body, fingers curving, his thumb catching in her navel, pressing gently before his hand insinuated itself between her legs, pulling up the cotton until the swollen folds, still pulsing from his previous attention, were bared.

And pleasure, she mentally added to the list of things to be found in Caine's world as he found her clitoris. There was a lot of pleasure for a woman invited into Caine's world. Her breath hung up in her lungs as those long, lean fingers circled, plucked and flicked.

"And that's the other thing you need to understand, Gypsy," he whispered in his deep drawl, continuing with his point. "I touch you and your breath catches. Not because you're seeing dollar signs, or because I paid you for the pleasure, but simply because it's my hand on you."

His fingers contracted, his cock pushed, spreading her muscles, forging past the initial resistance, making a place for himself in her sensitive flesh. Her cry was involuntary, a volatile welcome to the slow invasion. His hum of satisfaction came right behind it. "There's no purer gift a woman can give a man, Desi, and so long as you don't mess with that, I won't mess with your pretending."

She panted through the first level of his possession. It was the longest speech he'd ever given, and with her eyes closed and all her senses focused on his voice, there was no mistaking the sincerity. She wiggled her butt back, hampered by her position. With her toes barely touching the floor, she was helpless beneath him. "Maybe I won't pretend after all."

His laugh puffed over her ear, sending tingles down her spine. She opened her mind to the sensation rather than trying to control it. It skimmed the surface of her awareness for a moment before catching on something and then burrowing in, leaving her open and receptive for more.

"I'd prefer it."

And she believed him. For the first time ever, she really believed he just wanted what she felt as she felt it, without worrying that as he touched her he saw the handprints of those who had gone before. It was wonderfully liberating. She tilted her head to the side, facilitating his nibbling kiss, letting those shivers go where they wanted, letting them build the pleasant glow.

"Caine?"

"What, baby?" He was clearly distracted.

"Make me yours tonight."

His lips left her neck. "You already are."

"Not like either of us need."

"You know what you're asking for?"

"Literally?" She opened her eyes and strained to see his face. "No, but I trust you."

His fingers bit into her buttocks as his cock waited inside her, pulsing with his heartbeat, his anticipation. "Don't ask this of me, Desi, if you've got any doubts. I won't be able to let you go if you give yourself to me like that."

She arched back into his possession. "Who asked you to?"

It came out more gasp than question.

He caught one of her curls around his finger and measured it, as if it held all the secrets of the world. "You were raised with fine things. Meant for them."

"And yet the only thing I've ever truly wanted was to be yours." She dug her toes into the floor and pushed up. "Make me yours."

For three heartbeats he didn't move, just rose above her like a wonderfully cast statue embracing everything masculine and primitive that made a man a man. And as she watched from the corner of her eye, all that control shattered, and for the first time, she got to see the man she'd married without the reserve he wore like a shield. Possessive, carnal, intent on dominating her. Fear tempered her excitement, but even the fear was good because it just sharpened the latter.

Caine cupped her pussy, all the possession and dominance in his expression doubled in his touch. "Don't let me scare you."

She brought her hand around, placing a finger to his mouth the way he did to her when he wanted her attention focused. He was such a worrying man. "Scare me, excite me, pleasure me." She traced the contour of his firm mouth, smiling when he captured the tip of her finger between his teeth. "Whatever you want."

He made a noise like a growl in his throat, his fingers leaving hers to clasp her buttocks, spreading the soft flesh even as his thighs pushed at her. "Open."

The words came from her soul. She needed this, needed to know she could handle him when he let go. Needed him to know it, too. "Make me."

With a hard curse, he pushed up and away. First one

and then the other of her hands were anchored above her head, captured in his. He pressed them into the mattress beside her head, sounding completely savage as he asked, "Is this what you want, Desi? Me to love you like I've been dreaming about, all stretched out beneath me, helpless to do anything but take me as I command?"

A hot bolt of lust tore through her, stealing her voice.

She managed a nod.

"It'll be hard and rough." He nudged her thighs apart.

"Maybe too much like you used to fear."

She shook her head, sure of this. "It'll be nothing like I'm used to."

"I've only got so much control, Desi."

"That's what I'm hoping."

"You haven't a cautious bone in your body."

"I've got a lot." She stretched her fingers out as far as she could, imagining the freedom that would soon be hers. Freedom from fear, freedom to enjoy. "I just don't need them with you."

"You goddamn well better be sure."

He didn't give her time to respond, just made that sound deep in his throat again. His fingers sank into the soft cheeks of her ass as he thrust into her pussy, separating the full curves, stretching her anus in a whispery caress as his cock forged into her tight sheath. The familiar burn of his possession spread over her in a welcome scald. Her channel struggled to accept his size, answer his demand. And deep inside the wildness gathered, waiting to be unleashed.

"Relax, Desi."

She tried, but it was always that way at first, her body fighting what it wanted. She closed her hands into fists and pushed her forehead into the mattress. Swallowed by his heat, surrounded by his strength, frustration joined the chaos within. "Just do it."

His hand came over her fingers weaving between her splayed ones. His lips brushed her ear. His serene "Just follow my lead" smoothed over the wildness, calming it, controlling it.

At first it wasn't easy to follow the shallow, seductive pulses of his hips. Not when everything inside demanded violence. Force. Action. Caine didn't allow her any choice. He held her still for the brush of his lips over her ear, her neck. Kisses so faint, she had to still to feel them. Kisses that made her focus on him in a desperate effort to anticipate where the next would land. Kisses that seared as they progressed down her neck and over her shoulder in a string of tingling sparks, stopping midway between her shoulder blades. The touch of his tongue burned deep.

"Such a pretty, responsive little wife. Are you going to come for me when I tell you to?"

She didn't hesitate. More than anything she wanted to come. "Yes."

"Good." Again he moved away from her, depriving her of his heat, letting the wildness out from under his control. She dug her hands into the sheets, holding on against the urge to do something crazy. Like throw herself back and end this torment.

"Just lie there and enjoy the feel of my cock for a minute. Just a minute more, and then I'll give you what you need."

It was the understanding in his use of the word *need* that gave her the strength to contain the impulses coming at her, all of them strong, none of them smart. All of them once again quelled as he released her hands and centered her attention with the touch of his fingertips on her forearms in a feather-light summons.

He was connected to her at three points, his fingertips to her forearms and his cock to her pussy, forming a triangle of need inside of which chaos reigned. It didn't make sense that so little could cause so much havoc, but it did. Tiny hairs rose on her nape. Goose bumps sprang up her arms before racing over her torso, dragging anticipation in their wake, peaking her nipples and shortening her breath.

His fingers followed the path of the kisses, the hard calluses abrading her skin, reminding her of the violent life he'd led, everything of which he was capable. Unlimited pain, unlimited pleasure.

Every nerve ending in her body tracked those fingers' path over her shoulders, down the ladder of her ribs, the trail narrowing until they nestled into the well of her spine. They stopped for one heart-seizing second before continuing up the rise of her buttocks.

Desi had a gorgeous ass. Caine palmed the white surface, frowning at the faint marks marring the smooth skin. He traced one line that ended in a curve. The edge of a buckle? He placed his palm over it, blocking it from his sight. The past had no place between them. Right now there was just him and her and the passion between them. And the care with which he needed to proceed.

"Caine…"

He ignored the frustration in the plea. "The way I want, baby."

"You don't like this."

"You don't have a clue what I like, but if you relax and follow my lead, you'll find out."

She wiggled that enticing butt at him. His cock jerked and for one minute, he was tempted to just push through the resistance of her body to the searing heat beyond. He knew how she'd feel, tight and smooth like liquid silk. He tucked one hand under her hips, finding the damp nest of curls before sifting through to the swollen lips of her sex. Her clitoris rose to his touch. Her cry flowed like a riveting melody. He leaned back over her so he could feel the next cry vibrate against his chest.

"That's it, right there, isn't it?" He rubbed and teased. She bucked, and little by little, relaxed. On the next pass of his fingers, her muscles unlocked. His shaft popped into the tight sheath. Her nails scraped across the sheets as she struggled with the shock, the pleasure.

"That's it," he encouraged while massaging her clitoris. "Take me."

She did. Deeper and deeper. He increased the strength of his thrusts. Her sheath rippled around him, tugging a tendril of the lust past his control. Caine's next thrust wasn't nearly as gentle. It lodged him deep in her flesh, deeper than he'd gone before. Her cry froze him in place. Damn, she was so small. He pulled back.

Her hand snaked back and her nails dug into his thigh, halting his withdrawal. "Oh, God, please, Caine, do that again."

The ecstatic spasming of her pussy echoed the plea. He could give her that. He thrust back in, hard and deep. Desi's voice broke on his name, an exultant little feminine expulsion of joy he wanted to hear again and again. Another hard thrust and her back arched. A hoarse scream echoed through the room. She was so close, so close.

Caine wanted this climax for her. He wanted her to have every bit of pleasure he could give her in this life. Every pleasure there was. He worked his cock out, his balls pulling up tight to his body as she fought with the only thing she could. Her inner muscles clutching at him, bringing the friction to unbearable. His balls burned. Sweat dripped in his eyes. He didn't know how much longer he could hold back, but he would. He would not come before she did.

He slammed back in, hard enough that she bounced on the bed, hard enough his grip on her slippery little clit slipped. They both moaned. He yanked out just as fast before plunging back into her steamy depths, her grunts of "Yes" on every down thrust rising to a chant that summoned the primitive lust within. The lust he swore she'd never see. Lust he was helpless to contain as she begged with her body, her voice. "More," she jerked. "Hold still, baby. I'll give you what you need."

He gave it to her, and still she didn't come. He shook his hair out of his eyes and reached for the jar on the bed stand, pressing high and deep inside her as he flipped the lid. He dropped the jar on the bed before scooping some of the smooth cream onto his fingers. He spread her buttocks. The little rosette winked at him.

"Hurry," she gasped.

The same urgency was beating at him. He touched his finger to the tight ring of muscle. It clenched immediately. "Relax, Desi."

She whimpered, and a shudder shook her from head to toe, sending an equally fierce convulsion through him. He pressed his finger in, the small circle flattened and spread as the lubricant eased his way. His finger sank into that tight portal. It seized like a fist around him. He pushed deeper, spreading the cream around, easing his passage.

She was tight. Hot, tight and delicious and he wanted her ass like hell on fire. He worked his cock out of her pussy, keeping his finger tucked inside her. "Such a sweet ass, Desi."

"Oh, God."

"Perfect to give a man pleasure." He sank his cock back in. She was closer now, taking him in a luxurious expansion of muscles and delicate flesh.

He pinched her clit between his fingers, stretching it out before letting it retract as he slowly fucked her ass with his finger in counterpoint to his thrusts; once, twice, three times. On the fourth, he tested her with another finger, watching his cock slide into her body as her anus stretched to accept his demands.

"Caine."

There was a touch of uncertainty underlying the desire. "It's all right. Just relax."

It had to be all right. He was heading out tomorrow. If things went wrong, he didn't want to die without claiming her totally.

"You said you wanted to be mine."

A slight pause, then, "I do."

"Then push back and let me make you feel good."

Another squeeze on her clitoris, another pulse of his cock and she took his fingers to the second knuckle, panting as she struggled with the sensation. He wasn't doing much better. The heat of her pussy and ass were melting his control. She was so perfect, so responsive.

"It's going to be rougher now, Desi." She'd be lucky if he didn't pound her into the mattress. "But stay relaxed."

Her hand flailed, found his thigh, dug in and held on, pulling him to her, inviting him to take more. "God, yes!"

Like a flower she opened to him. Fingers clenched in the sheets as she arched her back, relaxed and did everything she could in her limited ability to move, to entice him. Her dark channel milked him in pace with his manipulation of her clitoris, squeezing and relaxing, rippling and smoothing over the ultrasensitive tip of his cock, tearing at his good intentions. Tearing at his control. He could hear every break in her breath, every hitch of anticipation. He kissed her ear, letting his lips linger as she moaned.

"Stay still, baby."

He didn't want to come at her like an animal, but she wasn't leaving him much to hold on to. She was all hot, willing, trusting woman. It was the trust that gave him the strength to hold back. She was close, so close. He removed his fingers from her rear and scooped up another dollop of cream. He added it to her already greased hole, soothing it in with one finger, two, then three. Pressing down on her back when she struggled, easing her through her adjustment with a sprinkle of kisses on her neck and tiny teasing pulses of his cock, waiting for that betraying tension that would tell him it was time.

He had to wait a good two minutes, but then it was there, holding her within its merciless grip, suspended above the pleasure he wanted for her. "Come for me, Desi."

He shoved his fingers in as he drew on her clit. She erupted around him, her ass and pussy clenching on his fingers and cock. Caine pulled all the way out, and then plunged back into the center of her climax, taking her shock as his she milked him with strong, rhythmic contractions, her body pleading as hard as her voice.

"Come, please come."

"Not yet." He wasn't coming yet. Tonight might be his only time to be with her the way she wanted. Completely.

She turned her head. He kissed her cheek, ignoring the pain in his arm from the awkward position.

"That's my girl."

He pulled his cock free. Her mewl of disappointment followed.

"Just a minute and you'll have me back."

He lifted his cock and aimed it at the slick little starburst. When their flesh touched, she jumped. He waited until she settled before pressing in. He brought his arm up and tucked it under her cheek, supporting her as she shuddered under the dual impact of the residue of her climax and this new possession. She tightened and he stopped.

He kissed her neck, her ear, the corner of her mouth, just letting her get used to him. The cream had a short-lived numbing agent. A little more time, and she'd be fine. Gradually, she relaxed. The tight muscles gave, and she took a little more.

"That's it. Just a little at a time until you have it all."

She shook her head. Her voice was strained. "I can't."

"You can, sweetheart. Nice and easy."

With a pop that had her crying out, he won the unequal battle. Again he held her, nursing her compliance with slow draws of his fingers and soft kisses. The only word he could get from his mouth as he sank into that dark channel was, "Mine."

And through the shuddering gasp that expanded her ribs as he worked deeper came the one response he needed.

"Yes."

It was almost dawn. Caine slipped from the bed. The others would be at the barn getting ready to ride. He needed to be there. Beside him, Desi slept, stretched out on her stomach, worn out from their lovemaking. He propped himself up on his elbow. The purity of her profile, the way her hair tumbled about her face, enthralled him. She was so damn beautiful. He brushed the hair aside. A pink spot on her neck drew his attention. He rubbed his jaw. Whisker burn. He'd have to remember to shave more often.

Caine pulled the sheet down farther. The hollow of her spine beckoned, feminine in its delicacy, strong in its line. He traced it to the cleft of her buttocks. She shifted and sighed. He dipped between, his fingers gliding easily along the slick flesh. He covered the pucker of her anus, holding his seed inside, liking the idea that when he was gone, part of him would stay with her in a warm, potent memory.

He slid lower. Her pussy was wet and inviting. He rubbed his thumb around the well of her vagina. He'd been like a green boy with her, unable to hold back, wild, fucking her insatiably. Her flesh showed it, swollen and sensitive, wet with his seed and her juices. As he rubbed, a selfish hope blossomed in his chest. Maybe she was pregnant.

He eased his fingers in. Her pussy was wet and inviting. She took two easily. She was still open and primed. And he was still hard and ready. He glanced at the sky beyond the window. And then back at Desi. There wasn't time. Desi sighed and shifted, arching her hips back into his probe, thighs falling apart in wanton invitation.

Fuck it. He'd make time. He drew the sheet down to her knees. She moaned when he rolled her over. "Shh, don't wake up. Just lie there."

A shift of his hips and his cock fell into place. He bore down. Her muscles parted. "Just lie still, baby. This will be nice and easy. You're all soft and wet and ready. And I need you just one more time."

She caught his hand and brought it under her cheek, eyes closed, still half-asleep, welcoming him. He slid his cock in to the hilt with a slow and steady glide, holding himself high within her pussy as she stirred, not wanting to wake her. She sighed and relaxed. He took it as his cue. He pumped leisurely between her thighs, savoring the hot pleasure, the knowledge that she was his wife, the knowledge that when he left this time, he was leaving something behind. Something to come back to. A wife and maybe a child. A family to carry on. Someone to remember him.

Caine lowered his lips to her ear as his climax washed over him, cupping her breast in his hand and rolling the plump nipple between his fingers, his orgasm devastating for all its easy prelude. "Come for me, Desi. Give me a memory to come back to."

Her small cry shattered his soul as she came, sucking the seed from his body, pulling it deeply into hers. He collapsed on top of her, taking his weight on his forearms and knees.

God, he wanted to give her everything she was used to—diamonds, chocolate, peace and safety—but those were out of his reach. The only thing he could give her was the security that came from knowing the men who'd hurt her could never touch her again.

He eased his cock from her body, cupping his hand over the flood of moisture that immediately escaped. By the end of the week, she'd have that and then…

He sighed and got to his feet. It wouldn't be long after that before she realized what a poor deal she had, and when that happened, she'd be looking for outs. He tugged on his socks, deciding then and there when she asked to go, he'd let her. He picked up her hand and kissed the back, the long elegant fingers marred now with new callus. He touched a blister. She wasn't made for this life.

Caine pulled on his pants, ignoring the weariness in his muscles. Desi moaned and reached across the bed. He pulled the blankets up over her shoulders and pressed a kiss on her cheek. "Sleep, Gypsy girl. I promise when I come back, all will be right in your world."

23

Tracker and Sam were waiting for him in the barn.

"For a man about to deliver an ass-kicking, you're not looking too happy," Sam observed, tightening the cinch on his saddle.

Caine shrugged and opened Chaser's stall, grabbing the bridle off the hook. Down the way, the stallion screamed. To the left, Lily whickered. The place was growing fast. Next year, if he got that mare and the stallion settled, they were going to need a bigger barn. He wasn't going to take any chances with his mares getting pregnant by accident or being brought down by predators. Chaser greeted him with a snort.

"Morning, fella. Ready to ride?" The big horse ducked his head for the bridle, nuzzling his pocket for sugar cubes. Caine slipped the bridle over his ears and shoved his head away. "Desi sure has you spoiled."

Desi was trying to bribe her way out of fear with the horses by bringing them precious cubes of Tia's sugar when she thought he wasn't around. He didn't know why she tried to hide what she was doing, but since it wasn't hurting anything and she stayed away from the stallion, he didn't put an end to it. Much to Tia's disgust. At the top of the shopping list Tia had shoved into his hand when he left the house that morning—just in case there was time when he finished business—was sugar, in three times the amount they usually bought. Her glare had dared him to complain about the expense.

He led Chaser out of the stall. He wasn't going to complain. His wife was used to better. No doubt she hadn't even considered how dear sugar was when she'd chosen it as a treat for the horses. He swung the saddle off the sawhorse and up onto Chaser's back. Two sharp tugs and he had it in place.

"Who're you leaving in charge of Desi?" Tracker asked, tucking a food pack into his saddlebag.

"Shadow."

"Shadow's babysitting?" Sam grinned and turned as he lowered his stirrup.

"He's the best when it comes to up-close-and-personal discussions."

"You think someone's going to get close enough to Hell's Eight to need that kind of defense?"

Caine cinched the saddle. "Judging by the number of hopeful collectors we've had to take care of this last week, I think one thousand dollars is a hell of an incentive to forget common sense."

"Son of a bitch."

Caine couldn't agree with the sentiment more. "Eventually, someone with some real skill is going to give it a shot, and I don't want anyone getting too close for comfort."

"Which is why we're heading east to have a talk with the folk who set the bounty," Tracker added.

"Exactly." Caine tucked the excess strap into the knot and dropped the stirrup. "There's one man in particular we're looking for, though."

"Besides James and the bankers?"

"Yup." He checked his pistol and rifle. He double-checked the pack to make sure there was ample ammunition. "He's a smooth-talking bastard with an eastern accent."

"That's not much to go on," Sam said.

"Desi never saw his face, but from what she said, I get the impression he's the head honcho creating the threat."

Sam and Tracker cut him a glance, paying more attention to what he didn't say than what he did. Tracker's mouth settled to a thin line, Sam's brow went up. "And when we find this easterner, is he dying fast or slow?"

Caine swung up into the saddle, settling his weight as leather creaked, and kneed Chaser toward the door. "Slow. Very, very slow."

HE'D LEFT HER. Without a word, without a goodbye, without even an explanation. He'd left her. Desi stood in the kitchen, frying bacon and potatoes for the men, and stared at Tia.

"When did he leave?"

"This morning." Tia motioned to the pan. "If you do not turn the bacon, it will burn."

She forced herself to care. Caine had left her. He'd made love to her as if there was no tomorrow, and then he'd left her. She flipped the bacon pieces one at a time as she absorbed the knowledge. He'd told Tia he was leaving but he hadn't said a word to her.

"Did he go alone?"

"Tracker and Sam went with him."

Tia's brusque tones were colored with sympathy, which just served to rub salt into the wound. Everyone but her had known her husband was leaving. Everyone but her knew why. That could only mean one thing. She turned the other rasher of bacon. "He went after James, didn't he?"

"You could not expect him to let them be."

No, but she'd asked for it. "It's dangerous."

A snort came from the direction of the table. One of the new men, she didn't know who because she'd been distracted when they were introduced, stared at her over his coffee. He tipped the cup in a small salute.

"Begging your pardon, ma'am, but if those three have set their sights on someone, the only one in danger would be this James fella."

Desi slammed down the fork on the stove so hard, the metal grates rattled. They all acted as if they were immortal when in reality, they weren't, and things went wrong all the time. "Do I know you?"

He tipped his hat. "Shadow, ma'am."

Desi turned to Tia. "Tracker's brother, right?"

"Yes."

Desi could see the resemblance. Same big-boned build, same deadly darkness, same exotically handsome features, same just-give-me-a-reason attitude that belied the lazy way he slouched against the chair back. "I met you my first day."

"Briefly."

"It's a pleasure to meet you face-to-face."

His lips twitched at the formality. "Same here."

Tia's smile was fond as she looked over at Shadow. "He and the rest of the boys came in a few days ago. It has been many months since all have been together."

Ordinarily, in most households, that would call for a party, but no one was here to celebrate anything. Desi picked up the fork and flipped the bacon, thinking hard as it sputtered and spit. "Why are they all here?"

"Because Caine asked us to come."

She shot the man a glare. Now that the formalities were over, she didn't want to hear from him, the living proof that Caine didn't regard her as an equal. She directed her question at Tia. "Where are the other three?"

"They are guarding the passes."

She stirred the potatoes with a quick jab. "Why?"

Tia didn't answer, just folded a dish towel, her face set in that impassive, stubborn way Desi had learned meant she disapproved of something. The man who called himself Shadow didn't look up from his coffee.

"For heaven's sake, if it involves me, I should know about it."

"Caine does not wish you to worry."

Desi grabbed at the back of her apron and untied the strings. Wadding it into a ball, she tossed it to the scarred worktable. "Too late."

She grabbed a shawl off the hook by the door and stormed out onto the porch. Boone raised his head. As she stomped down the steps, he whined and followed. His nose pushed into her hand as she crossed the yard. She tried to find comfort in the gesture. There was none.

James was coming after her. Caine was going to try and stop him, but he couldn't. She knew he couldn't, because James was a snake in the grass. And if James was coming after her then so was *he*. The horror of it bled into her soul. She looked around the stronghold, sending her gaze higher than she normally did to include the cliffs above, spotting the silhouette of a man. She'd felt so safe here, but she wasn't. She wasn't ever going to be safe. Her heart raced. And now Caine was in danger because he saw it as his duty to protect her. Boone whined again. She patted his head. "It'll be all right, Boone."

Dear heavens, she was no better than anyone else,

lying to the dog so he wouldn't worry. As if he could understand her. As if he had anything to worry about.

"It really will be all right, ma'am."

She spun around, her hand going to her throat as the man loomed above her. He was even more threatening up close. Taller than Caine with the broad-shouldered lean-hipped build that carried a lot of muscle. His long black hair, contained by a red bandanna tied around his head beneath his hat, whipped around his face with the wind, adding to the impression of wildness barely contained.

Boone snarled low in his throat. Desi's fingers clenched in his scruff. She hadn't heard Shadow follow her out of the kitchen, which should have been impossible even with those knee-high moccasins he wore. "No wonder they call you Shadow."

He touched his finger to the edge of his black hat before cutting the dog a glare. "If you don't shut up, I'll be using you as target practice this afternoon."

He adjusted his grip on his rifle. Desi couldn't tell if he was serious or not. Boone didn't care. He just kept on snarling. She placed herself between the dog and the man. She couldn't control much, but she could control this. "You'll do no such thing."

Shadow stared at her. His eyes were brown, she realized. A deep, almost black-brown. And hard. Like all the Hell's Eight men, they were a reflection of his life's experience, and his life had made him deadly and cold. Very cold.

His "Who's going to stop me?" was a flat inquiry. She pulled her shawl around her. "I will."

He pushed his hair back, revealing a handsome face to go with those too-cold, too-old eyes. "Uh-huh."

He didn't have to sound so amused. Just because he'd

grown as big as a mountain didn't mean he couldn't be taken down a peg or two. She spun on her heel, hauling Boone with her by her grip on his scruff. When they were a safe distance from Shadow, she released him. The hound skulked in apology, which forced her to stop and pet him to let him know she wasn't mad at him. "It's okay, Boone. You were a good boy standing up for me."

His head came up, and his face sagged in bliss that he'd pleased her.

The man behind her scoffed. "That dog's still as useless as the day he was born."

There was no point arguing with him. Everyone seemed to be very set in their opinions when it came to Boone, but she knew there was more to him than what they saw. She petted the big dog's head and kissed his nose. "I like him."

She didn't leave any room in the statement for argument. She headed across the yard at a brisk pace, trying to work off her anger and frustration. The man followed. She glanced over at him.

"Don't you have something better to do?"

"Nope."

"I have a sister that's missing."

"Tracker's handling that."

"He needs to get on it." Every day that passed her sister suffered.

"He will."

She rubbed her hands up and down her arms. "Not fast enough."

The set of his mouth softened. "Don't worry, ma'am. He knows what she means to you."

No one knew that. She kept walking. Shadow fell into step beside her. "Any idea where we're going?"

She blew out a breath. *"I'm going for a walk."*

"Before breakfast?"

"I am."

"Then go eat."

He shrugged. "Can't rightly do that seeing as I'm to guard you."

"I don't care."

"Yes."

His stomach rumbled. She steeled herself not to feel guilty as she asked, "You're dead set on skipping breakfast?"

"Well, hell!" He cradled his gun in the crook of his arm, muzzle pointed away from her. "Now Caine's going to have my hide for sure."

She sighed, because he clearly wasn't going to shut up until he got to his point. "Why?"

"Because he said specifically that I was to make sure you didn't get upset and miss meals."

"If he didn't want me upset, he should have told me he was leaving and why."

"I won't argue with you there, ma'am."

"Desi," she corrected, slowing her pace. That agreement in his statement might have been genuine.

He nodded. "Desi, it's just a suggestion, but you might just consider how Caine is before you go getting mad at him for doing what comes natural."

"Lying comes naturally?"

The corners of his mouth twitched in what could have been amusement. "Sometimes."

They'd reached the barn. Shadow reached around her to open the door. She stepped aside. Unlike Caine, he made her nervous. She wasn't going inside a dark barn with him. Boone slipped between them. She covered her nervousness by petting his head. She turned the other way, leaving Shadow holding the door. She didn't want to hear Shadow's explanation. She didn't want anything to mitigate her anger at Caine. She wanted to hold on to her anger. That way she didn't have to hurt.

Shadow was as good as his name, following her, nagging her with that silent patience that seemed bred into the men out here. Every footfall, every breath he took, prodded her common sense until finally she stopped dead just short of the henhouse, folded her arms across her chest and practically spit, "Just get it out."

He had the gall to look innocent. "What?"

"Whatever it is you think I should understand about Caine."

There was nothing obvious about the shift in his expression, but she still had the impression that he felt he'd won. It didn't take but a second to figure out why.

"I'd be more comfortable talking over breakfast."

"Then we can forget it."

He motioned her forward with a smooth gesture. "Shall we continue with our constitutional then?"

Constitutional. A fancy way to put running away. Desi pulled her shawl tighter against the morning chill. Ahead of her, Cantankerous strutted, ready to fight, beyond him in the woods, men might be waiting to take her hostage. Beside her stood a stranger ready to give his life for hers simply because her husband had asked him to. A man who apparently was willing to talk about her husband, the one man she wanted to understand above all others. She was annoyed at being manipulated and stubborn by nature, but she wasn't a fool. This was a golden opportunity. She spun on her heel and headed to the house, ignoring his soft chuckle as she said, "I think I'd rather have breakfast."

NORMALLY HE HATED KILLING on an empty stomach, but he could make an exception today. Caine crept across the roof of the building containing James and his cronies, being careful not to disturb the shakes. It was just pure dumb luck that the men he wanted to visit had called a meeting above the warehouse the night he'd come hunting. Now that evening was upon them, the time of reckoning was at hand. Below, he saw Sam slip into the building through a side window, gun drawn. Around back, he knew an equally lethal Tracker was taking care of the other escape route. His smile spread cold and easy. The rats were trapped. He swung down off the overhang, dropping onto the balcony below. The wood rocked under his feet. He crouched, holding his pistol up, waiting to see if the structure held. Having the balcony collapse was not part of his plan. When he was sure it would hold, he crept up to the window beside the door.

"What in hell is so important, James, we had to miss our dinners to hear it?"

Caine recognized the voice coming through the thin glass of the window. It belonged to Bryan, the fat banker. He shifted his position to get a better view of the inside of the room. Judging from the crates stacked along the walls, it was used for storage, which meant the men were taking no chance on being overheard. He could see James and Bryan clearly. The other occupant was merely a shadow cast by a lamp.

"Maybe he's heard word about the sister," the shadowy figure offered in a softer, almost effeminate voice. The other banker, Carl?

"Hell, no. She's more than likely just a corpse rotting in the sun."

And from the sound of it, James couldn't care less. Caine cocked the hammer on his gun.

"It was stupid to let her go in the first place," Bryan retorted.

"I didn't see you reaching in your pockets to keep her put." James ran his hand over his hair, none of that false charm on his face now. The shadows from the lamp narrowed his features until he looked exactly what he was: a well-dressed snake.

"I didn't know you were going to bungle things to the point we'd lose the first," Bryan sneered, reaching in his pocket. He pulled out a can of snuff.

If looks could kill, the one James cut Bryan would have severed his head. There was definitely trouble in paradise.

"We only needed one."

For what, Caine wanted to know.

"But if we'd had both, we would have had insurance."

"You worry too damn much, Carl."

So Carl was the shadow.

"After my last meeting with our associate, I don't think you're worrying enough."

Caine eased closer. The associate was the one he wanted.

"He was angry?" Bryan asked, an edge to the question.

"I wouldn't exactly call him pleased. We wired and told him it was settled, and now we don't have the woman he wants, and we can't confirm the other is dead."

"She's dead. If she wasn't fucked to death before she cleared the territory she sure as shit was once she hit Tejala's land."

Bryan's lip curled as he tucked his snuff into his cheek. "But you don't have proof, do you? And he wants proof."

"Then he can fucking go get it himself. Tejala's territory is not a safe place for any gringo."

"Here's not going to be safe, either, if we don't get this settled."

If they'd just give him a name, Caine would settle it for them right now.

A match flared in the corner, casting dancing shadows on the opposite wall. "We still only need one, and we know where she is."

"Hell's Eight land isn't much better than Tejala territory," Bryan said.

"Not everyone is as chickenshit as you," James sneered.

"What does that mean?"

"It means that for the right price, anything is possible and our little problem should be taken care of by this time tomorrow."

Caine stiffened and eased back against the wall. They'd sent someone for Desi?

"How much did it cost?" Carl asked.

"More than you cheap bastards wanted to pay."

Carl waved, the shadow of the movement exaggerated against the far wall. "It doesn't matter what it costs anymore. We need her back. Our associate is not pleased with the delay."

Bryan was a banker to his toes, and his "It wouldn't hurt to know who he hired and at what cost" clearly indicated he didn't trust James.

"I hired Apache Jack."

"I thought he was dead."

James cut the man a pitying glance. "Apparently not. For twenty-five hundred, he's going to bring the girl back."

Rage burned hot in Caine's chest. Apache Jack was

about as low as a man could go. Scorned by both races, Apache and white, he had a penchant for torture and killing that reflected nothing less than the sheer joy he got from both. He exercised his skill to the extent he'd devised his own brand of killing for those that got on his bad side. A series of knots tied so that when a victim couldn't stand anymore, or tried to get free, he strangled to death, slowly and agonizingly, brought down by their own weakness one way or another. And they'd sent that monster after his Desi? Son of a bitch.

"Alive?" Bryan asked, the lecherous twist to his mouth indicating where his interest lay.

"That cost another five hundred."

"Did you pay it?"

James laughed. "Hell, yes. I've got a score to settle with the little bitch."

"You can settle your score after I get through with her."

"You got that big a taste for our little Desdemona?" James asked, his scorn for the banker as evident as the banker's for him.

"I liked having her at my disposal."

And helpless, Caine bet. The fat shit. It was all he could do not to put a bullet in the man's brain. His stomach roiled at the thought of what Desi had endured at the man's hands. Hell, it was a miracle she'd let him touch her, let alone responded. He knew Tracker and Sam were at the other side of the door, no doubt hearing the same thing he was. He hoped to hell their disgust didn't get the better of them. He needed the accomplice's name, and it would be a hell of a lot easier to pick up in conversation than to get it by force, though—he touched the knife in his belt—the latter did have its attractions.

"About the only thing that would have made it better

would be to have both those women together," Bryan said, fingering his snuff can. "Identical twins. I've never had that before."

Bryan visibly shivered with the force of his own fantasy. James wasn't far behind. "Shit, yeah."

"How soon is this Apache Jack going to have her back?" Carl interrupted, no lust, no nothing in his tone.

"We'll have her back tomorrow, the day after if he runs into trouble."

"Alive?"

"That's what I paid for."

"But you're not sure?"

James, the oily son of a bitch, just shrugged. "You know Desdemona. She has a way of trying a man's patience, and with Apache Jack, it's anybody's guess whether he'll find cutting her throat or collecting the rest of the reward more suiting."

"Hard to believe she'll have much fight in her after servicing the Hell's Eight men." Bryan licked his lips. "Think she spread her thighs for those Indians, too?"

A floorboard creaked. Carl came into view now. A slender dandy in a gray suit, looking too innocuous to be as cold-blooded as he was. "What I think is that it doesn't matter anymore."

There was something strange about how he was holding himself. Caine shifted to get a better view of his arm as Carl headed for the door. Carl pulled something long and thin from his pocket. Too big to be a cigar. It took Caine the same split second it took Bryan and James to recognize what Carl held in his hand. Dynamite fed with a very short fuse. As he reached the door, Carl stated calmly, "You two have become a liability."

Bryan threw up his hands. "Hold on, Carl. There's no need for this."

James's eyes locked on the deadly stick. "That solicitor won't be happy if you do this. He needs us."

Carl touched his smoke to the fuse. Sparks shot out on his face. "Who do you think gave the order?"

He tossed the sizzling explosive at their feet.

Shit! Caine gave the emergency whistle and dove for the edge of the balcony. As he flipped over the edge, holding on to the handrail, he caught a glimpse of Carl's shock when he opened the door and saw Sam standing there. Saw Sam's quick assessment of the scene and his grim smile as he hurled the smaller man back into the room. The door closed. Caine dropped and, above him, the sky exploded.

CAINE HIT THE STREET hard. His knees buckled as pain shot up his calves. He covered his head and rolled into the lee of the building as pieces of wood pelted the ground around him. Through the roaring in his ears, he could hear women's screams and men's curses. A bell clanged the alarm. Footsteps ran by him. His shoulder collided with the edge of the porch. Caine uncovered his head. People were spilling out of shops, staring in shock at the building above him. Caine got to his feet. His gun was lying three feet away. He picked it up. No one challenged him. He dusted off his pants.

"You all right?" Tracker asked as he came up beside him.

"Yeah. How about you?"

"A little scorched but fine."

He looked around. "Where's Sam?"

"Checking on things."

Caine looked up at the flames devouring the pending night. "Christ, no one could survive that."

"You know Sam. He just has to be sure scum meets its end."

"You heard?"

Beside them, men formed a brigade, tossing buckets of water into the inferno.

Tracker nodded. "They didn't deserve to die so clean."

"No, they didn't." There weren't words to convey the rage he felt at that. Sam came around the building, melding naturally into the shadows. At Caine's questioning look, he nodded. The men were dead.

Tracker swatted aside a burning ember. "It'll be damn hard to find out who the head of this mess is now, with all his men dead."

"Not that hard," Caine countered. "Whoever that solicitor is, he still wants Desi. And now he'll have to come after her."

"Or send someone else."

Caine shrugged. "Then they'll lay a new trail to backtrack." He jerked his chin over his shoulder. "Right now I'm more concerned with what those three set in motion." He glanced at Sam. "He sent Apache Jack after Desi."

Sam spat smoke out of his mouth. "I heard."

Caine stared to the west, unease eating at his gut.

"He's good."

"Shadow's better," Tracker said in a flat statement of fact.

"Not to mention that Desi's got a mean temper on her," Sam added, scanning the crowd.

Fire crackled and popped. Heat drove them back.

"She's just a woman." A tiny, frail woman who deserved more than violence and danger.

Sam smiled, his teeth very white in his soot-darkened face. "I saw her practicing with you, and anyone thinking she's going to be easy pickings is in for one hell of a shock."

"She's no match for Apache Jack," Tracker stated.

Caine followed the flight of a hawk as it soared westward, heading where he needed to be. He remembered Desi's battle with the men who'd kidnapped her, the honor with which she'd upheld her vows to him despite her experiences, the strength with which she met each challenge. He remembered the way she'd defended Boone and then Cantankerous, the way she'd demanded he teach her to fight. But mostly, he remembered that little smile on her face as she'd missed her target to win the booby prize of his kiss. As the hawk disappeared into the horizon, Caine whistled for Chaser. "You're right. She's a match for anyone who takes her on."

24

Desi was no match for this. Tired from lack of sleep, grumpy from the inability to take Caine to task for how he'd left, Desi stared at the chicken coop and the rooster guarding it. She held the pacifier in her hand while Cantankerous strutted and dared. They both knew he could take her. They both knew she could bribe him. The problem was she was having a hard time falling into Caine's habit. Bribing with sex, she was discovering, was against her nature. Maybe because she'd just realized Caine used the same techniques on her when he wanted her to look away from what he was doing. And, according to Shadow, a veritable font of information, he hadn't wanted her to know a bounty had been put on her head, so he'd kept her distracted with orgasms while he went out and risked his life. When he got back, she was going to kill him.

Cantankerous clucked. Boone, sitting by her side, whined anxiously, his attention totally focused on the feathered demon.

"Don't worry, you won't have to come save me this time."

The dog leaned his big head against her, knocking her off balance. The wind blew against her nape and unease prickled across her skin the way it had when she was a child and she'd thought monsters lived under her bed. She glanced toward the outhouse. Shadow hadn't come out yet.

She glanced at the house, and suddenly her plan of gathering some eggs to make a cake for supper while he took care of business seemed foolhardy. He'd told her to stay in the house, but when Tia had gone off to take care of Ed, who'd just ridden in, the prowling restlessness had taken over, sending shards of energy through her body. She'd needed something to do and Shadow had given it to her. He was a lean man, fresh off a hunt, and he was always hungry. Getting eggs to make him breakfast seemed a good idea. The henhouse was well within the stronghold and Shadow was only a shout away. How dangerous could it be?

The wind blew again, and the unease left. She was letting the overprotectiveness of the men influence her. She wanted Caine home. Wanted to scream at him, slap him and then hug him and hold him tight. Until she saw him ride through the pass, the only thing she knew for sure was that she'd be on edge and jumping at shadows. She looked down at the red pacifier in her hand and then at the dog. "What do you think, Boone? Should we throw away our scruples or make a stand for what's right?"

Boone eyed the rooster. It spread its wings and crowed. Mid-crow, Boone shivered and let out a moan of pure terror.

Desi glanced at the outhouse. Shadow would be popping out of there any minute now, which meant expediency was her best bet if she didn't want a twenty-minute lecture. "You're right. We don't have time for scruples."

She tossed the pacifier on the ground. Cantankerous

went for it with unholy zeal. She shook her head as he hopped onboard. "That's just not right."

She didn't have any more time to ponder why. Keeping her eye on the rooster, she dashed for the henhouse. She made it to the top of the little ramp and almost inside when a hand wrapped around her wrist. With brutal force, she was yanked behind her and almost inside of the ranch spun out of focus as her scream was killed off at birth by the huge hand that slapped over her mouth. She had time for one breath before she was slammed up against a hard body. A god-awful stench filled her nostrils as she kicked out. Her feet met only air.

Oh, no. No!

Fingers pressed against her neck. Stars splintered before her eyes and then everything went black.

She blinked and screamed in her throat, looking wildly around, but no one could help. She bit at the hand covering her mouth. All she needed was one squeak of sound. Boone came around the corner, freezing when he saw the tableau. His hackles rose. Something flashed in the corner of her eye. The big dog collapsed, a knife buried in the side of his chest.

THE FAINT SOUND OF a hound's baying floated across the plains. Caine pulled Chaser up short. The only hounds he knew in the area were Hell's Eight. "Recognize that bay?"

Tracker tilted his head. "Can't say that I do, but whatever the scent, that dog's going hell-bent for leather on it."

There was something about the bay, a familiarity in the warble and the way it hitched from one note to the next.

"Boone's pa had a bay like that," Sam offered.

"Boone's pa is dead." Caine squinted against the sun, a sick feeling in his stomach.

"Boone's not."

"He's coming fast up the other side of the pass."

"Only thing I know that gets that dog moving is Desi," Sam stated.

"And Apache Jack's looking to collect that bounty."

That's what Caine was afraid of. He kneed Chaser up the ridge. "He'll collect when hell freezes over."

Tracker grabbed Chaser's bridle, pulling him up short. Caine's gun was in his hand before he acknowledged the thought.

Tracker didn't move as the muzzle centered on him. "Think, Caine. The dog's on the scent. From the sound of the bay, they're coming this way. There's no way we passed them. Country's too open for that, which means they're holed up between the two passes."

Caine eased his finger off the trigger, but he couldn't put the gun away. He'd promised Desi he'd keep her safe, and now she was out there somewhere with pure evil. He couldn't wrap his mind around how scared she must be, what she might have already suffered, what still might be in store for her. The gun in his hand was shaking. He stared at it, not comprehending why.

Tracker eased the gun from his grip. "We'll get her back, Caine."

Sam came up on his other side. "Not if we go charging up that ridge like a bunch of greenhorns, we won't. Apache Jack is one mean son of a bitch with the devil's own smarts. Charging up the hill isn't going to do anything except maybe get us all killed."

He was right—they were both right. Caine held out his hand for the revolver. After a pause, Tracker handed it over. Caine holstered the gun, images of Desi trapped beneath Apache Jack's scarred body, struggling against the man's brute strength—calling for him, needing him—filled his mind.

Shit, he couldn't focus on that. He scanned the ridge, projected the trajectory of the hound's path with what he knew of the terrain. And he knew plenty. This was Hell's Eight land.

"There are only two places where it'd be safe to hide. The caves along the ridge and the blind canyon."

"Apache Jack isn't the type to get himself trapped." Sam pulled out his makings, rolled the pouch between his fingers and then tucked them back in his pocket.

"He's in the caves then."

"There's only one big enough and dry enough for two."

"And fortunately," Tracker said, checking the load in his rifle, "it has a back entrance."

Caine smiled. "Indeed it does."

He listened to Boone's bay and felt the same aggressive urgency beat within him, along with a bone-deep agony he hadn't experienced since he'd watched his father fall under the first volley of bullets and his mother pick up the gun to defend their home. Time was not their friend. He kneed Chaser up the trail, sending one thought-prayer ahead of him. "Hold on, Gypsy. Just hold on."

A BLOODY CORPSE LANDED at Desi's feet. "Cook dinner."

Desi looked down at the bleeding rabbit carcass and then back up at the man who'd kidnapped her. He wasn't a prime specimen of masculinity by anyone's definition. He was obviously of Indian descent, but unlike Tracker and Shadow and Tucker, he didn't radiate that sense of strength and honor that inspired trust. This man reeked of evil from the top of his bandanna-covered head, with its greasy shoulder-length hair, to the soles of his stained knee-high moccasins. She looked at the offering at her feet, fighting back her gorge. And he wanted her to cook a rabbit.

She didn't reach for the carcass. "I don't know how."

A knife stabbed in the soft dirt between her feet. Her start was internal. She wouldn't give the bastard the satisfaction of letting him know how much he scared her, or how much the sight of that knife made her grieve for Boone.

"Then you'd best git learning fast."

The threat wasn't lost on her. She kept her fear hidden right along with her disgust. She had no doubt her kidnapper would enjoy punishing her for not doing it right, but she was also reasonably sure he would punish her even if she got it right. There was an unnaturalness about him, a twisted pleasure in his flat brown eyes that told her when this was all over, she wasn't walking away alive. And between now and then, the sick son of a bitch intended to make her suffer.

She prodded the knife handle with her toe. It fell over, lying in the dirt like so much deadly temptation. "For that to happen, I'm going to need a teacher."

Amusement lit deep in his gaze as he picked up the innuendo in the statement. "You want to learn from me?"

God, he was twisted. His perversion just oozed out of his pores like some sort of foul wind, raising goose bumps along her skin as her senses cried a warning. As if she hadn't already figured out she was in trouble. She adopted her most serene expression and told the truth. "I don't particularly want to learn to cook at all, but as I'm assuming there's a consequence for not learning, I'm open to suggestions."

He gave her the evil eye. It just might have been his normal stare, but it was vile, no doubt about it.

"Pick up the knife and skin the rabbit."

He was completely unconcerned with her being armed. Desi glanced at the muscles in his arms and chest, the heavy scars beneath his open leather vest and on any visible surface. She also remembered the easy way he moved. He might be a true outlaw, but he was a skilled one. And from the slashing line of the majority of the scars, one who preferred to fight with knives. Whereas she only used them at the table. She sat forward and picked up the knife. It fit her hand with surprising balance. She put her other hand on the still-warm carcass. "Were do I begin?"

"At the neck and cut down." He turned away, and looked at the entrance, presenting her with his back.

She did as he ordered. When he looked back, there was a touch of respect in his gaze. "You did not try to use the knife on me."

"I'm not stupid. I recognize a trap when I see one."

He smiled, revealing broken teeth. "Those sissified bankers taught you well." He motioned with his hand. "Cut down the legs."

So he was taking her back to *him*. "They were satisfied."

His head canted to the side. His shoulder-length hair slid in a greasy hank over his shoulder. "But not well enough. There is no respect in your tone."

She'd been trying to keep everything out of her tone.

"If you show me disrespect, I will hurt you."

He said that in a completely matter-of-fact tone of voice that scared her. She tucked the emotion deep inside and focused on the rabbit. "I know."

His finger came under her chin, forcing her face to his. His breath hit her cheek in a fetid promise. He studied her expression for three heartbeats. "You look very much like your sister."

Her hand jerked. The knife slipped and sliced the base of her thumb. She dropped the knife and pressed her palm against the wound. "She's alive?"

"She was last time I saw her."

She hardly dared breathe when she asked the question, certainly didn't dare look away from his malevolent face. "When was that?"

"When I was coming in her."

If she hadn't dropped the knife, she would have gutted him on the spot, common sense be damned. And from the flare of amusement in his eyes, he knew it. "I think, little pretty, that you're going to scream for me just like she did when I come."

"I wouldn't count on it." She wasn't known for giving anyone but Caine that satisfaction.

He didn't remove his finger from under her chin. Something cold and metal slid up the inside of her calf beneath her skirts. "I think you will."

The knife. He'd picked up the knife. It grazed the inside of her knee and moved down her thigh. Horror took her in a cold shudder as his meaning sank in.

From afar she heard a faint sound, almost a howling. It came again, sinking through the terror in her mind to form a recognizable pattern. A dog on a scent. She only knew one person who kept hounds. Caine. He was coming for her. "Shouldn't you be escaping?"

The knife left her skin. She breathed a sigh of relief. "Not yet."

She mustered her courage. "Caine is going to kill you for taking me."

"There's something you'd better understand, pretty thing, or you're not going to last long."

She lifted her chin. "What?"

"Men don't risk their lives for whores."

The potential for truth in his words cut deep. She set her lips against the pain, refusing to give him the satisfaction of seeing he'd hit dead-on her insecurity. She was Hell's Eight. Caine would come for her. "He'll come. And when he does, he won't be alone."

The man let go of her chin and stood. His touch lingered like a bruise. "Actually, I'm counting on that pride of his dragging him after you. I've got a score to settle with that bunch."

He dropped the knife into the dirt at her feet and motioned to the rabbit. "Finish skinning that and then slit the middle and take out the guts."

Whoever was coming after her—Shadow and Tucker maybe?—was riding into a trap. She needed to think.

She picked up the knife and went back to work.

"What's your name?"

He reached for his rifle. "Jack. Why?" He raised his eyebrows. "Looking to get more friendly?"

"Just want to know what to put on your grave."

The man laughed, actually laughed. "If it comes to that, there won't be a grave to mark. Hell's Eight aren't known for their mercy."

She shrugged, tugging at the knife where it stuck under the leg of the rabbit. "Probably."

With a move so quick she never saw it coming, he took the knife, severed tendons and disemboweled the carcass. "That's how you do it."

She stared at the gore oozing at her feet, willing back her gorge and her terror. "Thank you."

He didn't give her back the knife, just stared at her,

grunted and then picked up the carcass to skin it. The bay came at her again, fluctuating with the wind, faint but determined, bringing hope. Caine would come. He would come because it was his nature. Because she was his wife. She remembered that last night, his dominance, his need, his tenderness. He'd come because he cared.

She hugged the certainty to her, letting it grow as the next bay rose in volume. She just had to stay alive long enough to benefit. A sharpened stick landed in the dirt in front of her. The now skinned carcass was shoved into her hands. "Put this through the meat and then hold it over the fire to cook it up. I don't like to fight without an offering."

"You're superstitious?"

"The spirits reward those who remember them."

She didn't want to know what gods he prayed to. She stabbed the point through the carcass and held the heavy mass over the small fire.

Jack leaned over and lashed her wrists together with a stretch of rawhide. The thin leather bit into her wrists. The rabbit wobbled and almost fell. She held on to it for dear life, sensing the need to hurt building inside him with the tension of the approaching battle.

Jack collected his rifle and stood. "Your sister had more spirit."

He was a very tall man and everything about him was dark—his hair, his eyes, his personality. She remembered how he'd drawn the knife up her leg. Imagined her sister in the same situation, helpless at his mercy. She gripped the stick so tightly her nails bent. "As you said, I'm better trained."

SECONDS PASSED LIKE MINUTES, minutes like hours. Desi hunched in the cave within the restraints Jack had fashioned from rawhide, her legs and back aching as she held the excruciatingly uncomfortable position in which Jack had left her and waited. She counted heartbeats and hope, holding on to the hound's bay like a lifeline through the terror. The outlaw had left the cave ages ago, dressed to deadly perfection: bullets across his chest, knives strapped to his hips and thighs, guns riding his belt. After a token cooking and tossing an offering in the fire along with some sweetgrass and prayers, he'd stood, relieved himself on the half-cooked carcass and kicked it across the dirt to her with a "help yourself."

Over the next hour the stench of urine had intensified, but if Jack thought it would demoralize her, he had another think coming. Some men were pigs. Being reminded of it with every breath kept her strong and she needed that, because when the opportunity presented itself, she was going to kill him. Preferably with the same knife with which he'd tormented her.

The hound's bay was close now. Loud, echoing signals that would lead anyone following to the network of caves on this ridge. A rifle shot ricocheted through the canyons, the echo marking the cessation of the hound's bay, reminding her of that moment when Boone had gone down. Boone. She closed her eyes. She was probably the only one who would mourn him. Everyone thought him worthless, but he'd been such a good friend to her. She imagined she could feel his silky smooth fur under her fingertips, hear his moan of doggie bliss as she scratched behind his heavy ears. And the inner rage grew.

She flexed her fingers, but couldn't tell if she'd accomplished the move. She'd lost feeling in them thanks to the way Jack had tied the knots. Any movement on her part created tightening somewhere along the system. Soon she wouldn't be able to move anything at all.

More gunfire exploded down the ridge, each repercussion making her heart jump because the fact that it didn't stop meant Jack lived and each successive shot meant someone she knew and cared about was a target. She refused to let her worry focus on Caine. Doing so would devastate her ability to function, and she needed to function.

She tested her bonds. The knots were set up in an intricate system. Her hands were trapped down around her hips yet connected to the bonds on her feet and around her neck. Any attempt to stand resulted in the knot tightening around her neck. But it didn't loosen when she bent back down. The knot was already uncomfortably tight. A hanging truss, Jack had smiled and called his system that marked him as the devil he was.

Before he'd left, he'd even suggested she might want to take that way out rather than waiting for when he got back. She got the impression he wouldn't care either way, that whatever torturous death she accepted would please him in the same way most men reserved for sex.

He was sick and intelligent, but he wasn't perfect, and she'd used the time since he'd left to find the holes in his system. She tugged on the ties, holding the strand that would tighten the knot. There was give, which was the hole in the trap that she'd need. If Jack hadn't been so uncouth as to urinate on her dinner, she might have missed her one possibility of escape, but he had and now all she needed was the opportunity.

The gun battle raged fast and furious. Jack wouldn't be coming back anytime soon, which meant it was time. Inch by inch, she worked up the material of her skirt. Twice she had to straighten a bit to get the excess material out of her way. Both times the tether around her neck tightened until her breathing became a hoarse strain.

She ignored the pain in her hands and the slow strangulation and kept going, her goal a clear picture in her mind. Three inches from her salvation, she came to a stop. She needed more room. She wasn't going to get it without strangling. A cessation of gunshots made the decision for her. She tightened her neck muscles, took a deep breath and yanked the material up under her bonds.

The rawhide tether viciously bit into her throat, choking the air from her lungs. She coughed, a painfully aborted effort that only tightened the noose more. Warm liquid trickled down her neck. She forced herself not to fight, to suck thin trails of air in and out on a hoarse wheeze as she worked her hands between her legs. She couldn't pull down her pantaloons, and for a heartbeat, she couldn't do what she needed to do. It was just so intrinsically repugnant, so against everything she'd been taught. A bullet winged off the cave entrance, slicing though the interior with a high-pitched whine, and one thing became clear. If she didn't do it, she was going to be dead.

She closed her eyes, took another careful breath and let her bladder go, wetting the rawhide, working her hands as she did, cringing and sobbing as the leather loosened but not enough. Not enough. Forcing a deep breath she held it and shoved her hands up against her body in an effort to soak the leather. The noose bit deep. She couldn't let her breath out. Couldn't get another in. The leather gave. She yanked at her hands, using the blood seeping from the cuts to grease the ties more. She ripped her hands free, her scream at the agony it caused trapped in her throat.

Spots danced before her eyes as she clawed at the leather severing her wind. It loosened slightly but she couldn't get it free. Across the cave, beside the fire, there was a glint of metal. The eating knife. Jack hadn't taken it with him.

She hobbled toward it, fighting the wave of black coming at her faster than she could move. She fell to her knees before it, grabbed it with both hands and brought the edge up against her throat. The flat side slipped between the leather and her skin, cutting a thin line of pain. More wetness spilled down her neck. With all her might, she pressed outward. The leather stretched, gouged her neck from behind as it held to its intent.

C'mon, she prayed. *Give up already.*

The leather held. More gunfire roared around the cave. Men's voices peppered the silence in between, no distinguishable words, just staccato notes of anger that beat on her calm with merciless precision. And still she pushed and still the rawhide resisted. Her vision went to black. Her "No" welled silently within. She gave another soundless scream and one last thrust.

The knife flew out of her numb hands as the rawhide severed. She fell to her hands and knees, head hanging, dragging gasp after gasp into her tortured lungs as the knife clattered against stone. "Oh, God. Oh, God."

She needed the knife. Another bullet whined through the cave. She crawled in the general direction of the weapon, sprawling twice along the way as her wet skirt wrapped around her legs. It hurt to breathe, to move. She kept on, whispering as she went, only realizing the name she was invoking with every breath was Caine's. If he was here, she had to help him. She wouldn't let Jack kill him. She blinked. The knife was right in front of her. She watched her fingers curl around the hilt, unable to feel it in her numb hand, so she just tightened her grip until her knuckles showed white. At some point, it would occur to Jack that he could use her to disarm the men of Hell's Eight. She couldn't let that happen. She had to think.

A glance at the section of the cave where she'd been hidden was dimly lit. That had possibilities. She cut the ties from her feet and waist, grimacing at the strong smell of urine wafting with her every move. Even though there wasn't anyone around to know she'd wet herself, and even though she'd done it for a good reason, humiliation still flooded her soul.

She grabbed up the rabbit carcass, almost vomiting as she touched it. She also grabbed up a couple of rocks and the stick before limping back to the spot where Jack had tied her. She took off her dress and shawl. She laid the dress out as she would be if she'd fallen, making sure the head was up under the shadow of the rock. She stuffed the carcass down the sleeve and the rocks up under the torso. She broke the stick in half and then braced the pieces under the hip and shoulders, before carefully draping the shawl around the rest. She stepped back, rubbing her bruised throat. It wasn't perfect, but anyone taking a quick glance and expecting her to be there might be fooled for a split second. Which meant she now had to decide what to do with her split second.

A volley of shots rent the air and then the sound of someone coming up the hill preceded a curse. The accent and foreign words identified the intruder. Jack was on the way back.

Everything faded as Desi's sense of survival kicked in, fear amplifying every nuance of the world around her. She could hear the sound of feet scraping up the hill, metal striking on rock, dislodged pebbles skittering down the hillside. Jack was armed to the teeth and going to be here any second. She squelched panic and kicked her brain into a gallop. She only had seconds.

She ran to the mouth of the cave, her breath sounding unnaturally loud in her ears. Grabbing up a large rock, tears seeping from her eyes at the agonizing tingle from the returning circulation in her arms, she held it above her head as she pressed her back against the wall. Her breath sawed in and out of her lungs and a trembling began deep inside.

She was panicking again. She couldn't afford to panic. Desi made her next breath slow. It didn't lessen the sound, but it gave her a focus for the adrenaline charging through her limbs. The footsteps came closer. She formed a picture of Jack in her head, building each detail with precision, paying special attention to his height. As she heard his gun bang against the outside of the cave entrance, she opened her eyes.

Jack's shadow entered the cave first. A sinister stretch of black that crept up the wall. His foot followed next, then his body and then his scent. Rank like the rest of him, suiting the evil that was so embedded inside him. He didn't turn or focus anywhere but where he'd left her. Time slowed as he stepped past her. He brought up his revolver and pointed it to the corner where she'd piled the clothes.

Desi snuck behind him, soundlessly whispering Caine's name, which had become her talisman. With unemotional precision Jack pulled the trigger. Noise exploded in the cave as he fired into her clothes with a dispassionate disregard that would be her life he was taking.

Fury erupted from deep down. She reared up on her toes and brought the rock down with all her might as more explosions ripped through the cave, along with her name, Jack jerked and crumpled as something whizzed by her side and pinged off the rock behind her. The sound of the gunshots faded, but not the sound of her name. It lingered in her ears and in her heart in a harsh masculine echo. She blinked past the tears of relief welling and peered toward the back of the cave.

Caine. He stepped out of the dark shadows like an avenging angel. Gun at the ready, he moved soundlessly across the floor. On the next step, light caressed his face, highlighting the three-day growth of beard and the lethal tension in his face. "Step away from him, Desi."

The order was given in that flat, deadly voice with no warmth to let her know what he was thinking, what he thought about her.

Desi stepped back. Rock pressed against her back. And still Caine advanced. He kicked the gun away from Jack's reach. With a foot, he pushed him over.

Desi gasped and put her hand over her mouth to hold back her stomach as blood poured from him in a river. Caine had shot him through the heart.

The small breathless sound brought Caine's attention back to her. His eyes ran over her from head to toe, stopping along the way at her neck, the ropes dangling from her waist, the blood on her wrists. His expression spasmed in a way she couldn't understand before he pointed to her feet. "Stay there."

Two strides and he was at the cave entrance. In rapid succession, he fired off three shots.

He turned back. She flinched from the coldness of his glare. The move set off another olfactory reminder of what she'd done. Humiliation chased away relief. It didn't matter why she'd done it. She did not want Caine to see her this way. "Keep back."

Caine stopped. She could ask anything of him in that

moment, and he'd give it to her. She was alive. He stood there and absorbed that fact. As he stood, he memorized everything about her, the shaking in her upraised palm, the wildness in her eyes and, worse, the humiliation that had her gaze dodging the directness of his.

It took his last reservoir of strength to subdue the need to snatch her up in his arms. She'd been through a trial. She was hurt, outside and maybe inside. If she needed a minute, he'd damn well give it to her.

"James, Carl and Bryan are dead."

She blinked. "How?"

"Dynamite."

He expected her to ask for an explanation. Instead, she just stood there and said, "Oh." He clenched his hands to fists as a drop of blood welled at the abrasion on her neck. He watched it swell until it got too heavy and then dripped down her neck, following the path of the drops before, bleeding into the thin white lawn of her chemise.

He'd promised to protect her and he hadn't. He didn't blame her for not wanting him near.

"Did he hurt you, Desi?"

Her chin came up. "What if he did?"

"Then I want to go back in time and kill him all over again. Real slow like."

He wanted to do that anyway.

"And me? What about me?"

"You I'm taking home and tying to the bed."

"I've had enough of being tied up."

She eyed him warily as she brought her hand down and rubbed her wrist. The one the bastard had broken. The one Jack had tied.

"Then you're just going to have to suffer being wrapped

in cotton wool, because I am never going through this again."

"I was the one who was tied up by some evil monster who likes to see people suffer."

He closed his eyes slowly, accepting the weight of the truth in her words, the blame.

"He killed Boone."

"No, he didn't."

"I saw the knife."

"It'd take more than a shoulder wound to keep Boone from coming after you."

Her smile was shaky. "I told you he was special."

"Yes, you did."

"You'll have to make it up to him for misjudging him."

"He can have steak every night for the rest of his life."

"Don't."

Why the hell were they talking about the dog? He took another step forward, drawn by the need to hold her, to know she was real and unhurt, that she hadn't strangled to death in one of Jack's specialized knots. Her hand came back up.

He stopped, letting pain sear his soul. He'd broken his promise to her to keep her safe. He didn't deserve anything more. Another trickle of blood chased the previous. He watched it with morbid fascination, barely, just barely able to honor her request. "Why?"

He needed to hear it, needed that salt rubbed into the wound, needed all the pain she had to vent. Though there'd never be enough to make up for his failure, it was better he bear it than she.

"I'm dirty."

"Jesus." She couldn't think that. He wouldn't let her

convince herself of that. "You get that right out of your head, right now. No matter what happened, there isn't a more pure woman walking this territory than you."

She blinked and then with a grimace, waved away his assumption. "He didn't touch me like that."

Relief collided with exasperation. If Jack hadn't touched her, then Caine didn't understand her problem. She wrapped her arms around her waist and shivered, the haunted shadows in her eyes calling to him. She need to be held. And he needed to hold her with an ache that wouldn't stop. "Then why in hell am I standing over here?"

It came out harsher than he intended. So harsh he didn't initially hear her response. He had to ask her to repeat it. She did, with her head down and a flush covering her torso.

"I smell."

He blinked. She expected him to care that she'd picked up a few odors through her ordeal? He took a step closer and she scooted away, hand up, face averted. The cold stone skimmed her back and she shivered. She was going to freeze to death if he didn't get her covered. Caine would force the issue if he had to, but he hated to after all she'd been through.

"Explain."

The gaze she cut him was resentful. "He tied me up so I had to stay bent over or strangle."

"Jack's hanging truss."

"You know about that?"

"Yes."

She rubbed her hands up and down her arms, casting him a glance from under her lashes while a flush rose up her chest. "I don't think he cared which way I died. I think he just wanted me to suffer."

A woman shouldn't have to live knowing there were men like that in the world. "He did."

She stared at her toes. "I refused to give him the satisfaction."

"That's my girl." He wanted to touch her so badly, wipe the blood from her neck and kiss the tears from her cheeks. "I'm not going to be patient much longer, Gypsy. I need to hold you, so if what you got to say needs saying before I hug you tight, you'd best be about it."

She fingered her wrist. Her expression was anguished, pleading for his understanding. A flush rose to her cheekbones. It tore his heart out that she thought there was anything she needed to do to survive that he'd hold against her.

"There's nothing you can tell me that I'm not going to applaud. Whatever you had to do to stay alive, I'm backing it one hundred percent, so there's no need to worry."

Those fingers rubbed faster, fingering the old break. He took a step forward. Her eyes flew wide. She tried to take a step back but she'd boxed herself into a corner. Her lower lip slipped between her teeth as she searched for options.

"The only place you've got to run is into my arms." She shook her head and took a deep breath. "The ropes were made of rawhide."

He nodded, waiting for the rest.

"The kind of rawhide that stretches when it gets wet."

She looked hopeful, but he wasn't getting it. Her grip on her wrist was brutal, smearing the blood, leaving white dents. "I had to urinate on the ropes."

He blinked. "What?"

"It was the only way."

If a hole had opened up in the floor at that second, he was sure she would jump through it while he just stared at her in wonder. He'd buried three outlaws and one seasoned Ranger who'd fallen victim to that bastard. Hardened men, knowledgeable about survival, and not one of them had had the wits to get free of the hanging truss, their expressions in death mirroring the helpless horror of their battle. But his prim little greenhorn wife not only had the mental wherewithal to figure out a way, she'd had the fortitude to see the job done.

He closed the distance between them in two long strides, ignoring her "Oh, no" and upraised hand. He hooked his hand behind her head and pulled her to him, kissing her hard and hot, thrusting his tongue into her mouth, absorbing her start, her taste, the sheer wonder of her. She squirmed for all of two seconds, until he hooked his hand under her butt and lifted her the rest of the way into his embrace, not ending the kiss, letting her kick her feet for as long as it took her to realize he didn't care. He was never letting her out of his sight, out of his arms again.

He tilted her head for a better angle, needing to be deeper in her mouth, in her heart, in her soul, pulling her closer, offering her his heart, his soul, her freedom. Whatever she wanted. The rush of emotion was too wild to contain, breaking over the dam of his restraint, bursting through him on a brilliant wave of understanding that crashed against his reality, rupturing with soul-deep certainty against the softness of her lips in a hoarse whisper. "Goddamn, Desi, but I love you."

A good man deserved a scandalous woman. Caine had told Desi that once and she'd scoffed, but as Desi slipped inside the warm barn she realized the truth in those words. A man did deserve a woman who put him first, a woman who matched his passion in bed and out of it, the same way every woman deserved a man who saw her as beautiful, worthy and smart. The way Caine saw her.

Caine was everything her father had warned her against growing up—out for all he could get with no respect for propriety or a woman's delicate sensibilities, demanding in bed and out of it. Elementally protective, brutally honest. Caring. Special.

In other words, exactly what she wanted. And he had the crazy idea that if he pushed her away, she'd get a sudden hunger for the empty life she'd led before and catch the next stage back east. That was never going to happen. She'd been home since the first touch of her feet on Hell's Eight land. It'd just taken her a bit to realize it.

She shooed Boone back, stealing herself against his big eyes and drooping wrinkles. Closing the barn door quietly behind her, pausing for her eyes to adjust to the gloom, she braced her hand on the wall as she tugged her skirt out from under her feet. Without the proper undergarments, the bottom hung too low, something she hadn't considered when she'd launched this plan. If she made it to Caine without making a fool of herself by tripping over the hem, it would be a miracle.

Arranging her skirt decorously about her bare thighs, she looked around. Golden streams of sunshine filtered through the slats in the wall, highlighting the lazy drift of dust motes between her and her destination. She straightened the lace collar of her new shirtwaist, her fingers lingering on the luxury. It wasn't the finest lace she'd ever worn, nor the most intricate, but it was fast becoming the most cherished. Simply because Caine had given it to her.

Two stalls down, a horse's hooves stomped with nervous fervor—probably the new mustang they'd brought in, the one Caine was so determined to tame. That horse was crazy, unlike her sweet, placid Lily, who was more inclined to droop than walk. She had yet to see that horse on more than two legs. If it wasn't kicking, it was rearing, lashing out against captivity without compunction, unfazed by any kindness extended to it.

She jumped as something hard landed against wood, the sound snapping like a pistol shot out of the interior. Immediately thereafter, Caine's deep drawl rumbled out of the shadows, rising and falling on a subtle cadence, soothing the fuss to quiet. She shook her head, walking toward the commotion. As determined as the horse was, it didn't stand a chance. Caine wasn't one for letting a case of the stubborns get between him and a good thing.

It was a philosophy she was thinking of adopting. At least, when it came to her husband. She fingered the lace again. No one had ever bought her something just to make her smile. She'd been given gifts for birthdays, for bribes and for fun. Gifts casually bought with the excess of money available, but no one had ever sacrificed a part of their dream to make her happy. No one except Caine. This bit of lace had set back his plans to buy his brood mare, and when she'd found out, she'd been furious. She was Hell's Eight now, the ranch's future was hers, just as it was his, and she didn't need lace more than the ranch needed that brood mare.

In the course of the argument, she'd rejected the present, and indirectly, according to Tia, him. She hadn't understood how much Caine had needed to give her the lace. How his pride demanded it. His guilt commanded it. She mentally sighed. Men and their pride. She'd have to learn to handle Caine's better if she wanted a peaceful marriage.

She passed her little mare's stall. The horse whickered a greeting and stuck her nose over the top bar. Desi gave her a pat in lieu of the sugar nugget she usually brought and kept going, her steps getting shorter and slower as she got closer to Caine's location, until, finally, she came to a complete stop just shy of the door. She owed him so much more than an apology that she didn't even know where to begin. Hopefully, though, the next couple hours would open the door to a discussion on the matter. Certainly at the end of it she intended there'd be no doubt she was staying.

She tugged her skirt from between her legs. If not, she was giving Caine the job of rubbing ointment on her chafed inner thighs. Bloomers definitely had their uses, and doing without made that fact abundantly clear.

"You going to stay out there and spy or come in here and talk?"

How did he always know where she was? "Do I have a choice?"

"You've always had a choice."

She was beginning to understand that. "Will you think less of me if I tell you I'm too chicken to come in there?"

There was the sound of a soft pat of a hand on horse-flesh, another murmur and then Caine slid through the cross poles that made up the stall door, replacing the middle one before leaning on his arm against the top, hat tipped down too low to see his eyes. He crossed his ankles, nothing but lazy nonchalance in his posture as he answered, "Not if you tell me it's the horse that has you clucking."

The turn of phrase made her smile. Then again, Caine always made her smile. "I'm not afraid of *you*."

He pointed to the spot in front of him. "Then come here and prove it."

She shook her head and pointed to a spot in front of her. "You come here."

He pushed his hat back, revealing the natural stern-ness of his expression and the hint of laughter etched in faint lines around his eyes. "Make me."

She cocked her head to the side, keeping her own smile hidden with difficulty. "Do you think I can't?"

He eyed her from head to toe, pausing a fraction longer on her breasts than anywhere else, before coming back up to her face. "What I think, sweetheart, is that I've got about a hundred pounds on you."

"Uh-huh."

His right eyebrow rose at her open purloining of his favorite expression. "You don't think that's going to make a difference?"

She shook her head. "Not a bit."

He straightened, pushing his hat back farther, his attention honing in that indefinable way he had. The way that made a person feel in the center of a tornado, with judgment whirling all around, the delivery at his discretion. It was a scary feeling having that attention focused on her when he was angry, but with the edges of his mouth softening with desire, all it did now was remind her how thorough he was in the bedroom, how particular he was when it came to her pleasure. The tiniest of shivers quivered through her womb, reverberating outward on a tendril of anticipation, peaking in her nipples, drawing them tight with the first sweet hum of desire.

His gaze dipped to her chest again. His smile turned knowing. No doubt he'd noticed her body's response.

"You don't say."

She reached for the fastening at her collar. "I do."

He didn't say another word, just watched expressionlessly as she got the first, second and third buttons undone, but she wasn't fooled. By the time she'd reached the fourth his cock was halfway down his thigh, straining the tough cotton of his pants. By the time she got to the fifth, he'd found his counter to her declaration.

"It's going to take more than a glimpse of skin to get me to see things your way."

She popped the sixth button, dipping her fingers inside, stroking lightly in the shadow of her cleavage, allowing herself another small smile when the muscle by his cheek twitched. "Uh-huh. Well settle your mind on it, Caine Allen, I'm staying."

The blouse opened over her abdomen, exposing her blue corset, the one he liked best because it fit just a little too snugly around the chest, pressing her breasts in and up more than was fashionable, but perfect for his mouth. Or, she glanced down, the jut of his cock.

She held his gaze and shrugged her shoulder, letting the material slide down her arm at its own easy pace, letting him hope, just a little, before slipping her hand across her breast to catch the edge just above her elbow with her fingertip. Leaving her hand splayed suggestively over her left breast, she glanced at him from beneath her lashes. "I'm just hoping the right incentive will get you over your stubbornness."

"It's not a matter of being stubborn."

"It's not?" She dipped her right shoulder.

"Nope." His gaze narrowed, lending a dangerous edge to his expression as the other sleeve began its slide.

She caught that one, too, just above the gather of her loosely tied chemise—very loosely tied chemise—that gaped obligingly.

A little of the nonchalance left his stance. "You're playing with fire, sweetheart."

She just loved the way he drawled the endearment, as if it were a threat and a promise at once. "I am?"

He pulled the hat down over his brow and straightened. "Oh, yeah."

She strove for innocence as she pointed out, "I'm just trying to get your attention."

He nodded toward her chest. "You've got it."

"Good."

She turned, giving him a view of her back, and let the blouse go. It slid off her arms in a whisper of enticement. As soon as it cleared her hands, she reached for the fastening on her skirt, feeling every bit the fast woman she'd been accused of being as the outside button came undone. She decided she liked it.

From the husky edge to his drawl, Caine liked it, too. "You know the others will be in here in about five minutes to rig up?"

She nodded, more concerned with the stubborn button than the conversation.

"I'm going to have a real problem with my wife strutting before them in her unmentionables."

She glanced at him over her shoulder as she freed her skirt, liking the possessive emphasis he always put on "wife." Liking even more the way he looked. Big, mean and ready. For her. Her smile broadened as his hand dropped to his fly. "Then I guess it will be up to you to make sure they don't get too much of a show."

Her skirt hit the floor with a soft rustle. She wasn't wearing anything underneath except the chemise and corset, and ankle boots topped with knee-high stockings tied with a bright pink ribbon just below her knee.

His curse hit her ears a lot harder. Deep, dark and sexy—a hot erotic prelude to the touch of his skin. In the next instant, he was there behind her, his big body propelling her forward, toward the stall wall. His hand splayed across her stomach, pulling her up short before she connected, giving her a moment to catch herself, and then he was up against her, crowding her between the hard wood and the heat of his body, the rough cotton of his open fly abrading the naked curve of her buttocks, the thick hot length of his cock pressing hard between. She wiggled back, working him deeper into the crease of her buttocks, gifting herself with the hot stab of arousal.

"Does this mean I'm staying?"

"It's a hard life."

"It's a challenging one," she corrected.

"You were meant for better."

"I swear if you make me say this again, I'm going to box your ears."

His laugh puffed beside her ear. "Box my ears?"

She nodded. "And before you get to laughing, you should know that Tia offered to teach me to do it right."

He gave an exaggerated shudder. "Really."

She smiled against the cool wood. "But only if you prove stubborn."

"I'm never stubborn."

He was so full of it.

His right hand climbed the light boning of her corset.

"How much time do we have?"

"You said yourself, five minutes." God, he felt good against her—all hard muscle and banked power. His left hand headed south, tugging up the bottom of her chemise, finding the flesh beneath, stroking a path from hipbone to hipbone, the rough calluses dragging on her stomach before stretching to tangle in the curls topping her mound. His right had reached her breast, covering it completely, cupping the nipple within his palm, the heat of his touch carrying the remembered promise of pleasure, as slowly, oh, so slowly, his fingers contracted.

Pleasure speared deep as her flesh shaped to his touch compressing and shaping as he willed.

"Uh-huh."

His fingertips coasted up the smooth slope until he captured the taut nipple between his thumb and forefinger. Tiny flutters of eager sensation broke off as he pinched the tight bud through her chemise, swooping down to feed the hungry expectation of her pussy, stroking the ache, the need…whispering of more to come. Her sheath clenched and cream flowed as the worn cotton amplified every brush of his thumb, every press of his finger, every squeeze of both. He rubbed the sensitive nub lightly, then harder, knowing what she needed, coaxing her nipple from plumped to hard with a light pinch that shot the sharp, sweet sting of joy winging straight to her core. Lower down, that teasing finger traced the curve at the top of her mound. "Now, tell me the truth."

She dropped her head back onto his shoulder, and tilted her hips up into the stroke of his finger, wanting it, needing it lower. "I declared the barn off-limits all morning."

His hands stilled, and his chest pressed against her back as he sucked in a slow deep breath. Had she gone too far?

And then he bent, his breath reaching her first, wafting over her ear in a shivery caress that found a friend in the shudder that raced though her. It hadn't taken him long to discover how sensitive she was there. To realize that just the feel of his breath across her ear pulled her nipples tight and readied her pussy. Goose bumps sprang up over her skin as he drawled, "You, sweetheart, are a scandalous woman."

The smile was back in his voice, along with that low, sexy rumble. "So, what does that make you?"

His finger worked between the plump folds of her labia, sliding into the slick crease between. "A very lucky man."

He drew lazy figure eights on her sensitive flesh, alternately circling her vagina and her clit, touching neither, as if they had all the time in the world, as if her skin wasn't catching fire from the drag of his calluses on her intimate flesh.

His finger dipped into the well of her vagina, circled the tender opening to gather silky moisture before he drew his finger back up to her swollen clit, nudging it lightly as he milked her nipple with a slow, easy rhythm that was anything but easy on her equilibrium. Simply put, the man made her burn.

"Caine."

"Right here, Gypsy."

And he was. All around her. She leaned into his hands, trusting him to hold her up. "Do it right."

His "I wasn't aware I was doing it wrong" reflected his amusement and his intent. The man was not in a hurry.

Another little nudge, but this one followed by a slow circle, equally as frustrating as the engorged nub of her clit strained, every nerve ending leaping to life, training on that one spot, waiting for the deliverance he withheld. "You know what I mean."

"Maybe you should elaborate, just to be sure."

She had to wait a second to explain, her voice stolen by the hot kiss he pressed into the curve of her shoulder. She canted her head to the side, giving him better access. "You're teasing me."

Her reward was a strong suction that brought her up on her toes, followed by a sharp sting that had her dropping back down. He caught her weight in the cradle of his palm, cupping her pussy while two fingers slipped into the crease of her buttocks, finding her anus with unerring accuracy.

His smile pressed against her cheek as she gasped and bore down, instinct overcoming caution as he countered, "I'm pleasuring you."

She braced her hands against the wall and pressed back into the thrust of his cock, rubbing her ass back and forth against the solid length, grinding her clit against the heel of his hand, the silk of her cream making them both slick. "I need more."

She needed him bare and in her hands, her mouth, her pussy.

"Like this?" The tip of one finger left her ass while another dipped back to her vagina, not entering, just stroking in that aggravating, maddening, mind-shattering way. She dug her nails into the wall, holding on as a bolt of desire seared her control. Her knees buckled. The finger at her pussy pierced her in an inexorable culmination. Her muscles clamped down on the tip as the one at her ass strained for the same pleasure. It wasn't enough. She shook her head helplessly.

"Do you ache, Desi?" Another finger probed.

She bit her lip as her pussy flowered to the hot query. Would he take her gently or thrust fast and hard, filling her the way he did, to the delicious point of a pain that only hurt in a way that always satisfied. "Yes. Damn you."

His breath bussed her ear, then his lips and lastly his tongue, tracing the whorls with liquid fire as a shiver shook her from head to toe. Her whimper was a cry for mercy. He had none. His grip tightened on her nipple, squeezing until knife-edged pleasure burst into an erotic arc of sensual bliss. Her head snapped back, then forward. He did it again. Harder. Faster. Sharper. He pulled the nipple out, holding it as she gasped and twisted, fucking herself on his fingers, pleasing herself in his hands, letting her build her own need until it was razor sharp before just...letting go.

A glance down revealed the full curve of her breast suspended in the golden light, hanging taut and swollen, and his dark hand below, hovering just below the nipple that sat atop the white mound like a bright red cherry, begging to be plucked.

She groaned, thrusting her breast into his grip, soundlessly begging for more.

He didn't respond, just stood there waiting. She added her voice to the plea of her body. "Pinch my nipple, Caine. Please."

His knee wedged between her thighs, spreading her

as a second finger joined the first at her pussy, probing. He flicked her nipple with his nail, watching her as she watched her breast shimmy before settling into the V of his thumb and forefinger a split second before the sizzle of electricity speared through her.

"How do you want it?"

"Hard." It was difficult to speak clearly with her focus on the glittering shards of that flick. "Oh, God, do it hard."

"Like this?"

Again that sharp mix of pleasure and pain, stronger, more piercing than previously, shot inward, too close, too perfect to fight, too wonderful to waste on speech. Her "Yes" was a mere ghost of sound, but he heard.

He did it again and again, not letting her direct, not letting her help, forcing her to take her pleasure as he delivered it, absorbing her start as her muscles convulsed when he added a twist to the strong, milking motion.

"Relax, baby."

She tried, but it wasn't easy. Not when everything in her wanted him so badly. His thumb brushed her clitoris. She jerked up onto her toes, her back arching at the shock. When she came back down, he was waiting, his cock precisely aligned. She hesitated, anticipation almost as good as the real thing. Then he was whispering in her ear again…senseless words, encouraging words, intimate words…creating the illusion no one else existed. That it was just the two of them. Here, now. And all he wanted in the world was her.

She took him that first little bit in her pussy, holding on to the illusion, shuddering as the burn spread outward, knowing for her there'd never be another as good as him.

"Finish it."

The guttural order drove her hips down those few crucial inches, wanting the pleasure, groaning as her muscles parted, sighing as her heels hit the floor and his cock spread her in that first biting rapture. She leaned back into his strength, eyes drifting closed. Good, so good.

"Again."

"Give me a minute." She pushed down a little harder, taking—God, yes!—just a little more, the stretching ache blending with the pulse from her breasts, lodging in her womb in an ever-tightening, ever-expanding knot of desire.

"Now."

She shook her head, everything focused on the point of their joining, the intimate adjustment, the knowledge that there was more, as much as she wanted, more than she could take. It would take a miracle to get her to move right then. Or so she thought.

In reality, all it took was the natural dominance of a man used to being obeyed. The swat on her hip caught her by surprise, sharp and sweet. The sensual sting blended into the rapture. The second came harder, not so sweet, but, dear heavens, as good as a fuck in the heat it delivered. She kept her feet firmly planted on the floor through the third and fourth, controlling the mesmerizing torment, the lust through sheer force of will, but the fifth... Oh, God, the fifth. That one didn't come from the side, but from the front to land on the pad of her pussy. She squealed and arched back, rising into the next as he plunged upward, knees buckling as it landed, hot and just right on her sugar spot, tearing another cry from her lips, another pulse of cream from between her thighs.

The tight, rough growl of his voice blended with the

howl for more that rang in her ears as he cupped her pussy and yanked her back onto him. "Goddam, you're going to burn us both up, Desi girl."

She didn't care as long as he was with her, as long as he didn't stop, didn't leave her hanging with her whole body attuned to his pleasure. She spread her legs wider, arched her back farther, offering her breasts and her pussy as a sacrifice to his desire.

"Again, sweetheart?"

"Yes." *Please, yes.*

"Look at me."

She did, turning her head to the right as his cock worked out, almost flinching at the primitive intensity of his gaze.

"Don't look away." He worked his cock out that last inch, stopping with the flared head throbbing just inside the snug grip of her opening, her channel flexing in time with the pounding of his pulse. He leaned back and his hand came round to stroke damp fingers over her anus, a smile touching his lips as she jumped at the flare of delight. He tested the point of their joining with something thick and firm—his thumb? He swirled it in the cream spilling freely from her body before returning to her ass.

"You're going to like this."

She swallowed hard, knowing what was coming. He pushed against the tight ring, hard enough to tease, to worry. The give in the muscle echoed the give in her soul as she angled her hips up, moaning as the pressure changed. His chest came down over her back, sheltering her from the storm of her own conflicting needs. His mouth touched the corner of hers.

"That's it, Desi. Push that hot little ass back. Tempt me into giving you more."

She didn't know if she could take more, but she tried, wiggling and struggling to adjust to the foreign stretching, the intense longing that came hot on the heels of the insistent ache for more. Always more. She held her breath as the dark moment loomed, trapped between heaven and hell, hovering in an agony of suspense, before, with a low-voiced "Now," he took her past her inhibitions to the glory beyond.

His fingers, tight on her breast, anchored her as his cock tunneled high into her pussy, forging deep as his thumb made a place in her ass, neither accepting resistance as the steady onslaught continued, nor stopping until he had her full surrender. She collapsed against the wall, a hoarse cry ripping from her throat as she battled to handle the dual penetration.

"Easy, girl. Just relax and let it feel good."

She shook her head, too many conflicting impulses to sort through to relax.

"Yes, you can." A small pulse of his hips centered her attention. "Push back and relax."

She searched his eyes, needing to see him right now. He didn't hide from her, letting her seek for what she would find—his desire, his satisfaction and underneath it all, something softer, that special something that wove through all their interactions and gave her hope. His love.

"You can take me, baby. You know you can."

She wanted to, but he was so deep like this, feeling so much bigger with the insertion of his thumb. "No."

Her denial was for her own abilities, not him, but he responded to the challenge with the implacable resolve that was so much a part of him. "Yes."

She shook her head again, seeing the set of his chin out of the corner of her eye, thrilling to the knowledge that he wouldn't let her cheat herself, opening her body and soul to the proof he was the one man who could deliver this moment, grunting as his thumb pumped in time with his hips, pulling out only to plunge back in, two short thrusts to one long thrust of his massive cock. Rejoicing as he said in a voice that brooked no refusal, "Come for me."

Her body took control from her mind, rising to his demand, nerve endings swelling and opening until her whole body felt as raw and as exposed as her pussy. She caught her breath as his grip dropped from her breast to her labia, parting her, holding her open. Cool air blew over her clit. She saw his shoulder flex, his arm raise just enough, and then there was only the green of his eyes, the heat of his desire as the scandalous slap landed where she needed it most.

The wet sound of his hand meeting her sopping pussy reverberated around them, the sensual snap of his fingertips on her clit what she'd been waiting for.

Shock held her immobile for a split second as the coiled tension exploded outward, ripping the air from her lungs and control from her grasp. She bucked as the high, sweet pain joined the burning ache lodged in her womb, swelling it beyond being bearable, forcing it outward. Too big to contain, too intense to endure alone.

She bucked and twisted in his arms, crying out his name as her pussy clenched in agonizing pleasure to the rhythm of his strong thrusts, each one taking him deeper, each one bonding them tighter, each one more than the one before until there wasn't him and her, just them, together. Striving for that moment when nothing else mattered but the feelings that bound them.

She buried her face in the arm he wedged between her head and the wall, buried her teeth in his wrist as he lifted her into his careful thrusts, holding her as she fell apart, soul exposed, keeping her safe as reality narrowed to the grinding pleasure that held her in its grip. And when the violent spasms mellowed to ripples, he kissed her cheek softly, her mouth gently, and whispered, "Again."

She shook her head, too sensitive to bear more.

He sat on a grain box and cradled her against his chest. The worn wood creaked a protest. Behind them a horse snorted. Beneath her hips his cock throbbed with the promise echoed in his gaze. The touch of his lips to hers was as light as a feather, belying the urgency that cocooned them in residual heat. She closed her eyes, absorbing his tenderness as he whispered, "Definitely, yes."

His fingers trailed down her neck, over her collarbone and around the side of her breast. She opened her eyes and looked down. His hand was very dark, very big as it cradled her breast. Her nipple looked beyond fragile as he caught it between his fingertips, containing the echoes of her orgasm that throbbed through the tight bud, amplifying them inward in a hot rebound that rekindled the fire. She bit her lip as he squeezed to the lingering pulse, luring back the violent need with minute compressions. His other hand skimmed up the inside of her thigh, leaving goose bumps in its wake. Her breath caught as he grazed that sensitive spot high at the top.

She touched his forearm, surprised she had a voice left at all. "I can't."

The bit of his smile she could see from the corner of her eye was sin personified. "You can do anything you want."

He hooked his ankles over her calves as the side of his hand nestled into the engorged folds of her pussy. "And you want this."

She struggled, but he held her pinned, enthralled to his whims. She couldn't go up, couldn't go back, couldn't do anything but beg with her eyes and her body as he drove her over the edge again with a touch on her clit that was so gentle she'd never have felt it if he hadn't primed her so well. This orgasm wasn't as devastating, but it was sweet, so sweet because of the care in his touch, his eyes. As he turned her, she wrapped her arm around his neck, pressing kisses to the pound of his pulse, murmuring apologies and promises as he stroked her spine. When he eased her back, she pushed his hands away, reaching for his big cock, being careful as she lifted him, stroking him soothingly as she straddled his lap.

She ran out of height about halfway up.

His laugh was as tight as his expression as he realized her dilemma. "Spread your legs and hold on."

He didn't give her time to do anything else. He simply tucked his hands under her arms and hefted her up. She clutched at his biceps, marveling at his strength, delighting in his power as he centered his shaft.

"Oh, God." She loved this. The special first moment every time they joined, the struggle to take him in, the knowledge that she would. Could.

He scooted back, jostling her out of her rapture.

"Kneel on the box."

She had to release him to do so. Her involuntary moue of disappointment heated her cheeks and fired his passion.

"Damn, Gypsy." His hand slipped behind her head, dragging her forward to the searing heat of his kiss. She relaxed into his possession, accepting the thrust of his tongue, the outright dominance in his claim, understanding why he needed it, giving him her acceptance as she went compliant in his arms, opening her legs to his command, gasping as the fat head of his cock centered on her vagina.

"I love how you feel," she whispered into his mouth.

"Not nearly as much as I love how you feel. Soft, wet and hot." He emphasized his point with a pulse of his hips.

Oh, yes, that's what she wanted. She caught his wrists in her hands, holding on tightly as the pressure increased, her whisper of his name a plea for more. "Caine..."

"No one else." His hips lifted as he guided her down on his cock, forcing her to take that first vital inch with his hands, his need. His "Never anyone else" was a gut-tural reflection of the depth of his desire

No, she realized as her tender muscles parted beneath the onslaught, stretching to give him what he wanted, there would never be anyone else for her. Not now, not in the future. She bent her knees, working him deeper as he groaned with the agony of holding back the strength of his desire. For her. Because he worried that taking her any other way than gently would remind her of *them*.

As if she could ever confuse Caine with *them*.

She leaned in, circling her hips as she pushed down, kissing his lips, his chin, his throat, groaning herself as he lost control and thrust up. His big cock wedged deep, stroking that spot only he had ever reached. More. She wanted more. More of his passion, his pain, his tender-ness. Even more of that damn stubborn nature he wore like a shield. She wanted everything that made him the man he was. She held his gaze as she took him, letting him see her determination along with her pleasure, her want.

As she watched his. The aggressive desire he held in check, the concern, the anticipation as the broad head of his cock spread her wide, tunneling into her eager channel, dragging on the delicate muscles that clutched a welcome. His hands shifted to her hips, stopping her descent. "Easy, baby. Not too much. Give yourself time to adjust."

She didn't want easy. It was time he understood that. Time he understood she'd healed. "Caine?"

His fingers flexed as she squeezed as best she could with her inner muscles. He stretched her too finely to have much control.

"What?"

"I didn't just come out here to play."

"You didn't?"

The way he lifted his right brow just begged for a kiss. She gave in to the impulse, following the arc to his temple, measuring the rapid beat of his heart with her lips before tucking her face into the curve of his neck. Being scandalous left her feeling open and exposed. "No."

Two tugs and she had his hands on her breasts, relaxing into their heat, taking strength from the familiar feel. She settled back onto him, for the first time taking him with nothing—no worries—between her pussy and his cock except the liquid silk of her desire. She ran her fingers up over his chest, skipping over the collar of his shirt to his face, pausing to stroke the lines carved beside his mouth by the sun and experience before moving on. His hair was cool against her fingers. She didn't stop when she reached the barrier of his hat, just continued up, pushing it off, wrapping her arms around his neck as the full force of his attention centered on her. "I came to get fucked."

His hand spread open over the small of her back as she dropped her forehead to his. He was always ready to support her if she needed it, ready to give her whatever she required. The knowledge gave her the courage to say what they both needed to hear. "By you."

His smile was infinitely gentle, infinitely understanding. "My wife doesn't get fucked."

"What does she get then?"

He touched his nose to hers and his drawl when it came was low and intimate and loaded with feeling. "Ah, sweetheart, she gets loved." His right hand slid around to her back, tucking her against his heart. "All I can give for as long as there's breath in my body. Can you live with that?"

She searched his eyes, for once seeing him without his defenses, without his shields, seeing nothing but pure love pouring out over her from a man who didn't know how to do anything by halves, a man who appreciated her smiles and her frowns, who'd share his fortune and his triumphs. A man who saw her as his partner, his lover, his treasure, his wife. She brushed his hair off his face, her fingers naturally finding the hint of anxiety tightening the skin by his eyes. Silly man. She slipped her arms around his neck. "Will you be mine?"

His eyebrow arched and his hand came up to cup her head. "Who else's would I be?"

She tried to arch a brow back, but gave up when his lips quirked in a small grin. She played with the hairs at the back of his neck. "Mine to love, honor and obey, in sickness and in health, for better or for worse?"

The smile left to be replaced by an intensity that would have scared her in the old days, but now just filled her with peace. This was her man and everything he did, he did with his whole heart, including making his wedding vows, this time with nothing but his own desire forcing his hand.

"To love and cherish," he drawled, his deep voice rich with nuance and commitment, his eyes a brilliant green as he made his vows there in the shadowed barn, the air redolent with their commitment, the rhythm of their desire still pounding in their blood. "Until death do us part."

He tilted her head back for his kiss. "I love you, Desi Allen."

Just before their mouths connected, in that instant when their breaths mingled and anticipation reigned, she whispered back, "And I love you."

The edge of his lips teased hers. "Did you mean that part about obeying?"

She tickled his upper lip with her tongue and confessed, "I had my fingers crossed on that part."

His laugh was pure sensual pleasure, flowing into her mouth, her heart. She loved to hear him laugh.

"That's my Gypsy."

Epilogue

April 5, 1858

Dear Ari,

I don't know how to start this letter, except to say, "Thank God you're alive."

So much has happened in the last year. Not all of it good, but some of it so special, there aren't words to describe it. I'm married. Happily so to a man of whom Papa would never have approved. He doesn't have money, doesn't have social position and doesn't care a fig about mine, but he is everything I never dreamed big enough to desire when we used to sit under the apple tree imagining the perfect husband. A heart that knows no limits, a sense of honor that can't be compromised and a love for me so rich, I'll never be poor. He's Hell's Eight and if you're still living in the Texas Territory when this letter finds you, you know what that means. If not, you're in for a treat. The men of Hell's Eight are a breed apart. A standard on which to build legends, for all they'll scoff at you if you tell them so.

My husband's name is Caine Allen, and he's the one insisting I write this letter. He believes in family and in my intuition. Though everyone says you're dead, he says my gut feeling is good enough for him, and he's promised finding you will be Hell's Eight's number one priority. He can be high-handed at times, but in the best ways.

I'm sorry I can't introduce you to the man handing you this letter, but you see, I've made seven copies and entrusted them to seven different men with the hope they'll find you: Tucker, Sam, Tracker, Shadow, Luke, Caden and Ace. Like your soon-to-be niece or nephew, my husband and yourself—though you don't know it yet—they're Hell's Eight, and I'm asking you, Ari, to put yourself in their care because each one of them has made a promise to me, one they've sworn to uphold.

You see, they've promised to bring you home, Ari. Home to Hell's Eight, where there's no past, no recriminations, no judgment, just peace and a place where you can breathe easily. After what we've been through, I know it sounds like a preacher's description of heaven—illusive and unreal—but I promise you, there is a way out of hell and if you haven't already found it, I'll help you.

Trust no one but them, Ari, because father's solicitor, Harold Amboy, is the one who arranged for us to be attacked initially, and he has men hunting for you, too. He intends to control father's money through one of us. But you can trust any of these men. Absolutely and completely with everything you hold dear.

I'm crying as I write this. I can't imagine what you've been through. I can't forget how we parted, my nightmares—which must have been your reality—the sense of helplessness as I stare at the night sky wondering if you can see the same stars, wondering if you're healthy, happy and most of all, safe.

Do you remember the game we used to play at the summer house as children when things didn't go our way? How we'd go find a patch of daisies dappled in sunlight, link our hands in our special way and then just spin until we didn't care about anything else? I just want to see you again, Ari, find a patch of daisies, grab hands and spin until laughter takes over and all the bad falls away. Though it's irrational because I have no idea how long it will take the men to find you—days, months, years—I have to say this.

Hurry home, Ari. I've planted a patch of daisies and it's waiting.

* * * * *

Try these Healthy and Delicious Spring Rolls!

INGREDIENTS

2 packages rice-paper
spring roll wrappers
(20 wrappers)

1 cup grated carrot

¼ cup bean sprouts

1 cucumber, julienned

1 red bell pepper, without
stem and seeds, julienned

4 green onions
finely chopped—
use only the green part

DIRECTIONS

1. Soak one rice-paper wrapper
   in a large bowl of hot water
   until softened.

2. Place a pinch each of carrots,
   sprouts, cucumber, bell
   pepper and green onion on the
   wrapper toward the bottom
   third of the rice paper.

3. Fold ends in and roll tightly
   to enclose filling.

4. Repeat with remaining
   wrappers. Chill before
   serving.

Find this and many more delectable recipes
including the perfect dipping sauce in

NTRSERIESJAN

REQUEST YOUR FREE BOOKS!

2 FREE NOVELS
FROM THE ROMANCE COLLECTION
PLUS 2 FREE GIFTS!

YES! Please send me 2 FREE novels from the Romance Collection and my 2 FREE gifts (gifts are worth about $10). After receiving them, if I don't wish to receive any more books, I can return the shipping statement marked "cancel." If I don't cancel, I will receive 4 brand-new novels every month and be billed just $5.74 per book in the U.S. or $6.24 per book in Canada. That's a saving of at least 28% off the cover price. It's quite a bargain! Shipping and handling is just 50¢ per book.* I understand that accepting the 2 free books and gifts places me under no obligation to buy anything. I can always return a shipment and cancel at any time. Even if I never buy another book, the two free books and gifts are mine to keep forever.

194/394 MDN E7NZ

Name _____

(PLEASE PRINT)

Address _____ Apt. # _____

City _____ State/Prov. _____ Zip/Postal Code _____

Signature (if under 18, a parent or guardian must sign) _____

Mail to The Reader Service:
IN U.S.A.: P.O. Box 1867, Buffalo, NY 14240-1867
IN CANADA: P.O. Box 609, Fort Erie, Ontario L2A 5X3

Not valid for current subscribers to the Romance Collection
or the Romance/Suspense Collection.

Want to try two free books from another line?
Call 1-800-873-8635 or visit www.morefreebooks.com.

* Terms and prices subject to change without notice. Prices do not include applicable taxes. N.Y. residents add applicable sales tax. Canadian residents will be charged applicable provincial taxes and GST. Offer not valid in Quebec. This offer is limited to one order per household. All orders subject to approval. Credit or debit balances in a customer's account(s) may be offset by any other outstanding balance owed by or to the customer. Please allow 4 to 6 weeks for delivery. Offer available while quantities last.

Your Privacy: Harlequin Books is committed to protecting your privacy. Our Privacy Policy is available online at www.eHarlequin.com or upon request from the Reader Service. From time to time we make our lists of customers available to reputable third parties who may have a product or service of interest to you. [ ] If you would prefer we not share your name and address, please check here.

Help us get it right—We strive for accurate, respectful and relevant communications. To clarify or modify your communication preferences, visit us at www.ReaderService.com/consumerchoice.

MROM10R